AGAINST THE DYING LIGHT

LIGHT

THE SUCCOURI SAGA

MERIDITH GIBBENS

CONTENTS

PROLOGUE

While others might have found solace in the night's stillness, to Donovan Bradshaw it screamed a warning that prickled across his skin. Every time he closed his eyes he saw it: the flash of light, the explosion of fire and debris, and the blood of his brothers in arms splattering on his fatigues. The sounds of carnage echoed in his ears: screams of terror and groans of desperate torment. Undergirding the deafening chaos, he heard laughter, a mocking voice he couldn't silence no matter how hard he tried.

The taunting resounded with the voices of his mother and father, menacingly synchronized with the scoffs of a wicked enemy who stood over him, rejoicing as he watched blood pour from his open wounds. Triumphantly, he kicked him in the side, believing him dead. And indeed, in that moment, he hadn't been sure himself, but he'd been close enough to play the role flawlessly, knowing that if he indicated otherwise, his enemy would be sure to leave him with no doubt.

"You've thrown your life away," the chorus declared.

"You were meant for more than dying with your face in the dirt."

But then, there came another voice, repeating a whispered prophecy he'd heard for as long as he could remember. "Take courage. You are a guardian, a keeper, a protector for the one who is chosen."

As he lay dying, Donovan had wondered why this voice spoke now as his life ebbed away like a wave retreating from the shore. It was too late to repeat this incomprehensible call. It was over. He'd done his best and laid down his life to protect the country and people he loved. Wouldn't it now relent? Wasn't this sacrifice sufficient?

A rustling in the bushes just beyond the reach of the house lights brought him back to the present. Contrary to what he'd believed possible, he had survived that dreadful night nearly two years ago; that is, if you could call this existence survival.

As he had trained himself to do, Donovan tuned out the voices, focusing solely on his task. He crouched lower, using his night-vision goggles to peer into the thick darkness. Someone was there, but he was crafty, perhaps trained like himself in camouflage. Unhurried, his enemy plotted each movement carefully, staying in the shadows and using the occasional gust of wind to mask his footsteps. But Donovan knew the game well.

Noiselessly, he used the cover of the rock wall that circled the governor's home to maneuver into the darkest recess of the sprawling front yard. He needed to get behind the intruder and ambush him, leaving him no time to respond with deadly force.

Patiently, Donovan waited, but there was no movement from the bushes. It appeared the enemy had no plan to attempt a breach of the home itself, knowing the effort would be fruitless as security was far too tight. Instead, he was content to wait for the governor, or perhaps his wife, to come to him. Whether the intruder was the author of the frightening death threats against the family or merely a hired gun was unclear, but that distinction didn't change Donovan's mission. After tonight, he wouldn't trouble this family again.

Though the governor already employed a team of personal bodyguards, Donovan had been hired for his skills at technological surveillance, specifically his training in undetectable sensors and cameras capable of alerting security personnel to an approaching threat. And in this case, the near-invisible technologies had done their job. Donovan had easily tracked the intruder's movements once he breached the property's boundary, giving him plenty of time to intercept him before the threat became critical.

Despite the echoes from the past and the merciless pain that throbbed through his body, his experience and training overtook competing distractions, sharply focusing his senses. Use the environment, keep silent, time your approach, fade into the ambient noise, take cover in dark corners and shadows, and control your breathing.

Moving heel-to-toe, he advanced, each step corresponding with nature's own utterings: the hoot of an owl, scurry of a nocturnal critter, rustling of dry leaves, and clashing of woody branches.

Arcing a wide circle, he moved steadily but deliberately until he was twenty yards behind the intruder. After glancing one last time at the sensors' feedback on his dimmed screen to confirm the exact location of the intruder, he lowered himself onto the ground and inched forward on his stomach, approaching like an invisible serpent slithering in the underbrush. His breaths barely stirred the air, but as he advanced, Donovan could hear the enemy's respiration, and he timed his own to coincide.

When the distance between them closed in on ten yards, something scurried a few feet behind him, its hasty retreat igniting a sudden shuffling of leaves and an audible clamoring of rocks. Donovan flattened to the ground, and the skittish gunman whirled around, squinting into the darkness, affording Donovan a look at the man's face thanks to the advantage the night-vision technology afforded him.

Too high, Donovan mentally chastised the man as he watched him strain his neck, focusing on the dimly illuminated space between the underbrush and the lower limbs of the trees. Perhaps this guy wasn't as skilled as he'd given him credit for.

Don't worry about what you can see. Worry about what you can't. Donovan winced, recalling the critical lesson he'd learned the hard way.

Unbreathing, Donovan remained motionless as the man weighed the threat, at last returning to his crouched position facing the house.

Big mistake.

When the man's shoulders relaxed, Donovan resumed his advance, patiently strategizing each motion. Luckily, the man was restless, and his repeated shifting gave Donovan ample sound cover as he moved stealthily, halting when he was just a few yards behind him.

In the distance, a train whistle blew, and he seized the opportunity to stand, sheltering behind the trunk of a sturdy tree and sliding off the goggles. Remaining statuesque, he allowed time for his eyes to adjust to the darkness as he began to plot his surprise attack.

This was not a battlefield and, as of yet, the only known

crime this intruder had committed was stalking and issuing death threats. Until that changed, terminating him was not an option. But he was armed and had murderous intentions, which meant he would put up a fight if he got the chance.

During his brief glance, Donovan had determined his height, five feet ten inches, and his weight, one hundred ninety pounds. His stature was smaller than Donovan's six feet three inches, giving him an advantage in a takedown if he could maintain the element of surprise. But he would need to plot each footfall as he rushed him, staying undetected even as he acquired enough momentum to sweep him off his feet and capture him in an inescapable stranglehold.

Listening to his enemy's breathing to ensure he remained undisturbed, he risked a quick glance around the tree, needing no more than half a second to capture a mental image of the terrain. Right foot down in the soft dirt just beyond the sprawling tree root. Left foot, heel first, into a moldy pile of limp leaves. Then the controlled slide, letting his own weight and momentum propel him forward as he swept beneath the man's bent legs, knocking him off balance and enabling Donovan to capture him in a tight grip.

It all sounded so easy, a textbook takedown, but in his experience, nothing ever went quite that smoothly. Contingency planning was as important as plotting the first strike. One last time, his mind hovered over the mental snapshot he'd taken during his brief glance, zooming in on each rock and twig until he had rehearsed three ways to defend against an unforeseeable error or unexpected countermove.

Sliding his hand down his side and into his boot, he fingered the grip of his nine-millimeter then the handle of his knife, fervently hoping lethal force would not prove necessary. He'd done his share of killing, and unless that defense became inescapable, he had no stomach for unnecessary violence.

Gratefully, since he'd retired from military service and begun his work in private security, he'd not been forced to kill anyone, though he couldn't claim to have avoided inflicting serious injuries in a few cases. After watching his brothers, fellow SEALS, die in torment and enduring his own brush with death, he feared losing himself, the part of him that remained tenderly human.

Though the call to serve was as much a part of who he was as the blood that coursed through his veins, he'd seen too much to deny the impact on a soul that occurs when the soldier identity begins to take over the heart of a man. In his estimation, humanizing virtues like kindness, compassion, forgiveness, and mercy were not discardable, even when they interfered with the demands of soldiering. It was a precarious balance to sustain in his chosen occupation and, before he'd become critically injured and subsequently released from service, he'd felt himself losing his footing in that struggle. Throwing aside moral restraints may provide a kind of strength and resolve necessary for survival as a warrior, but at the end of that dark road lay a hellish existence, one more frightening than any battlefield he'd encountered.

Therefore, when his injuries ejected him from the life he'd once believed to be his destiny, he'd resolved to find a new way to satisfy the need to serve, rooted deep in his soul, while also reclaiming as much as he could of the man he'd been before he'd become an expert at the art of killing.

But Donovan couldn't deny that most of the time, he struggled with unanswerable questions as he sought an ever-elusive inner peace. Why was the call to defend so relentless, even now when he'd served and sacrificed so much? And, almost equal in its uncompromising demand, came the dire warning to stay true to who he'd been before he'd donned the soldier's uniform.

Each time the blinding pain of his battle wounds shot through his body, fresh anger seized him, but he had no one to fairly blame for his misery. He'd signed up for this life, disregarding his parent's warnings and sharp rebukes, and despite the consequences, he did not regret his choice. His head spun as he wrestled with conflicting questions, which he'd assuredly not live long enough to resolve with any degree of satisfaction.

Setting his jaw, Donovan determinedly refocused on his present task, knowing if he allowed himself the slightest equivocation, his mission would fail, potentially costing him, and perhaps those in the house, their lives. Taking one last noiseless breath, he mentally counted down from three, then sprang from his hiding spot, letting the soldier in him have its way.

CHAPTER I

VOICES FROM THE PAST

Interstate 495 was gridlocked as Donovan entered the Greater Boston area, heading for his infrequently inhabited apartment. Though he'd technically resided there for over a year, he rarely spent more than a few days at home, his work keeping him continually traveling. As he had no one to come home to anyway, he felt no sentimental attachment to his residence, evidenced by the unpacked boxes still occupying a substantial part of his living room.

Though he'd grown up in the area, besides a few childhood friends who'd also joined the service, he maintained no relational attachments to anyone from the past, even family. At eighteen, he informed his parents of his decision to join the military and, because this conflicted with their pre-determined course for Donovan's future, they disowned him, explicitly stating they no longer considered him their son.

His mother and father had grown up under the sheltered cloak of opulence where work was more about prestige than earning a living or fulfilling a calling. Certainly, the idea of service to others or to a greater cause were not concepts they considered as they envisioned which occupation was suitable for their only son and heir.

Donovan's father had a law degree from an Ivy League university, but he had never officially practiced law, unless having an unyielding opinion on every conceivable topic counted as such. He used his education to justify his arrogance toward anyone who lacked equally prestigious credentials and as a means of legitimizing his station in life, mostly to himself, concluding that he'd earned his wealth through such personal achievements.

As for his mother, she wasn't burdened by a need to legitimize her privileged station. Uninhibited by compassion for the less fortunate, she readily enjoyed every luxury available to her, which seemed an inexhaustible list. Even when he was young, she spent most of her time traveling the world, typically aboard cruise ships with an equally entitled and indulgent group of heiresses.

His mother's idea of charity and service was donating an occasional designer outfit from her overpopulated closet, not because it was worn, but because it was no longer stylish enough for her finicky taste. The act was carried out with notable fanfare as if she were donating an organ or relinquishing her last penny.

Shaking his head, Donovan blew a breath through his lips, recalling how she'd made the same overexaggerated fuss when donating clothes he'd outgrown, as if giving them up was a praiseworthy act of sacrifice. Consequently, it was little wonder that when he grew up and decided to pursue a calling that demanded genuine, rather than conjured, sacrifice, his parents couldn't abide the thought and thus had turned their backs on him.

Though he couldn't deny their rejection had disappointed him, perhaps pained him, he was thankful it had liberated him from a fate much worse than the one he now faced. For truly, he'd rather die young in pursuit of a noble cause than live to a ripe old age, languishing in an entirely meaningless existence.

Unconsciously, Donovan touched his bruised ribs as he waited for traffic to let up. Though executed flawlessly, his ambush of the governor's stalker three nights ago had left him with this new injury. The sweep had caught the man off guard, knocking him backward, but before Donovan could secure his hold around the man's neck, the lunatic had managed a strong elbow jab. For an instant, it had knocked the wind out of him, but as he was well practiced at dismissing the distraction of physical discomfort, he quickly rallied, subduing and securing the assailant seconds later. The governor was grateful, generously praising him for his work and vowing to spread the word about his competence to others who would inevitably need his services at some point in their public careers.

But Donovan was weary of protecting politicians and celebrities. That wasn't what he'd had in mind when he started this venture. The praise of the powerful meant little to him; that was his parent's game. He wanted to help ordinary people, those who couldn't defend themselves from an evil they'd inadvertently stumbled upon. Women with obsessed stalkers or abusive ex-husbands, victims who'd narrowly escaped the horrors of sex-trafficking, or those who'd turned state's evidence against hardened drug dealers or other heinous criminals: these were the people and circumstances he most wished to defend.

As traffic at last eased, Donovan heard again the familiar voice, calling him to something he couldn't define, a destiny as distinctive as the warrior heart he'd been born with, despite his progenitors and upbringing. He squinted his eyes, as he tried again to grab ahold of whatever was drawing him, calling his name, but he couldn't fix on it.

Not that it mattered anyhow. Worse than an indiscernible calling was the reality that, even if he understood it, he wouldn't get the chance to fulfill it. He was a man living on borrowed time, the final grains of sand slipping through the narrow funnel of the ominous hourglass that was his life.

Perhaps it was fortunate he was estranged from his parents. His premature death wouldn't disrupt their reverie. The ones he'd saved were his legacy, though, to most, he was an anonymous, impersonal rescuer. Besides his brothers in arms, he'd had no time or opportunity to become anything more to another human heart. When death found him, whether that day or the next, though some may honor him for his service, not a single heart would mourn his absence.

GRACE SOPHIA WATCHED HER FRIEND, Callie LeVray, carefully. At this late hour, everyone had gone home except herself, Ms. Essie Jones—a close family friend of the LeVrays—and Callie's seriously hot new boyfriend Ben Sawyer.

Callie's father, Ronald LeVray's funeral that afternoon had been a fitting tribute, though there was no adequate way to rightly honor the man. He was the perfect father, kind and loving, sacrificing his own needs for Callie and her younger brother Lee, as well as his community.

Since she'd befriended Callie over three years ago, Mr. LeVray had adopted her, treating her like family. Upon meeting her, he immediately assigned her a nickname, "Amazing Grace," and though no one else adopted it— Callie clinging to "Gracie" as her favorite affectionate reference—whenever Mr. LeVray called her that, it brought a smile to her face and warmth to her heart. She loved Ronald LeVray, with his contagious laugh and his incomparable wisdom, which he unfailingly lived out daily.

When Grace found out about Ronald's stroke and later visited him in the hospital, she not only struggled with worry and grief for her dearest friend, but also for herself as she couldn't imagine a world without him in it. Her own parents had divorced when she was nine, and she could count on one hand the number of times she'd seen her father since then. Her mother moved on quickly, but she was incurably inept at picking decent men. Until Grace left for college, her homelife featured an endless parade of degenerative men: some addicted, some abusive, and some just plain lazy or stupid. It was a relief to at last leave home, escaping the unending pageant of goons and clowns.

Though she felt sorry for her mother, there was no curing her of her poor taste. She liked these irredeemable specimens that one could not fairly refer to as human, even when they treated her like garbage. Grace didn't get it and, after several unsuccessful attempts to get her mother help, she'd given up and channeled her energy into ensuring she never fell into that trap. After a brief lapse in judgment when she first tasted the freedom of life on her own, she wised up, deciding she didn't need a man, though she couldn't deny that some, present company included, were pleasant to look at.

"Gracie, thank you for being by my side today, for your words of comfort and support," Callie said as she lowered herself beside her on the couch and put a hand on her shoulder. Grace could still see the abrasion on her cheek, a morbid reminder that just a little over a week earlier, the dearest person in the world to her had almost been killed. A soulless monster had shot her best friend on her porch, and the police still didn't know who or why. Ben and Lee had found her and, through nothing short of a miracle, gotten her help before it was too late.

Grace turned tear-filled eyes to Callie. "Girl, I love you. Your dad, he gave me something to believe in, you know? He was the first man I've ever known who was genuinely good."

"He *was* that," Callie agreed nostalgically, then briefly glanced Ben's way. "But there are other good men out there, my sweet friend. I promise you. You're going to find one soon. I know it."

Following Callie's gaze, Grace watched Ben as he spoke with Lee and Ms. Essie.

Callie had met Ben Sawyer a few weeks before, thanks to a romantic twist of fate. Since then, they'd barely spent more than a few hours apart. Without question, they belonged together, behaving as if they'd known each other all their lives. Ben was drop-dead gorgeous, almost inhuman looking in the flawlessness of his features. And he was taken with her best friend, incurably head over heels, even if, due to her significant visual impairment, Callie couldn't see well enough to recognize the telltale look in his eyes.

The first time Grace met Ben, he'd stopped by Mr. LeVray's hospital room while she and Callie were chatting. Immediately, Grace was unsteadied by his good looks, but as she watched him interact with Callie, the genuine expression of love in his striking blue eyes endeared him to her. The pure devotion she saw was a stark contrast to the hollow affection her mother's degenerates offered, and Grace herself had never been fortunate enough to experience anything close, not even from men she dated for a much longer period of time. It was difficult to resist feeling jealous, more of the rare, devoted affection he displayed than of his undeniable attractiveness.

But beyond being thoroughly smitten by her best friend's gracious heart and beauty, Ben was genuinely kind-hearted, even if he remained something of a mystery. With his humble, gentle nature, one couldn't help but like Ben Sawyer, which was fortunate for him as, if she'd felt otherwise, Grace wouldn't have held back in expressing her disapproval. Since the beginning of their friendship, Grace had been protective of Callie LeVray, perhaps partly because of her visual limitations, but there was more to it than that.

They'd met in college, both girls participating in their university's orchestra program; Callie playing cello and Grace the violin. Immediately, they'd hit it off, quickly becoming more like sisters than friends. Both girls had the unmistakable feeling that the universe had meant for them to be family. Having no siblings of her own, Grace didn't know how her heart recognized the connection, but she was certain of it. There was something behind it all, a purpose that Grace was meant to fulfill in Callie's life and vice versa. The details weren't clear to her yet, but she was sure of the bond, and she knew Callie was as well. No matter what came their way, they would be friends for life.

"Not everyone has the good fortune to meet a prince, Cal. But I've certainly met my fair share of frogs, so maybe I at least have a chance at finding a human being sometime soon." She crossed her fingers and pressed them into Callie's palm, knowing she wouldn't see the gesture.

Callie laughed sweetly but shook her head vigorously, her copper curls swishing around her face. "I won't rest until my best friend finds the happily ever after she deserves, a good man worthy of her beautiful heart."

"Like"—Grace raised an eyebrow and gestured toward the opposite side of the room—"the one who's stolen *your* beautiful heart?"

Though she smiled, a tear escaped the corner of Callie's eye. "I couldn't have made it through these days of sorrow without you, Lee, and Ben. Love has filled my heart so full it's impossible to despair, even though I miss Dad desperately."

"I just wish you'd had the chance to say goodbye, you and Lee."

A strange look flashed across Callie's face, and she lowered her head. "I'm at peace with his passing, Gracie. It will take time to heal, but there's... there's a lot to be thankful for."

Perplexed, Grace straightened, once again watching her friend carefully. There was something Callie wasn't telling her. She'd felt that way since the shooting. From the beginning of their relationship, they'd told each other everything, no secrets between them. But now, Callie was holding something back, something important, and Grace had a strong suspicion it had something to do with the gorgeous, yet mysterious Ben Sawyer.

Donovan tossed his keys on the counter and picked up a teetering stack of mail his landlord had collected for him over the weeks he'd been away. Going to the cabinet, he pulled out a glass, one of only two that occupied the space, and filled it with lukewarm water from the tap. During his tour of duty, cold beverages had been scarce, so he'd become accustomed to, and now preferred, beverages at room temperature or warmer.

After a few sips, he set his cup on the counter and began sorting through the stack, separating the bills from the advertisements. As he moved through the pile, a small envelope caught his eye, halting his progress. He took it in both hands, leaning back and squinting at it as if his eyes were playing tricks on him. In the top left corner, the names Ivan and Clarice Bradshaw appeared atop a familiar address. Setting it down on the counter in front of him, Donovan blinked at it, feeling more anxiety over the harmless envelope than he had when facing an erratic gunman in the dark woods of Georgia.

What was this? He hadn't heard from his parents in over ten years, so what could be prompting them to reach out now? Running a hand through his hair, still cut short but grown out beyond the military-approved buzz cut, he turned away, feeling too weary and caught off guard to face the letter's contents. Maybe after a good night's sleep, he'd have the strength to read it, or maybe it was best to leave it be. Knowing his parents, he doubted the motivation that prompted them to contact him after all this time was benevolent. It was more likely the letter's content would cause him further disappointment and heartache, and he'd had more than his fill of that for a lifetime. If he wasn't long for this earth, he intended to spend whatever time remained in worthy pursuits, not digging up past grievances or resurrecting sorrows he'd long since put behind him.

A familiar ache began to throb, starting in his head,

then spreading throughout his body. Sleep was what he needed. He'd deal with the letter another day.

With a groan, he bent to retrieve his knapsack, then headed for the bedroom. Exhaustion and ceaseless pain made him feel like a man in his seventies, rather than the twenty-nine-year-old he actually was. His condition was growing worse by the day. Perhaps he should take some time off, give his body a break, at least allow it to heal from the most recent injuries. The idea made him feel weak and frail, which he detested, but he wasn't sure he was well enough, at present, to do what was required of his physically demanding occupation.

Just as he entered the bedroom, his phone buzzed. Placing the bag on the bed, he pulled the phone from his back pocket. Only a handful of people had his personal number. In his line of work that was an essential safeguard. As he stared at the screen, he was, for the second time that night, caught off guard, but this time, the surprise was a pleasant one.

Shaking his head, he chuckled and sat down on the bed. "I guess today's my day to face voices from the past," he mumbled as he accepted the call.

"Ben Sawyer?" he greeted, unable to hide the curiosity that mixed with delight in his voice.

"Donovan, my friend." A warm laugh resounded on the line, a sound that pleased Donovan, though it was unexpected. "Yes, it's me. I'm sure I'm the last person you expected to hear from today."

Though the voice was familiar, the tone didn't match that of his friend, whom he hadn't seen or heard from in several years. Ben Sawyer was a kind, but downcast soul, though Donovan had easily befriended him and long admired the courageous heart he instantly recognized.

Generous, humble, and extraordinarily compassionate, Ben had nevertheless always been heavy in spirit, as if carrying the world's weight on his shoulders.

But the voice on the line was much lighter, almost contented, which brought an easy smile to Donovan's face as he carried a deep affection for Ben and had worried about him after his mother's tragic suicide six years ago.

"Unexpected, but very welcome," Donovan replied, his smile carrying in his tone. "How are you?" he asked cautiously, recollecting Ben's hesitancy to share personal information at their last encounter.

"We'll get to that, but first, I want to hear about you. I looked you up and discovered you'd returned to civilian life, started your own security business. That's fantastic, but I can't deny I was surprised. I know you loved your work as a SEAL, and our country was a rich benefactor of your service."

Sighing, Donovan unconsciously rubbed his aching ribs again as he answered. "I appreciate that, Ben," he replied softly, lowering his head. "Unfortunately, circumstances prevented me from continuing my military career, but I have no regrets."

"Are you… Are you alright?"

The question was asked with such genuine concern that it made Donovan yearn to tell his old friend everything, spill out his woes in a way he'd had no opportunity to do since returning home. But he hadn't seen Ben in years, didn't know the reason for the call or his new, lighter tone. Though the changes in his friend appeared to be positive, he wanted to know more before putting the weight of his own problems on someone who'd already endured more than his fair share of tragedies. And if this was a one-time thing, a quick check-in with no plans for further contact, it didn't feel right to reveal something so personal.

"War is messy, my friend, and few of us who partake in it come out unscathed."

The line fell silent for a breath. "I see. I'm sorry for what you've been through, Donovan, but I'm honored to know someone with such courage. I'm hoping… I suppose I was hoping you might consider being a part of my life again and letting me be a part of yours. I've been a most neglectful and selfish friend, but—"

"It would be my honor," Donovan interjected, his enthusiasm unrestrained, even as his curiosity over the radical change in Ben's demeanor rose by the minute. "You've been suffering yourself for a long time. Some of it I understand, some of it I don't, but all I ever wanted was to walk through the battlefield with you, lend you my shoulder to lean on."

A heavy sigh preceded Ben's response. "I'll never be able to express how much your friendship has always meant to me, even though, for the most part, I've been unable to accept your generosity. Until a few weeks ago, I was… I was sleepwalking through my life. I couldn't trust or heal or reach out to anyone. It's complicated, Donovan. Some of it arose from the sorrow regarding my mother's choice, but there is more to it than that. There are burdens I carry that… that make it almost impossible for me to stay in one place or let people get too close. But none of that is related to my sincere affection for you, my friend, or my gratitude for the ways you've reached out and tried to help me."

Stunned by the casual reference to his mother, a topic Ben had been vehemently unwilling to so much as mention at their last encounter, and confused by the rest, it took Donovan a moment to formulate his response. "Forgive me.

I feel like I'm talking to a different man than the one I've known for over a decade, so I'm a little tongue-tied here, but I have to know. What's happened to you? Something's changed you, Ben Sawyer, in the best of ways."

Ben chuckled. "It's a little cliché, but still just as true. I met a girl, a wonderful, beautiful, extraordinary girl who has changed my life!"

Donovan nearly dropped the phone into his lap. "Uh, wow! Where? How?"

"It's a long story I'm anxious to share with you, preferably in person. But that topic brings me to the urgent matter that inspired my sudden reentry into your life this evening. I need your help, Donovan."

"I... Of course. Whatever I can do but—"

"I'd like to hire you, at once, if you're available. And, as you know, cost is no obstacle."

"Hire me for what?" Donovan was confused, trying to stay focused as the drastic change in his friend, the admission that he'd fallen in love, and now the alarm and anxiety rising in his voice, left Donovan scrambling to keep up.

"For what you do best: protection."

"Are you in trouble?"

"Not me, her. Callie, the woman I love, was shot a little over a week ago, and the police informed me this afternoon that her killer is on the loose and won't be giving up until he's accomplished his evil goal. Donovan, I can't lose her. I'll happily give up my life for hers, but that might not be enough to keep her out of danger. I—"

"Hold up," Donovan interrupted putting up a hand, even though Ben couldn't see it. "Start from the beginning. Who shot your lady, um... Callie, and why?"

Ben inhaled deeply, attempting to calm his nerves so he could offer a clear explanation. "Callie's father was the prosecutor in this town. He recently worked on a case that ended in the conviction and life sentence of a wicked drug dealer and murderer. Just a few days ago, her father passed away after suffering a severe stroke. The police believe someone close to the criminal is out for revenge and since they can't take it on Callie's father anymore, they've set their sights on her. Callie has a younger brother as well, but they don't appear interested in him, just her. The failed attempt seems to have heightened their resolve. But solving this case is going to be hard and take time. An officer advised me this afternoon to get her out of town until they apprehend the shooter. I'd like to bring her to my former residence in Boston, as I have unfinished business related to my past to face and sort through there as well. It's far from here, and the security measures already in place are substantial. But it's not good enough. Though I have certain... skills that can be useful in keeping her well, I don't have your training and technical know-how. And I trust no one else, Donovan, not with Callie's life."

Determined yet desperately tormented at the thought of losing the woman he loved, Ben's voice shook with conviction, and Donovan's heart rejoiced for the love Ben had found, a treasure that had somehow unlocked the prison doors of his captive heart. Yet at the same time, his own heart constricted in empathy at the dread Ben expressed.

This was exactly the kind of work Donovan sought, protecting the innocent, the ordinary person who'd found themselves in a situation outside their control. And if he could preserve his friend's newly awakened heart at the same time, that would make the victory even sweeter, for it wasn't hard to discern that, if his friend lost this girl, the newfound peace he enjoyed would very likely die with her.

Revitalized by the positive changes in his friend and passionately determined to keep him in such a state, Donovan resolved to do whatever he could to secure Ben's happiness. This must be one extraordinary girl, well worth protecting. A few years back, he'd tried to break his friend out of his personal hell, but he'd failed miserably. Now, he had another shot at helping him. Despite his injuries and physical exhaustion, he'd rally everything he had as, pressed by his conscience and the demanding voice in his head, it was unthinkable to offer Ben anything less.

While Donovan processed the circumstances Ben described, a quiet moment lingered, and Ben cleared his throat. "However, I do understand if you are already otherwise obligated or—"

"Absolutely not!" Donovan rushed to assure him, realizing that Ben had interpreted his silence as reluctance. "Actually, I just finished a case, so the timing couldn't be better. And I'm in Boston right now, just walked into my apartment a short bit ago. My skills are at your disposal. We'll keep her safe, I promise you. But we need to meet. I need more details, and we need to put together a solid plan."

"I'm in your debt." Ben exhaled in relief. "I'll book you a flight for tomorrow morning. I haven't told Callie about my plan to take her out of town yet. Her father's funeral was today, so she's had enough to deal with. I'll talk to her before you get here in the morning. This will be hard on her. You see, Callie has limited eyesight and because of that, being away from her familiar environment is more challenging than it is for the rest of us. I'm hopeful she will grant me enough trust to do what I need to do to protect her, though it isn't a fair thing to ask."

"If this lady is the inspiration behind the change in you,

she must be very special. But so is my long-lost friend. She'll give you her trust, and it will be well placed. Shoot me a text with the travel info, and I'll begin working the case on my end at once. Ben I... I'm glad you called. It's good to hear from you and to witness such a change... to hear new life in your voice. I look forward to seeing you again and meeting the miracle worker who brought my long-lost friend to life."

CHAPTER 2

PARTINGS AND REUNIONS

Grace sat staring out her kitchen window, mindlessly stirring her bowl of cold cereal. She longed for the coming of spring. Dreary and cold, the view made her moody and restless.

When she was a child, she loved Saturday mornings, sleeping late, then enjoying a leisurely breakfast in her pajamas. But now that she was an adult living alone, the weekends were lonely and far too quiet. Though she enjoyed cooking, preparing a big, fancy breakfast for one seemed a waste of time and the few times she'd indulged, eating it alone had deepened her sense of isolation.

Callie was blessed to have a brother, Grace thought wistfully. Though her father's absence would leave a hole in her heart, Lee would be there to talk her through it and empathize. And, of course, now she also had Ben.

Despite her proclamation that she didn't need a man, Grace craved the company of people, being naturally social and extroverted. But her busy life left her little time for relationships. In addition to her full-time job, which often kept her working well into the evenings, Grace managed Heart-

Strings, a musical trio group that performed throughout the community and had recently begun to gain substantial popularity.

The group included Callie and herself as well as Lobster, their quirky pianist. Before Callie was shot and they'd had to cancel many performances, they had enjoyed a steady inflow of bookings, averaging two or three a week. Without their trio and the frequent opportunities it granted her to visit with her friends, Grace had to admit her life would be plagued with loneliness. She had little to no contact with her dysfunctional family, and though she enjoyed her job, it couldn't fill the abiding craving in her heart for something deeper than casual connections.

After obtaining her marketing degree, Grace landed a job with a prestigious firm, coordinating the advertising campaigns of several well-known brands. She was good at what she did, and the popularity of their music trio in the community was further proof of her talents. Leaving the music selections to Callie and Lobster, Grace handled the marketing, scheduling, and paperwork. The three of them were a terrific team, and their tight friendships made the extra work of this side job well worth it; indeed, she preferred the work she did for HeartStrings to that of her day job as it offered more meaningful rewards than a simple paycheck.

But even with her busy, successful life, there was a hole that nothing she had accomplished thus far had filled. There was something more she was meant to do, but she didn't know what it was. Presently, sitting in the silence of her kitchen, the mysterious hollowness ached more acutely than usual.

As she moved to deposit her bowl in the sink, her phone

vibrated, and she backtracked to retrieve it from the table and glance at the caller ID.

"Hey, Cal."

"Gracie!" Callie's voice shook, and Grace put a hand to her heart, as it began to pound at the sound of her friend's distress.

"What's wrong?"

"Gracie I... Someone tried to kill me again this morning."

"What? Are you—"

"I'm okay. I'm okay. Ben saved my life. They shot up into the window of my bedroom just before dawn. The police are pursuing them but..."

"I thought you had police protection, Cal?" Her voice rose in anger. "Where were they? Taking a nap?"

"It happened so fast. The car came out of nowhere and by the time security responded, it had sped off. If Ben hadn't been there—"

"Is he okay?"

Grace heard Callie's relieved exhale. "Yes, thankfully. His shoulder was grazed, but he'll be fine. But he could have been killed."

Once again, Grace wasn't surprised Ben had saved her life. Protectiveness was part of the deep devotion she'd observed and admired.

"Thank goodness neither of you were seriously hurt. I'm coming over, right now, Cal. I need to see for myself that you're alright."

"That's what I was about to ask. There's something I need to tell you and Lobster."

Whatever it was, it didn't sound good. "Something more than the shocking news that someone just tried to kill you again?"

"Related to that. We'll talk when you get here. Thank you, Gracie." Gloom oozed from her voice, and Grace began to worry in earnest.

"Are you sure you're alright?"

"I will be. See you soon."

Saturdays were popular days for travel, so Donovan was grateful Ben had arranged for a private flight. Bypassing the crowded parking lots, busy terminals, and long security lines, he made his way to a smaller, private airport nearby and, without much trouble at all, soon found himself heading west, relaxing alone in the spacious cabin of a Gulfstream G150.

Like himself, Ben grew up surrounded by wealth and luxury, though one would never guess it from his humble demeanor. After his mother died, he inherited an enormous family fortune, overnight becoming one of the wealthiest men in the country. But, like Donovan, Ben had no love or desire for the lifestyle or prestige of high society. Their mutual disdain for the entitled snobbery that often accompanied wealth had been a contributing factor in the rapid development of their friendship. Neither wanted that life and though, unlike Donovan, Ben hadn't successfully dodged it, there was no doubt in his mind that his friend would use his fortune to better the world while staying uncompromisingly true to who he was. Assuredly, if there was anyone who had the necessary temperament and character to manage the burden rightly, it was Ben Sawyer.

Despite the silver spoon, much of Ben's ingrained humility was forged in his childhood. The consequence of a careless night of drinking, Ben grew up with the stigma of being unplanned and unwanted by his parents. As far as

Donovan knew, he'd never met his father. Ben's mother was a confounded mess, despite being astonishingly beautiful. Afflicted with incurable depression and narcissism, Adalynn Sawyer was incapable of attachment and affection, even in regard to her only son. Apart from what she could selfishly gain from his inexhaustible loyalty and kindness toward her, Adalynn showed virtually no interest in Ben whatsoever, to the point of cruelty. Even after he miraculously survived leukemia as a young boy, she didn't change her behavior, remaining singularly focused on her own world, treating her son like he was virtually invisible.

Their families were acquainted, so Donovan and Ben had occasionally interacted through the years, but it wasn't until late high school that the two became close friends. When Donovan's parents rejected him because of his decision to serve in the military, Ben took him in. Though he and Ben quickly became as close as brothers, during the months he lived in the Sawyer home, Donovan often agonized as he watched Ben suffer at his mother's cold detachment, even as Ben did all he could to aid her in her unending sadness. Admittedly, as he observed Ben's one-sided faithfulness, Donovan felt some guilt at how quickly he'd given up on his parents after their rejection. However, though he and Ben shared many personality traits, it was a rare soul who could endure such constant neglect yet remain so consistently devoted. It was one of many qualities he admired in his friend.

In addition to the weight of his mother's issues, after living with him for a short while, Donovan discovered that there was something else that haunted Ben Sawyer. He kept his distance from people, not because he lacked compassion, for he certainly had no shortage of that, but because he was sincerely frightened to let others get too close. For reasons unknown to him, Donovan was somewhat of an exception to this rule, allowed more access to Ben's inner world than others, though there were still a few impenetrable barriers he'd never broken through. He guessed the awarded exception had something to do with the easy, instantaneous bond that had formed between them when they'd started spending time together in their late teens.

In Donovan's presence, Ben was lighter, less guarded, yet there were still secrets that remained locked away, beyond even Donovan's reach. On a few occasions, he had cautiously probed, inquiring about the mysterious dark corner of Ben's existence, but when the questions elicited panic and a reaction of sorrow, he backed off, not wishing to be the cause of more pain in his already troubled friend's life. Instinctively, he knew his role as Ben's closest friend was to be a comfort, a defender of sorts for this unique soul. Therefore, he couldn't risk doing or saying anything that compromised the trust between them, no matter how altruistic the motive.

After Adalynn's tragic suicide, Donovan had hoped that, despite the pain of her loss, the removal of the burdensome obligation he felt to cure his mother's depression would ease the discernible heaviness he carried. That hope had inspired him, several years ago, to reach out to Ben, though they hadn't been in touch for quite some time because of Donovan's overseas assignments. Upon witnessing his alarmingly troubled state, Donovan had begged Ben to stay in one place, to come and live with him for a time while he was stateside. The profound pain he was suffering was evident in his lifeless eyes, and Donovan knew he desperately wanted to accept the offer, but, in the end, Ben turned him down. He would never forget the tormented look on Ben's face as he turned to leave.

"I can't be fixed, Donovan. I'm a hopeless cause. I'll always be alone," he'd said, his eyes filled with a despair so raw it mirrored the desperation Donovan had seen too many times in the dying.

Grabbing his arm, Donovan pleaded with equal fervor. "It doesn't have to be that way, Ben. There's help, healing. You helped me once. Please, let me return the favor. You're like a brother to me. I can't let you just walk away, not like this."

His friend's deep blue eyes filled with unshed tears, as he slowly shook his head. "I wish... If things were different, if I wasn't..." He huffed in frustration, leaving the sentence incomplete.

"If you weren't what?" Donovan pleaded, trying to understand what torturous truth kept Ben on the run. It had to be something besides his mother's death. "Please, tell me what's holding you captive, keeping you from healing and finding the happiness you deserve. I want to help you. Please, my friend." The anguish in the plea was entirely genuine. The mysterious dark corner he'd observed in the past had taken over his friend's life, trapping him inside its locked doors. Ben was a prisoner now to this unknown master, and with everything in him, Donovan wanted to break him out of that hellish dungeon. More than a desire, it was a need. He had to help him. The urgency of the calling was as strong as the one he'd heeded when he'd joined the service.

For a fleeting second, the light of hope flickered in Ben's eyes, and Donovan thought he was finally going to trust him with the whole truth and let him into his hidden world. But as quickly as it had brightened, it faded again.

"It's my burden to carry, not yours. I won't force my

dearest friend to join me in living under the unbearable weight of my curse."

At that, he'd turned, rushing from the room before Donovan could answer. For a long time, he'd stood there, heartbroken and confused. Curse? What was he talking about? A sad representative of the Biblical warning, Ben was a man who had gained the world but had somehow lost his soul, though Donovan was confident it wasn't by his own choosing or fault.

Since that encounter, a day hadn't gone by without Donovan wondering about his old friend, always praying he would not follow in his mother's tragic footsteps and would someday return to take him up on his offer.

As his plane began its descent, Donovan smiled, a piece of his own heart mending at the hope that Ben had indeed found someone he could trust with his secrets. Shaking his head, he wondered what kind of remarkable woman had managed to convince him to stop running and start living. Donovan was certainly anxious to find out.

Fifteen minutes after she hung up with Callie, Grace pulled into her friend's driveway, gawking at the police presence surrounding the home. Patrol cars were everywhere, and uniformed officers meandered about, deploying metal detectors as they searched for evidence.

As she unbuckled her seatbelt and opened her door, Lobster pulled in behind her, and she waited for him to meet up with her before moving toward the door. Lobster —whose real name was Roberto—was an awkward, yet kind soul. Though he always looked unkempt—a problem Grace kept trying to remedy—his hair was particularly unruly today, likely a result of the short notice they'd been given when Callie called to summon them to her home.

Prior to Ben's entrance into their lives, he and Lobster had met before, though Grace hadn't heard the story yet. Whatever the history, since the day before when Callie at last officially introduced them, unaware of their prior connection, Lobster had begun acting even more strangely than usual. When in the same room, Lobster barely took his eyes off Ben, as if he were waiting for Ben to do something spectacular and didn't want to look away lest he miss it. It was odd, but that described virtually everything Lobster did.

"Can you believe this?" Grace lamented as she raked her fingers through Lobster's unruly black hair, trying to bring order to chaos. Perhaps because he was a few years younger than her and Callie, or perhaps because he simply needed taking care of, Grace had a motherly affection for him.

"She's okay though," he stated, sounding unsurprised by the fact.

"But she wouldn't have been if Ben hadn't been there. And he could have gotten himself killed as well." Her anxiety starkly contrasted with Lobster's calm demeanor.

He shook his head, the action causing her to give up on her attempts to tame his wild mane. "Not likely." He smiled tenderly at her, reversing the roles as he now looked like a parent trying to soothe an anxious child who was innocently ignorant of how the world works.

Grace crinkled her forehead, confused and a little indignant. "What does that mean?"

With a coy smirk, Lobster shrugged and began moving toward the front porch. Before joining him, she momentarily stared, then threw up her hands and sighed. She was used to the inadequacies of Lobster's communication skills but nevertheless baffled by his lack of distress or surprise.

As they approached the porch—the police officers watching them—Ben opened the front door and stepped out. Gesturing toward them, he spoke to the nearest officer, and afterward, the uniformed group descended the steps and moved past her and Lobster as Ben smiled and beckoned for them to join him.

"I hear you nearly got yourself killed today," Grace said, with a tone of mock scolding. Then she smiled. "But for a very worthy cause." Her expression sobered as her eyes locked on Ben's. "Thank you for saving her life."

Placing a hand on Grace's shoulder, Ben's eyes blinked as the emotion in his words unsteadied his composure. "I love her, and I owe her a debt I'll never be able to repay. As long as I'm alive, what happened to her a little over a week ago, will never happen again, Grace. You have my word on that."

Studying him silently, she smiled, admiring Ben Sawyer more with each encounter. "I believe you."

Ben shifted his gaze to Lobster, who grinned at him, as if sharing a private joke. Curious as he took in Lobster's expression, Ben nevertheless patted his shoulder as well. "Callie's waiting for you both. I'll let her fill you in on the plan, but I just wanted to assure you of my commitment to do whatever it takes to keep her out of harm's way." He stepped to the side. "Come on in."

When they entered the living room, Grace rushed to her friend's side, her heart dropping as she took in the tears on Callie's cheeks. "Girl, I'm so sorry. This is awful." She embraced her, and Callie leaned against her shoulder for a long time, before finally pulling back and taking Grace's hands.

"I'm alright," she forced out, then laughed at the ridiculousness of the attempted ruse. "The shock is wearing off, but the consequences are almost as difficult to accept."

Lobster stood over them, uncomfortable as he took in their raw emotions. Grace pointed to a nearby chair. "Have a seat," Grace commanded, and he happily complied, rubbing his hands on his knees nervously.

She turned back to Callie. "What consequences?"

"I have to leave, Gracie; get far away from here. An officer told Ben it would likely be a while before they'll catch whoever's after me and as long as I'm here, it's too easy for them to find me." She looked Lobster's way briefly. "I'm sorry."

"Leave? How can you leave? I mean, who will help you? What about your job and Lee and—"

"Ben's going with me. He has a plan and has arranged for a secure place for us to stay."

Grace rose to her feet. "Wait, wait. Callie, you know I like Ben and all, but you don't know him that well and he's not trained at protection or…" She squinted her eyes, recognizing she didn't actually know anything about Ben's background. "Is he?"

Callie smiled through a sniffle. "Not exactly, but he has an old friend who was a Navy SEAL. He'll be here in a few minutes to help us refine the plan, and he'll work with Ben to provide protection when we get to our destination. Between his training and Ben's… unique skills, I'll be well cared for, Gracie. And it's only for a little while. We're coming back. Ben wants that as much as I do."

Grace folded her arms. "Where are you going?"

"I can't say. Only a few know, and it's safer for everyone that way, but I'll be safe. Ben has saved my life twice already. He's not going to let anything happen to me. Please, don't worry."

Twice? Until this confession, Grace hadn't been entirely sure Ben was directly responsible for Callie's survival the night she'd been shot, but now her suspicion was confirmed. How had Ben managed to single-handedly save her from dying of two gunshot wounds?

Slowly, Grace returned and sat beside Callie once more. The mysteries surrounding Ben were piling up. But all Grace saw in Callie's eyes was unwavering trust, a firm belief that her life was safe in his hands.

"But you just got shot. You're still recovering and your dad just…"

"As we talked about before, timing doesn't always work out very conveniently. Sorry, HeartStrings will be forced to take a hiatus, but I will be back, Gracie, I will."

Grace shook her head, dizzy with a mix of emotions. On the one hand, she understood the urgency to get Callie out of town and away from this monster. But on the other, she knew how hard that would be, especially for her. For the last three years, Grace had helped her friend negotiate new environments, unfamiliar places and people. It had taken Grace months to learn how to be most helpful to Callie as she gradually gained an understanding of what she could and couldn't see. Ben had barely had enough time to begin that process and now Callie would be dependent on him. But her friend appeared unconcerned. In fact, though she was sad at the prospect of leaving, she showed no hesitation in placing her life in Ben's hands.

Swiping her index fingers under her eyes, she stared at Callie. "There's a lot more going on here than I know about, Isn't there?" Her own question surprised her, but as she took in Callie's guilty smile, she recognized that it had been precisely the right one to ask.

Remaining silent, Callie dropped her gaze. Grace looked over at Lobster, who appeared perfectly at ease, once more grinning as if he knew exactly what was going on. She raised her eyebrows at him, but he only shrugged. There were moments when she really wished her odd friend was more talkative, and this was definitely one of them.

At last, Callie looked back up at her. "Yes, that's true," she admitted hesitantly. "I'll share the details with you both at some point." Callie turned to Lobster. "Perhaps some of it is already known. Now's not the right time though. Not when we're leaving. Please just trust me when I tell you that I'm in good hands, and I'll be safe."

Leaning forward, Lobster put his hand on Callie's shoulder, a shocking gesture coming from him as he rarely touched anyone. "You will," he said simply, then rose and left the room, evidently having heard all he needed to hear.

So, there it was. Lobster did know something, something about Ben from the past that inspired his goofy grin.

As they watched him leave the room, Callie looked nearly as caught off guard by Lobster's behavior as Grace was, but her look held more comprehension than Grace's expression of total confusion. "I... I don't understand," Grace stammered, and Callie refocused on her.

"I know, and I deeply regret the confusion. You're my dearest friend and keeping you safe must be my highest priority right now. But, you know me well. You know I wouldn't make a decision like this recklessly, and I'd never leave Lee unless I was sure that was best for him too. Please, Gracie. Trust me and trust Ben until we are free to tell you more."

Sighing, she relented, having no legitimate arguments to offer in response. Callie LeVray was one of the smartest, most well-reasoned and practical people she knew. While Callie's heart trusted more easily than her own and always saw the best in people, Grace had to acknowledge that she herself hadn't detected anything in Ben's character or behavior that gave her cause for concern, so she had no grounds to doubt the words he'd spoken on the porch. "Alright, but you'd better stay in touch as much as you can, as I'll be worried sick." Another tear threatened to slide down her cheek as she imagined the long days of worry ahead, fretting over Callie's safety.

After ringing the doorbell, Donovan stepped back, surprised by how emotional he was about his and Ben's impending reunion. Despite the attachment they'd formed in their late teens, it had been years since they'd been a significant part of one another's lives, but the lapsed time hadn't dulled the affection he had for his friend and the reverse appeared to be true as well. Since Ben's phone call, something in Donovan had reignited, a familiar feeling he'd experienced before in Ben's presence. It was almost like déjà vu, but rather than the sensation of reliving a prior experience, this was more like a strong premonition of a fated future event. The odd feeling baffled him, just as it had years ago when Ben had visited him and he'd tried to convince him to stay.

When the door opened and his eyes met Ben's, Donovan couldn't hold back his smile. Ben's eyes were alive with hope and life and his smile revealed an inner peace.

"Donovan, my friend." Ben greeted him with enthusiasm, but for a moment, all Donovan could do was stare. This was indeed a different man than the one he'd known.

Observing his stunned expression, Ben chuckled and put one hand on Donovan's shoulder while extending the other. "It *is* me, your old friend, in the flesh."

Somewhat robotically, Donovan lifted his hand, but he didn't look away from Ben's eyes. In that moment, he was so overtaken by delight in the manifest change in his friend's life that he could have sworn he felt something tangible in Ben's touch. Though he knew he was imagining it, it was like a flood of warmth, like light, heat, or strength flowing into him. The ever-present aches that riddled his being momentarily vanished. Simultaneously, a look of grave concern flashed across Ben's face, and he released Donovan's hand and stepped to the side, beckoning him to enter.

"I can't tell you what it means to us to have your help. I'm anxious to catch up and introduce you to Callie and her brother and—"

Shaking off the surprise and confusion of the imagined experience, Donovan at last found his tongue. "Ben, you... You've truly changed. I barely recognize you."

Smiling, Ben studied his friend. "No doubt. You, however, haven't changed at all. You have the same kind smile I envision whenever I think of you. It's good to see it in person again. Thanks for coming all this way."

"I would have happily made the trip, just to meet the new man before me. It's everything I hoped for you."

Humbly, Ben lowered his gaze, but his smile remained.

Stepping back, Donovan folded his arms, his smile becoming crooked as he adopted a teasing tone. "So, do I get to meet her or is she too busy walking on water or raising more dying souls to life?"

Shaking his head, Ben laughed joyfully. "You most definitely get to meet her. She's in the living room with her friend, Grace, but I wanted to update you quickly on our current situation first." Soberly, Ben informed Donovan of the most recent frightening attempt on Callie's life and the status of the pursuit.

"I saw the police presence outside and assumed something was up," Donovan noted with concern. I'd like to meet with the officer in charge of the case before I leave town and get read in on the evidence and the leads they're pursuing. I may need to delay my return trip until I acquire the necessary information from relevant sources here."

"I'll let the pilot know to standby for your call. I'm sure it won't be a problem."

"Were either of you injured in this morning's attack?"

"A bullet grazed my shoulder, but I'm fine."

Donovan grimaced. "I've been grazed on several occasions, and it's no small matter, Ben. Were you checked out by a doctor?"

Shifting his weight, Ben appeared uncomfortable with the question. "It's nothing more than a scratch. No need for concern, I promise."

"Well, you were both very lucky then. Let's be certain neither this guy nor his associates get that close again. As I know your place in Boston well, I've already put together a plan for enhancing security. As soon as I'm done here, I'll get the tech installed and have it up and running before you get there with Callie."

"Perfect. I've informed Rosa and Leo—you remember they care for the house?—about your work there. They're anxious to see you again."

"Such kind people," Donovan said nostalgically.

Ben clapped his hands satisfactorily. "With that order of business taken care of, let's move forward with introductions, shall we?"

"By all means." Donovan gestured for Ben to proceed ahead of him as they moved into the living room.

CHAPTER 3

FAMILIAR STRANGERS

A few minutes after the doorbell rang, Ben entered the room, quickly approaching Callie and taking her hand as she rose to her feet. With pride in his voice, Ben introduced Callie to a man Grace couldn't presently see as her view was blocked by the two of them as she remained seated on the couch. When the stranger spoke, introducing himself and offering words of assurance, something in his voice caught Grace's attention.

Ben stepped aside and gestured toward her, and she politely rose, her vision still blurred by tears.

"And this is Callie's friend, Grace."

Blinking hard and making one last attempt to clear the tears with her thumbs, she at last looked up into the brown eyes that were intensely focused on her. Stifling an involuntary gasp, she stared, disoriented by a wave of unanticipated feelings.

The stranger was gorgeous, though not inhumanly so like Ben. His short hair was blond, though darker than her ashy shade, and his soft brown eyes glinted with flecks of the same golden hue. The rest of his facial features were strong, almost stern, but the eyes betrayed the conjured disguise. Several faded, vertical scars, one along the line of his right jaw and one above his left eyebrow, humanized him, enhancing rather than diminishing his appeal. He was tall and very fit, and when he stepped toward her and took her hand, she couldn't breathe.

Smiling at her, he lifted her hand to his lips, kissing it softly. Like the eyes, his smile also betrayed him, shattering any impression of harshness his other attributes may have conveyed.

Callie had told her this man was Ben's good friend, and indeed, there was a distinct resemblance in the two souls, though physically they looked nothing alike. In truth, though it surprised her to admit it, Grace judged Donovan more handsome, as his minor imperfections rendered him more real and relatable.

Or maybe it was something else entirely. As they remained locked in an unbreakable stare, Grace had the sudden impression that she'd met the man before, that she knew him, and he looked at her with the same inquisitive expression. But no matter how hard she tried, she couldn't recall meeting him, and she couldn't imagine, if she had, she would have ever forgotten the encounter.

At last, Donovan released her hand and stepped back, momentarily breaking eye contact to glance over at Ben. "Wow! How did you get so blessed as to be acquainted with such lovely women?" As soon as the last word was spoken, his gaze returned to Grace, and she felt her cheeks warm.

Though the conversation continued, Grace had no idea what was being discussed. Donovan's incredible eyes held her in some kind of spell, and she couldn't speak or move. Though he appeared unable to look away from her for more than a second, he managed to participate in the friendly chatter. Inwardly, she tried to free herself of the paralysis, realizing she must seem nearly as odd as Lobster, standing there mute and unresponsive. But it was no use. She was a captive to his eyes, and some previously dead or slumbering part of her heart awoke and rejoiced at its captivity.

At last, Callie politely excused them, took Grace's arm, and gently tugged at her. With one last smile, and a slight bow of his head, Donovan finally looked away, freeing her body to obey her commands again.

When they were outside, Grace sucked in a deep breath, the first full inhale she'd taken since meeting him. "Who was that?" she asked clumsily, the question too simple for the vast information sought by the inquiry. "I mean, I know his name and that he's an old friend of Ben's but..." She put both hands to her heart, noting that it still pounded irregularly. "Wow! He's... Wow!"

Callie smiled, but didn't respond, and Grace knew her muddled words had left her friend confused. "Where's he from?"

With an apologetic grimace, Callie shook her head. "No. Sorry. Still trying to keep everyone safe by not giving out too much information. If I can, I'll get you his number or give him yours."

Sighing, Grace relaxed, trusting her friend to carry through on the promise. "And here I was, worried you got the last knight in shining armor." She giggled. "Guess there's at least one more out there."

Callie embraced Grace, and the two women lingered in a sorrowful farewell.

As she drove home, she tried to make sense of her dizzying thoughts and calm the raging emotions in her heart. Genuine terror for her dearest friend gripped her soul. It felt wrong to let her leave, though Grace logically understood why she had to go. The protective instinct she had for Callie left her with a displaced sense of guilt for not acting to secure her safety, though she had no idea what she could possibly do.

Then there was Donovan. What had possessed her to stare at him like that? She'd never acted so ridiculously. Sure, she had been known to behave swoony around cute guys before, but this wasn't some girlish crush. Though his good looks had disarmed her, it had been his soul that held her prisoner, an instantaneous connection that was deeper than anything she'd experienced before.

Her last significant relationship lasted six months. From the beginning, she'd felt little attraction for him. He was reasonably good-looking, but there wasn't anything particularly interesting about him, no heart connection. When he began pressuring her to advance their physical relationship, she broke it off. She'd watched her mother freely give herself to one unworthy despot after another, and after suffering a few heartbreaks herself, she'd determined not to follow in her footsteps, vowing never again to give herself to anyone who wasn't worthy of her whole heart. Well aware that her standards were ridiculously high, she nevertheless had no intention of compromising or lowering them. It was safer that way as no man would or could ever live up to her expectations, so she easily avoided the temptation to relinquish her heart. That was, until that day.

"Grace Sophia," she scolded, speaking out loud as she drove. "You just met the man. You barely know his name." Laughing, she conceded that she actually didn't know his last name. Looking in the rearview mirror at her reflection, she continued the rebuke. "Stop acting like a silly schoolgirl, or"—she grimaced—"like your mother. He could be a serial killer, an irredeemable loser, or the embodiment of a million other unflattering descriptors. You'll probably never see him again anyway."

But her heart knew none of it was true. Ben wouldn't befriend a criminal, and no one with those gentle eyes harbored evil in his soul. Callie had said something about him being a soldier, and that would explain the scars and the tough-guy façade. But she'd instantly seen right through it, perhaps because his heart had experienced the same connection to hers as hers had to his. As he'd awakened something new in her, a part of her heart she didn't know existed, she wondered if, as she looked into his eyes, she likewise was the first to witness a part of him that no one before her had ever aroused. Despite the reasoned warnings she'd spoken to herself, she smiled, unable to do anything else as she softly spoke his name out loud for the first time. "Donovan."

Just before seven o'clock, Donovan left the police station after meeting with Officer Joe Evans, who was in charge of the investigation into Callie's assailant. Alarmed by the deadly hornets' nest she and Ben had inadvertently stepped right in the middle of, he was all the more determined to employ every skill he had in the effort to keep them safe from harm.

Relieved that they were now out of town and confident in the security plan the three of them had devised, Donovan pulled into a local deli to grab a quick bite before heading to the airport to catch his flight back to Boston. He had an hour, and he intended to use it wisely.

As he leisurely enjoyed a turkey sandwich and a bowl of potato soup, he combed through his notes from his meeting with Officer Evans, committing to memory each crucial piece of evidence they'd gathered thus far. The threat against Callie was so dire and the suspects so dangerous that he had already decided to bring in some additional help, including consulting with his contacts at the FBI. Though his skills were advanced, this enemy was connected and altogether soulless. Drug dealers were among the worst manifestations of evil humankind could produce, rivaled only by radicalized terrorists. He hated the thought of the sweet woman he'd met today, or his dearest friend, being hunted by such depravity.

Callie had turned out to be everything he'd hoped she'd be: tenderhearted, trusting, kind, and lovely. And there was no doubt that she was deeply in love with and unwaveringly devoted to Ben. They were a match made in heaven, a perfect pairing, and Donovan delighted in his friend's well-deserved happiness. The only lingering fear he had was that, if this all went bad and Ben lost her, it would permanently destroy him. Callie was his anchor, the solid ground keeping him from sinking into the quicksand he'd spent his whole life trying to escape. So, this mission was as much about saving his friend as saving his friend's girl.

The restaurant was quiet with just a few other patrons chatting softly in the spacious dining area. Pulling up past case files on his laptop, Donovan tapped a finger on the table as he considered who he might bring in on the case. He needed someone with knowledge and experience regarding the inner workings of this particular drug ring.

After cutting and pasting several contacts into his active case file, he looked up briefly, considering returning to the cashier for a cup of hot coffee, when someone at the counter caught his eye.

It can't be, he thought. Her back was to him, but the

silky, long blonde hair cascading over her black blouse was an unmistakable piece of the mental image he hadn't been able to remove from the front of his mind since his eyes had captured it. When she turned to the side, the profile confirmed his suspicion. It was her!

Though he'd done his utmost to forget her stunning face so he could focus on his mission, his training and practice at capturing every detail of a scene had worked against him this time. In perfect clarity, he recalled her light blue eyes framed by the longest and most delicate eyelashes Donovan had ever seen, her perfect nose and full pink lips, and her flushed cheeks as she imprisoned him, like a chained captive in her gaze. A few centimeters shy of five feet seven inches, she was a slim one hundred twenty-five pounds.

But more than these cold statistics he'd been trained to automatically assess, this young woman was enchanting, instantly shaking up his well-ordered world. Donovan had never been in love and, with his health situation and lifestyle, had spent little time considering the idea, but if there was such a thing as love at first sight, this had to be it.

As they'd stood in Callie's living room staring at one another, another emotion surfaced. Suddenly, he was certain that he knew the woman, that they'd met before, but he couldn't place when or where. Alongside her unshakable image, this impression had occupied his thoughts, but he was no closer to solving the mystery than he'd been when it first arose. But perhaps this coincidence was his chance to do so.

Leaving his laptop at the table, Donovan rose, his heart pounding as he noiselessly approached. Just finishing her order, she pulled a few napkins from the dispenser and reached into her small purse.

Closing the gap, he came up beside her, catching the eye of the teenager behind the counter. "It would be an honor to buy this lovely woman's dinner, if she'll graciously oblige me," he said, turning to her and bowing his head as she gasped in surprise.

"Donovan?" She put her hand over her heart as the shock of his unexpected appearance worked its way across her features.

Folding his arms, he smiled teasingly at her. "So, you do speak, ma'am. I'm relieved, but I'm even more delighted that you remembered my name."

Still gaping, her cheeks reddened. "I… Yes, Well, I…" She shook her head, having no idea what to say next.

Desiring to put her at ease, he held up both hands. "I don't wish to cause you any undue stress, but since fate has seen fit to bring us to the same restaurant this evening, it seems only right to indulge it by"—he gestured toward his table—"sharing a meal? If you would consider granting me the great honor."

Straightening her posture, she smiled, at last composed enough to play along. "Who am I to argue with fate, but if you buy me dinner, some might consider that a date."

Chuckling under his breath, Donovan glanced down at the small salad and cup of coffee on the counter. "Treating a woman to such inadequate sustenance most assuredly wouldn't be my idea of dating, ma'am. This situation could hardly qualify as anything more than a casual, friendly encounter, orchestrated by forces beyond our control."

Putting one hand on her hip, she stepped back from the counter. "Well, alright then. Since we're nothing more than helpless victims of circumstance…" She gestured toward the cashier, and Donovan nodded in gratitude as he requested an additional cup of coffee, paid the bill, and then picked up the tray.

"After you, ma'am," he said with a smile of satisfaction as they moved away from the counter.

When they'd settled and Donovan had closed and set aside his laptop, he retrieved his coffee from the tray and leaned back in his seat. "Now, first things first. I believe a full and proper introduction is in order. I'm Donovan Bradshaw, and you are Grace…"

"Sophia," she responded, looking appreciative of the clarification.

Closing his eyes, he pondered silently, trying to match the last name with any prior connections but, at last, he shook his head, confident he'd never encountered anyone with that name before. "Unfortunately, that doesn't solve the mystery," he said, trying not to become trapped again by her soft blue eyes.

"Mystery?" she inquired, picking up her fork and placing a napkin in her lap.

Donovan took a sip of coffee before answering. "Your face is so familiar, Miss Sophia. I'm sure we've met before. It's been confounding me all day, but I can't place the encounter."

Grace's eyes grew wide. "I've had the same feeling."

Setting his cup on the table, he leaned forward. "Then there must be something to it. Have you had more luck at recalling the connection?"

Her lips turned up in a shy smile as she shook her head. "None whatsoever."

"Then I suppose we'll have to remain in contact with one another, at least until we've resolved the quandary. It would be improper to leave the matter unsettled."

Her smile grew. "I suppose it would."

For several heartbeats, they held each other's gaze. The sense of familiarity intensified, frustrating him as, despite his teasing, he was sincere in his desire to discover its source.

"Mr. Bradshaw," Grace said at last, breaking the spell as she looked down at her salad.

"It's just Donovan, ma'am."

Grace giggled sweetly. "But you keep calling me ma'am, so it seems only fair that—"

"Forgive me. I'm a little old-fashioned, and my military training has rendered certain practices habitual, but I... I very much enjoyed it when you called me by my first name." Feeling awkward about the admission, he nervously shifted the cup in his hand.

Her easy smile dispelled his discomfort. "Donovan it is then." She sighed, and her smile withered. "I know you can't say much, and I'm not asking for details, but..." She blinked as her eyes grew moist. "I love Callie like a sister, Donovan. Will she be alright?"

Wishing he could take her hand, but knowing that would be way too forward, he did his best to offer her the most compassionate expression he could muster. "I won't lie to you, Miss Sophia. Miss LeVray's in significant danger, but she has two vital advantages. First, Ben Sawyer. I've known Ben for a long time. He's smart, resourceful, and strong. I can guarantee you he'll give up his life before letting any harm come to her. Second, every resource and skill I have is at her and Ben's disposal. I've been doing this kind of work for a long time and, at the risk of sounding arrogant, I'm good at my job. There's no absolute guarantee, but she's in good hands."

Her shoulders relaxed, but tears still glistened in her eyes. "Are they... Did they leave?"

"Yes, I saw them safely out of town myself a few hours ago and followed them until I was certain they weren't being trailed. They'll be on the move until they reach their destination and that will keep them out of danger."

"And you'll be there when they get to wherever they're going?" There was a plea in the question, and Donovan was honored by the solace this idea brought her.

"Affirmative. And I will stay nearby and actively engaged until this crisis has passed. I give you my word."

Pressing her lips together, she nodded appreciatively. "Will you stay in touch with me, let me know they're alright? I mean, I hope Callie will be able to call me herself too, but..."

"It would be my pleasure, but might I also submit a personal request for your consideration?" He smiled teasingly, even as a protesting voice shouted inside his head. What he was about to do wasn't wise, but he couldn't resist his heart's urging.

She raised her eyebrows.

"When this is over, and your friend returns home safely, may I have the privilege of escorting you on a real date, Miss Sophia, with real food and formal attire, the whole package?"

Silently, she considered his request as she chewed on a bite of her inadequate dinner. Then she smiled at him, the expression saturating the dry places in his heart as it conveyed genuine affection. "I suppose a worthy deed, like rescuing my best friend from a heartless monster, deserves a just reward. But I do generally like to know more about a man before entrusting myself into his care for an evening." She smirked. "You know, basic stuff, like where he's from."

Apologetically, he shook his head. "I'm afraid that one has to stay under wraps for now, but I'm happy to oblige your reasonable expectation by providing you with as much information as I can"—he paused to glance at his watch—"in the next fifteen minutes as, unfortunately, I will need to leave soon to catch my flight. What would you like to know that would set your mind at ease?"

Momentarily frowning in disappointment, she recovered quickly, sweeping her hair over her shoulder as she adopted a determined expression. "So, it will have to be rapid fire then. Are you sure you're prepared?"

Leaning back again, he held out his hand. "Fire away."

Grimacing, she shook her head. "Don't say I didn't warn you. Despite your military background, I doubt you've ever met an interrogator quite like me. I can be ruthless."

Donovan couldn't stifle the chuckle that escaped his lips as he stared at the delicate, slight woman across the table, who, paradoxically, possessed the spirit of a lion. In truth, he found the combination extremely attractive, but it was nevertheless difficult to take her warning seriously.

Taking a deep breath, he forced a somber expression and set his hands flat on the table, as if bracing himself. "I can take it."

Looking doubtful, she plotted her approach, taking a slow sip of coffee before speaking. "Are you currently married, engaged, or otherwise involved romantically with anyone?"

"No, ma'am."

A smile momentarily weakened her no-nonsense demeanor. "Have you ever been convicted of a crime?"

"Negative."

"Are you addicted to any substance: drugs, alcohol, nicotine, or the like?"

Donovan lifted his cup. "Nothing but coffee, ma'am."

She offered him a crooked nod. "Coffee is acceptable."

He swiped a hand across his forehead, relieved at the allowed exception.

"Have you ever been unemployed for more than six months?"

"Not unless you count the years before I was of an employable age."

A quick shake of her head reassured him that his answer was satisfactory.

"Do you expect a kiss, or perhaps more, on a first date?"

"I expect nothing from a woman, at any time. A kiss isn't worth receiving unless it is freely and enthusiastically given."

Though her lips remained straight, her eyes sparkled.

"Do you believe in any weird superstitions that control your life, like not sleeping when there's a full moon or never eating pancakes on Wednesdays?"

Amused, Donovan squinted his eyes, curious about the origin of this question. "None of which I'm consciously aware."

"Do you presently or have you ever practiced any variety of witchcraft?"

"As I consider myself a man of faith, that too is a hard negative."

"With that answer, I can skip the next two questions," she informed him with an approving nod.

"By all means, continue, but as a side note, we must someday converse about the irregular men you've been acquainted with who have inspired the need for, as well as the content of these questions," he said with a mixture of amusement and sincere concern.

She lowered her gaze to the salad in front of her as she responded. "Perhaps someday," she whispered. "But for now, I'll just say that, in my experience, the number of men who can make it this far into the questioning without striking out is infinitesimally small." Raising her eyes to his, she at last offered him a smile with a hint of flirtatiousness. "I believe you are the irregular one, Donovan Bradshaw, and I believe your friend is as well."

"Any measure of comparison that places me in the esteemed company of Ben Sawyer is a most welcome honor." He placed his elbows on the table and folded his hands together. "Please. Proceed."

"Which is more important to you, people or money?"

He allowed a few seconds of silence before responding. "Well, Miss Sophia, considering I walked away from a guaranteed fortune in order to serve my country, I don't think there can be much doubt about which I favor."

Surprised, she was quiet for an awkward moment. "That's... I'm sorry."

"Don't be," Donovan said casually. "It was one of the best decisions I've made in my life, even though..." He dropped his hands onto the table and lowered his eyes, hoping she wouldn't ask him to finish the sentence, though, in fairness to her, he undoubtedly should.

Silence hung between them as Grace considered her response. What was he doing with this poor girl? He should tell her the whole truth, that he was a dying man, not likely to live long enough to offer her anything but a broken heart.

Grace slowly inhaled, then sighed, the sound conveying satisfaction. "I don't need to ask you any more questions, Donovan."

He shook his head. "Truly? Lovely lady, if you think that qualified as vigorous interrogation, I'd like to introduce you to my drill sergeant from basic, or a few like him who tormented me during SEAL training. Mercy was not a concept they were familiar with," he said, whistling a breath of air through his lips.

"Oh, there were a lot more probing questions," she defended, raising a finger in the air. "But I don't need to ask them because I'm reasonably sure I already know the answers."

"Oh?" he questioned, but she only smiled.

Appearing quite at ease now, she lifted her cup, took a sip, then placed it back on the table, apparently having nothing more to say on the matter.

Donovan glanced at his watch. "Regrettably, I only have a few moments left so..."

She took another sip of coffee, put her elbow on the table, and rested her chin on her hand. "So..."

Pleadingly, he touched his palms together and locked her in his gaze. "Miss Sophia, if I may be permitted to know, please relieve my suspense."

"Suspense?" Though he had thought she was teasing him, she now looked genuinely confused.

"Your answer, ma'am, regarding my invitation to escort you on a real date when the matter with our mutual friends is resolved."

Giggling, Grace briefly reached across the table to touch his arm. "I'm sorry, Donovan. I thought... I guess I thought my answer was obvious, even before the interrogation began."

"Far from it," he admitted, lowering his arms to the table to make it easier if she should happen to want to touch him again. "I'm afraid I still remain stranded in the dark."

"I'm sorry," she repeated, the apology mingled with another soft giggle. "I guess I'm not very good at this." She cleared her throat and forcefully sobered her expression, though she couldn't entirely restrain her disobedient smile. The look was so endearing that, once more, Donovan fought the impulse to reach for her hand. "I accept, as I would enjoy the opportunity to get to know you better, Donovan Bradshaw."

Blowing a relieved breath through his lips, he sat back once more. "So, I passed the test?"

"With flying colors."

CHAPTER 4

MYSTERIOUS SHADOWS

To define Grace's mood as she drove home as 'floating on cloud nine' would be an understatement. Though part of her still engaged in some gentle self-rebuke at her unbridled exuberance, the dominant voice in her head argued that it was justified, as the odds of finding anyone like Donovan were so small that she'd long since given up on the possibility. Gorgeous, kind, and good were a combination of traits not commonly found in any single human being, much less men of her generation.

Though she wasn't entirely sure how to respond to it, having never encountered such behavior, Donovan's old-fashioned, gentlemanly way of communicating was refreshing and extremely charming. In his presence, she felt like she was living in a different time, an era when men treasured the company of a lady and felt obliged to show her the utmost respect through impeccable manners and genuine deference. If more men knew how attractive that kind of treatment was to a woman, it might not be so uncommonly practiced, though Grace guessed few men could pull it off with such sincerity. Donovan wasn't putting on an act. That was genuinely who he was.

Still, there was a cautious voice that warned her this was too good to be true. There must be a catch. But then, Callie had found Ben, and there didn't appear to be anything insincere about him.

"Just relax, Grace," she admonished as she pulled into her driveway. "Don't cheat yourself out of enjoying this." She did have a way of ruining a good thing by overthinking it until her negative expectations latched onto something to justify their existence. This was particularly true when it came to men. She expected them to let her down, and indeed, every single one she'd dated had done just that.

As she got ready for bed that night, she took a moment to stare at herself in her bathroom mirror. "Don't do that to Donovan. He's a good man. Give him a real chance."

Just before falling off to sleep, Grace's phone buzzed, and she retrieved it from its charging station on her night-stand. Her heart pounded when she saw Donovan's name in the notification of a new message.

> I hope you don't think me too forward, Miss Sophia, but though it was fate that brought us together this evening, I find myself grateful for the chance to get to know you better and enthusiastic about continuing to do so, if that would be of interest to you. After all, you may decide some of those probing questions you omitted are indeed important, and I wouldn't want to give you grounds for changing your mind about our anticipated date by being unavailable to answer them.

Smiling as her heart sped up, she tapped out a response.

> While I'm willing to consider continuing our
> dialogue, I do have one condition.

> Name it.

> You must, at least sometimes, call me
> Grace.

A full minute passed before Donovan's response came.

> I accept your terms… Grace.

She laughed out loud, knowing how difficult that was for him.

> I appreciate the concession. Have you left
> town?

> Affirmative, though admittedly with more
> regret than I anticipated feeling when I
> arrived there this morning.

Though she was alone in her bedroom, her cheeks warmed at the implied compliment.

> How long have you and Ben been friends?

> Our families were acquainted, so we
> interacted casually a few times as children,
> but it wasn't until late high school that we
> became close.

Pondering, Grace realized she had no idea how old Ben was, much less Donovan.

And that was... how many years ago?

I'll make you a deal, ma'am. I'll tell you my
age, but first, will you allow me to guess
yours?

Guess away.

Twenty-four. No, I think twenty-three, but
soon to be twenty-four.

Squinting at her screen, she was stunned by his
answer.

How did you...?

Does that mean I'm correct?

Exactly right. My birthday is late next
month. But seriously, how did you know?

I was trained to assess visible stats about
people quickly. I could also tell you your
exact height and weight, but I don't think
that's a dignified thing for a gentleman
to do.

I appreciate that, but you've got me at a
disadvantage, Donovan Bradshaw. I don't
possess those skills.

I'll gladly provide you with the information,
as that's only fair, but perhaps you'd
surprise yourself if you ventured a guess.

Shaking her head, Grace was doubtful about his
prediction.

I'll skip the weight part as that's certainly
none of my business, but alright, I'll oblige
you. Give me a moment to think…

At your leisure, ma'am.

She did her best to concentrate, but picturing his handsome face and fit physique caused her mind to wander into areas she probably shouldn't entertain, so she threw up her hands and tapped out the first guess that came to mind.

Six feet three inches and… twenty-eight?

Miss… Grace! You are much better at this
than you gave yourself credit for. The height
is right on, and the age is only one year off.
I am twenty-nine.

Wow! It was a complete shot in the dark,
though our mutual sense of familiarity,
along with other factors, may have caused
me to be more observant than usual.

Grace's finger lingered over the 'send' button, as she feared this message might be too bold, but it was the truth, so in the end, she chose to proceed. When there was a significant pause before her phone buzzed again, she began to regret her decision.

A sense of familiarity isn't the only mutual
feeling between us, Miss Sophia. But I am
nevertheless impressed by your
observational skills. So, returning to our
original discussion, Ben and I have been
good friends for over a decade now, though
distance and circumstances have kept us
apart for the majority of that time.

Though flattered by the implied compliment, Grace was relieved that he didn't linger there but instead returned the conversation to topics more suitable to their current level of intimacy.

> Because you were overseas?

> That's a big part of it.

> How many years did you serve?

> Just shy of ten years.

> And you're retired now, permanently out of
> the military?

> Affirmative.

> May I ask why you left?

No response came, so Grace sent another message.

> I'm sorry, Donovan. It isn't my business.
> Please disregard my question.

Another minute passed, and Grace began to worry in earnest, but at last, her phone buzzed again.

> It's a perfectly reasonable question, and
> you had every right to ask it. I was injured,
> quite severely, and that resulted in my
> discharge from service.

Recalling the scars on his face, Grace's heart fell and she wished she had never broached the subject. But ignoring it now without explanation would make her appear cold and uncaring.

Donovan, I'm truly sorry. I didn't mean to broach a topic so painful or personal. My heart aches at the revelation, but I recognize this isn't the right time or communication method to further this delicate conversation, so please don't think me indifferent if I redirect in order to give you the appropriate space and privacy on this matter.

That is most kind, ma'am.

Though Grace's heart continued to ache as she couldn't help but wonder about the suffering and trauma this good man had endured, it didn't take long for the conversation to regain its easy, playful tenor.

When they at last said good night, Grace lay in her bed staring at the ceiling. For the first time in her entire life, she felt... well, she wasn't exactly certain what she felt, but whatever it was, it was unlike anything she'd ever felt for a man before. Attraction, certainly, but not just to his body. Donovan had a beautiful heart, a genuinely kind soul, and she found herself wanting to know everything about him, even the parts of him that had been singed by pain. It was clear that his years in the service had left him with deep scars, not exclusively of the physical kind. But the fact that he had suffered such hardship, yet remained capable of such gentleness was extraordinary. Even his present career, protecting innocents from evil, had to frequently place him in situations where righteous violence was necessary. How did he keep his soul intact, his humanity?

Suddenly feeling as if she lived a sheltered, pampered life in comparison, Grace acknowledged that she knew nothing of Donovan's world, the soldier's dilemma that must confront so many who have served and sacrificed as he had, though she wanted to try to understand. But it had to be his choice, on his timeline. He didn't really know her yet, not enough to trust her with such deep wounds.

And as much as she rejoiced in at last meeting someone worth pursuing, the truth was she had her own baggage to contend with, past prejudices about men and relationships to wrestle. As long as she maintained the strict belief that there was no man on earth worthy of her heart, she didn't have to face those demons. But if there was one, a man whose goodness had been tested by fire yet had survived unconsumed, his mere existence would inevitably force her to confront her past hurts. The thought frightened her, but if he was strong enough to thwart the darkness, perhaps she could be too.

The following evening, Donovan sent her a message asking for permission to call her, rather than text, and she granted his request.

"Have you... Have you heard from them?" she asked hesitantly after a few minutes of light conversation.

"Not directly, but I'm following their progress as I clear the trail behind them, erasing credit card records and the like. They're alright, Grace. Don't worry."

"I tried Callie's phone today, but it didn't go through."

"Out of concern that their old phones may have been compromised, they have only a burner for the trip. I'll be setting them up with new secure phones when they arrive. I'll be sure you get Miss LeVray's new number."

"Thank you, Donovan." A sigh accompanied her words. "And, thank you for keeping my best friend safe from this... this..."

"It's my pleasure and privilege, ma'am. This is what I'm

meant to be, do. Which reminds me, despite all our introductory conversation, I have no idea what you do for a living. What's your passion, Miss Sophia?"

Hesitating, Grace felt insecure about sharing this information as, in comparison to his calling and work, hers seemed superficial. "I... I studied marketing in college, and I currently work for a local firm. But what I really enjoy is managing and promoting the performance trio Callie and I are a part of, along with our unique friend whom we affectionately call Lobster."

"Smart and beautiful. And apparently talented as well. What's your part in the trio?"

"I play the violin, Callie the cello, and Lobster the piano. Our group has become something of a household name in this town, but the best part is getting to perform with my dearest friends."

"I very much look forward to hearing you play if you'd consider issuing me an invitation to one of your performances when Miss LeVray returns. And I'd enjoy the chance to meet your friend, as I'm curious about that unusual nickname and the characterization of him as *unique*."

Grace laughed. "He's a character alright. Incredibly, Lobster actually knows Ben, I mean, he knew him prior to Callie introducing the two of them a few days ago."

"Oh? How's that?"

"I'm not sure of the details. I haven't had the chance to hear the full story yet, and..."

"And?" Donovan prompted, curiosity in his tone.

"Donovan, you've known Ben for a long time. Do you... Do you ever get the sense that there's something... I don't know, mysterious about him? I mean, Ben is kind and good, there's no doubt about that, but there's something he carries, a shadow of sorts. I think Callie knows what it is and so does Lobster. The way Lobster looks at him, it's peculiar, like he's his hero or something."

There was a moment of silence on the line before Donovan responded. "As I noted yesterday, Miss Sophia, your observational skills are unusually keen. I know precisely what you're referring to, but I can't offer you clarity as I've never solved the mystery myself, though I've tried on several occasions. Ben had it rough growing up, not materially, but in the way of affection. The fact that he turned out to be so kindhearted is an outright miracle. But even with that background, it doesn't explain the invisible yet easily discernible burden he carries. I've endeavored to help him by offering to shoulder some of it, but I'm afraid my efforts have been unsuccessful. If what you say is true, if Miss LeVray knows, I'm glad as that would explain the remarkable change in him, which I was ecstatic to observe yesterday. If he's found in Miss LeVray someone to trust with his secret, someone who will love him unconditionally, then I'm quite content in knowing my friend is at last happy and at peace, as no one could be more deserving."

Hearing the raw emotion and deep affection in Donovan's voice, Grace's respect and admiration for him grew. "You feel for Ben what I feel for Callie. The attachment goes deeper than friendship. It's like... family, well, what I suppose family should properly be."

Grace heard Donovan's sympathetic inhale. "There's pain behind that statement, Miss... Grace, that I won't presently pursue, as you've granted me the same courtesy, but I am nevertheless moved by it and can, perhaps, relate to it. And yes, I couldn't love Ben any more if he were my blood brother."

"Well, then, perhaps you and I should make a pact based on the mutual affection we have for our friends."

"I'm intrigued."

"With the danger they're facing, they could use all the love and support we have to give. As I am confident enough in your character to grant you my full trust in regard to your judgments of Ben, I will vow to extend my affections and loyalties, which I presently hold for Callie, to Ben as well. After all, it appears near certain that the pair are permanently linked. And perhaps you will consider granting the same extension of affection to Callie?"

Donovan chuckled softly. "Already done."

The following evening, Donovan sat at the island in Ben's Boston home, double-checking the advanced security equipment he'd spent the day installing, looking for gaps or malfunctions. Having lived there before, the process had been easier than usual as he already knew the layout of the land, including pre-existing features, like the iron entrance gate on the south side of the property and the river on the north. Though Ben had told him he had more than one reason for choosing that location, it was nevertheless a good decision to bring Callie there as the home's numerous natural barriers made it virtually inaccessible, except directly through the locked gate. The cameras and sensors were conveniently linked to a secure app on his phone, which he had also installed on Ben's new one, making it easy to monitor unexpected or suspicious activity.

In addition to setting up the equipment, Donovan had made several phone calls to contacts at the FBI, only to discover that the case was already active inside the agency, under the supervision of an agent named Wes Taylor, someone with whom Donovan was unacquainted. An hour earlier, he'd left a message on Agent Taylor's voicemail but was still awaiting a returned call.

"Sure is good to have you here again, Mr. Bradshaw," Rosa said with a warm smile, setting a bowl of soup in front of him.

Donovan smiled at the kind older woman who, along with her husband Leo, had, as far as Donovan knew, been the only loving influences in Ben's childhood. The caretakers of the enormous home, the caring couple had been far more parental than Ben's biological mother, treating him and, by extension, Donovan like family.

"It's a pleasure to be back"—he lifted a spoonful of soup—"enjoying your exquisite home cooking and your kind company, ma'am, though I do wish it was under better circumstances."

"You'll have this sorted in no time," she said confidently with a wave of her hand. "I'm just thankful he's comin' home at last. My heart's achin' to see him." Her eyes shadowed. "How is he, Mr. Bradshaw? Leo and I been worried sick since... Well, you know."

Donovan placed his hand on top of the old woman's rough and wrinkled one as he looked her in the eye. "Changed, Miss Rosa, and all for the better. Miss LeVray appears to be the healing salve his broken heart needed."

Her eyes filled with tears, even as she returned his smile. "I'll be!" she exclaimed. "I'm anxious to meet the girl who could accomplish such a wondrous miracle."

Chuckling, Donovan picked up his spoon again. "She's as special as you might imagine. I'm looking forward to getting to know her better myself."

Wrinkling her brow, Rosa's expression shifted, conveying mischievousness mixed with genuine curiosity.

"And you, sir? Has your heart been touched by a special young woman?"

Donovan dropped his gaze.

"It has. Then why the sadness?"

Avoiding the woman's eyes, Donovan stared at his soup. "I just met her recently, but she's... extraordinary! I feel like I've known her for years, and she appears to feel the same." He looked up, shaking his head as the strain in his voice grew thick. "But I shouldn't have pursued anything with her, let it get even this far, Miss Rosa. Grace is beautiful, spirited, smart, and kindhearted, everything I could want in a woman, but I've not been honest or fair to her. I have no choice but to end it. I have nothing to offer her, no chance at a future. I..."

This time, Rosa reached over and put her hand on Donovan's, her dark, weathered eyes sorrowful, yet determined. "Nobody knows the future, Mr. Bradshaw, and if she's as wonderful as you say, all she's wanting is your heart, and you got that to give her. Trust her enough to tell her 'bout whatever's troubling you. Let her be the one to decide."

Just then, Donovan's phone buzzed with a text message, and Rosa patted his hand before quietly leaving the room. Glancing at the screen, Donovan easily recognized the number as that of the burner phone he'd given Ben.

Almost there. Stopped for dinner. Be there late, probably after eleven. Would you be able to meet me at the house at eleven thirty? Something important to discuss.

Affirmative. Security's all set here. Ready for your arrival.

Fantastic! Thank you, my friend. Just let
yourself in tonight as Callie will likely be
asleep. See you soon.

When Donovan returned to the Sawyer home late that night, he was pleased and relieved to see Ben's vehicle with his own eyes, even though he had already been alerted to their arrival by the home's new and enhanced surveillance system.

Quietly, he let himself into the Sawyer mansion, but there was no sign of Ben, so he wandered into the kitchen and helped himself to a tepid glass of water.

A few minutes later, Ben appeared in the doorway, looking disheveled and utterly exhausted.

"Ben!" Donovan exclaimed, staring at him in surprise. In slow motion, Ben approached, moving gingerly as if he were in as much pain as Donovan always was, but lacking Donovan's practiced façade.

Rushing to his aid, Donovan offered Ben a supportive grip on his arm, and Ben accepted the help, nodding in appreciation. "What in the world happened to you? Are you alright?"

Smiling weakly, Ben leaned into Donovan, and they slowly made their way to the nearest stool. When they'd sat down, Ben exhaled, the sound conveying relief as much as weariness. "It's a very long story, but we made it in one piece, and that's the important thing."

"Did something happen on the trip?" Donovan pressed, scrutinizing Ben's appearance as his heart pounded with worry.

"Nothing related to the threat against Callie's life. In

that regard, the trip went smoothly." Ben waved a hand in the air. "Everything's fine. In fact"—he managed a nearly full grin—"I made a decision this morning that I'll need your help with, primarily as a friend, but also as the man in charge of security around here."

Baffled by Ben's casual attitude regarding his debilitated state and quick change of subject, Donovan struggled to adopt Ben's enthusiasm. "Um, of course, but..."

"I'm going to ask Callie to marry me."

Straightening, Donovan's mouth fell open. "Um... I... That's outstanding, Ben. I couldn't be happier for you both, but..."

Ben put up a hand. "Not now, after this is all over, but I need to go out tomorrow morning and pick up the ring. I'll make it early and quick, so hopefully she won't get suspicious as she'll likely sleep late since she's almost as tired as I am." Ben leaned on his elbows. "But, under no circumstances will I leave her unprotected. Would you be available in the morning to be here with her, just for a few hours?"

"Of course, I'd be happy to, and it will give us a chance to get better acquainted, but..." Donovan held out an open hand, subtly waving it in Ben's direction. "You must tell me what happened. I know you well, Ben Sawyer. You don't get sick, weak, or tired. If something transpired on the way here, I need to know about it as I'm now responsible for your and Callie's safety. Please."

With a look of affectionate gratitude, Ben tried again for a reassuring smile. "Last night we came upon some people who needed our help. We were able to render aid, but it was... it was a bit more difficult than we anticipated." He leaned away. "It cost us a night of sleep and Callie... Donovan, she was amazing; she saved my life, really. When I first met her, because of fear, I almost walked away, unable to believe she was everything she seemed to be. I didn't think she could love someone like me." His eyes moistened, and Donovan's heart was deeply moved by the intensity of the emotions in his friend's voice. "But in the end, I realized I couldn't live without her, so I took a chance, even though I knew, if she couldn't accept me, love me back, it would kill me."

Without thinking, Donovan nodded, relating to Ben's dilemma as ironically, despite his lack of understanding regarding Ben's mysterious references, he presently faced a similar choice.

Slowly, Ben shook his head, his smile still firmly in place, even as his eyelids drooped from weariness. "Until yesterday, I still had doubts, still wasn't confident she could carry the heavy burdens partnering with me would unfairly place on her. But I have no more doubts now, my friend. Despite it all, she still loves me, wants me. She's the one, made for me and me for her." At the proclamation, his eyes brightened, and he sat up straighter, the truth visibly strengthening him as Donovan watched, still astounded at how dramatically love had transformed his friend.

Reaching over, Donovan patted Ben's arm, his voice hoarse as he responded. "Your happiness brings me more joy and satisfaction than I can express. I'll be here first thing tomorrow, and I'll protect Miss LeVray, the future Mrs. Sawyer, with my life."

As Donovan drove home, he meditated on Ben's words, turning them over and over in his mind. Much of what he said made little sense as he still had no idea what the "burden" he referred to was or how Callie had saved his life. He'd spoken the truth when he'd said Ben didn't get sick, tired, or weak as, in all the years he'd known him, he'd never seen him in any of those states. Whatever the "shadow" was, as Grace called it, Donovan was now sure it had nothing to do with his mother or her death. Now that Ben was back in his life, Donovan's need to understand, to solve the mystery was more pressing, and seeing his friend in such a weakened state exacerbated that feeling.

But momentarily setting aside that issue, Ben's statements about trusting Callie despite his fears, deciding it was better to take a chance than to play it safe and let his heart wither and die from the loss of her, repeated on a torturous loop in his mind. But wasn't Donovan's situation different? Wasn't the fact that his doctors had given him a literal death sentence, no hope or chance of survival long term, a deal breaker?

Though he'd only known Grace for a few days, something deep in his heart told him she was his Callie, the one made for him and he for her. It was crazy to feel so certain of that so quickly, but in twenty-nine years he'd never come anywhere close to feeling that way about a woman. This wasn't a naïve, boyish fantasy. He'd lived too long and too hard for that kind of immaturity. He and Grace had a soul connection that couldn't be understood with the mind, only the heart.

But he'd found her too late. Five years ago, pursuing her would have made sense, and could have been justified. But now, his life was all but over. Very possibly, guarding Callie and Ben would be the last case he'd ever see through to the end. As it was, the doctors had advised him weeks ago to quit his job and check into the hospital. But he saw no point in spending his last months rotting away, no matter how bad the pain. If this was the end, he wanted to go out in service to others, giving his last ounce of strength to keep someone safe from evil. They couldn't do much for him in the hospital anyway and lying around depressed and futile would only accelerate his end.

But he couldn't deny that his body was weakening by the day and the pain was becoming unbearable. He wouldn't be able to keep up the act much longer, even though he'd become quite skilled, able even to fool his best friend into thinking him strong and well.

Nevertheless, the truth was, his kidneys were failing, damaged beyond repair by the blast and bullets that had nearly blown them out of his body. And that was only one of a myriad of life-threatening conditions. Soon, he'd have no choice but to surrender, to lie down and wait for death to come and take him. There was no escaping this truth, so why was he behaving as if there were? Why was he dooming Grace to certain disappointment, or if she indeed felt for him what he already felt for her, much worse?

But the idea of reversing course, cutting off all contact with her flooded him with a kind of hopelessness and despair even his dire prognosis hadn't evoked. Into the bleakness of his rapidly darkening world, Grace had shone a light, and without her, he had no will to go on.

Nevertheless, Rosa was right. He needed to tell her the truth. It was immoral to keep her in the dark, to let their connection deepen, even for one more day. Though selfishly he wanted to conceal the matter, pretend it didn't exist so he could keep her in his life, that wasn't the kind of man he was.

As the day had been busy, he and Grace hadn't had time to exchange more than a few casual text messages, and now it was too late to call her. But he would speak with her soon, maybe try to catch her before she went to work. Somehow, he'd find the strength to tell her the truth.

As he thought about their chance encounter and some of the peculiar questions she'd asked him, he grimaced, wondering what her response would have been if she'd had the notion to ask him the most important question of all. "If I should give you my heart, can you promise not to turn around and break it?"

CHAPTER 5

CALLINGS AND QUESTIONS

Donovan saw Ben off early the following morning. Though he still looked tired, his enthusiasm regarding his errand provided him with an ample supply of compensating energy. Once more, Donovan gently pressed him for an explanation for his weakened state, but Ben simply patted his shoulder and told him not to worry.

But Donovan was worried. Something in his gut warned him that the situation they'd gotten involved in was fraught with more consequences than they were willing to acknowledge, even to themselves. Lending a helping hand to a stranger and thereby missing one night of sleep wouldn't have resulted in that extreme state of debilitation. Ben could barely walk, and he looked as if he'd missed weeks of sleep. It didn't add up. Why Ben was being resolutely ambiguous about the details was puzzling, but then, if this was related in some way to his mysterious secret, the elusiveness wasn't entirely unprecedented.

Nevertheless, if Donovan were going to successfully protect them, he needed all the facts, as that could make the difference between life and death. Sitting at the kitchen island watching his screen for any signs of danger and eating a plateful of Rosa's legendary pancakes, he wondered if Callie might be more open about the matter. While he didn't want to cross lines or betray his friend's trust, keeping them safe was his priority.

As he was carefully considering how to approach the matter with Callie, his phone vibrated, and he tensed when he saw Grace's name on the screen. First thing that morning he had left her a message, asking her to call at her earliest convenience. Though it was the very last thing he wanted to do, he had to tell her the truth and let her go. Anything less would demonstrate selfishness, not love or kindness. With paralyzing dread, he accepted the call.

"Good morning, Miss Grace."

"Morning, Donovan. Is everything alright?"

"Yes, ma'am, I..."

"Did they arrive safely?" Her voice was frantic, and Donovan realized she'd interpreted his message as potentially bad news about her friend's safety.

"My apologies for worrying you. Yes, they arrived late last night, safe and..." He was about to say 'well' but realized he couldn't truthfully claim that. "Tired, but grateful to be here."

Grace audibly exhaled. "That's a relief! And everything's ready there; secured, or whatever you call what you've been working on?" She laughed lightly at her ignorance.

"Affirmative. They're safe here, and so far, there's been no cause for concern. Please, put your mind at ease."

"I'll try," she promised, but the tone was tentative. "Is Callie okay? Does she seem afraid or uncomfortable with being in a strange place?"

"I haven't seen Miss LeVray yet, but I should shortly."

"But you saw Ben?"

"Affirmative. Late last night after Miss LeVray had already gone to sleep."

"And he said the trip went smoothly?"

Donovan didn't answer.

"Donovan?"

"I can tell you that they are presently alright, and I will be sure it stays that way."

"What are you not telling me?" Though they'd only been acquainted for a few days, Grace already knew him well enough to detect his evasive tone.

But Donovan didn't know what to say as he was still sorting through the matter himself.

"Please, Donovan. Unless telling me would put them in danger, I need to know. I don't know why, but I feel... There's something inside me, an instinct, a need to protect her, watch out for her. I recognize that it makes no sense but..."

"Actually," he interrupted, "it makes perfect sense." Since the moment he met Ben, he'd felt the same unexplainable impulse, but he was nevertheless startled by the coincidence of their parallel callings. "I feel the same. First for Ben, but now for Callie as well."

"Then if you understand, please tell me what's concerning you."

Unsure as to whether he was doing the right thing, Donovan sucked in a slow breath as he carefully considered his words. "Ben arrived last night looking... utterly worn out, almost unable to stand. In all our years of friendship, I've never seen him like that. When I inquired about it, he brushed it off, said something about helping people who were in need. Though I questioned him further, he assured me that this had nothing to do with Miss LeVray's stalker and that they were simply tired from missing a night of sleep."

"But you don't believe him." Grace stated, confident in her reading of his tone.

"I don't believe he's lying, but he's not telling me everything either and my instincts tell me the details are important, even if Ben doesn't believe they're relevant to my work here."

There was silence on the line as Grace considered his analysis. "This is about his... his mysterious... thing, isn't it?"

Astounded by how closely her thoughts tracked with his, Donovan began to understand why a connection had formed so quickly and effortlessly between them. "I believe so. No matter how close Ben and I became, I've always felt it wasn't my place to pry into that part of his life as even the slightest reference to it inevitably provoked panic. But, Grace, if I'm to protect them, take on the responsibility of being their guardian, I'm not sure I can afford to be ignorant any longer. Something traumatic happened to them on that trip, and I need to know what it was, so I can be absolutely certain it didn't place them in greater danger."

"And if you explain this to him, that you need this information to keep them safe, do you think he'll still put you off?"

"He's convinced that the two situations are unrelated, and truthfully, I have nothing but my intuition to counter that notion."

"Perhaps, if we are right about Callie knowing his secret, she'll be more willing to share."

Donovan rubbed his forehead, feeling uncomfortable with the idea, though it had already crossed his mind. "It doesn't feel right to go behind Ben's back." He paused to tap his finger on the counter as he struggled with opposing voices in his conscience. "I'll subtly inquire of her, but I won't push her to betray his trust. That would be a breach of our friendship and unfair to her."

"You're a good man, Donovan Bradshaw." At the compliment, Donovan's heart soared and sank simultaneously. "You're in a tough spot, but I know you'll do the right thing. In the end, keeping them safe is the most important thing. Shoot! I have to head to work. Can we talk again tonight?"

"Well, I..." he stammered, ashamed of himself for getting sidetracked. Not only had he failed to tell her what he'd committed to reveal, but he'd actually allowed their connection to deepen by taking her into his confidence.

"Is there something else?"

"Grace, I... I must speak with you about something important. It isn't related to our friends or their safety. This is about me."

There was no response.

"I know you need to go, so I'll call you tonight. We'll talk about it then."

"Donovan?" Her voice was tremulous, and he ached to take her in his arms as he knew she was imagining the worst about him, and indeed, she should. Though he knew none of the details, it was clear that Grace had been hurt, particularly by men. Her willingness to take a risk and trust him as much as she had was a compliment of the highest order. Now, he felt her distress that offering that trust had been a mistake, that Donovan was no different from all the others who had disappointed her. The thought of letting her down, having her remember him as another foolish choice, pulled the air from his lungs, but by hiding the truth, he only proved himself to indeed be exactly what she feared.

"I'm sorry, Grace. I didn't want to, never meant to… We'll talk about it tonight. Good day, Miss Sophia."

Mortified by the way he was handling every aspect of the mess he was solely responsible for creating, he ended the call, not knowing what else he could do or say. Putting his head in his hands, he sucked in a shaky breath as he began to feel the abiding emptiness of returning to a world without Grace. Though that reality had been in place for all but a few days of his short journey on this planet, it was suddenly unbearable. Why had he let himself become emotionally attached? He couldn't fathom what he'd been thinking when he approached her in that deli. What right did he have to toy with this beautiful woman's heart as he had? It was cruel and wrong, and it would end in pain for both of them.

His self-incrimination was interrupted by the sound of voices approaching. Rising to his feet and wiping at his eyes, he gathered his composure just as Rosa and Callie entered the kitchen, chatting and laughing as if they were lifelong friends.

Clearing his throat, Donovan approached. "Good morning, ma'am. It's nice to see you again. I'm glad you and Ben had a safe and pleasant trip."

Donovan watched Callie's face as his comment registered. She smiled in greeting, but there was undeniable tension in her expression.

After exchanging additional pleasantries, Donovan offered Callie his arm, then escorted her to a stool before seating himself across from her. Rosa served her a generous plate of breakfast and then left the two of them alone to talk.

"Did you sleep well?" Donovan asked. Though Callie looked tired, there was no comparison to the extreme physical weariness and weakness he'd observed in Ben.

"It was a little hard getting settled," she admitted. "But the accommodations were very comfortable."

With wide eyes, she glanced around the room. Ben's childhood home was not only enormous, but it was peculiarly decorated, the result of his late mother's eccentric taste. The furniture was stiff and formal, and everything was blindingly white. Ben had always hated it, and indeed, it was impossible to find a spot anywhere in the house that was comfortable to recline and talk. The kitchen stools were the best option, which was why they were the most used seats in the house.

"This is quite a place," Donovan said, a sarcastic chuckle accompanying his words.

"Yes, it is. I had no idea Ben grew up like this."

The fact that Ben hadn't informed Callie about his wealth didn't surprise Donovan. To Ben, this wasn't who he was. This was his mother's world, a lifestyle he wanted nothing to do with. Besides being both well-educated and well-mannered, there wasn't anything in Ben's character that would readily associate him with the pampered and privileged class from which they both came.

Again chuckling, Donovan tried to imagine how she must have felt when they pulled up to this sprawling mansion. "I bet it was quite a surprise. If I'd met Ben apart from knowing about his family, I'd never have guessed he came from this kind of environment either. Ben is so different from all of them."

Her brow crinkled in confusion. "What do you mean, 'all of them'?"

Donovan explained how their families had been

acquainted and how generations of inherited wealth had not brought out the best in any of them. Callie listened with great interest, continuing to look caught off guard by each revelation. It was clear she knew little about Ben's past, but the fact that he'd chosen to bring her here, straight into the belly of the beast, demonstrated his readiness to share this painful part of his past with her.

"That certainly isn't true of Ben or you, Donovan. I am grateful for your service to our country and now to Ben and me. I want you to know how much Ben admires you and how highly he regards you, and I the same."

Though her lovely green eyes struggled to read the expressions on his face, genuine warmth and kindness radiated from her in a way that was almost tangible, like the comforting heat from a cozy fireplace. Without difficulty, he understood how this woman had disarmed Ben's defenses, as she had a way about her, a sweet vulnerability that engendered instant trust.

"I sincerely appreciate that, but I have to tell you that I believe you to be a great hero in your own right, ma'am. When I met up with Ben a few years ago, he was afflicted. I tried my best to help him, but I couldn't get through to him or break down his defenses. From the start of our friendship, he's always been a downtrodden, though incredibly generous soul, but after the last time we were together, I thought he was lost beyond the point of return. I've seen people suffering, in a bad way, soldiers with PTSD. Ben was not far off from that. It troubled me as I've always thought he possessed a uniquely courageous heart."

Pausing, Donovan watched her carefully. As she nodded, comprehension and empathy reflected in her eyes. She knew exactly what he was talking about, and more than that, she knew the source of Ben's turmoil. He was sure of it.

"I tried to get him to move in with me, to remain in one place for a while, and he genuinely seemed to want to, but he couldn't accept my help, even though he had helped me in much the same way early in our friendship."

Lowering her gaze, she softly spoke her response. "I know. When I first met Ben, it was very, very hard to break through his walls." Compassion resonated in her voice. Truly, this woman loved Ben with all her heart and soul, and whatever his secret, knowing it had served to enhance that love and devotion. Though he'd already assured Grace that his affections for Ben had been extended to include Callie, he found himself feeling honored to know her, and profoundly touched by her boundless dedication.

Proceeding cautiously, he dared to press just a bit further. "I don't mean to pry, and certainly don't feel obligated to share anything you're uncomfortable sharing, but can you tell me what Ben was running from? I get the sadness and I, of all people, understand wanting to escape from the way we grew up, but there was just more to it, something I couldn't put my finger on or figure out. It was like he was running from himself."

Her eyes grew moist as she did her best to focus on his face. For an instant, Donovan was certain she was going to give him the information he sought, as she appeared desperate to relieve his anxiety. But then, she averted her eyes, and a sigh escaped her lips. "I can only say that I understand your confusion. I've felt it, struggled with it. There are reasons, and Ben turning down your help and running had nothing to do with you. He thinks of you as a brother; he told me that. He admires you for your choices in life and your courage to serve despite opposition. The reasons why Ben ran are complex. He did want to accept your help; even now, he wishes he had."

As she raised her eyes to his again, her distressed expression pleaded with him to understand her dilemma. On the one hand, she wanted to share the secret, empathizing with the confusion brought on by a lack of understanding. But on the other, her primary loyalty was to Ben, and this wasn't her secret to tell. Despite his disappointment, Donovan couldn't fault her in the least. In truth, if she'd thoughtlessly blurted out the information without Ben's consent, he may have lost some of the respect for her he'd recently acquired. Ben had given her all his trust, and indeed, that trust was well placed. Though he continued to worry about the situation that had led to Ben's weakened condition, he had no choice but to let the matter drop, as he wouldn't press either of them further.

Shifting the topic away from the sensitive subject, Donovan enjoyed the rest of their conversation, finding her easy to talk with. She was curious about Ben's absence that morning, but Donovan played it off with humor, hoping Ben had a believable explanation prepared. Casually, he inquired about how she and Grace had met, and Callie beamed as she spoke of her friend, her deep affection evident. He couldn't help but wonder what Callie might think of him if she knew about the information he was concealing, and how its revelation would wound Grace. The shame of what he had done and was still doing made him feel physically sick, adding to the multitude of pains he already unceasingly suffered.

By the time Ben returned, he and Callie had spent enough time together to establish a firm foundation of friendship, augmented by their mutual love for Ben.

"That lady of yours is... much more than you deserve,"

Donovan teased Ben as he headed for the door, anxious to return some voicemails that had accumulated during his conversation with Callie. He didn't plan on being away for long, but as there was no sign of trouble at the house, he wanted to take advantage of the calm to do more research and follow up on potential leads.

Observing the genuine admiration in Donovan's expression, Ben smiled. "There's no doubt about that. She most definitely is."

"Mission accomplished?" Donovan asked, lowering his volume even though Callie was still speaking to her brother on her new, secure phone in the kitchen.

"Yes," Ben whispered. "Everything's set." His eyes danced with anticipation.

"You're a lucky man, my friend. I'll head out for a bit, but I'll be monitoring. Be back later."

With a nod of appreciation and a friendly pat on the back, Ben hurried off to join Callie, and Donovan drove back to his apartment.

For several hours, he played phone tag with Officer Evans and agents at the FBI, but at last, he successfully connected with Agent Wes Taylor, who informed him of some rather shocking news.

"We believe we know who shot Miss LeVray," he declared, his voice strained as if the information affected him personally, which Donovan found odd. Most of the FBI agents he'd known had been skilled at remaining unnaturally unexpressive.

"I worked undercover for years, inside this drug ring. I knew the man Miss LeVray's father prosecuted. You don't get more evil than him, but his cousin, Charro Ruiz, comes in a close second. He's brutal, Mr. Bradshaw, soulless and smart, which is a deadly combination."

"I know the type all too well," Donovan responded, leaning back in his chair and stroking his chin as he took in the news. "Any information on his whereabouts?"

"Two weeks ago, he visited his cousin in prison. That's how we connected him to Miss LeVray's case, because of his relationship to the prisoner and the confirmation that he was in the area around the time of the shooting. That gives us motive and opportunity."

"If they had eyes on him, why wasn't he taken into custody?"

"You know how this works, Mr. Bradshaw. We have pieces of evidence connecting him to a number of open cases, but we haven't been able to make any charges stick yet. Some of our best undercover agents, one in particular who replaced me when I left the field, are working hard, putting their lives at risk to gather indisputable evidence so we can get this demon off the streets, but it takes time. Truthfully, this situation with Miss LeVray might be the break we're looking for. If we can pin an attempted murder charge on him, we might be able to make some of the other charges stick as well."

"But we have to catch him first. And before he harms Miss LeVray or Mr. Sawyer. Any leads on his present location?"

"Unfortunately, no. There's been no sightings of him in the last forty-eight hours, including by our undercover agents, but we're reasonably sure he's no longer in Miss LeVrays hometown."

Distressed by the revelation, Donovan's voice tightened as he spoke. "That's disconcerting considering his disappearance coincides with the timing of Miss LeVray's and Mr. Sawyer's departure."

Agent Taylor offered no immediate response, but after a

moment had passed, he cleared his throat and spoke, the distress in his voice palpable. "Mr. Bradshaw, it's my understanding that, in addition to providing security for Mr. Sawyer and Miss LeVray, you are personally acquainted with them. Is that correct?"

Donovan was taken aback by the question. Though he knew it wouldn't have been difficult for an FBI agent to uncover that information if he intentionally sought it out, he had no clue as to why Agent Taylor would have the notion to do so.

"Affirmative," he answered hesitantly. "Ben and I are old friends. I've only recently become acquainted with Miss LeVray, however."

"I see." As he continued, his voice resounded with what sounded like sorrow, though without seeing his face, it was hard to be sure. "And are the two... romantically involved?"

"Affirmative," Donovan answered, increasingly uncomfortable with the personal nature of the questions.

"They must be quite attached for Mr. Sawyer to risk his own life by associating himself so closely with her. Ruiz is no ordinary criminal. He's cunning, lethal. As his friend, would it not be wise to advise Mr. Sawyer to leave Miss LeVray in the care of your protective custody and temporarily disengage so as not to put them both in such great peril?"

Tightening his jaw, he fought his instinct to raise his voice at the man for suggesting that Ben leave the woman he loved to save his own skin. Though Agent Taylor had evidently done enough research to uncover his connection to Ben, it was clear he knew nothing of his friend's character.

"Agent Taylor, I assure you, my friend and client would rather die than do as you've suggested, and I would never insult him or his integrity by proposing such an action."

Though he heard Agent Taylor take several deep breaths, the man took his time responding. "Understood. I'm making this case my top priority. As your reputation precedes you, I'm confident that the security you're providing is adequate for the time being. I've got agents throughout the country looking for Ruiz. We'll track him down. I'll keep you apprised of new developments. In the meantime, I'll forward you a picture of the suspect and all available information. It's my understanding Mr. Sawyer caught a glimpse of Miss LeVray's attacker. If he could confirm our suspicions with a positive ID, that would be most helpful. I'll be in touch."

Though Rosa's cooking was superb, Donovan had little appetite when he returned to Ben's house for dinner that evening. Confusion regarding Ben's secret, dread over his upcoming conversation with Grace, alarm over Agent Taylor's warnings regarding the brutality of Miss LeVray's stalker, and frustration over the increasing pain and fatigue of his deteriorating health prevented him from staying focused on the light conversation going on around him. On several occasions, he caught Ben's concerned gaze, and though Donovan did his best to offer subtle nods of reassurance, by the time the meal was over, Ben's distressed expression told Donovan he was unconvinced.

At last, as they cleared the dishes and Rosa and Leo took over the cleanup, Donovan dropped the pretense, his solid nod communicating that there was indeed something the three of them needed to discuss. Retrieving Callie from the kitchen, they sat back down at the dining room table, and

Donovan took a deep breath, pained by the fear in their eyes.

With as much calm and compassion as he could muster, Donovan relayed the content of his phone call with Agent Taylor. Pulling a file from his briefcase, he presented Ben with a picture of Charro Ruiz, and Ben quickly confirmed that this was the man he'd seen through a car window just a few days before Callie was shot. Though Donovan knew Callie's poor eyesight prevented her from a detailed view of the man's face, she nevertheless winced when Ben slid the photograph in front of her.

"But if they know who he is now, that sounds like good news, not bad," Ben observed, confused by the distress in Donovan's demeanor. He couldn't bring himself to tell them about Taylor's grim descriptions of the man's cunning and brutality, though he guessed Ben saw it in Ruiz's cold eyes.

As he explained Ruiz's connection to the criminal Callie's father had prosecuted, his alleged prior crimes that made him a person of interest to the FBI, the confirmed sighting of him in Callie's hometown, and the unfortunate present reality that the authorities had lost track of him at about the same time that the two of them had left, Ben's jaw tightened and he put an arm protectively around Callie's shoulders.

"Does this mean... Donovan, do you think he knows where we are?"

"Unlikely. It doesn't sound like you two left tracks behind, and I've been sure to erase evidence of hotel reservations and credit card use, so I can't think of any way for him to have tracked your direction."

Though the statement was delivered in a tone of confidence, his words didn't alleviate the fear on their faces.

Simultaneously, they broke eye contact with him and looked questioningly at one another. Donovan's heart sped up. So, something did indeed happen on that trip; that much was certain. And it appeared that, whatever it was, they both suddenly had apprehensions regarding its ramifications. Despite Ben's denials, Donovan's instincts had, once again, been proven right.

After an awkward moment of silence, Ben at last returned his gaze to Donovan. "Donovan, could you please give Callie and me a moment, and then we'll get right back to you?"

Caught off guard by the unexpected request, he nevertheless complied, moving into the front room of the house, and staring blankly out a window. Were they deliberating about whether or not to tell him about the incident that occurred during their trip or about Ben's lifelong secret? Maybe both. Just a few hours ago, he'd been desperate for this information, but now, for some unknown reason, he felt terrified of the truth, sensing that the knowledge might change everything, irrevocably shifting the ground under his feet.

Apart from Callie, Donovan was Ben's closest confidant, the relationship more like brothers than friends. Yet for over a decade, Ben had hidden this part of him, called it a curse, and been so frightened of its exposure that he ran continually. He'd nearly let the thing destroy him, and if it hadn't been for Callie, Donovan had no doubt it eventually would have.

Try as he might, he couldn't fathom what it could be, but as he stood there, awaiting their decision, he felt the weight of sharing in it fall heavy on his shoulders. What if Ben had committed some terrible crime before Donovan knew him? Or maybe he witnessed something unspeakable and the running was his attempt to stay safe from the grip of the perpetrator. How would Donovan balance his own conscience and responsibility to justice with his desire to protect his friend if he were made aware of either of these scenarios?

But none of those possibilities rang true given what he knew about Ben Sawyer. Gentle, yet just, Ben wouldn't protect himself at the expense of others. He'd never allow a violent criminal to run loose. So, if all such explanations could definitively be ruled out, what was left?

When Ben appeared in the doorway, the look on his face and the resolve in his vivid blue eyes left no doubt about their decision. They were going to tell him everything. Ben's love for Callie, which included his willingness to sacrifice whatever was necessary to keep her safe, was greater than the fear of exposing his secret.

Despite the fierce battles he'd fought and the depraved enemies he'd faced, as Donovan walked behind Ben back into the dining room, he wasn't sure he'd ever felt as uneasy as he did in that moment. For, somehow, he knew that, once he learned it all, his life would never be the same again.

CHAPTER 6

NEVER THE SAME AGAIN

Donovan had no idea how he'd made it safely back to his apartment, as he couldn't remember a single thing about the drive home. Rummaging through his bathroom cabinet, he retrieved a bottle of Tylenol and eagerly swallowed three pills with an accompanying mouthful of water. His doctors had prescribed much stronger pain medication, but though it relieved his agony more effectively, it rendered him drowsy and unfocused, preventing him from doing his job, so he rarely indulged. Besides, he'd known too many injured soldiers who had become addicted to such easy relief, and though he empathized, he didn't want addiction to be the title of his life's final chapter. Nevertheless, there were times he craved the numbing bliss strong narcotics provided, and this moment certainly qualified.

Overtaken by physical agony and utter confusion, he flopped onto his bed, putting both hands over his face. When Ben had touched his arm, for the first time in years, Donovan remembered what it was like to live without constant physical torment. He could breathe easier, sit up straighter, and glimpse the strength of the youth he'd long since left behind. When Ben withdrew his hand, and the pain flooded back over him like an inescapable tidal wave, the truth of what he'd lost hit him hard.

But that torment was a small part of his present distress. What Ben and Callie had told him, and he'd tasted himself, was impossible, utter foolishness. This was the real world, not some kind of fairy tale. In his short life, Donovan had witnessed too many indescribable horrors: men's shattered bodies, suffering children, and ravaged women, to believe in something so fantastical. The world was a cruel place, but it was real, predictable, and ordered.

But hadn't he just told Grace that he was a man of faith? He'd always believed in God, a being who exists outside of nature and its rules and confinements. But that was different. Ben wasn't God. He was a man, flesh and blood like himself. Donovan had grown up with him, known him since childhood. It was true that he was one of the kindest people Donovan had ever known, but that didn't place him above humanity.

But then, Ben wasn't claiming to be more than a man. He called what he possessed 'a gift,' something he himself didn't fully understand yet, but he believed it had passed to him from another when he was a boy. And truly, Ben had a quality, something almost inhuman about him. Not a single blemish or scar could be found on him, and his features were perfectly proportioned. Though too humble to notice, Ben turned the heads of every woman he passed.

But beyond the physical, there was something else, something deeper in his eyes, a presence, like one was in the company of royalty, but of the most noble and benevolent kind. Though Donovan had grown accustomed to it over time, he remembered being startled and somewhat overawed by the feeling when he and Ben first began spending significant time together. Perhaps it was this soothing quality that eased his mother's depression whenever she troubled herself to spend a few minutes with her son.

But lots of people had flawless features and a charismatic persona. That didn't mean they could perform miracles.

When Ben and Callie told him everything, they saw the doubt in his eyes, and it prompted Ben to come and sit beside him, informing him he already knew about Donovan's serious injuries. Then he asked Donovan for permission to touch his arm. When he reluctantly granted it, Donovan felt something flow into him, a heat that moved from the point of contact throughout his entire being, sweeping away every twinge of pain and leaving refreshing wholeness behind. It was the same sensation he had experienced when he shook Ben's hand during their happy reunion in the foyer of Callie's home, but the handshake hadn't lasted long enough to clear all the pain away. At the time, he'd convinced himself that he imagined the whole thing, that it was nothing more than a euphoric reaction to seeing his friend happy and settled, but now, he didn't know what to believe.

Massaging the sides of his aching head, Donovan groaned, both from the pain that was moving like fire through his body, but also from the mental anguish of the choice he faced. He either had to throw away reason, everything he'd solidly believed about life and science, or he had to reject his dearest friend, labeling him a liar or lunatic, and Callie along with him. Though the first choice was uncomfortable, the second was impossible.

There was, in his heart or perhaps his soul, a binding

connection between himself and Ben Sawyer. As if yoked together, Donovan had always felt that he was destined to share Ben's burden, even when he had no idea what that burden was. Despite his present confusion, the bond between them would never permit him to turn his back and walk away.

Still, he wished he had more to go on than his own unexplainable experience. Though some might accept personal anecdotes as the most convincing kind of evidence, Donovan's deference toward Ben made him doubt his own senses.

Abruptly sitting up, Donovan considered that there may indeed be a way to verify Ben's claims. The fire.

In the course of their explanation regarding Ben's secret, Ben had told him why he had arrived in Boston drained and weak. The prior evening, as they drove through the eastern part of Ohio, they'd come upon a farmhouse on fire. Though a woman had escaped the flames, her husband and baby remained inside. Ben had entered the house and rescued them, nearly losing his own life in the process. When help finally arrived, suspicions arose as no one could comprehend how Ben had accomplished the seemingly impossible rescue. With Ben nearly unconscious, Callie had rushed them away and compassionately taken care of him until he regained enough strength to emerge from his stupor.

The next morning, they'd become aware that the man they'd saved had spoken to the media, and a newspaper article had subsequently been written and circulated about the incident. Upon hearing that Ruiz might know they had left town and was likely searching for them, Ben decided that telling Donovan about this incident was unavoidable as the media coverage may have left a detectable trail.

For the next two hours, Donovan sat with his laptop at his kitchen counter, combing through newspaper articles and copying and pasting any and all references to the incident into a single file. Then he transcribed a brief television news segment, which aired the day after the rescue. When he was confident there was nothing else out there to find, he printed his multi-page document and retrieved two highlighters, marking statements that revealed details about Ben's and Callie's identities but also evidence in support of Ben's claims about his gift.

Focusing on the firsthand testimony of Nathan, the man Ben had rescued, Donovan highlighted several phrases as he read.

I tried to get to my son, but I passed out on the stairs 'cause the smoke was so thick and it was hotter than hell in there. When I woke up, I could breathe! Easily. This... man, who looked like some kind of angel with those bright blue eyes, was holding my arm. It freaked me out at first, so I pulled away, but when I did, I started coughing uncontrollably and my head started spinning, like right before I passed out. He grabbed my arm again, told me I had to hold on to him. All I could think about was my boy, getting him out of there before the whole place went up in flames, but I eventually got it through my thick skull that this guy was trying to help me do just that. I can't tell you how he did it. It's nothin' but a miracle! He saved my life and my boy's too. He held my son in his arms the whole way out. Doctors say there's no damage to my boy's lungs, no sign that he was ever in a fire, but that's impossible. It was black as night in there, no air to breathe, and the heat alone should'a killed us, quick like. But the only one suffering was him. As I held onto him, I got stronger and he got weaker. It was like, he was givin' us his strength, sacrificin' himself to get us out alive.

Switching to the statements of the responding emergency teams, Donovan continued his highlighting. One of the first firefighters to arrive on scene confirmed the severity of the fire.

When we got there, the house was completely engulfed in flames. We broke a window in one of the front rooms and pulled them out, just as the flames closed in, within feet of overtaking them. We never would have attempted a rescue under those conditions, even in full gear.

One of his colleagues offered a statement as well.

This man had nothing, no protective clothing or oxygen, but he pulled two people out safely, and he seemed to be the only one significantly harmed, though the fact that he was alive at all was an outright miracle.

A paramedic added his perspective.

When we broke the front window and pulled him out, the man was covered from head to toe in soot and grime, so I can't give you a description, but he was out of it, eyes closed and unresponsive. Yet those he rescued were in exceptionally good shape for what they'd endured. I tried to get the man to come with me to the closest ambulance so he could get the help he needed, but he didn't seem to hear me or understand what I was saying, and the next thing I knew, he had vanished.

Every statement expressed the same bewilderment, agreeing that the rescue itself was impossible and the condition of the man and child, after spending upward of thirty minutes in an unsurvivable environment, were beyond comprehension.

As he read the transcript of the television news segment, a quote from Nathan caught his eye.

When I grabbed his arm, it felt like heat moved through me, like my insides were on fire, but in a good way. As long as I kept ahold of him, that heat stayed put, and I could breathe and move with the energy of a man half my age.

Dropping his highlighter onto the counter, Donovan stared blankly at the wall. That was exactly how he'd felt, precisely how he would have described the experience when Ben made contact with his arm.

The remaining content of the articles and news blurb consisted of a variety of proposed theories about the hero's identity and whereabouts. Nathan remained unwaveringly convinced that his savior wasn't human, and the fact that he'd seemingly vanished into thin air compelled even the most reasoned witnesses to consider the outlandish idea.

Returning to his laptop, Donovan pulled up the final scene of the television interview. Nathan and his wife stood —the rubble of their house behind them—their eyes filled with tears as they held their son in their arms.

If it weren't for Ben, I'd be dead. My son would be dead. We owe him our lives. We were strangers, no one to him, but he gave us all his power at his expense. Wherever he is, I hope he's alright. We don't care what anyone else says or thinks, he's our guardian angel, and we'll never forget his compassion and sacrifice.

For a long time, Donovan sat in silence, staring at the paused image of the family on his screen. Putting aside the many descriptions of impossible conditions and miraculous happenings, for Donovan, it came down to one thing. The hero this man described was unquestionably his best friend, Ben Sawyer. That was his heart, his character. Ben had nothing to gain by risking his life to save this family and everything to lose. Though he hadn't focused on this aspect of the media coverage yet, the broadcast details about him, though thankfully few, would assuredly increase the danger for him and Callie. But even if Ben had known about the ramifications of helping these people, Donovan knew it wouldn't have made a difference. He still would have saved them.

Shaking his head, his heart constricted at how very close he'd come to losing his friend. Ben had said that Callie saved his life, and though he didn't understand how this... magic worked, he didn't doubt she had as every person who saw him after the rescue believed his life was at risk.

Blowing out a long, resigned sigh, Donovan leaned back in his seat. He believed. He didn't understand, but he believed, nonetheless.

When the vibration of his phone startled him, he glanced down at his watch. It was after ten. Grace! In his frantic research, he'd lost track of time.

Lifting his phone, his heart ached as he read her message.

Donovan, I don't understand what has
happened to cause you to pull away, but I
want you to know that I believe you to be a
good person, and I'm so grateful you're the
one taking care of our friends. I wish I'd had
a chance to get to know you better, but if
you no longer desire that, I understand, and
I just wanted to say, thank you for
everything.

Her words were kind, despite the obvious pain he was causing her. He didn't know what to do. Though he desperately wanted to call her, he knew he couldn't hide anything from her. She read him like a book. If she heard his voice, she'd instantly detect the raw emotions he was feeling.

Now that he knew Ben's secret, his responsibility to his friend went far beyond guarding him and Callie from Charro Ruiz. Bound by the trust they'd placed in him, it was now his obligation to protect his secret, even from Grace. But he needed time to absorb the shock of it, regain control, so he could adequately pull off a believable mask of ignorance, one that could fool even Grace. Right now, that was impossible.

But he couldn't tell Grace about his health situation in a text message. That would be cowardly, and cruel.

Lifting his phone, he tapped out several renditions of a message before finally settling on the best one he could conceive of.

Please accept my apology, Miss Sophia. I
received some news pertaining to our
friends' situation today, and I've been
following up on it all evening. I completely
lost track of time. As it is late, and I have
more work I must do, would you consider
giving me a second chance another
evening to explain myself and redeem my
poor manners?

"Of course, Donovan!" came her immediate response, and Donovan couldn't help but smile in profound relief. This lovely woman was so gracious, which made the pain of losing her all the more unbearable.

I won't keep you and I know you probably
can't tell me the details, but should I be
worried?

Gritting his teeth, he hated to admit the truth, even to himself. Though he'd been involved in dozens of cases like this, he'd always been compassionate while remaining largely emotionally detached, but he was finding that impossible this time.

I am doing everything in my power to
ensure their safety, and I've got some
additional help on board now. But if you are
a person who regularly practices prayer, I
encourage you to put that habit to
good use.

Oh, Donovan! I will do as you suggest, but
there must be more I can do to help.
Anything at all?

He hated scaring her, but it wasn't right to lie to her. Though he was certain that Ben's extraordinary gift shifted the balance significantly, he didn't know enough about it yet to determine how much of an advantage this afforded them in their present situation.

> Just keep the faith. Callie is in good hands. Tomorrow, I'll be moving into the house full time to be available around the clock. I'll do my best to be in touch tomorrow evening, but if I don't call, it will be because I'm engaged in this important work. It won't be long until this is resolved. I'll continue to do what I can to put your mind at ease.

> I understand. What you're doing there is the important focus right now. There will be time for the rest later. I'm comforted to know you'll be nearby, keeping a close eye out, and I appreciate you keeping me in the loop but, Donovan, can I ask one more thing of you?

> If it is in my power to give you, Miss Sophia, I'll happily oblige.

> Please be careful! Ben and Callie aren't the only ones I'm worried about now.

Donovan felt something warm spread through his being. More than a casual interest or a source of information about her friend's safety, Grace cared about him, his well-being, and though this made the impending conversation that much harder, it awakened a dormant corner of his heart, a place he'd believed beyond revival. If she only knew that the true threat to his life wasn't from without but from within...

I'll do what I can to comply with your kind
request, ma'am.

Grace didn't sleep at all that night. She tossed and turned,
unsure if her anxiety for Callie's safety or Donovan's was
more acute. There were two layers of protection guarding
Callie but the only thing protecting him were his skills and
experience. He was the tip of the spear, expected to risk his
life without hesitation. While she appreciated and
respected him for that, she had to admit that he had
become much more to her than a means of staying abreast
about her friend's well-being.

His odd statements that morning disheartened her, and
then, when he didn't call, she was sure he'd changed his
mind about continuing their relationship. The depth of
disappointment and sadness that thought provoked had
taken her by surprise. He'd only been in her life for a few
days. Surely, she could easily forget him.

But when he responded to her message, the last one she
thought she'd ever send him, her heart began to beat again,
came back to life. Though it was foolish, and she knew it,
she couldn't hide the truth of what she felt for him, at least
not from herself.

But there was an undeniable cloud hanging over their
happily ever after, something more than the risks of his
dangerous job. Reminiscent of the situation with Ben,
Donovan had secrets of his own. If they hadn't gotten
distracted by their conversation and she hadn't needed to
rush off to work, she suspected he would have revealed it
during their phone call that morning. But when he crypti-
cally referenced the topic, his tone was decidedly despon-

dent, like telling her would mark the end of their association.

A part of her wanted to know, to get it over with. If he was planning to walk away, the sooner she knew, the better, before her heart became any more entangled with his. But another part of her craved ignorance. As long as she was in the dark, she could imagine it was nothing; some silly event from his past or trivial character flaw that she could tease him about, then dismiss out of hand.

But even as she hoped that that was the case, Grace knew Donovan wasn't the kind to make a mountain out of a molehill, and that fact, alongside her fear for everyone's safety, haunted her throughout the night.

A MISERABLE NIGHT, plagued by merciless pain and conflicting voices shouting in his head, caused Donovan to move slowly as he got up and prepared for the day. Still struggling to absorb the unbelievable truth of Ben's secret, the exhaustion made it tough to sort through his emotions.

And then there was the situation with Grace. Amid the chaos, he couldn't summon the courage to tell her a truth that would drive her away forever. Though he could endure a body racked with excruciating pain and a mind reeling with confusion, right now, he couldn't tolerate a broken heart. Grace was the solitary soothing voice amidst a chorus of senseless shouting, and, for the first time in his life, he feared, without that tether to sanity, he might succumb to the madness.

As he packed a bag with several days' worth of clothing, he began to worry in earnest about his ability to physically carry through with his job. Though the threshold of pain he'd trained himself to endure was much higher than most could abide, what he was presently suffering was pushing his limits. While he didn't want to acknowledge it, it was time to check himself back into the hospital and undergo another round of treatments to temporarily ease his symptoms, but the timing couldn't be worse.

In preparation for such an eventuality, he had assembled a list of contacts, men who were skilled and smart, but he hated the idea of turning over responsibility for Callie's and Ben's safety to someone else. Now that he knew Ben's secret, he was uniquely capable of adjusting their plans with that consideration in mind. But he certainly didn't want to put them at risk by being weak, too debilitated by pain to adequately protect them.

Huffing frustratedly, he filled an insulated mug with fresh coffee, hoping it would quickly work its magic in dispelling the fatigue of his restless night. He'd give it the day, see how he felt in the morning. If the pain persisted, he'd speak with Ben. After all, they already knew about his condition, and, though they were much too kind to bring it up, they had to be concerned about how his fragile health might impact his work, and thus their safety.

On the way out the door, Donovan glimpsed the small envelope, the unexpected letter from his parents, still lying on his kitchen counter. With all that had transpired since its arrival, he had forgotten about it, and he certainly didn't have the emotional fortitude to face it now. Without knowing why, he picked it up and tossed it into a side pocket of his knapsack, bemoaning the fact that there was yet another piece of his life that was unresolved and fraught with emotional pitfalls.

Anxious faces met him when he returned to the Sawyer home. Undeniably, he'd been shocked and skeptical when he'd learned Ben's secret, but they surely believed he would come around and offer them his unconditional support. The idea that Ben may have had genuine doubts about his friendship and loyalty pained him more than his present physical torment.

Sitting awkwardly in the uncomfortable furniture of the home's front room, Donovan chuckled, trying to put their minds at ease. "Ben, I think we might be more comfortable sitting on the floor."

The tension on both their faces eased. "Comfort wasn't one of my mother's priorities," Ben noted with uncharacteristic bitterness. Being back in that house was taking a toll on him, which was understandable as the vast majority of memories there elicited nothing but pain.

"It was a weird world we grew up in, Ben, a very weird world. And speaking of weird worlds." He smiled and opened the file folder he was holding. "I read the articles and watched a short news blurb that aired the following day. Big picture, it gave away your vehicle and your first name, Ben, and a very basic description of you, but I saw no mention of Callie's name anywhere, though they did report that there was a woman with you. The story was"—he leaned forward, looking at his friend with admiration—" remarkable, unbelievable really. Anyone who read it or heard it likely wouldn't believe most of it." He chuckled. "Well, as I also didn't."

Unblinking, his friend's eyes pleaded, and though Ben's doubts tore at his heart, he was also honored by how much he valued Donovan's acceptance. With the exception of Callie, Donovan guessed there hadn't been anyone else in Ben's entire life who had known everything about him, much less supported him as he carried the burdensome weight of his extraordinary secret. Though Ben earnestly hoped Donovan would be capable of it, he could read the apprehension in Ben's eyes, the fear that had inspired nearly a decade of running. Ben knew that what he possessed was so unfathomable that most people could never wrap their minds around it. But as it was fundamentally who he was and who he had been for the majority of his life, a rejection of the gift was a rejection of the man. As he held Donovan's gaze, he witnessed his friend's frantic fear that, though he knew Donovan cared deeply for him, this was a step beyond where Donovan could go. Thankfully, Ben's fears were unfounded.

"It was a shock to find out that my long-lost friend was a superhero, but I'm very honored and a little intimidated to have been trusted with this sensitive and sacred secret, and I consider it a privilege to come alongside you both, primarily as a friend, but also as someone in the fight with you as we continue to keep Callie safe."

Donovan extended his hand, and with tears of joy and relief shining in his eyes, Ben firmly grasped it. As Ben's strength pulsed healing throughout Donovan's body, offering him a coveted easy breath, something old and new began to stir within him; that nonsensical calling that had repeated in his mind whenever he faced danger. It whispered the same prophecy, exhorting him to "defend he who was chosen." Could Ben be that person? In some ways, that made sense given Donovan's present role and their tight connection. But chosen? What did that mean? Once this was over and Callie's attacker was behind bars, how and why would he need Donovan's help? After all, Ben was the one with miraculous powers.

Compassionately, Ben held onto Donovan longer than one would typically sustain a handshake, his distressed expression revealing he knew Donovan's condition was worsening. When he at last let go, he watched him apologetically, his eyes mournful as Donovan's pain returned. If he could, he knew Ben would drain himself dry to the point of unconsciousness, just as he had in that fire, to keep him well. But there was no chance whatsoever Donovan would let that happen. Though powerful, the fact that his touch couldn't permanently cure—neither his pain nor Callie's blindness—was a tremendous burden of regret Ben had no choice but to shoulder.

Lowering his eyes, Ben spoke softly. "I appreciate the kind words but, truly, I'm the one who's been honored, for a long time now, to enjoy the friendship of a real-life hero."

As Callie smiled at the affection between them, Donovan put a hand on Ben's shoulder, waiting to speak until he looked back up into his eyes. "Anyone who would run into a fire like that to save people he didn't even know... well, you're a fellow soldier in my book."

Too humble to fully embrace Donovan's praise, the compliment and its implications nevertheless provoked such strong emotions that Ben had to wipe his eyes and take several shaky breaths before he could speak. Until that moment, Donovan hadn't been certain that the affection and dedication between them was entirely analogous, but now he knew that it indeed was.

Over the next hour, they discussed revisions to their security plan in light of the new information. His decision to move into the house full time comforted them, and after informing Rosa about it, she hurried off to prepare a room for him. Ben invited him to use the private office space in the house and whatever other resources he needed. He also told him they had plans to drive to Cape Cod the following day.

"It's regarding a matter related to my Succouri identity," Ben explained, but Donovan shook his head.

"Your what?"

Ben laughed. "In all our explanations, I guess we failed to tell you what this gift is called. I'm a Succouri." He grimaced. "Not that I know much about what that is yet. Until very recently, I knew nothing about any of it. I thought I was the only one with these odd abilities."

Donovan was taken aback. "So, there are others like you, who can do what you can?" Accepting his friend's superhuman powers was disorienting enough, but finding out that he wasn't alone, that this was a named phenomenon, took that acceptance to a whole new level.

"It seems so, though, believe me, that was as much of a shock to me as it presently is to you. I need to know more about what I am, and that's part of what tomorrow's trip is about. But if you think it unsafe—"

"On the contrary," Donovan interjected. "Take a different vehicle, but in truth, you're probably safer there than here, since it's somewhere you've never been and have no known connections to."

Ben considered Donovan's advice. "Alright. If anything happens to change your recommendation between now and then, please let me know. Callie and I have some... some ghosts from the past to face today, but we'll be nearby."

Knowledgeable enough about Ben's troubled past to grimace in empathy, Donovan placed an encouraging hand on Ben's shoulder. "Courage, my friend. What's ahead of you is so much brighter than what's behind you."

"Without question, that is the truth, Donovan, for both of us."

Smiling at the reciprocal offering of encouragement, Donovan nevertheless knew that, in his case, there was no chance of it being true.

CHAPTER 7

DOUBTS AND REGRETS

Grace had all but given up on hearing from Donovan that evening, but just after nine thirty, he called.

"Good evening, Miss Grace," he greeted, but his voice was tense, and weary.

"Donovan? Are you alright?"

"A bit tired, but all was quiet around here today, so that's encouraging."

"Yes. I was able to reach Callie earlier. She sounded worn out too, but she feels safe there with you and Ben."

Donovan managed a weak chuckle. "I think we're all going to sleep for days when this is over."

"Any luck at solving the mystery?"

"Mystery?"

"About Ben."

Silence fell for a long moment. "My main focus, at present, is keeping Ben and Callie out of harm's way. In my line of work, distractions can be fatal."

Confused, Grace hesitated, not sure if the distraction he was speaking of was her. "Alright. I..."

"Apart from worry for Miss LeVray, is something else troubling you Miss Sophia?"

"Well…" She again fell silent, unsure how to voice her concerns in a way that didn't put him on the spot.

"Please, Grace. What is it?"

Though she didn't doubt his sincere concern, she could hear the weight of the responsibilities he was carrying in his tone, and she didn't want to add to them.

"Ugh! I hate doing this on the phone, and I hate the distance between us."

"I wholeheartedly concur, but since this is our only option right now, please…"

"Donovan, I'm not good at subtlety, and I've had too many dead-end relationships to ignore the signs, so I'll just be straight with you. I like you, think you're amazing, actually. You're the first man I've met in… maybe forever who I genuinely want to get to know better, in a real way, a way that's meaningful. But, from previous conversations, I get the feeling you're not in the same place, and I don't want you to feel obligated to call or text just because of your job or our mutual friends. I…" A lump caught in her throat, halting her awkward outburst.

"Grace!" He breathed out her name, speaking it in a way that at last felt intimate rather than the formal manner with which he typically addressed her. "I assure you, in the strongest of terms, my hesitancy is not a result of disinterest." He let out a sorrowful sigh. "You have no idea how having you in my life, even with the distance between us, has awakened my heart. I can't get your beautiful face out of my mind, nor can I comprehend the connection my soul feels with yours. From the moment I met you in Miss LeVray's living room, you've been continually in my thoughts."

Putting her hand to her heart, Grace breathed unevenly as she absorbed his words, elated at the unexpected confession, yet confused by the hesitancy that still saturated his tone. "But, then, why—"

"I'm not well, Grace," he blurted out, his voice so strained it was barely recognizable. "I... I can't be what you want, what you deserve, no matter how much I want to be. I'm deeply sorry."

Brokenhearted at his obvious distress, Grace sucked in a shaky breath. This man had given nearly his entire adult life in service to his country. He'd suffered a catastrophic injury that appeared to cause him continuous pain, and now, he felt duty bound to forfeit love too? Though she had no idea how serious his condition was, in that moment, a singular conviction broke through the dense fog of confusion and fear. Whatever his injuries or prognosis, it didn't matter. She wanted him in her life, regardless.

Clearing her throat, she spoke softly, but without a hint of equivocation. "That doesn't change anything, Donovan. I feel what I feel, and we can work the rest of it out together if you'll let me in, trust me enough to share the burden of whatever you're going through."

For a long moment, he said nothing, but Grace felt his struggle in her heart. He wanted to say yes, but in a battle between his heart and mind, she wasn't sure his heart would win.

"Grace, I... I'm terribly sorry, I need to go. I'm getting a call from the FBI. I have to take this. I... I can't tell you what your words, your kindness means to me, but you don't understand what you're getting yourself into. I'll get back to you when I can. Good night."

And then he was gone.

. . .

ANOTHER SLEEPLESS NIGHT PLAGUED DONOVAN. The call from Agent Taylor had been alarming. Ruiz had been sighted that afternoon in Ohio, not far from where the fire rescue had occurred. There was now no doubt he was tracking them. At this point, Ruiz had to know Ben's full name, and because of his fortune, it wouldn't be hard to find information on him. As Ben owned many properties, it might take some time to fix on the right one, but he was indisputably resourceful and determined.

As he tossed and turned, Donovan considered changing his recommendation regarding their trip to Cape Cod but, in the end, he decided his original advice was still sound. Having them out of town for the day, in a place completely disconnected from any known past or present associations, was a safe plan and would buy him the time he needed to make the adjustments necessary in light of his recent decision.

After speaking to Agent Taylor, Donovan had grudgingly decided he had no choice but to step down from the case and turn it over to another; the man at the top of his contingency list, an extremely skilled and experienced defender who would guard them well. As the man, another former soldier, was finishing a case in California, he couldn't get there until the day after next, but with Ben and Callie's plans to be away for most of the day, and Agent Taylor's promise to have help on standby, Donovan felt confident he could hold on and do his job effectively until his relief arrived. There had still been no sign of trouble in or around the property.

Despite its necessity, he hated his decision, feeling he was abandoning his friends in their greatest hour of need.

But the alternative was to leave them vulnerable because of his pride, and he would never be able to live with himself if that cost them their lives. His body was betraying him, shutting down. It was impossible to maintain the façade of health and strength for much longer, as he could barely breathe from the agony. If he weren't on duty, his watch and phone set to alert him if the security equipment detected the slightest sign of trouble, he would take the prescribed pills and escape into the bliss of oblivion, at least for the night, maybe longer.

Grace's radiant face floated across the center screen of his mind's eye. He wasn't sure which was more painful, the revelation that she cared enough to blindly accept the unknowns about his health condition or the ugly truth that even that selfless offering wouldn't save their doomed romance. No matter what either of them did, it would end before it had barely begun.

As a dark hopelessness closed in around him, Donovan did the only thing he knew to do. He whispered a prayer, not for himself, for he had chosen his life, his fate, but for the people he cared about, the ones he'd promised to protect but could no longer adequately defend, though he would nevertheless continue to give his last ounce of strength in an effort to do so.

THE FOLLOWING EVENING, after work, Grace sat sipping a glass of white wine as she tried to settle her nerves. Besides the nagging questions that Donovan's admission about his poor health had evoked, something else was bothering her; a sense of doom, as if something terrible were about to happen. Still mostly in the dark about Ben and Callie's present situation, she nevertheless knew Donovan was worried, which meant something had changed, increasing the threat to their safety. She wished she could be there with them instead of sitting at home helpless and riddled with anxiety.

A soft knock at the door pulled her from her compulsive fretting. When she opened the door, she was surprised to see Lobster standing there. Though they'd been friends for years, he'd visited her house only once or twice, just to drop something off. But as he stood awkwardly staring at her, his hands were empty. Despite the February chill, he wore a wrinkled, short-sleeve shirt and no coat.

"Lobster?"

He shifted his weight but said nothing.

"Come in." She stood to the side, beckoning energetically as the cold air from the open door made her shiver. Hesitantly, he stepped inside, staying close to the door, suggesting he didn't intend to stay long.

"Is everything alright?" she asked after a minute had passed and he'd volunteered no explanation for his unexpected visit.

"Have you heard from them?" He didn't look worried, more curious.

"I have. I talked to Callie briefly, and Ben's friend, Donovan, who's been coordinating their security, has kept me updated. The situation seems somewhat precarious of late, but Donovan is skilled and smart. He'll keep them safe, Lobster. Don't worry."

"And you like him," Lobster announced, studying her carefully and grinning.

"I... How?" Grace sighed in exasperation, but eventually put up her hands, surrendering to the truth. "I suppose I do."

"But?"

Shaking her head, she was astonished at how her nearly mute friend, who seemed clueless about ninety percent of the time, had suddenly turned insightful.

"I don't know. There's something... something standing in the way. I'm unclear about the details, but whatever it is, it troubles him, and I don't know what to do." This was, by far, the most personal conversation she and Lobster had ever had, and it was uncomfortable.

"If you care about someone, you stay by their side, no matter what. That's how you know it is love."

Stunned into silence, all Grace could do was stare. Who was this person and what had he done with her quiet, aloof friend?

"I... You're absolutely right. Is that what you came all the way here to tell me?"

With another lopsided grin, he gently patted her shoulder. "I guess it was. And also, don't worry about Callie. She'll be fine, but not because of your new friend's skills. Ben's with her, so you don't need to worry." Without further explanation or a goodbye, he turned and reached for the doorknob.

"Wait!" Grace called after him. "What does that mean? What do you know about Ben, Lobster?"

He put his finger to his lips. "You'll find out." And with that, he left, as she looked after him in bewilderment.

THOUGH THERE WAS STILL no sign of trouble, that afternoon Donovan manually rechecked every piece of surveillance equipment he'd installed around the property. His replacement, though skilled in other ways, didn't have the same technical training he did, so it was important to leave everything in perfect working order. As he finished and began walking back to the house, he received another call from Agent Taylor, this one making him second guess his decision to step down from the case.

"We think Ruiz may be in the area," Agent Taylor said through clenched teeth. Perhaps his personal distress regarding the case was due to his former undercover work inside the drug ring, but still, Agent Taylor continued to surprise Donovan with how emotionally affected he was by each new development. "The information is second hand, so it isn't conclusive, but I wanted to make you aware. I'd like to send some additional security your way, but it will take a couple of hours to free up the personnel, get the paperwork filed, and then get them out there." He paused and when he spoke again, his voice was thin and hoarse. "I need to attend to a personal matter, but then I can head your way, probably get there before the protective detail arrives."

"You're planning to come yourself?" Donovan was sure he must have misunderstood what the man said.

"Yes. I'll stay out of your way, but I want to be there when and if Ruiz shows up."

Besides being highly unusual, having Agent Taylor there as well as others would complicate things, even though it would provide added safeguards.

"Miss LeVray and Mr. Sawyer are presently out of town, which is fortunate if your intel is accurate."

"Right," he said simply, and Donovan halted in his tracks surprised as, evidently, Agent Taylor was already aware of that fact, though Donovan certainly hadn't told him.

Despite an extended moment of silence, Taylor didn't elaborate, so Donovan had no choice but to move on.

"They should be returning shortly. Everything is quiet

and locked down here, and I'll be on site until early tomorrow morning. I'll get your men up to speed and introduce them to my replacement when he arrives."

"You're... You're leaving, handing the case over to someone else?" Taylor's tone verged on panic.

"With great regret, that's affirmative."

"May I ask why? You're the best in the business, Mr. Bradshaw, and I know you care about their well-being."

"I have a personal matter that demands my immediate attention. I have no choice."

After an extended pause, Taylor spoke, the tension in his voice notably stronger. "That's regrettable. I'll expedite my efforts to get there as soon as possible."

Not long after Donovan completed his equipment check, Ben and Callie returned to the house. Intending to pull Ben aside to discuss his phone call with Agent Taylor and his need to step down and bring in a replacement, he went out to meet them as they pulled into the driveway, but when he saw Ben's face, he changed his mind.

Whatever they had experienced or learned that day had upset him. His eyes were red, and he looked nearly as tired as he had the first night he'd arrived in Boston.

"Donovan? Is everything alright?" Ben asked as he in turn scrutinized Donovan's appearance.

Unwilling to heap more stress on his friend's shoulders, he nodded dumbly. "Rosa has dinner waiting, but let's talk afterward."

Sustaining eye contact, Ben tilted his head. "Are you sure?"

Though Donovan confirmed that, presently, their situation was secure, Ben kept a concerned eye on him during dinner. The pain had become intolerable, preventing Donovan from effectively hiding it any longer. Relentless and excruciating, it throbbed through every part of his body, slowing his movements and disordering his thoughts. He was thankful Taylor's men would be there in a couple of hours, as now he could no longer adequately do his job. As soon as help arrived and he got them up to speed, he would head straight to the hospital.

Dinner was quiet as everyone was consumed with their own thoughts and worries. No one ate much, which Donovan hoped wouldn't offend Rosa, but as she worked on the cleanup, her looks of somber concern told him she understood that their lack of appetite was caused by their troubled hearts.

On her way out, Rosa stopped to squeeze Donovan's shoulder as she looked on him with motherly concern. He did his best to smile reassuringly, but it didn't ease her worry.

"Alright, my friend, what's going on?" Ben asked at last, when the three of them had settled with cups of coffee and tea around the kitchen island.

Unable to look Ben in the eye as he delivered the bad news, Donovan stared at nothing in particular. "Regrettably, I need to step away for a bit, but I've got someone coming tomorrow to take over security here. He's very competent, Ben, and he'll ensure your and Callie's safety."

Doing his best to force Donovan to look at him, Ben casually dismissed the shocking revelation with a wave of his hand, as if it were incidental. "That's fine, Donovan, but that's not what I meant. What's going on with you? You don't look well."

This was the heart of his friend, the one-of-a-kind compassion he'd often admired, a kindness that understated the significance of his own concerns and focused instead on helping others with their troubles. And Callie had the same heart. As soon as Ben's words registered in her mind, she looked up at him and tears formed in her eyes. But this was the wrong time to employ that compassion. Their safety and possibly their lives, were in danger. Focusing on themselves was critical right now.

"I'm not. I need to check back into the hospital for more treatments. I don't want to leave you vulnerable here in any way so…"

Lowering his gaze, Ben softly interrupted. "I'm sorry. You don't know how much I wish my gift could permanently heal." Years of accumulated pain, forged by this regret, resounded in his voice.

"Is there anything we can do? Anything at all?" Callie gently inquired.

"Well, ma'am, I could use a new kidney and a few other spare parts if you've got them lying around." It was a badly timed joke, delivered with a tone of bitterness that was not meant for her. Yet, as he watched their faces, he perceived that they'd offer him all that and more without hesitation.

"Ben, I'm kidding. I doubt they'd give me a kidney as there are too many other things going awry to justify accepting a donation." It was the truth as his doctors had already informed him that a transplant wasn't an option.

A strange look passed between Ben and Callie as Donovan watched, feeling regretful about his misdirected irritation and inappropriate attempt at humor.

"We will do everything we can to help you; you know that. You name it; we'll make it happen." Though Donovan had no idea what they could possibly do, he got the feeling that they had something in mind. Considering neither of them knew much about the details of his injuries, he was perplexed about what they could possibly be contemplating.

"Right now, let's focus on keeping you two safe." Donovan relayed the most recent news about Ruiz's whereabouts, and advised them to stay within the confines of their tight security for the time being, assuring them that it likely wouldn't be long now before the FBI would have him in custody.

"Alright," Ben agreed with a resigned sigh. "We'll stick around the house for the time being."

"My replacement will be here at eight a.m. tomorrow, and I'll get him up to speed before I leave and..." As Donovan rose from his chair, intending to give them some privacy and step outside to place a phone call to check on the ETA of the FBI team, he felt a sudden wave of dizziness wash over him. Gripping his head, he heard an involuntary moan pass through his lips just before everything went black.

WHEN HE CAME TO, the familiar heat of Ben's healing touch was saturating his entire being, like being submerged in warm water. The alleviation of pain was so thorough that even the memory of it was hard to retrieve. He couldn't recall ever feeling this strong and healthy, even before he'd been mortally wounded. As his mind gradually regained full consciousness, he heard Ben speak to Callie who was kneeling on the floor beside him as they hovered over Donovan.

"I'll need to drop the security and open the gate."

"No!" Donovan interjected forcefully, attempting to sit up, but Ben put one hand on his chest, holding him down.

The uncompromising look in Ben's eyes prompted Donovan to yield to his wishes.

"Ben, don't! No one's watching the cameras. Dropping our defenses is not an option."

With tears in his eyes, Ben gazed at him with such deep affection that Donovan had to look away as he felt entirely unworthy. Not only was his collapse putting them in danger from Ruiz, but he was literally stealing his friend's strength to keep himself well. Second by second, he could see the drain taking a toll as Ben held tightly to his arm. His face paled, and his hands began to tremble. And to think, just a little over a day ago he'd struggled to accept the truth about a gift that was now saving his life.

A fierce self-loathing seized him as this was the opposite of what he wanted to do, was supposed to do. It was his job, his duty to defend Ben, not the other way around. He'd sooner die than watch his friend suffer because of him, but he knew Ben would never allow that.

"At least let me call and get some backup here," Donovan argued, desperate to do something. The help Agent Taylor was sending wasn't scheduled to arrive for another hour or two. But that might be too late.

Without waiting for Ben's consent, he reached into his pocket with his free hand and retrieved his phone. It was hard to work it with one hand, but he at last reached a receptionist at the Boston FBI office. The woman promised to relay a message, but the lack of urgency in her tone didn't put Donovan at ease. He tried Taylor's direct number, but it went to voicemail, forcing him to leave a message.

Grunting in frustration, Donovan hung up, his mind racing as he tried to figure out what to do.

"You need to relax," Ben implored. "I know it doesn't

feel like it but your body's undergoing trauma, and you need to stay still and calm."

Ben was right. It was hard to remember that he was injured at all as he felt healthier than he had in years. The sense of horror he was suffering at the idea of leaving them unprotected was much worse than his concern for his physical well-being. Why did this have to happen now? Another few hours and they would have had ample protection. If anything happened to them, it would be his fault, a result of his grave miscalculation regarding his ability to manage his condition. He wouldn't, couldn't let harm come to them because of his foolish mistake.

Callie whispered something, and Ben nodded and whispered back. Donovan could see the concern in her eyes for both him and Ben and now, the tremble in Ben's hands was more intense.

Not only would Donovan leave them unprotected, but he'd also leave Ben so weak that he wouldn't be capable of defending Callie if necessary. As panic and anger consumed him, he set his phone on the ground and balled his free hand into a fist, trying to figure out how to convince Ben to let go of him and put his and Callie's safety first.

"Someone will be here, but it might be a while. You can't drop the security. Please, I'll be fine, and..."

The definitive shake of Ben's head halted his plea. "You won't be fine," Ben declared, his voice strong despite the trembling that was now spreading, causing his whole body to shake. "You don't understand. That's not how this works. It's not a cure, remember? If I let go, the symptoms will return. We have to get you help, and they have to be able to get in here."

Donovan gritted his teeth. Without question, he'd

rather suffer the pain for a hundred years than watch his friend suffer it for a single minute in his place.

Callie put her hand on Ben's back as, noticing his trembling, her concern for him grew. Helplessly, Donovan watched and listened as she moved her hand, resting it on top of Ben's, which visibly relaxed him, and stilled the trembling. Looking at each other with surprise, Ben smiled at her and her green eyes danced in delight and relief.

Despite his mental anguish, Donovan couldn't help but be astonished by the miracle of Ben's gift and confused by Callie's apparent role in it. "This whole thing is amazing! How is she helping you?"

Breathing easier, Ben managed a chuckle. "That's a little complicated. We haven't told you about all the perks of this Succouri thing yet." Though there was amusement in his tone, a light shone in their eyes that heightened Donovan's curiosity. Whatever it was that they hadn't told him brought them considerable pleasure.

Callie turned her attention to the phone she held in her right hand. "They're two minutes out," she whispered, and Ben's expression sobered.

"Okay, my friend. I don't want to let go of you, so you have to use your phone to drop the security and open the gate."

"No! Let's find another way. It's not a good idea..."

"Please," he softly pleaded. "I'll let go and do it myself if I have to, but I don't want to do that until the paramedics are here, so please. It will only be for a few minutes. I'll get it back up as soon as you're on your way to the hospital." Ben's eyes begged Donovan to comply, but he couldn't. He wouldn't be the cause of putting them in danger. Disabling the sensors was one thing, but opening the gate for a significant period of time without anyone paying attention to who entered was unthinkable.

"Maybe I'm okay now. I mean, maybe it was just a quick head rush," Donovan argued, desperate to persuade Ben to let go of him and focus on his and Callie's safety instead.

Shaking his head, Ben sucked in a strained breath. "Donovan. I feel the draw. It's not gone. Please, trust me. Even with Callie's assistance, I can't hold on for much longer, so we need to get you some permanent help."

The desperation in Ben's eyes, cut him to the core. Whatever the draw felt like, it wasn't specific enough to pinpoint the exact source of the infirmity, but it evidently did alert him to the severity of the condition. And from what Donovan saw in Ben's expression, he was in real trouble.

For a long moment, he wavered, willing, even wanting to die if it meant keeping them safe. But there was no chance whatsoever Ben would allow it. He wouldn't let go of him, even if it killed him, not until he knew Donovan was in good hands. And he'd carry through on his promise to temporarily let go and drop the security himself if need be. So, in the end, though he abhorred the forced choice, Donovan did as Ben requested.

When the paramedics arrived, Ben leaned over him. "You're my dearest friend. I just got you back in my life, and I don't want to lose you again. Please, fight hard. This is not the end, but the beginning. This time, it wasn't your charge to be our guardian. But that time will come. Hang on to hope and take courage."

And then, Ben let go.

. . .

Grace paced back and forth in her living room all evening. Unable to eat or sit, she unconsciously massaged the spot where her aching heart throbbed in her chest. Something dreadful had happened. Of that, she was certain.

At eight o'clock she tried calling Callie, but there was no answer. Then she texted Donovan, but again, no response came. Just after nine, in desperation she called him, but her call went straight to voicemail. What else could she do? She didn't have Ben's number or she would have tried to reach him too. For a moment, she considered calling Callie's brother, Lee, but in the end she decided against it, not wanting to worry him unnecessarily.

At eleven, she tried everyone again, but still nothing. Sleep was impossible, so she knelt beside her bed. Following Donovan's advice, she spilled out her heart in a frantic prayer accompanied by a stream of unchecked tears. Whether it was Callie, Ben, or Donovan she wept for, she didn't know, but she feared that, before this night was over, each of them would be forced to look death directly in the face, and she could only hope and pray they would survive the encounter.

CHAPTER 8

GRIM ACCEPTANCE

By the time the sun peeked over the horizon the following morning, Grace was so overcome with exhaustion and worry that she, for the first time ever, called in sick to work. Dragging herself to the bathroom, she filled the tub with hot water, hoping a bath would soothe her frayed nerves, but it offered little comfort. Still unable to eat, her stomach churned, and she was sure, if she attempted even a light breakfast, she wouldn't be able to keep it down.

At ten o'clock, her phone lit up with an incoming call and before it had a chance to vibrate, she grabbed it. "Callie!"

"Grace? Are you alright?"

"Me? What about you? I've been worried sick."

"Why?" The question expressed curiosity, without denying its relevance.

"I've had an awful feeling, Cal, since I got home from work yesterday. Please tell me you are all okay."

"We are okay. That's... That's ironic that you felt that way because we, well, we had a rough night, but it's over,

Grace. The guy who was after me was killed last night, though he tried very hard to kill us first." Her voice quivered at the memory.

Sinking into a chair for the first time in hours, Grace covered her face and breathed in and out, as Callie's words sank in. "What happened? Did Donovan kill him?"

"No. Actually..." There was a hint of something like joy in Callie's tone, although Grace was sure she had to be imagining it.

"Callie?"

"Ben's father killed him."

"Who? I thought Ben didn't have any family."

"Ben had never met his dad, didn't know who he was until he showed up and saved both our lives." Callie laughed lightly. "It's a very long story that I'm too exhausted to tell in detail right now, but it's truly wonderful, Gracie. He's a kind man; looks just like Ben, same amazing blue eyes. It makes my heart so happy to watch them together. And"—her pitch rose—"there's more good news."

Though Grace heard the elation in her friend's tone, she was having trouble keeping up. How did Callie know Ben's father looked just like him? She had to get very close to people to see the details. In particular, Callie had often lamented about her inability to see people's eye color. If they'd just met this man the night before...

"Gracie, we're engaged, Ben and me! We're going to get married!"

Grace stopped breathing. Her tired brain couldn't track with the tidal wave of extraordinary news.

"Uh... What?"

Giggling, Callie repeated herself, slower this time. "Ben

and I are engaged. He asked me to marry him this morning, and of course, I said yes."

"Um, Callie LeVray, that's... That's wonderful. No, it's magnificent! I couldn't be happier for you both but..."

"I want to tell you everything, the whole story, but not over the phone. We'll be coming home soon, and we have a wedding to plan. I'll need your help, Gracie. So much to do in such a short time and..." Her voice bubbled over with joy and, despite the fact that there was still a dark shadow hovering in Grace's soul, she couldn't help but get caught up in her friend's celebration.

"You know I'll do whatever you need me to do, Cal. Just name it."

"Alright then"—she giggled—"be my maid of honor, in like, ten days."

"Um... ten days? Wow! I... Alright then, ten days it is. We'll make it happen."

"Thank you. From the bottom of my heart. I gotta go. So many calls to make, but we'll talk soon."

"Cal, wait. Can you tell me where you are now, and... You said Donovan didn't kill your stalker. Was he hurt? Is he alright?"

Callie's extended silence made Grace's heart pound.

"We're in Boston," she said, her voice now soft and somber. "Ben grew up here, so we're staying at his child-hood home. Donovan is..."

Grace put her hand to her mouth, gasping for air as she waited for Callie to finish.

"He collapsed yesterday, just before my stalker showed up and tried to kill us. He's in the hospital, Grace. It's serious. Ben's making phone calls right now, and checking on his condition is at the top of his list, but I don't currently know what his status is. But he was alive when he left in the ambulance. With everything that happened last night, we didn't have a chance to inquire about his condition."

Overcome, Grace's head spun. What if Donovan didn't make it through the night? What if he died alone? Her heart broke at the thought. "Which hospital?"

"I'm not sure, but I'll ask Ben and send you the info. We'll visit him today. I promise. We'll make sure he's okay and we'll stay in touch with you."

When they ended the call, Grace went to work, not willing to wait for Callie to send her the information. She contacted every hospital in the Boston area until one finally acknowledged that Donovan Bradshaw had been admitted.

"Can you tell me if he's alright?" she asked, trying to control the sobs that threatened to overtake her. Pushing them down, she determined to stay in control until she had exhausted every avenue in her attempts to find out about his condition.

"Are you family?"

"No, but..."

"I'm so sorry. I can't give out health information to anyone except immediate family."

"Can you just tell me if he's alive and stable," she begged, yielding to a few tears that she could no longer control.

"I... I probably shouldn't tell you even this much, but he is, at present, a patient in this hospital, if you catch my meaning. That's all I can say."

Lowering her head and relaxing her shoulders, she released the breath she'd been holding. "Thank you."

When the call ended, she sat for a long time considering what she should do. Her instincts told her to get on a plane and fly to Boston. But that seemed too forward, inappropriate. No matter how much her heart told her he was made for her and her for him, the truth was they'd had one thirty-minute encounter that wasn't even a date and had exchanged a few text messages and phone calls over the course of a couple of days. If she showed up at the hospital and he was unconscious or didn't want to see her, they likely wouldn't let her into his room.

But she had to do something. Too exhausted and over-wrought to think straight, she gave in to the torrent of emotions that had flooded her heart for hours. Without holding back, she sobbed until she had nothing left inside her. Then she lay down on the couch, worn out and empty, and closed her eyes, surrendering to a few hours of sleep.

Donovan blinked, disoriented and momentarily unable to focus his vision in the dim light.

"That's it, my friend," a familiar voice encouraged. It took him several minutes to rouse enough to turn his head.

"Ben," he whispered, his throat dry as tubes forced oxygen into his nose.

Smiling, Ben placed a hand on his shoulder. "Welcome back. You gave us quite a scare." With a guilty expression, Ben glanced over his shoulder. "If anyone comes in here and asks, I'm your brother. It's the only way they'd let me in here to see you, and I figured, it's pretty much the truth anyway."

Donovan tried to smile, appreciating the sentiment but amused as no two people could physically look less like brothers. As he focused on Ben's relieved expression it all began to come back to him: Ruiz, his sudden collapse, and Ben's rescue of him. With a paralyzing wave of regret, he remembered that he'd left them unprotected and vulnerable.

"Callie! Ruiz!" he stammered, trying to sit up as panic seized him.

"She's safe, and Ruiz is dead. Please, go easy. There's nothing to worry about. Best not to move around too much until the doc gives permission."

"Dead? How?"

A subtle smile raised the corners of his mouth. "Agent Taylor took him out. It's over. Now we just need to get you back on your feet."

Donovan relaxed into his pillows, overcome with relief that, though he'd let his friends down in the worst way, they were safe and the danger had passed. Agent Taylor must have tracked Ruiz down before he found out where Ben and Callie were staying. But it surprised Donovan that he had killed him. The man must have gotten violent, put up quite a fight when Taylor tried to arrest him.

"How long have I been..."

"Nearly two full days, but I think some of that was intentional sedation. Your body needed rest." Ben lowered his eyes. "We almost lost you despite my..." He lifted an eyebrow and held out his hands. "It almost wasn't enough."

Taking a deep breath, a brief shudder shook his body as he began to feel hints of the familiar pain as well as some new, sharper ones. The lingering effects of the sedation and likely some IV-administered narcotics were restraining their potency, but the tormentors were there, ready to resume their torture as soon as the medication wore off.

Concerned, Ben set his hand on Donovan's arm. "Are you in pain?"

Though the flow of healing into him was refreshing, he couldn't bear to watch him weaken again. Patting Ben's hand, he shook his head. "No. I'm alright. Please. You've done more than enough, my friend."

For a long moment, Ben watched him closely, but at last, he relented, understanding the urgency in Donovan's plea. "If that changes, and you need help…"

"I'll be alright. I… I owe you and Callie an apology. I failed you. You came to me for help, put your trust in me, and I let you down. I thought I was well enough, thought I could…"

Emphatically, Ben shook his head. "You didn't fail us, and there's no need for an apology. What you suffered, are suffering, is the result of selfless sacrifice. My trust in you was well placed, and nothing that has occurred has diminished that trust in the slightest. Quite the contrary. I couldn't be prouder to call you my friend."

"But, Ben, I…"

"Everything worked out. And, actually, if things hadn't happened the way they did, I may never have met my father."

"Father?"

Ben chuckled and smiled broadly. "It turns out Agent Thomas Weston Taylor is my father."

Donovan squinted at Ben. "Wha… How in the world?"

"It's a very long story, but if you saw him, you'd know it was undoubtedly true. He looks just like me."

"I thought… I wondered why he was so interested, so emotional about this case. But I never imagined…"

"His dangerous undercover work prevented him from being in my life when I was young, and then recently, he couldn't track me down because of my constant running. He seems sincere in his desire to get to know Callie and me, be a part of our lives, but it will take time to build trust." Ben sighed. "But right now I want to focus on getting you better and out of this place. After all, you'll need to be back on your feet so you can fly back home with us to attend a very special occasion, happening in eight days."

Confused and still reeling from the shock of Wes Taylor being Ben's father, Donovan stared questioningly at Ben's unhindered grin.

"I asked Callie to marry me, and though I can't fathom why she deems me worthy of such an honor, she said yes."

"Ben! Finding your father and getting engaged, all while I was off taking a nap. Miss a day, miss a lot," he teased. "That's fantastic. No two people could be more perfectly matched."

Inquisitively, Ben stared at him. "There's a girl out there who is your perfect match as well. Perhaps closer than one might think." Donovan got the feeling Ben already suspected he and Grace had been communicating.

Donovan dropped his gaze, wondering if Grace knew what had happened. Surely Callie had informed her by now about the severity of his condition, and how he'd failed them. She would assuredly want nothing more to do with him, and though the reality of that made him feel as if his heart were being torn from his chest, it was inevitable, and far better for her in the end. She deserved happiness and he could only offer pain.

Before Donovan could respond, a nurse entered and seeing that he was awake, she rushed back out to retrieve the doctor.

"I'll let you get some rest, my friend, but I'll be back tomorrow."

But Donovan reached out and caught his arm before he could turn to go. "Ben, thank you for saving my life, you and Callie. But please, I have to know. Right before you let go of me and the paramedics took over my care, what did you mean by what you said?"

Ben looked blankly at him. "I... I just wanted you to know how happy I am that we've found each other again. Your friendship is important to me, and I'm going to do everything in my power to get you well so we can enjoy it for years to come."

"I appreciate that, but I'm referring to the other part, the part where you said this wasn't the time for me to be your guardian, but that time would come. What did that mean?"

"I..." Wide-eyed, Ben shook his head. "I don't remember saying anything like that. I recall telling you to hang in there, have courage, but..."

Releasing Ben's arm, Donovan ran his fingers through his hair. "Do you... Do you remember telling me that this wasn't meant to be the end, but the beginning."

Once more, Ben shook his head. "I'm sorry, I don't, but I do agree with that sentiment. We're going to figure this out, get you better. I won't lose my friend again."

"I don't understand," Donovan said, his voice just above a whisper. "I distinctly remember you saying those words to me, and the way you were looking at me... I..."

"Your body was in a state of extreme trauma, and they've given you a lot of pain medication. Give your mind some time to clear the cobwebs. From recent experience, I well understand the confusion of waking up after being unconscious for a while. It's hard to know what's real and what's your mind playing tricks on you. It will all settle soon."

The doctor stepped into the room and Ben picked up his coat from a nearby chair. "I'll be back, brother," he said with a playful grin. "And I'll be expecting to hear that you're being released soon so we can reserve that flight for you. No chance I'm getting married without you there."

Offering him a weak nod, Donovan watched his friend leave the room. Despite Ben's proposed explanations, Donovan was certain of what he'd heard. Why Ben couldn't remember was a mystery, but that didn't shake his conviction that his experience was real, burned into his memory in vivid sound and color, like the first time he saw Grace.

As the doctor somberly informed him of what they'd done to his body in the last forty-eight hours to stabilize his condition, and then mournfully described his bleak prognosis—offering him very little that was new or unexpected—Donovan continued to ponder the strange experience. Ben had said he knew almost nothing about his gift, that he'd just recently learned what it was called. Could Ben's lapse in memory be related to his miraculous ability somehow? After all, Ben was actively using his gift, giving Donovan his strength when the conversation occurred. How could Donovan be unwaveringly confident he'd heard those words and Ben be equally sure he hadn't spoken them? Ben Sawyer wasn't a liar. So, if Ben didn't say those things to him—the Ben who'd stood by his bedside just a moment ago—who did? And another question was equally pressing. What in the world did the words mean? The message spoke of a future, another chance to be a guardian for Ben and Callie. It referred to the present as the beginning. But Donovan had no future, as the doctor who was currently speaking solemnly reconfirmed. So, what could it all mean?

"Mr. Bradshaw, do you understand?" The doctor's woeful inquiry redirected his focus.

"I understand," he answered, having heard it all before. "When can I leave?"

"Leave? No, Mr. Bradshaw. If you'd like to transfer your

care to the veteran's hospital, we can arrange for your transport, but..."

"Doctor, you just informed me there's nothing you can do for me, correct?"

A sigh preceded the doctor's response. "We can keep you out of pain, keep you hydrated, use dialysis to counter some of the lost kidney function, and—"

"But it's all just delaying the inevitable."

"Well, yes, but it will prolong—"

"I'd like to leave tomorrow."

"Mr. Bradshaw!" The doctor shook his head in protest. "The high dose of narcotics required to keep you out of pain needs to be administered under supervision and—"

"After one more night of rest, I won't be needing narcotics."

The doctor's eyes grew wide. "You'll never be able to tolerate the pain. You don't understand. Your injuries are so severe that—"

Donovan put up a hand. "I'm well aware that I'm a ticking time bomb and that everything in my body is coming apart. If I have one more month, one more week, or one more day, I accept that, but I don't want to spend it here. My fr... brother is getting married. I'd like to witness that. I'll tolerate the pain, as I've been doing for a long time. Thank you for patching me up, giving me a chance to catch my breath, but I'm not going to die in a hospital, not today anyway."

Though astonished and reluctant, the doctor at last agreed to release him the following morning. When he left the room, Donovan closed his eyes, feeling foolish about groping in the dark, searching for a thread of hope too flimsy to cling to. He was going to die, very soon, and the best thing he could do for himself was accept that fact and get his affairs in order. There was no time or justification for pursuing anything else.

For the rest of the day and most of the night, Donovan escaped into the fog of sedation and potent pain medication. Despite his resolute pronouncement to the doctor, it was exceedingly tempting to simply let the final grains of sand drift peacefully into the bottom of the hourglass, while remaining too drugged to notice or care. But he owed his friend this one last effort. Ben wanted him at his wedding, and he'd be there.

By seven the next morning, Donovan was fully awake, the pain's return dispelling any remnants of peaceful bliss. As he waited for the doctor to sign his discharge papers, a nurse brought in a bag with his clothes and personal items. As he dressed, he paused to look at himself in the mirror, something he generally avoided at all costs. His body was marred by deep, ugly scars, courtesy of burns, bullets, surgeries, shrapnel, and knife wounds. Even his face hadn't been spared. Grimacing at the disfigured man he saw staring back at him, he found it a wonder that anyone as beautiful as Grace would or could ever have taken an interest in him. But then, she didn't know about all of it. The scars on his face weren't so hideous.

Hurriedly, he finished dressing, and despite his determination to forget about her, he pulled his phone from the bag, sure it had to be out of charge. Surprisingly, it lit up when he touched it. At the top of his screen, her name appeared in three consecutive notifications, and his heart twisted in his chest.

Ignoring the objectors screaming in his head, he opened

the messages in the order they'd come in, the first dated the night of his collapse.

> Donovan. Please call me when you can. I have a terrible feeling something bad is happening or is about to happen. I'm worried about all of you. Please be careful.

Donovan looked up from his phone. How had she known? The timing was uncanny. Eagerly, he scrolled down to the next message, which she'd sent the following morning.

> Donovan. I heard from Callie this morning. She told me about everything; that Ben's father saved their lives by killing that horrible monster and about your collapse. I called every hospital in Boston until I figured out where you were, but they won't tell me anything except that you're alive. Maybe you're unconscious or too ill to talk, but as soon as you feel strong enough, please call me. I'm worried, more than worried. I want to come there, make sure you're alright, but I don't know if you'd want that or if they'd let me in to see you. Please, at least let me know how you are.

Profoundly touched by her genuine concern for him, Donovan wanted to call her, tell her how much her words meant to him, but that would be pure selfishness. He desperately needed her, but she needed to move on, let go of any attachment she'd formed to him, and find happiness elsewhere.

But there was one other thing from her message that caught his attention. She said Taylor saved their lives.

Clearly, there was more to the story of Ruiz's demise than Ben had relayed.

With an anguished sigh, he read the final message, sent fourteen hours ago.

> Donovan. Callie told me you're awake and recovering. I'm overjoyed and relieved. I know this might be too forward, but may I come and see you? I'm done with the long-distance thing, and my heart is telling me I need to be there. But I won't disrespect your right to privacy. I know you're trying to protect me by keeping me at a distance, but please, let me make my own choice about what my heart can and cannot endure. I'm tougher than you think. I await your response, but either way, I want you to know you're not alone.

Erasing the evidence of his unchecked emotions, Donovan swiped at his cheek with the back of his hand. If only she knew how much he wanted to oblige her, to not just permit her to come, but beg her to. Worse than any physical anguish he suffered was the agony of having found such a treasure, a rare, beautiful, kind woman much too late.

A soft knock, followed by the sound of a man clearing his throat interrupted his dismal thoughts. When he looked up, he knew immediately who the stranger was. A thick head of dark hair lightly peppered with gray, a muscular build, and unusually vivid blue eyes were dead giveaways.

"Agent Taylor," Donovan greeted, rising to his feet and extending his hand.

Taylor smiled and gripped Donovan's hand firmly as he looked him over. "Indeed. But I see the intelligence I received was faulty. I was told you'd be here for… for the foreseeable future."

Donovan chuckled. "I don't do bed rest well. I didn't leave them much choice but to let me go."

With admiration, Taylor nodded. "I came by because I wanted to put a face with a name and because my son speaks so highly of you that I was compelled to meet you in person. In the last year, I've heard your name mentioned numerous times, Mr. Bradshaw, always with the highest regard. When you abruptly withdrew from the LeVray case, I figured the circumstance that pulled you away must have been serious. I was sad to learn that I was correct."

Feeling a bit exposed by Taylor's obvious awareness of his health condition—likely a result of his easy access to his aforementioned intelligence—Donovan quickly changed the subject. "I'm gratified you were able to step in for me, meet your son, and save his life," he replied, hoping the prompt would lead Taylor to tell him more about what had occurred the night Ruiz was killed.

Taylor's eyes shadowed and he looked to the side. "I've wanted to meet him for years, but I wouldn't put him in danger to satisfy that desire. Then for a while, I couldn't find him, even with my access to intelligence. When I finally learned he was back in town, at his childhood home, I hoped… prayed he might give me a chance, but when I showed up there and found Ruiz, holding a loaded gun six inches from my boy's head"—he took a deep shaky breath —"I can't express how that felt."

Taking a step back, Donovan lowered himself into a chair, horrified by what Taylor was describing.

"Mr. Bradshaw!" Taylor stepped toward him. "Are you alright."

"Um, yes. Just a little dizzy."

Taylor pulled a folding chair over and sat opposite him, watching with concern.

"Why did Ruiz target Ben rather than Callie?" Donovan asked, his voice strained, despite his attempts to control his emotions so he wouldn't appear as ignorant as he was.

A proud smile filled Taylor's face. "You were right when you told me he would rather die than leave her unprotected. After the first bullet sank into his arm, my son wrapped his entire body around that girl, like an impenetrable shield. There was no way Ruiz could get to her without taking him out." He shook his head, as his eyes shone. "I've never seen love or courage like that." He briefly glanced toward the open door, then put a hand to the side of his mouth. "It's fortunate he's Succouri or I would have lost him, before I even found him," he whispered.

"You... You know about that?" Donovan stammered, his mind overwhelmed and his heart filled with remorse and guilt at the terror they'd faced because he'd left them defenseless. Ben had been shot? How had Ben waved this off, acting as if nothing serious had happened? How had he forgiven him so quickly when they'd nearly been killed?

Unaware of Donovan's inner dialogue, Taylor chuckled at his confused stare.

"Ben told me you just learned his secret. The shock and confusion are normal. All these years later, I still can hardly believe it's real, but when it saves your life, and then your son's life twice, there's no denying it."

"I... I don't understand."

With another light chuckle, Taylor stood and patted Donovan's shoulder. "I should probably let Ben be the one to tell you those stories. It's a pleasure to meet you in the flesh, Mr. Bradshaw. As my son and his fiancée regard you with the greatest affection, I have a feeling we'll have many more opportunities to get better acquainted. I'm obliged to you for lending them your skills, watching over them."

Leaning back, Donovan looked up into the older man's eyes. "But, Agent Taylor, I didn't. I failed them, miserably."

Empathetic compassion filled the man's eyes. "Mr. Bradshaw, I worked undercover for more than twenty years. My mission was to protect the innocent and bring the scum of the earth to justice. I gave everything up for that singular mission, including my only son. But still, I failed often. In the two decades I toiled in that cesspool of evil, I failed seventeen times. I saved hundreds of lives, put dozens of bad guys behind bars, but do you know what haunts me every hour of every day? The number seventeen."

He leaned over Donovan, looking directly into his eyes. "You've saved hundreds, perhaps thousands. You've given up far too much, suffered beyond the pale. You did not fail my son or Miss LeVray. Despite what we who bear the burden to defend others expect of ourselves, we *are* only human. This time, you needed a helping hand, and I am proud to have finished the good work you started. Callie LeVray and Ben Sawyer are alive, safe. They are not one of my, nor of your, seventeen."

Straightening, he softened his tone as he finished. "It's time to focus on yourself for a while. Let someone take care of you, fill your heart, and feed your soul. Life can't be all about giving out. That's a sure way to end up empty, of no use to anyone. You've poured your life out in the noble cause of defending others. For a little while, let someone else save the world, and go get your heart mended, Mr. Bradshaw." He smiled. "That's an order, soldier."

CHAPTER 9

A GLIMMER OF HOPE

When Ben discovered Donovan had been released from the hospital, he invited him to join him and Callie for an early dinner the following day, as they planned to catch a flight home later in the evening. Still weighed down with guilt over what had happened, Donovan tried to politely decline, but Ben wouldn't hear of it.

"We've got to work out your flight arrangements, and there's something important I need to ask you," he'd said excitedly.

Though he admired and appreciated his friend's forgiveness and endless compassion, it was difficult to look him in the eye as they sat eating dinner together. As she had greeted him with a warm, unhindered embrace, Callie also appeared to be harboring no resentment whatsoever, despite the trauma they'd endured. But after learning the truth from Taylor, he couldn't ignore what felt like the elephant in the room.

"I owe you both my life and an apology," he began. "I

was supposed to be protecting you, but because of me, you were both nearly killed."

Without any actual humor, Donovan chuckled at their matching expressions of surprise. "I forced the truth out of Taylor, your father, Ben. All that FBI training rendered impotent by parental love and pride."

With conviction, Ben again assured him that they did not hold him in any way responsible for what had happened, and Callie nodded in full agreement.

"Still, my situation put you in danger, and for that, I'm deeply regretful. I hope to make it up to you some day." Dropping his gaze, he thought about the words Ben couldn't recall saying; the promise that, in the future, he would get the chance to defend them again.

Ben sent him a mischievous smile. "I was hoping you'd say that. I've got an idea if you're interested."

Puzzled, Donovan stared at Ben's impish expression.

"Be my best man next Saturday. Stand with me and make sure I don't forget the rings or my lines or anything else important."

Donovan swallowed hard. Not only had they forgiven him, but now they additionally honored him with this request. It was more than he deserved, and he struggled to keep his emotions at bay. "I'd be honored."

Rejoicing, Callie clapped her hands. "Perfect! Grace has already agreed to stand with me, so we're all set."

Donovan sucked in a breath. "Grace?"

"Um, yes," Ben confirmed, picking up on Donovan's discomfort. "Is everything alright between you two?"

Despite Taylor's words and his heart's longings, he hadn't responded to Grace's messages. No matter which way he twisted the facts, he couldn't justify hurting her.

"I... Of course, that's fine, but I haven't answered her

texts for a few days so she might not be comfortable being around me, but..." He didn't know what else to say. Of course, Callie would want Grace to stand with her, but the idea of having to see Grace again, look into her hypnotizing eyes, how would he hold his resolve?

Callie reached across the table and set her hand on Donovan's. "I've known Grace for years. She's strong and incredibly loyal. She won't give up on you, and she won't be scared off by your health concerns. You can and should trust her heart."

Sighing, Donovan threw up his hands. "There's just no point. I like her, like her a lot, but I don't think I'm going to be around for long, so I'll just hurt her. I don't want to do that." His voice cracked. "I can't do that."

"I won't accept that as inevitable, Donovan," Ben countered. "There's always hope."

Shaking his head, Donovan covered his face with his hands. They didn't get it. There was no hope for him. "I sincerely appreciate that, Ben, but even your magic isn't enough to put Humpty-Dumpty back together again in this case." He blew out a breath of air, wishing they could change the subject, talk about something else, anything else.

Once more, Donovan observed a strange look, the same one he'd seen pass between them the night he'd collapsed in their kitchen. Then Ben looked at him as if searching for something in his eyes.

"I... I don't know if this is a real possibility yet, and I... we hesitated to bring it to you because of that, but there might be a way."

A way for what? What was he talking about? Donovan stared at Ben in confusion.

"It's complicated but if we can find a Succouri who is

willing and able to pass along his gift, the gift would cure you, heal everything that's broken, permanently. But there are consequences and costs, and I don't know if you'd want to change, become something else forever."

Stunned, Donovan froze, unable even to breathe for a long moment. He didn't understand. He knew Ben believed his gift came from someone else, and Taylor had hinted it was him. But what exactly was Ben suggesting here?

"Become... like you?" Donovan stammered, trying to make sense of Ben's words.

Slowly, Ben shook his head. "Well, no, not exactly like me. We've recently learned I'm... unique. But you'd become Succouri, gifted like me. It's a new identity and a whole new life, but with your background of service, you're ideal as a candidate if you—"

His head spinning, Donovan put up a hand. "I don't understand. How would becoming like you cure me?" He knew Ben had the power to temporarily heal others when he touched them, but Donovan's body was so damaged: bones, muscles, skin, and organs. Surely even his wondrous gift wasn't powerful enough to fix all of that.

Ben sighed and looked over at Callie. Then he slowly unbuttoned his shirt and removed it as Donovan watched in stunned silence.

"The night you collapsed, I was shot, right here." He pointed to the upper part of his left arm. "The bullet went deep into my arm, and I had to have it surgically removed by a doctor who specializes in working with Succouri. That was just a few days ago."

Still horrorstruck by the thought of Ben taking a bullet that should have been stopped or suffered by him, Donovan struggled to focus on what Ben was trying to show him. But as he investigated the spot Ben indicated, there was nothing to see. The skin of Ben's upper arm was smooth, no visible mark or scar, just as with the rest of him.

"But there's nothing there."

Ben smiled. "Exactly."

And then, Donovan understood. Ben's flawless complexion, his lack of illness or disease, it was part of his gift. The only physical suffering that came to him was when he gave away his strength to save others. But otherwise, he was, it seemed, nearly invincible.

All at once, he remembered Ben's childhood battle with leukemia. He remembered his parents talking about how his recovery was sudden and remarkable. Taylor had said that Ben's gift saved his life twice; once when it kept Ruiz's bullet from fatally wounding him, but perhaps also when it liberated him from the ravages of that awful cancer.

Donovan's eyes grew wide as understanding dawned. If the gift could cure leukemia, perhaps there really was a chance for him.

"What are the costs?"

"Let's wait on that until I can assess how real the possibility might be."

"Fair enough, but I don't know how much time I have left, Ben."

"As soon as we return from our honeymoon, I'll follow up on my lead. I promise I'll do my best, everything I can to help you. For now, hold on to hope, and please, consider trusting in Grace. Walking alone with your pain isn't healthy. Trust me. Grace won't give up and you'll hurt her by excluding her from your life and heart."

Though they tried to get him to fly out with them that night, Donovan wasn't ready yet. He had some loose ends to tie up in town, and he had to figure out what to do about Grace. Since seeing her again was unavoidable, he couldn't continue to put off answering her messages. And if there was hope, even if it was fragile, should he reconsider his decision to protect her by keeping her at arm's length?

Despite their kind hearts and best intentions, it was by no means certain he'd make it until they returned from their honeymoon, much less for the time it would take beyond that to arrange what Ben had in mind. And besides, he had no idea if he would be able to accept the costs. Until he'd met Callie, Ben had hated his gift, calling it a curse and running from it year after year. In addition to the obvious risk of exposure, there had to be other reasons why Ben had maintained such a lonely, desperate existence. Certainly, he didn't want to trade one variety of death for another.

However, after he met Callie, Ben's perspective radically changed. He found peace with who he was. Maybe partnership was an essential part of the life, as illustrated right before his eyes when Callie's touch calmed Ben's trembling. If he wasn't alone, if Grace would consider...

Shaking his head, he scolded himself. He was putting the cart way before the horse. There was no point in guessing about matters he had no knowledge of. And anyway, if he decided to reach out to Grace, his motives needed to be pure. He owed her complete honesty, and it would be improper to expect anything from her. Any and every step forward would need to be dependent on her uncoerced choice.

Yet there was one obtrusive barrier he couldn't figure his way around. Grace didn't know about Ben's gift, and it assuredly wasn't his place to reveal the information. It wouldn't take her sharp mind and her uncanny instincts about him long to figure out he was hiding something. How would they build trust with that gigantic secret in the way?

Nevertheless, the reality remained that in a few days, he

would see her, offer her his arm, and walk with her down the aisle. Questions and doubts aside, the matter could no longer be deferred.

LATE THAT EVENING, Grace accompanied Lee to the airport to meet Ben, Callie, and Ben's father, Wes Taylor. Despite her heavy heart, it was a relief and a joy to have her best friend back safe and sound, and Callie's exuberance over her wedding plans was contagious. Shocked by his close resemblance to Ben, Grace took an immediate liking to Agent Taylor, particularly when he showed such kind affection for Callie, already treating her like a beloved daughter-in-law.

But as she drove back to her house that evening, the weight pressing down on her heart quashed every positive emotion. It had been nearly three days since she'd last texted Donovan. Ben and Callie had informed her that he'd been released from the hospital, which brought her solace, but that meant he had undoubtedly read her messages and had chosen not to respond. Although she knew exactly why he was pushing her away, it broke her heart as his assumptions and fears were unfounded, and that miscalculation was cheating them both out of a chance at happiness. But what could she do? Without his permission or expressed desire, she didn't feel right about going to see him, even if her heart kept urging her to do so.

The following day, as she mindlessly dragged herself through her Monday routine, she did her best to put Donovan out of her mind, but the effort served to deepen her sorrow. She didn't want to forget him. Rather, she wanted to find a way to convince him that she was strong enough to handle whatever they faced. Though he was accustomed to protecting others from harm, this time, he needed to let go of that impulse and accept that loving someone always involved risk, the chance of a broken heart. She was willing to take the gamble because she cared deeply for him.

That evening, when she was ten minutes from home, to her delight and surprise, Donovan called. Quickly pulling off the road, her heart pounded as she grabbed her phone from where it was lying on the passenger's seat.

"Hello," she answered breathlessly.

"Miss Sophia." The sound of his voice eased the ache in her heart.

"Donovan," she said through a sigh. "Are you alright?"

"I... I suppose that's a complicated question. Are you off work? I mean, can you talk?"

"I'm in my car, but I pulled over, so, yes."

"I owe you an apology and an explanation, Miss Grace. I got your kind messages, and I wanted to respond, but I felt, I feel asking anything of you, even continuing our long-distance discourse, is pure selfishness. By pursuing our relationship, I stand to gain everything and lose nothing, but"—he let out an anguished breath—"the opposite is true for you. I have nothing to offer you, except heartbreak. I've already failed my dearest friend, and yours as well. I can't make the same mistake again; encourage those I care about to put their trust in me, only to disappoint them. I'm sorry, Grace. I'm sorry I—"

"Donovan, please," she interjected, speaking gently, but resolutely as tears began to form in her eyes. "You didn't let Ben or Callie down. You collapsed. That wasn't your fault. How could you have known—"

"But I did know, Grace. I've known for a long time, but I wanted to, needed to spend the time I had helping others, doing something I could be proud of so that when..." He fell silent, and Grace stifled a gasp as fear flooded her veins with adrenaline.

"Donovan," she whispered. "What did you know? Please, tell me exactly what you're facing."

"Grace, I'm dying."

Putting her free hand over her face, the tears began to flow as his words confirmed her worst fears. It was a long time before either of them spoke, but at last, hearing her soft sobs, Donovan broke the silence.

"I'm sorry, Grace. Sorry I approached you in that deli, sorry I encouraged us to continue communicating, sorry I've already hurt you, but maybe you understand now. I have to let you go. Sorrow is the last thing I want for you."

Straightening, Grace forcefully wiped the tears off her cheeks. "No! Donovan, I'm not sorry you did any of those things. Not sorry at all." Frustratedly, she grunted. "We can't do this over the phone. I need to see you. If you truly care about me, than grant me this request. Speak with me face to face, before you make up your mind about anything. I'll fly out, right now. I'll—"

"Grace!" He elongated her name, his voice tortured and tight. "If that's what you wish, I'll oblige, but there's no need for you to come here. I'll be there on Wednesday. Ben has asked me to stand with him at the wedding. Perhaps Thursday or Friday we could set aside some time to talk, but I'm not sure what more there is to say. Regardless of how I feel, what I want, I can't change the truth."

"I understand."

Another long pause lingered as they both processed their feelings.

"Grace." Donovan at last spoke, the ache in his heart spilling out in his tone. "Are you alright?"

"I... When I see you, when we talk, will you give me a

chance, Donovan? Will you hear me with your heart, not just your head or the soldier part of you that wants to protect everyone else, everyone but yourself?"

"I'm not sure I know how to—"

"Just promise me you'll try. That's all I'm asking. Please."

Grace heard him take a slow breath, in and out. "I will try, Miss Sophia."

To help Callie with last-minute wedding plans, Grace had already taken Wednesday, Thursday, and Friday off from work. Though it was hard to think about anything but Donovan, she did her best to fulfill her duties as Callie's maid of honor, including helping her clear out her late father's closet on Wednesday afternoon in preparation for her and Ben taking over the space when they returned from their honeymoon.

With the hectic schedule, she and Callie hadn't had much time to talk. Though Callie had given her the basics on what had transpired in Boston, as before, Grace felt there was a lot she was holding back. And likewise, Grace hadn't shared much about Donovan either. The emotional distance between them was growing and that troubled Grace.

After some light conversation, intended to keep Callie's mind off the unpleasant task, Grace was ready to speak up about their recent detachment, but Callie beat her to it.

"Gracie, I know you and Donovan were communicating, and I know he stopped when he fell ill. Are you... Are you alright?"

"Cal, I..." And with that, the dam broke, and the accumulated emotions of the past week flooded out in an unrestrained stream of tears.

Callie threw her arms around her, begging her to tell her what was in her heart.

"I like him, Cal, like him a lot, like maybe the forever kind of a lot. But he doesn't want to hurt me, and I don't know what to do. He told me"—a fierce sob shook her—"he told me he's going to die!"

"Oh Gracie!" Callie exclaimed, tightening her arms around her. After a few minutes, she regained enough composure to lean back and look Callie in the eyes. "I know he's coming here tonight. I was planning to ask you and Ben if I could pick him up at the airport: that way he can't run away from me."

"What are you going to tell him?"

"I know I will get hurt, crushed even, but I think… I think I love him, and I'll hold onto whatever time I have with him if he'll let me."

Callie smiled at her. "Somehow, my kindhearted friend, I knew that would be your answer. I told Donovan as much a few days ago. I told him that if he told you everything, you'd still want him." Callie shook her head. "You and I… When we fall, we fall hard and fast and we don't let go."

"I just wish…" Grace lowered her chin in despair. "I wish there was hope: an experimental treatment, a possible surgery, something. How can such a good man face such an unyielding fate?"

"There is hope. Please, don't give up."

There it was again. Looking into her friend's eyes, Grace saw that mysterious shadow, like the one she'd seen in Ben. They were both hiding something. Her best friend was in on it, and it was past time to fess up.

Straightening, Grace grasped Callie's arm. "Alright, Girly, it's time. Long past time, actually."

"Time?"

"Yes. Time to tell me your little secret, yours and Ben's, what you promised to tell me when you returned from your trip. I want to know why, when you're with him, you seem complete somehow, like you've known him for years? I want to know how Ben saved you when you were shot. I want to know why you were so confident you were safe with him, and why you're getting married so quickly, yet it seems completely natural and right that you are. Why do you look into his eyes in a way you've never done with anyone else, like you can really see him? Why does Lobster worship Ben like a god? Why did Donovan have a million questions about Ben just a few days ago, but now he seems to have no questions at all? Why—"

"Okay, okay," Callie put up her hands in surrender. "Ben once told me I had some very observant friends. He was right. Well, um, I don't know quite how to tell you this, but Ben is a…"

On the edge of her seat, Grace drew circles with her hand in the air, trying to get Callie to hurry up and finish the sentence. "A what?"

"Um." She bit her lip. "He's a real-life superhero of sorts. Ben has a gift. An extraordinary, beautiful gift he's had since he was a child. In simplest terms, Ben has the power to temporarily cure illness and suffering when he touches people. So, when I was shot, he touched me and stopped the bleeding and pain until help arrived. And every time he holds my hand, I can see, Gracie, see everything." She gestured into the open space around them.

Slumping against the wall of the closet, Grace's mouth fell open. Her first reaction was complete disbelief. Was her friend crazy? But as she looked into her eyes, and her mind replayed scene after scene where she noticed Callie looking at Ben in a way she'd never seen before in the three plus years she'd known her, she gradually began to allow the idea that this might actually be true to take root and grow.

"I know it sounds crazy but ask Donovan. Ben saved him too. And Lobster. Years ago, Ben saved his life when his car went off the side of a ravine. Lee knows and has witnessed it as well, and Ms. Essie."

Donovan knew? Grace's head spun. Did Ben save him when he collapsed? Is that when he found out? And he believed? Donovan wasn't the kind of person to blindly accept something so outrageous. And Lobster and Lee!

"So, I'm the last to know." Grace huffed, feeling bitter about the fact.

Callie grimaced apologetically.

Seeing that Grace's mind was open, Callie excitedly told Grace about how Ben had temporarily revived her father just before he passed away, so she and Lee could say good-bye. She told her how he'd taken a bullet for her in Boston and how he'd had to have it dug out of his arm without any anesthesia. With a kind of love in her eyes Grace had never seen before, Callie spoke of a special bond, a tie that linked her and Ben's hearts and minds in a way no ordinary human bond could. And then, she told her about Donovan; how Ben had held onto his arm and, with her help, kept him alive until the ambulance arrived.

Grace clasped her hands over her heart, captivated by her friend's stories, yet grappling with the unsettling realization that the world was far less ordered and logical than she had believed. This was the kind of magic written about in fantastical tales, not lived out by real people.

But in the end, she trusted Callie and had seen far too

many unexplainable things in Ben's presence to do anything but believe. But if this kind of magic existed, then —her heart took flight at the thought—maybe there was hope for her and Donovan.

"Cal, is there anything Ben can do to help Donovan. I mean, permanently?"

Callie's expression mixed sorrow and joy. "We are working on that, but I'll be honest with you, it's a long shot. Ben loves Donovan like a brother. He'll do everything humanly, and inhumanly possible to save his life." Pressing her lips together, Callie looked away, having said all she was presently willing to say on the matter.

Lowering her head, Grace felt disheartened as there wasn't much comfort to be drawn from that vague and unenthusiastic response.

Sensing her disappointment, Callie smiled and put a finger under Grace's chin, lifting it gently. "There is hope, Gracie." Though still cautious, Callie's tone rang with more confidence this time.

With a weak smile, Grace embraced her friend, gratified that there was no longer a chasm of secrets between them. No matter how distant the possibility, if there was the slightest chance, the dimmest illumination remaining in the fading light of hope, she'd struggle with all her might against its extinguishment.

CHAPTER 10

A CHANCE AND A CHOICE

Grace wrung her hands nervously as she waited for Donovan just outside his arrival gate. He was expecting Callie and Ben, not her, and she didn't know how he'd feel about her bold imposition.

Beyond this insecurity, she was anxious about their conversation. No matter how many times she rehearsed what she'd say to him, it never came out right. She didn't want to come across as patronizing, nor did she want to, in any way, diminish the seriousness of what he faced. Yet in terms of her desire to be in his life, she needed him to understand that whether he died today or lived for seventy more years, it made no difference. She'd made up her mind. For the pleasure of knowing him, perhaps even loving him, she'd face the pain of losing him.

Wiping at her eyes as a tear threatened to ruin her meticulously applied makeup, she blinked, and when her eyes refocused, her breath caught in her throat.

Standing, not ten yards in front of her, was Donovan. Their eyes locked on one another, and Grace's heart pounded furiously. There wasn't a hint of disappointment or irritation in his expression. On the contrary, what Grace saw in his eyes reminded her of what she'd observed in Ben's the day he'd visited Callie in the hospital. As improbable as it was, the only word that could come close to describing it was love.

In slow motion, they moved toward one another. It grieved her to see the pain he was suffering, evidenced in his guarded movements and the new lines on his face. Though it had only been a little over a week since she'd seen him, he looked older, though his gentle eyes were ageless.

When they were face to face, Donovan set his bag on the ground and reached for her hands, never looking away from her eyes. When she touched him, her hands small and fragile in his large ones, her fears and doubts vanished. This was right, meant to be, and nothing else mattered.

"Though your face hasn't left my mind, a memory can't capture the impact of your incomparable beauty or what those blue eyes do to me when I look directly into them, Miss Sophia."

Her cheeks warmed, and he released one of her hands to lightly touch her face. Grace had forgotten how tall he was. The eight-inch difference made her unconsciously rise onto her tiptoes as she tried to look him squarely in the eyes.

Donovan chuckled at her effort. "We may have to get you a stool, ma'am, or perhaps we could find somewhere to sit?" He looked questioningly at her, but his words didn't register as presently, all she could think about was how nice his skin felt on hers and how attracted she was to him, body and soul. Being this head over heels for a man was foreign, something she had thought herself immune to.

When a long moment passed and she didn't respond,

he smiled and stepped back, dropping his hand from her face. "As it appears I am at your mercy, may I ask what you had in mind?"

"Um." She shook her head, trying to clear her thoughts. "Dinner at my house. If that's alright."

Releasing her, he folded his arms and smiled. "Miss Sophia! If you cook dinner for me and take me to your house, I don't know how we can possibly avoid calling that a date."

Her eyes sparkled. "Let's just call it a quiet, private place to talk, shall we?"

"By all means," he said with another low chuckle. "Lead the way,"

The drive to her house was quiet, as they considered the upcoming conversation. But whenever Grace rested her hand on the center console, Donovan placed his lightly on top of hers, and the contact was comforting, yet thrilling, simultaneously slowing and accelerating the beat of her heart.

As she reheated the chicken parmesan she'd made earlier in the day and tossed a bowl of salad, Donovan took his time looking around before leaning on the counter opposite her and whistling. "Your place is very nice, ma'am. It seems you are a woman of many talents," He grimaced. "Puts my bachelor's pad to shame. I haven't even unpacked most of the boxes from when I moved in a year ago. But then, I'm not home that much. This place"—he gestured in the air—"feels like a real home. How long have you lived here?"

"Just over a year. After I graduated, I rented an apartment for a while to save money for a downpayment, but I couldn't wait to get a place that I could make my own."

Shaking his head, he maintained his grin. "So, we've

lived in our residences for about the same amount of time, yet you've accomplished all of this."

She stopped tossing the salad. "Well, my life is not so... complicated as yours. How many lives have you saved in that same time period, Donovan? Even if your answer is one, you've got me beat by a mile."

Humbled by the compliment, he momentarily looked down. "Don't underestimate the value of making people feel welcome, at home, and"—he smiled—"hungry. Dinner smells delicious."

Bidding him to sit, Grace set the food on the table and brought them each a glass of ice water. Courteously, Donovan waited for her to sit and take a few bites, before partaking enthusiastically.

"And the lady has yet another talent. To whom do you attribute your outstanding cooking skills?" he asked after they'd eaten in silence for a time.

Grace frowned. "That would have to be... me."

She laughed at Donovan's puzzled expression.

"My mother didn't cook when I was growing up, and neither did most of the so-called men she brought home. With very few exceptions, they had no useful skills whatso-ever, except sucking the life from my mother's soul and the money from her wallet." She put up a finger. "And that includes my biological father. I learned to cook because, if I wanted to eat, which I've always been rather fond of, I had no choice but to learn to do it myself."

Donovan lowered his fork and looked at her with compassion. "Is this... Are some of those so-called men, as you put it, the inspirations behind those questions you asked me during our last"—he cleared his throat—"meal together, which also was most assuredly not a date?"

Smiling, she wobbled her head. "Them, and a few

others I've had the misfortune to come across all on my own." She took a sip of water and diverted her gaze.

Quietly, Donovan studied her before continuing. "Are you in any way close with your family, at least your mother?"

"We speak occasionally. My mother is incapable of deep connection, and my father"—she sighed—"is not interested in me unless he needs something. Mr. LeVray was more like a father to me than any man I grew up with. He was the real deal, a genuinely good man." She looked back up into Donovan's eyes, touched by his focused interest.

Donovan picked up his glass, swished it around, then set it back down without taking a drink. "It's unfortunate I missed the chance to meet him. From your description, I believe I can detect his spirit in Callie. She's perfect for Ben, exactly the kind of person he needs, and I couldn't be happier for our mutual friends."

"For a very long time, thanks to my mother's consistently poor choices, I believed there was no such thing as a good man, but Mr. LeVray changed my mind, though I still believe they are exceedingly rare. In fact, I've met only two others I consider worthy of placement in that category." She paused and rested her cheek in her hand. "One has found the happiness he deserves, but the other... I'm not sure if he believes he deserves to be happy."

"Grace." He whispered her name as his eyes shadowed.

Pushing her half-eaten plate away from her, she reached for his hand, and he offered it willingly.

"I'd like to continue this dialogue, get to know each other, the good and the bad. I'm willing to share my heart with you, but first, I need to know you're... you're in this with me; that you're not planning to pull away again or run off."

"I still don't think you understand." Letting go of her, he rose to his feet and paced a few feet away.

She stood as well but gave him space. "Then please, help me understand."

"Even if I want this, want it more than I've wanted anything in a long time, it doesn't matter because..."

"Because you're..."

"Because I'm out of time, Grace."

Slowly, she moved to stand in front of him, and he looked at her with pleading eyes.

"Tell me what you know for certain."

His jaw tightened. "I have two malfunctioning kidneys, a broken-down liver, and pins holding my vertebrae together. And those are just the problems at the top of the mile-long list. I shouldn't be alive right now. Every day, every hour the pain gets worse, and every time I go into the hospital, the doctors tell me I won't leave there alive." He dropped his eyes and his volume. "I sincerely believe the next time it happens, they'll be right."

Despite her best efforts, Grace's eyes filled with tears. "But there must be something they can do, a surgery or..."

"I've had them all, more than I can count."

"But..." She turned away, not wanting him to see the tears sliding down her face.

For a long moment, he said nothing, but then she felt his hand on her shoulder. "Grace, this may be the only way to make you understand. Please, turn around."

Slowly, she complied. Her eyes grew wide when she realized he had removed his shirt. Though extremely muscular and lean, deep scars crisscrossed much of his abdomen. With a sigh of despair, he turned around, and Grace's heart broke in two as she took in the scars that covered his back, some of which didn't appear to be that old. Evidence of traumatic burns, long, jagged scars, and smaller, clustered ones covered his skin, leaving not even the smallest space unmarred. If she didn't know better, she'd think he'd been viciously abused.

Putting both hands to her mouth, she struggled to keep her knees from buckling, feeling sick as she imagined the horrifying circumstances that had inflicted such wounds and the inconceivable pain he'd endured. Whether from battle or the surgeon's knife, his body had been brutalized. A strange mixture of despair and pride overtook her. To know such a man, someone who'd literally sacrificed himself to protect others, was an honor she felt wholly unworthy of. But there was also a kind of anger that burned in the pit of her stomach. No one should have to give so much while others, herself included, lived in comfort and ease.

When he turned around and took in the tears and the expression on her face, he quickly pulled his shirt back over his head. "Now you understand. I'm sorry."

In a few hurried strides, he crossed the room and bent to pick up his bag. When Grace realized that he intended to leave, that he'd misinterpreted her tears and the shocked expression on her face— believing them sourced in repulsion and rejection—she rushed after him, grabbing his arm.

"Donovan, no! Please!"

He released his bag, but kept his gaze lowered.

"Please, come and sit with me. Don't go. You mistook the reason for my tears."

She took his hand, and though he didn't speak, he let her lead him to the couch. Wiping at her eyes, she took several deep breaths until she felt she'd regained control of her emotions. "I don't know if it will ever be possible for me to grasp what you've been through, but the evidence of what you've suffered, tears my heart into pieces. There's no experience in my life that could come close to comparing. We come from different worlds, have walked vastly different paths. But still, the first time I looked into your eyes, I knew you, saw your soul. You tell me you're dying, and I believe it. I understand that if I let myself fall in love with you, it will most likely end with the breaking of my heart. But even so"—she tenderly cupped his chin with her hand, and he looked up into her eyes—"I choose it anyway. It's my choice to make, my heart to risk. One day, one week, one year, or forever: you are worth it, Donovan Bradshaw."

He blinked hard, unable to accept her words. "But this isn't a matter of taking a chance. This is a certainty. Your heart will get broken. And for what? A few days, maybe a few weeks with me? I'm not worth it, Grace."

"I'm the harshest critic of men you will ever meet, and I say you most certainly are," she asserted without hesitation. She reclined against the back cushions of the couch. "And as for the rest of it, we'll see." She smiled crookedly at him. "Four hours ago, I didn't believe superpowers were real, but now, I kinda think anything's possible."

Donovan straightened. "Grace?"

"I'm not at all bitter about this, but apparently, I was the last person to find out that your childhood friend did indeed have a secret, and what a whopper of a secret it was!"

"You know!" he exclaimed, sighing in relief as he also relaxed against the cushions.

"Thanks to the barrage of questions I attacked Callie with this afternoon, I indeed do. The shock still hasn't worn off, and apparently, neither has the bitterness," she mused with a sarcastic laugh.

Despite the heaviness that still bent his shoulders, he

chuckled. "It took me twelve hours and a substantial amount of corroborating evidence to believe, so you're way ahead of me, Miss Sophia. The night you texted me, and I told you I'd lost track of time... That was true, but that was the night I found out, and I could barely think straight as I tried to make sense of what they'd told me. Of course, once Ben's gift saved my life, it was pretty hard to hold onto doubt."

"It would assuredly be impossible to question its validity after that,' she agreed with a giggle.

"But, Grace, that doesn't mean Ben can heal me. He can only offer a temporary fix, not a cure."

"I understand, but Callie said they're working on something else, something that would be permanent."

"They mentioned that to me as well, but it sounds like a shot in the dark, and even if it worked out, I'd become... what's the word... Succouri, which I know virtually nothing about at this point."

"That's the plan?" she asked, surprised Callie hadn't shared that information with her. "To turn you into... whatever Ben is?"

"Something like that." He turned his body to face her. "But, Grace, the odds of this happening are nearly zero. I may not last until they return from their honeymoon. If your choice is based on that remote possibility—"

"I made the choice because it's the one my heart told me to make. I will hold onto hope, because I believe there is always reason to do so, but I had already made up my mind before I spoke with Callie today."

"But why? Despite what you think, there are good men out there. Better men than I. I could introduce you to several who could give you a happy life, a future. Why would someone so beautiful, kind, talented—someone with her whole life in front of her—needlessly put herself through such torment?"

"That's simple. Because you're the first man I've ever met who awakened my heart. I see, or maybe feel, something when I look into your eyes. It's like finding something you didn't even know you were looking for, but once you've found it, you realize you've always needed it, that it fits perfectly in that oddly-shaped hole inside you." She put her hand over her face. "That's such a stupid way of describing it, but—"

"Not stupid at all," he said, gently pulling her hand from her face. "That's why we felt like we'd met before," he said, his voice full of wonder.

"You mean, you... you understand what I'm saying? Do you—"

"Affirmative." He smiled. "Though I don't think I could have put it so eloquently."

Though his compliment was sincere, Grace laughed. "I'm a lot of things, Donovan, but I've rarely been accused of being eloquent. Nevertheless, if we both feel it, there must be something to it."

"Perhaps," he conceded, though he still looked uncomfortable with her decision to risk her heart.

Allowing him time to process his thoughts, she waited. Though she had no reservations regarding her choice, Donovan must have the freedom to make his own. This would never work if he couldn't let go, trust her, and allow her to walk beside him down the dark road ahead.

Donovan closed his eyes, unable to think rationally while looking into hers. This girl baffled him. With her beauty and graciousness, she could have any man on the planet.

Why would she choose a dying one, one who could offer her nothing but pain?

Though it was an impulsive act of desperation, when he showed her his scars, the tears in her eyes and the expression of anguish on her face convinced him he'd finally gotten through to her, forced her to face the ugly truth. Yet here she sat, despite having witnessed both the undeniable proof of his affliction and the disfigurement of his body, as ready as ever to give him something he hadn't had the chance to earn and would never have the time to fully cherish.

The logical thing, perhaps even the moral thing, was to walk away and do what was best for her, even if she hated him for it. But what if she was right? What if this strange familiarity and sense of destiny they felt in one another's presence really did foretell of something consequential, something they could only accomplish together? A week ago, he wouldn't have entertained such a fantastical notion, but after accepting Ben's unnatural gift, he viewed the world differently now.

Throwing caution to the wind, he opened his eyes and forced himself to look deeply into Grace's soul. What he saw convinced him, beyond the shadow of a doubt, that it was already too late. If he walked away right now, it would hurt no more or less than if he died in a week or a month. And furthermore, without her, he wouldn't have the will to go on, suffer the agony for one more day. Without conscious effort and despite the physical distance, their hearts had formed a bond. Severing that tie would be like breaking a bone without the means or knowledge to set it properly. It may eventually heal, but neither heart would ever function properly again.

"Since the moment we met, it seems fate has been in

the driver's seat of our relationship, Miss Grace. We're hapless passengers along for the ride. But if you're willing to stay beside me, continue on with this perilous journey, though I can't fathom why you would make such a choice"—he took her hand—"In return, I offer you my heart, without reservation, for however long it keeps beating."

Grace threw her arms around his neck, then suddenly pulled back. "Oh, Donovan! I'm sorry. Does that... Did I hurt you?"

He laughed and drew her close, feeling pieces of his heart that had long been scattered returning to where they belonged. "I'm not that fragile yet, Miss Grace. Two weeks ago, I wrestled a two-hundred-pound man to the ground in less than ten seconds, so I think I can handle your... well, I did promise not to mention the number, so let's just say significantly lighter frame."

"Now there's a story I'll definitely want to hear." She laughed, the sound carrying relief and a note of pure joy that instantly calmed his fears. She clung to him for a long time, and he to her. She was so delicate, so fragile in his arms, yet this woman was the most courageous person he'd ever known.

When they at last released one another, for a few seconds, she lingered close to his face, and Donovan wanted desperately to kiss her, but he was afraid if he did, neither of them would be able to stay in control of their emotions and the accompanying desires that their new closeness triggered. They were alone, the circumstances much too tempting, but despite the fact that their time together would likely be abridged, he wouldn't rush her or treat her with less than the respect she deserved. He hadn't even taken her on a proper date yet. He wanted to know much more of her soul and her heart, before he had the right to know her body.

"Grace," he said hoarsely, pulling back and turning his head in an attempt to loosen the grip of passion that held them both. "I know the next couple of days must belong to our friends as we help them prepare for their wedding, but after that, may I escort you on a real date; one that we both actually acknowledge as such?"

"I do believe I already agreed to that," she said her face still flushed. "After all, you did survive my interrogation, though I'm evidently not as tough as I thought I was."

"Oh, you're plenty tough, but in a way that makes you strong and courageous, though perhaps not particularly intimidating."

Grace smiled.

For the next three hours, they talked, the conversation easy and peppered with frequent laughter. Much of the talk centered around their mutual friends as they were both still coming to grips with Ben's gift and confused about Callie's role in it. Donovan told Grace about Ben's mother and how he'd tried to help Ben several years ago. Grace told Donovan how Ben and Callie had met, and she shared Callie's story of Ben's revival of Ronald LeVray just before he passed, which gave Callie and Lee the chance to say goodbye. Donovan was blown away by the power of the gift, so potent that it could awaken a man from a deep coma, snatching him back from the brink of death.

"Shortly after becoming good friends, I began to feel this... I don't know how to describe it, responsibility maybe, to help him, try to lighten the burden he carried, though I didn't know what the burden was."

"Yes! Me too. That's what I feel for Callie. Do you think... Donovan do you think that's part of what's drawing us together? I mean, now that they're getting married, they'll always be a pair, so helping Callie means helping Ben and vice versa. Perhaps, whatever is coming, it will require both of us to help both of them."

Stroking his chin, he contemplated. "I think that's part of it, but there's more than just that. I think... I think the connection goes both ways, like we're a crucial part of their story, and they're a crucial part of ours."

"That's exactly it!" Grace agreed excitedly, awestruck and overjoyed by their shared premonition.

As evening turned to night, they spoke of their childhoods and families, but Grace never asked him about his time in the service or the scars. Though in some ways, that was a relief, he knew they'd never truly be close until he shared that dark, hidden corner of his past with her. He'd never spoken about it before, and somehow keeping it in the dark gave it a kind of power over him he resented. Bringing it out into the light was the only way to break those chains. But as brave as Grace was, he wasn't sure she could handle hearing about it. The last thing he wanted to do was traumatize her by introducing her to a world of evil and violence she'd likely never imagined existed.

As the hour approached two a.m., Grace yawned and rested her head on his shoulder. Fifteen minutes later, she tucked her forehead into his neck, and he wrapped his arm around her. Ten minutes later, he chuckled when she slurred her last few words, then fell silent, breathing deeply as she fell fast asleep on his chest. It had never occurred to either of them that Donovan should probably check into his hotel and see about renting a car for the remainder of his time there.

When you find something of infinite value, and you know your time is short, it puts everything in perspective,

Donovan thought as he leaned his head back. Before he closed his eyes, he stole one last look at the treasure in his arms.

As she'd grown sleepy and repositioned herself, she hadn't noticed that her dark purple blouse had lifted, exposing two inches of silky, smooth skin just above the waistline of her jeans. There, on her right side, nearly at her waistline, was a teardrop-shaped birthmark. It was tiny enough that if he was less of a gentleman, he could cover it with one of his fingertips. As he thought about the grotesque scars that covered his body, this endearing blemish comforted him. In the real-life rendition of *Beauty and the Beast* he was presently cast in, Beauty had a flaw, and although it was minuscule and inconsequential, its presence made him feel slightly less monstrous.

Being cautious with his hands, he pulled her shirt down, covering the mark that was now one of his favorites of all her many alluring attributes. He brushed a few stray hairs away from her face, finding it near impossible to accept that this gorgeous woman, whose heart was equal in its radiance, was willing to put herself through pain just to spend a short moment in time with him. Agent Taylor had urged him to go get his heart mended, and though he wished there was some other way to carry out that mandate, Donovan knew that Grace was the cure for what had long been broken inside him.

When he next opened his eyes, he was stunned to see sunlight streaming through the windows. He'd slept for hours, undisturbed. The tormentors in his body never allowed him more than an hour of uninterrupted rest, yet even with the awkward position he'd been in when he fell asleep, he had to have slept for at least five straight hours.

"Grace?" he inquired aloud as he sat up. But she was

nowhere in sight. Rising from the couch, he stretched, grimacing as the fire of the familiar pains reignited, sparing almost no part of his body. Nevertheless, he was gratified to have been awarded such a rare reprieve.

Listening for her footsteps, he walked around the couch, peered into the kitchen, then explored the dining room, but there was no sign of her. As he moved back through the living room and into the front entryway, he noticed that the front door was open. Her car was still parked in the driveway, so she hadn't left.

Where was she? If someone had come into the house, he was far too experienced at being alert and aware, even in sleep, to have missed them. But if she answered the door and someone...

Without allowing the thought to develop, he moved toward the back of the house, feeling the hairs on his neck beginning to stiffen, even as he told himself she was likely just getting dressed. But would she carelessly leave her front door open like that? Grace was a smart woman. That didn't seem like an error she'd commit.

When he reached the closed door of what he presumed to be her bedroom, he listened for a long moment but still heard nothing. Softly knocking, he spoke her name several times, but there was no response. Now his heart began to pound, and the soldier in him awakened, seizing him with more force than usual as his instincts to protect this partic-ular woman were significantly more acute than when he'd defended mere strangers. If anything happened to her... He clenched his teeth, not able to abide the thought, but confi-dent that anyone who harmed Grace Sophia wouldn't live to see another sunrise.

Once more he called her name, but when no answer came, he sucked in a breath and turned the doorknob. As the door swung open, another door at the far end of the bedroom opened simultaneously and Grace stepped out into the room, wearing nothing but a bath towel.

At the unexpected sight of one another, they gasped, and Donovan stepped back and put a hand over his eyes. "Grace! I'm so sorry. I knocked several times, called your name, but I heard nothing. Your front door was left open, and I thought… I worried… I'm sorry, truly sorry. I didn't mean to…"

To his surprise, Grace giggled. "My neighbor came by early to drop off a piece of mail that had accidentally been delivered to her. I guess I forgot to close the door, and I was trying to be quiet, didn't want to wake you."

"That's most kind of you, but please promise me never to shower with your door open or unlocked again. There's an abundance of evil in this world, ma'am, and I couldn't bear it if…"

"I'm sorry I worried you but"—she softly giggled again—"in my defense, I did have a Navy SEAL, a man who protects people for a living sleeping on my couch. I suppose I felt so safe that I got a bit careless. Please forgive the oversight."

Still holding his hand firmly over his eyes, he couldn't help but smile, grateful that his presence put her at ease. "I'll overlook it, this time, especially since I'm the only one who's actually violated your privacy, and thus I must also beg your pardon. I'll leave you be, and again, my sincerest apologies."

Before he could close the door, Grace spoke his name through another round of giggles. "I left you a fresh towel and washcloth in the hall bathroom if you'd like to shower. I'll try not to return the favor, but no promises."

"Much obliged," he responded, chuckling to himself as

her easy forgiveness and humor relieved the awkwardness of the situation.

Still, as he retreated to grab his bag so he could take her up on her offered hospitality, he knew it would be a very long time before he could get the image of her in a skimpy bath towel, her hair shiny and wet, out of his mind.

CHAPTER 11

A TIME FOR JOY AND HEALING

The next two days flew by as they focused on their duties as best man and maid of honor. Ben's father joined Donovan and Ben on several outings, allowing Donovan to get to know him better. Plagued by a mysterious, mutual insomnia that Ben suspected had something to do with his gift, Ben and Callie were exhausted as the big day approached, but their joy and love for one another kept them going.

When they weren't helping their friends, Grace and Donovan stole every spare moment, talking and laughing as they got to know one another better with each passing hour. The more they shared, the stronger the already unusually tight connection became, which worried Donovan. No matter how resilient she claimed to be, in the end, he would be the one at rest, incapable of feeling pain any longer, but she would be left behind to process the loss. That wasn't fair, but he was in too deep now to reverse course, and he'd already pledged her his heart.

Though Donovan did check-in at his reserved hotel, he spent very little time there as he and Grace continued to talk late into the night. Without speaking of it directly, the rapid flow of sand through the hourglass was always at the forefront of their minds, and neither wanted to waste a single moment of the finite time they had together.

Just before leaving the LeVray house Friday night, Ben pulled Donovan aside, smiling as if he were holding on to a secret. "There's a new light in your eyes, my friend. The way you look at Grace and the way she looks at you—I think I know its source."

Donovan's grin was all the confirmation Ben needed.

"As of tomorrow, I'll no longer need my apartment," Ben said with a twinkle in his eye. "I wondered if, perhaps, you might like to make use of it, stay in town for a while. As soon as we get back, I will hit the ground running on that plan we discussed and having you nearby would be"—he paused and averted his gaze—"convenient if..."

"If I need to make good use of your miraculous gift again," Donovan finished for him. "Ben, just so we're clear, it's not your responsibility to save me from a fate I chose. I appreciate what you've done and what you're doing to help me, but I'm here because of our friendship. Having said that, I'll gratefully accept your offer to use your apartment because I'd like to stay awhile and spend more time with my childhood friend. Well, that and..." Donovan gestured toward where Grace and Callie were cheerfully chatting.

Ben chuckled. "Understood. But let me be equally candid. My motivations are purely selfish. I won't lose my friend just when I've reunited with him, and my soon-to-be-wife couldn't bear to watch her best friend's heart break either. We're going to do our best to ensure a happy ending for everyone, Donovan. We all stand to benefit here."

Patting Ben on the back, he turned to look at the two women who were the anchors for both their hearts. "We're blessed, Ben. Richly blessed. Why the two loveliest women on this planet choose to grace us with their affections, I'll never comprehend."

"Amen to that," Ben wholeheartedly agreed. "The possibility of our lives, the four of us, being permanently intertwined is a most welcome prospect."

"Agreed."

"Though I can't help but feel, this"—Ben gestured between them and the two women—"was fated somehow, and that conviction gives me all the more confidence that we're going to succeed in our efforts to keep you with us."

Though Donovan offered a simple nod in response, the faint hope he had barely clung to began to grow, as Ben's words echoed the shared feelings he and Grace had experienced since meeting Ben, Callie, and each other. His words reenforced the idea that there was, indeed, a purpose, a destined future for them all.

Sunshine and unseasonably warm temperatures graced Ben and Callie's wedding day. Though she and Callie laughed and rejoiced as they got ready, Grace worried about her friend's obvious exhaustion. Putting her expertise at cosmetics to good use, she did her best to conceal the dark circles under Callie's eyes, but when she could offer no explanation for her lack of sleep over the past week, Grace's worry intensified.

At the church, they dressed in the bride's room. As they stood side by side in front of the full-length mirror, Callie smiled and put her arm around Grace. "I predict, in a very short time, we're going to be standing here again, only in reversed roles."

"What do you mean?"

She bumped Grace playfully with her shoulder. "You and Donovan."

Though she couldn't stifle her smile, Grace looked down, wishing she could feel as confident as Callie about their future.

"Grace, we're going to be back in a week, and then our entire focus is going to be on saving his life. We won't give up until we've found a way."

Not wishing to do anything to spoil the day, Grace tightened her hold on her friend. "Thank you. But today is all about you and Ben. No stress or worry allowed. You are beautiful, Cal. The prettiest bride I've ever seen, hands down."

"And blue is definitely your color, Gracie." Callie stepped back so she could admire the long, flowing gown that accentuated Grace's figure nicely. "Wait until Donovan sees you." She paused to smile sheepishly. "Sorry to be nosy, well, not that sorry since you asked me this same question not long ago. Have you two kissed yet?"

Grace laughed, remembering how, when she'd asked Callie this question, she had answered with, 'sort of, I'm not sure.'

"Not yet, but not for a lack of desire on my part. We haven't gone on an official date, and though we've spent a lot of time together in the last couple of days, I think we're both confused on how slow or fast to go. I mean, we haven't known each other long, and under normal circumstances, we'd just relax and let things happen in due time, but we may not have much time, and I don't want to waste a second with him just in case..."

Callie wrapped her arms around Grace. "We are going to figure this out. I promise. But regardless, one should never take a single moment they have with someone they love for granted. Tomorrow is never guaranteed. As I try to do with Ben, love Donovan today with all your heart, that way you'll never have a single regret. He's a good man, so you don't have to worry about determining whether or not that's the case. I can see how you're healing his heart and he yours. Don't be afraid to love with abandon. Despite the unknowns surrounding Ben's gift and the future, I have determined to hold nothing back in offering my love to him, and"—she gestured toward the image of them in the mirror—"look where that has brought me." Both women smiled at the truth. "It can be scary, thinking about how your heart could break if the 'what ifs' come true. Ultimately, what will weigh heavier on your heart: the anguish of giving him everything and suffering loss, or the torment of holding back to protect yourself, only to regret not seizing the chance to give your all?"

Sniffling, Grace nodded, conceding the point. "Without a doubt, much better the former than the latter."

"For me too. Thus..." Callie pointed again at the reflected image of her in her bridal gown.

"Well, let's go make it official then, shall we?" Grace teased, offering Callie her arm as they headed for the door.

When they entered the lobby, Donovan approached, and Grace smiled as she took in the sight of him. Dressed in charcoal slacks, a matching blazer, and a blue collared shirt that matched her dress, he looked dashing. Releasing Callie into Lee's care, she waited for him to approach and offer his arm, but for several seconds, he stood staring. "Donovan," she finally prompted.

"Grace," he said at last, the word escaping with an audible exhale as he stepped forward. "You're... You're stunning. The most beautiful sight I've ever seen."

Shyly, she smiled. "You look rather dashing yourself, Donovan Bradshaw."

As he took her arm, still staring, his posture straightened. They walked together down the aisle, and Grace's heart exulted at how strong and well he appeared. Whether it was the joy of the occasion or the new hope she'd begun to see in his eyes, something was reviving his soul, giving him a new will to live, and she prayed it would last.

The wedding was beautiful, the sanctuary itself tangibly warmed by the special love Ben and Callie shared. Grace had never seen her friend look so happy, and every time Ben gazed at his bride, his face glowed. Tears of joy flowed freely during the ceremony and the reception when friends and family stood to toast the happy couple, she and Donovan among them.

Sitting side by side at the head table with the bride and groom, they occasionally reached for each other, surreptitiously holding hands. At one point, Grace set her hand on Donovan's knee, and his smile communicated his pleasure at the action, though he didn't reciprocate. Lobster noticed, but after meeting Donovan and sharing some light conversation, he sent Grace several approving grins throughout the evening.

After the speeches, Grace stepped into the kitchen to refill several glasses of water, and Ben's father came up alongside her.

"Miss Sophia, may I speak with you for a moment?"

"Of course," she said with a smile, but as she looked over at him, his serious expression quickly shifted her mood. He gestured toward the empty dining room, and she set down the glass she was holding and followed him.

"During my time working with him on Callie's case, I developed a profound respect and admiration for Mr. Bradshaw. His reputation preceded him, hailed by all as the most capable and skilled defender for hire. But no one who had worked with him had a clue about his health situation. That's how good he was. When he went into the hospital, I went to see him and... learned about the extent of his injuries. Medically speaking, he shouldn't be alive, much less be able to endure what he's suffering, Miss Sophia. He's a walking miracle. He's given more for his country than anyone, with the exception of those who already rest in peace. I can see that you care for him deeply, as does my son; he loves him like a brother." He paused to hand her a business card with a phone number handwritten on it. "I'm leaving town in the morning, but if anything happens, if you need help, please don't hesitate to call me, day or night."

With that, he offered her a slight bow of his head and went to rejoin the festivities. Though she was puzzled, the gesture was meant kindly, so she tucked the card into a pocket in her purse and returned to the kitchen.

By the time Callie and Ben departed for their honeymoon and the festivities ended, it was nearly ten o'clock.

Wrapping her light shawl around her shoulders as they headed out the door, Donovan turned to speak to her. "I know you're probably very tired, but would you consider going for a short drive with me, Miss Grace? Perhaps we might find some stars to gaze at, and if not"—his eyes twinkled—"I'm more than satisfied to gaze at you in that fantastic dress for a while longer."

"Well, when you put it that way..." She smiled playfully at him.

They drove until the city lights faded into the distance and the sky darkened enough to showcase its treasure trove of shimmering jewels. Donovan found a remote spot to pull over, and for a long time, they sat quietly, enjoying the view and the comfort of each other's company.

"They will be happy, very happy," Donovan finally said. "Of that I'm certain."

"No doubt, they will," Grace agreed.

Donovan had opened the windows to let in the fresh night air, and though it wasn't that cold, Grace shivered in her thin dress.

"I'm sorry." Donovan started to turn the key so he could roll up the windows, but she shook her head. "I'll be okay. I like the fresh air."

Removing his seatbelt, he took off his jacket, and Grace's heart constricted when she saw him wince from the pain triggered by the contorted way he had to move in the tight space.

"Donovan," she said tentatively, as she pulled his jacket tightly around her shoulders. "Does it always hurt? Does the agony never relent, never give you a moment's peace?"

As he silently stared straight ahead, she knew he was pondering whether to tell her the ugly truth. "Yes. And never," he at last confessed. Then he turned to her, a weak smile playing on his lips. "With the exception of the night I spent with you on your couch. I haven't slept soundly like that in... in such a long time I can't remember when."

She reached for his hand, and he grasped hers eagerly, intertwining their fingers. "I... I wish we had more time. I don't want to push you, make you share anything you're not ready to share, but when you are, I'd like to understand, carry some of the burden if possible."

The stillness of the night hung thick inside the car as she waited for his response.

"Grace, I don't want to frighten you. It's a world so distant and foreign from this one it almost seems unreal to me now, even though the pain and scars remind me it indeed exists."

"Do you have nightmares about it?"

"Frequently."

Slowly inhaling, she stared up at the thousands of stars dotting the black canvas above them. "I'll do my best to be brave, though I can't promise dry eyes. If you could live through it and keep your soul, your humanity, I know I can find the courage to hear it."

"I almost lost my humanity, Grace. If I hadn't gotten injured, gotten out, I may have. It's still hard at times. When I click into soldier mode, become the killing machine I was trained to be, it can be hard to reclaim who I am. Sometimes, I literally have to speak my own name, out loud, in order to break free. It didn't used to be as hard, but after..."

Remaining quiet, she waited as he carefully chose his next words.

"After undergoing the rigors of SEAL training, I obtained additional skills in surveillance tactics and technology. I know how and where to put cameras and motion detectors so that they're virtually invisible yet very effective. As a result of this specialization, I was placed on an elite team that was dropped into some of the darkest pockets of evil on the planet, strongholds of radical, vicious terrorists. Our mission was search and rescue, saving captured innocents: journalists, fellow soldiers, sometimes women and children taken in revenge or simply because they weren't of the right religion or sect." He let out an anguished sigh. "The savagery inflicted on some of the people we rescued is sufficient to supply one with a lifetime of nightmares."

Before resuming his story, he took another deep breath.

Grace felt the tears already stinging her eyes, but she willed herself to remain quiet and in control. What he described was assuredly, scary, but it was a reality he'd faced, and it would always be a part of him. If she wanted to truly know the man, she had to find the strength to hear it all.

"Because of the heightened danger involved in such operations, including frequent engagements in hand-to-hand combat, my unit received extensive supplementary training. I'm an expert with a knife as well as a gun, and I can subdue a hostile in mere seconds without any weapons at all. But training's no substitute for real-life experience. Some of my scars, particularly the older ones, are from knife injuries, not life-threatening, but each one taught me a valuable lesson. When you get cut a few times, you get better at fighting, fast. Additionally, some of the remote terrorist cells that weren't as well resourced, employed crude IEDs. Those unsophisticated but nonetheless lethal explosive devices ejected thousands of tiny pieces of metal, glass, whatever they had on hand, with such incredible force that they sliced through everything—clothing and skin in particular—as if it were soft butter." He grimaced as Grace recalled the sliver-size scars in tight clusters on his back. "Some of my brothers lost their eyesight and worse after an encounter with one of those ruthless, cowardly inventions. I'd rather fight someone hand to hand any day. At least you can look your enemy in the eye."

Lost in memories, he stared out the front windshield, unblinking for a long moment before continuing. "Though we enjoyed our share of successes, all too many attempted rescues ended in the death or maiming of someone: soldier, civilian, or the hostage we were trying to save." He lowered his head. "The worst cases were those where we lost good men and failed to free the victims. If the hostiles saw us coming, more often than not, they'd slaughter those they held, just to deny us the satisfaction of victory."

Grace shivered at the thought.

"That's where my skills played a vital role. Two or three of us would go in under the cover of darkness, install the equipment, then watch and wait. We'd study the hostiles' movements, learn their habits, and watch for an opportunity. We waited until there were fewer of them, the hostages were being transported, or, if we got lucky, when they left them alone in a locked room. Any advantage we could exploit increased the odds of getting them out alive. The intelligence this specialized technology gathered was invaluable and saved a lot of lives. But nothing is fair or certain in war, Miss Grace."

For the first time since he began telling his story, he turned to look at her. Seeing her wet cheeks, he shook his head. "I'm sorry. I don't have to continue."

"No. Please. I'm okay. I need to hear it. It's part of you, Donovan, a part I'm so proud of, even if it's painful."

With gentleness, he wiped her cheek with his thumb, clearing away the lingering tears. In his eyes, she could see the pain of what was left to tell, and it was difficult to breathe as she braced herself, determined to stay strong,

"My final mission as a SEAL was in a hot zone, a place well known by military intelligence as a high-traffic area for terrorist activity, typically of the more well-funded, high-tech variety. Five hostages were being held in a walled compound. They were mostly locals, working with our military as spies, providing on-the-ground information about the enemy's activities. But there was a mole among their ranks. If the hostiles had been certain of their betrayal, they likely would have shot them on the spot, but the fact that they were holding them told us that either they weren't confident about the mole's accusations, or—and this was more likely to be the case—they were torturing them to extract intelligence. Either way, we needed to act fast. Rescue was our hope, but protecting our intelligence was paramount. As callous as it may seem, in situations like this, sometimes taking out the entire group, hostiles and hostages, with a targeted airstrike is the right call. Given the torture they're enduring, its actually an act of mercy, and the chances of getting that many out before the enemy slaughters them is close to zero anyway. But in this case, one of the captives was highly valued, so it was decided to attempt a rescue. But this was a complicated and risky operation. The compound was surrounded by walls, only one way in and one way out. Though satellite imagery and high-altitude drones gave us an idea of the layout inside, there was no way to get surveillance equipment beyond the external barrier. Thanks to the successful execution of a rather ingenious distraction technique, we did manage to place a camera near the entrance, but that was the extent of our eyes, from the ground anyway. We watched for twenty-four hours and found a pattern in guard shifts, but there wasn't much else to ascertain from our limited vantage point. In the end, our team leader decided to employ a two-pronged attack strategy. A team of paratroopers would land on the roof and take out hostiles as quickly as possible so the ground team, which was my unit, could enter and join the fight with hopes of getting to the victims as quickly as possible. Stage one went smoothly, a little too smoothly. Minutes after the paratroopers landed, we got the signal to go in. I was the second to last one to enter the compound, but from the time I passed through the gate, something felt... wrong, off. It was scorching hot, and with my gear and adrenaline, sweat ran into my eyes as I shifted my gaze, anticipating much more of a fight than what confronted us. I remember thinking that even the smell of the place was wrong somehow."

Pausing, Donovan swallowed hard, and his hand tensed.

"Following the soldier in front of me, I was about eight feet from entering the main building at the center of the compound when I turned around to look behind me. To this day, I don't know why I did that. I must have heard or seen something. I can't remember but that action saved my face, if not my life. In that exact moment, a bomb exploded inside the building. We all went airborne, blind and deaf from the burst of light and sound. The soldier ahead of me, who had barely crossed the threshold of the doorway, was projected backward with such force that he collided with me in mid-air, the blood of his dismembered body soaking me through, as if someone had thrown a full bucket of warm water my way. But when I at last hit the dirt, face down, it didn't take long for the flow of my own blood to overtake it. I knew immediately that my back was broken, and my entire body felt as if it were on fire. I couldn't move, could barely breathe, but as time passed and my hearing began to return, the desperate moans of the men around me, and perhaps my own as well, rang in my ears; a sound I won't ever forget."

Allowing the tears to flow unrestrained, Grace nevertheless remained quiet, save for the pounding of her heart.

"I don't know how much time passed, but the next thing I remember was hearing shouts and gunshots. As the language was the native tongue, I knew these weren't my rescuers. No more than five feet from me, the soldier who had been at the rear of our group moaned, then I heard two shots. After that, I never heard him moan again. I remember biting my lip, willing myself to stay quiet, as gunshots resounded all around me. Two new agonies burned in my lower back, and a man laughed as he stood over me. Since I was face down in what was now a muddy pool of blood, I never saw his face, but he definitely believed me dead, and for a moment, I wasn't sure he was wrong. But when his boot struck my ribcage, the fresh burst of pain assured me I was indeed still alive, though barely so. Though he kicked me again and again, I remained silent, confident that a single indication that there was still life in me would yield a bullet to the head. Eventually, he grew tired of gloating over his prize kill and moved on. The last thing I remember was the sound of more gunfire and a surge of hope when someone shouted in English. Then everything went black. When I woke up in the hospital, days later, the pain hit me so hard I vomited violently and repeatedly until they had to sedate me again to keep me from ripping open stitches or further injuring my broken ribs and back. That happened two more times before I finally learned to tolerate the pain. After delivering the grim news regarding the extent of my injuries and the continuous procedures that would be necessary to keep me alive, the doctor told me they'd almost lost me more than a dozen times already. He said each time they'd been about to give up, I'd surprise them and rally. I still remember his exact words, as they gave me strength through many rough days. He said, 'no matter how dim the light, you never let it die'. I suppose that stubborn streak my mother warned me about proved itself an asset in this case; that and the herculean efforts of those who cared for me. Their determination to save my life was no doubt inspired by the fact that"—he forced out a heavy breath—"I was the sole survivor of that disastrous operation. Whoever wasn't killed in the blast was executed afterward. The fact that I was covered in blood, face down, and managed to remain quiet saved my life, or at least delayed my death. Despite more surgeries and procedures than I can count, they told me I wouldn't live more than six months. That was almost two years ago."

A cold breeze blew through the open windows, as Donovan finished his story and fell silent, waiting for her mind and heart to absorb what she'd heard.

"What... What happened to the five men, the ones you were trying to save? Were they killed as well?" she asked, her voice shaking.

"They were never at that compound. Turns out the mole was playing us, not the terrorists. But we did find them eventually, their bodies anyway." He lowered his voice to a whisper as he concluded. "There's no need to speak of how they died."

Letting go of his hand, Grace covered her face. "Oh, Donovan! I... I'm sorry. Those words sound so trite, so inadequate, but I don't know what else to say. It's awful, horrifying! But, through it all, you're... you're incredible!"

He shook his head. "Just lucky. If I had been just a few steps closer to the door, or if I hadn't turned around at just the right time—"

"That's not what I mean. You found the strength to stay quiet despite unthinkable, blinding pain, which should have rendered you incapable of rational thought. At least twelve times, you beat the odds, fought to stay alive, even when the doctors had given up. You've already lived far beyond what the doctors believed possible, even though weaker men would have given up, accepted the relief of strong narcotics, and surrendered in defeat. You're the bravest, strongest person I've ever known, Donovan Bradshaw, and I love you."

Grace closed her mouth and looked down, stunned at the words that had come from her lips. There was no thought behind them; they sprang straight from her heart. At first, she thought to apologize, try to alleviate the awkwardness and free him from any perceived pressure to reciprocate. But that felt wrong and dishonest. She wasn't sorry she'd said it. She meant it, every word. Boldly, she lifted her eyes to his. He was already staring at her, but she couldn't interpret the look in his eyes.

Abruptly, he opened his door and got out of the car. She sighed, worried that she'd ruined everything, but then, her door opened, and Donovan reached into the car and lifted her into his arms, making her gasp in surprise.

"No, Donovan, no! You can't! Your back. You'll hurt yourself. Please, I—"

But she had no chance to finish the sentence. He pressed his lips to hers softly but with enough fervor to clearly communicate his passion. She barely had time to return the kiss before he withdrew and set her on her feet.

Wrapping his arms around her, he leaned close to her ear. "What kind of extraordinary woman hears a story like that, and is not only strong enough to take it in without running away in terror, but actually finds something good, something hopeful amid the ugliness? And then"—he brushed his lips softly across hers—"turns around and gives me a gift, one I have no right to ask for as I have had no time to rightly win it. Yet I believe, wholeheartedly, in its authenticity. What manner of good I've done in this short life to deserve the love of such a woman, I can't conceive, but if my death is indeed imminent, there will never have been a man, even one who's lived a hundred years, so richly blessed as I."

Rising onto her tiptoes, she smiled and kissed him

again. "Now see. How can I possibly not love you when you say crazy, beautiful things like that to me."

The gold in his eyes glimmered in the moonlight. "Grace Sophia, I love you with all my heart. I have since the moment I met you. You have freed me of a weight I've carried for a long time, and you are reviving the part of me I thought was dead. I believed no one could love me, accept my difficult past and my hideous scars. But I was equally sure I was no longer capable of giving love, that my heart had been seared by violence and the depths of wickedness I've witnessed in mankind. But you have reintroduced me to the man I used to be before I was a soldier. I'm immeasurably grateful that, when I die, I'll die as that man, not the tormented one who is, in many ways, still lying with his face in the blood-soaked dirt."

Gingerly, rising onto her tiptoes again, she put her arms around his neck. "That's the man you'll always be to me, the one whose gentle eyes see into my soul. But I'm not afraid of the other one either, Donovan. The soldier in you protects, saves, conjures up courage out of thin air; courage enough to buy you one and a half additional years of life. Accept and redeem him too, as you need both sides. And truthfully, I need that soldier right now. I need his strength to buy me just a bit more time with the man I love, so our friends can work their plan and save his life. You won't fight alone. I'm here, beside you, through good and bad. But please, keep fighting, keep being stubborn. I know the pain is awful, more than anyone could be expected to take, but I beg you to suffer it just a little while longer so we can have a chance at forever."

"I will endeavor to do any and everything you ask of me, ma'am."

. . .

It was after one a.m. when Donovan walked Grace to her front door. "I'll look forward to seeing you tomorrow, Miss Grace." He laughed at the absurdity of his next statement. "For our first date."

Fidgeting with her keys, her eyes grew wide. "You're leaving?"

"Ben offered me his apartment and I..." He stopped speaking when he saw the fear on her face. Just an hour ago, he'd told her a story straight out of a horror novel. But she'd been so composed, so brave. But maybe the idea of sitting alone in a dark house with those images in her mind was more than she could handle.

"Unless you'd like to employ me to defend you against an early morning visit from a well-intentioned neighbor," he teased.

Grace scrunched up her face. "Mrs. Johnson's got a real dark side. I might need you, soldier."

"The couch it is then."

Grace laughed. "I do have a spare bedroom with a real bed where you can stretch out your legs."

"Well then, I'll reduce my fee in light of such kind hospitality."

They both laughed as they moved inside.

Though they did indeed fall asleep in separate bedrooms, sometime during the night, Donovan awoke to the sound of footsteps.

"Donovan," Grace whispered, keeping her distance, likely scared of what might happen if she startled him. Her voice shook, and in the moonlight, he could see tears shining on her cheeks.

Without a word, he held out his arms, and she tucked

herself against him, her body lightly trembling. His heart broke at how much he'd frightened her, but he was gratified she wasn't afraid of him. On the contrary, she asked him to stay because she found comfort and felt safe in his presence.

Despite his regret at scaring her with the truth of his past, in that moment, he couldn't deny feeling happier and more at peace than he'd ever felt before. The ugly memories had lost their power over him. Now, he had dominion over them and, as Grace suggested, he could use the strength he'd gained during those traumatizing experiences. And he would use it. He'd bring every ounce of it to bear to buy himself as much time with her as he possibly could.

CHAPTER 12

A CRAZY IDEA

The hours slipped by much too quickly the following day, but Donovan treasured each one. In the late afternoon, he took her out for an early dinner, at last enjoying their long-anticipated real date. As they waited for dessert, Donovan mindlessly turned his water glass around in his hand as he took pleasure in the sight of her in the remarkable black dress she'd chosen for the occasion. The short sleeves hung low on her shoulders, offering an enticing view of her neck, collar bones, and enough bare skin below that to fuel the imagination. That view, along with the memory of her in a bath towel and the recollection of the alluring mark on her side, made staying focused on the conversation challenging.

"Donovan, can I ask you something?"

"Anything, ma'am."

"Do you have something against water?"

Scratching the side of his chin, he squinted at her in confusion. "Um, I don't think so. What—"

"This is like the third or fourth time I've seen you turn a glass of water around and around without actually drinking any." She smiled. "Are you waiting for it to turn into wine or something?"

Donovan laughed. "No, ma'am. I just don't like it cold. I guess maybe I unconsciously think I can warm it more quickly, melt the ice, if I move it around." He let go of the glass, realizing that the notion sounded nonsensical.

"No ice. Got it," she replied, drawing a checkmark in the air. Pondering, she momentarily looked to the side. "Not much ice available in the desert, I suppose."

Impressed by how quickly she made the connection, he nodded in response. "Even when available, it melted so fast it wasn't worth the trouble."

The waiter set two pieces of strawberry cheesecake in front of them. Grace took a few bites before she spoke again.

"I was wondering..." She waved her hand in the air. "Never mind."

"Grace? Please." He extended an open hand, inviting her to continue.

"It's just, I'm the last person who should be telling anyone how to handle their family situation, as mine is so dysfunctional, but..."

"But?"

"I understand how much your parents hurt you, and I'm not defending them in any way as I can't comprehend their choices, but if... I mean, do they even know you might...?"

"Not from my lips. I haven't spoken to them since the day they told me I was no longer their son."

"And they've never tried to... reach out, apologize?"

Sighing, Donovan started to shake his head. But then, he remembered the letter he'd shoved into his bag. "Actually, I'd almost forgotten about this, but the day Ben called me I received a letter from them, out of the blue." He chuckled at his next statement as, after all he'd been through, it seemed a strange juxtaposition. "I haven't worked up the courage to open it."

Sitting up straight, she looked at him with wide-open eyes. "Do you have it? I mean, here with you?"

"I stashed it in my bag when I packed to go stay at Ben's house. I presume it's still there."

"Aren't you curious?"

He blew a breath through his lips. "My parents are not warm people, Grace. In fact, I could say the same of them as you've said of your mother, that they are incapable of deep connections. They're wealthy and well-connected in circles of influence, and that's all they want from life. I just can't imagine there's anything but disappointment waiting for me in that letter."

With compassion in her eyes, she nodded. "I understand and can relate, but..."

He waited, but she didn't finish the sentence. "But you think I should open the letter."

"That's your choice, and I support you either way, but I had a conversation with Callie just before the wedding about choices and regrets, and I wouldn't want you to miss an opportunity if maybe they've changed somehow. After all, it has been over a decade."

"But even if they have changed and the content of the letter is positive, how do I reach out to them after all this time and tell them I'm dying? Their worst fears, the reason they forbade me to join the service, then subsequently disowned me when I did it anyway, have come true. What if..."

"What if they say, 'I told you so'? What if, instead of being devastated by the news, they're callously indignant?"

Donovan stared at her, amazed at how she'd articulated his concern with such accuracy.

"It's a risk," she acknowledged. "But if they didn't know about your injuries when they wrote that letter, you can at least be assured that wasn't the motivation for reaching out. If, after you read it, you aren't convinced they've changed, you don't have to respond, and you certainly don't have to tell them about your situation. But if you never read it, maybe you'll miss out on an opportunity, a chance for healing." With a shrug, she took on a casual tone. "Just food for thought. No pressure."

He reached across the table and took her hand. "I'll give it serious consideration, under one condition."

Her eyebrows lifted in curiosity.

"If I decide to proceed, we read the letter together, so I can continue to benefit from your wise counsel."

She laughed. "Wise and eloquent. You've now endowed me with two characteristics I'm assuredly unworthy of."

"You have a habit of underestimating your talents, Miss Sophia." He tilted his head to the side and grinned playfully at her. "But I feel confident that you were aware, when you chose that particular dress for our date this evening, how irresistibly attractive you are in it."

The compliment was rewarded with one of her carefree giggles. "A very clever, not to mention charming, way to shift the topic, Mr. Bradshaw. Now you've seen me at my best and worst; bath towel to evening gown and everything in between."

"There is no worst in any of those options, Miss Grace. The bath towel in particular."

"Is that so?" Her eyes blinked flirtatiously at him, making his heart race.

He cleared his throat as he did his best to redirect his

thoughts into safer territory. "Tomorrow night, after you get home from work, I'd like to cook you dinner." He raised his hands. "Don't set your expectations too high, but I'm pretty good at following instructions so—"

"Donovan, I'm not going to work, not for the foreseeable future."

"What do you mean?"

She put her hands in her lap and looked down at her plate. "I'm not going to miss one moment with you. I have loads of vacation time saved up, but even if I didn't, I don't care about work right now. It's not what's important."

"But, Grace..."

Looking up into his eyes, she shook her head. "I've made up my mind, and I have a stubborn streak too, so there's no point in arguing with me. It's not every day that you fall in love. I'm taking my best friend's advice to heart and making the choices that will leave no regrets behind. I believe we're going to get our miracle, but either way, I won't miss a minute with you or take the chance of not being there when you need me."

"Grace, I'm not expecting you to be there. If things don't work out with Ben's plan, and I go into the hospital again, you need to stay away. You don't need to watch me die. I would never ask that of you."

She set her jaw and looked at him with unyielding resolve. "I will be there, and that's non-negotiable. I will not, under any circumstance, leave you to suffer alone. They can try to throw me out because I'm not technically family, but they'll have to drag me out kicking and screaming. And even then, I'll find a way to be with you."

For a long moment, he watched her, overcome by her pledged devotion. Callie had spoken of her unparalleled loyalty, and she hadn't been exaggerating. An idea flashed through his mind, but it was too much to expect or ask of her.

"Unless you really don't... Don't want me to—"

"It's not that," he reassured. "It's not a fair ask, Grace. It will be miserable, painful. I don't want to do that to you."

"Much, much less miserable than being separated, knowing you're suffering and not being able to at least hold your hand."

He let out a resigned sigh. "As always, I'm astounded by your kindness. Your name was well chosen. Undeserved, unearned favor; that's what grace is, and that's exactly who you are."

"Just do me a favor."

"As always, anything you ask, I will oblige."

"Write something down, call someone, tell them I'm your sister or something, so I won't have to get violent in order to stay with you." She laughed, but there was a genuine concern amidst the jest. Maybe his crazy idea wasn't so crazy after all.

Grace loved the days but hated the nights. Each hour with Donovan flew by too quickly as they held hands, walked, ate, laughed, and talked. Besides Callie, she'd never been closer to another human being. When he told her how he'd come by his scars, a profound trust was forged between them, making it easy to share even the deepest secrets, hurts, and dreams.

But ever since she'd heard his horrifying story, she'd lain in bed at night, unable to sleep, tormented by the image of him covered in blood, lying face down in the dirt, as an evil, twisted demon kicked him mercilessly. As the scene played out, over and over in her mind, she felt physically sick, holding her hand to her side as if it were her instead of him on the ground. She couldn't shake the disturbing visions, and she suspected that had something to do with her real-life fear of watching him die.

The night he'd stayed with her and she'd slept beside him, the visions had ceased, but he'd never offered that comfort again, and she wasn't bold enough to come out and ask him to spend the night with her, nor did she want to make him feel regret for sharing his terrifying experiences.

Since the brief kiss they'd shared under the stars, he'd made no further moves in advancing their physical relationship whatsoever. He complimented her often, and many times, she caught him looking at her in a way that assured her of his attraction, but unlike the other men she'd dated, Donovan was more focused on connecting in mind and heart than in body. And while she appreciated that, even admired it, their time was short and she wanted to be close to him in every way. In truth, it was surprising, even to her, how intensely she wanted him. But as days passed and he didn't initiate anything in this regard, she began to wonder if, as a consequence of his extensive list of injuries, this was perhaps something he could not offer her.

On Tuesday afternoon, as they sat together on her couch, looking through old photo albums of her as a girl, Donovan's finger lingered over one particular photograph. She was dressed in a karate gi, striking an intimidating pose with a tight fist and high kick.

Donovan laughed as he tapped the picture. "I might have to take back my statement about you not being intimidating." He swiped a hand across his brow. "I didn't realize you'd been professionally trained."

"Hardly," she countered with a laugh. "I think I had

three lessons, then my mom ran out of money. I always wanted to learn self-defense." She leaned back and stared at him. "Donovan, would you teach me? I mean, don't hurt me or anything, and I don't want anything to do with a knife or gun, but like, basic stuff. That way, if I ever forget to lock my door and don't have my soldier around to take care of business, I'd at least have a fighting chance."

"With pleasure," he answered enthusiastically, setting aside the album.

They both put on a pair of sweats, and for the next hour, Donovan walked her through some simple techniques: basic attack strategies, how to escape a choke hold, and how to debilitate an attacker, leave him blinded or in pain long enough to escape.

"Alright, I'm going to come at you," he warned, as he stood five feet away from her. "Do your worst. Don't hold back."

"But," she protested. "I don't actually want to hurt you."

He laughed. "I promise, you won't, but try anyway."

He rushed toward her, and she jumped to the side, grabbing his arm and twisting it as she moved behind him. Instantly, as hard as she could manage, she rammed her knee into the back of his legs, and he dropped to the floor, which made it possible for her to wrap her arm tightly around his neck.

Donovan whistled as she released him.

"Nice work, Miss Sophia. We'll make a soldier of you yet. But I made that way too easy for you. I'll make it just a little harder this time."

Resuming their original stance, he smiled proudly at her before rushing at her, quicker this time. She caught his arm, but when she tried to move behind him, he turned with her and grabbed her other arm. She tried to wrench it free, but his hold was too strong, so she kicked at him, but as all he did was smile at her efforts, it was clear she was failing this test miserably. In desperation, she jumped at him, slamming into his body with her full force. He evidently was not expecting that, and though he countered by shifting his weight forward, he overcompensated, knocking her backward. As they tumbled to the ground, Donovan slipped his hand behind her head, so it wouldn't hit the ground without some cushioning, but he nevertheless fell directly on top of her.

"Grace! Are you—"

She burst out laughing at their awkward position and her feeble attempts to take down a Navy SEAL who'd been in more real battles than he could likely count. Seeing that she was alright, he laughed with her, making no attempt to remove himself from his place on top of her.

"I guess I'm going to need you to stick around, soldier. I'm not very good at this."

"You're better than you think, ma'am. That was quite unexpected, but then again, perhaps I have you right where I want you."

It was the first truly suggestive thing he'd ever said to her, and in that moment, she couldn't restrain her desire any longer. Forgetting all about his injuries, she wrapped her arms around his neck and pulled him to her, kissing him with a passion she'd never expressed to any man before because she'd never felt it. With equal zeal, he moved his lips with hers and tangled his fingers into her hair. But after a blissful moment of pure ecstasy, he pulled away.

"Grace, I... we..." He fell silent, unable to speak as he fought to catch his breath.

"Donovan, what is it? Is there something... Don't you want to..."

Still breathless, he sat up and leaned against the couch. "Of course, I do, more than anything. But I..."

Grace sat facing him and put a hand on his knee. "Is there something wrong, something related to your injuries?"

Looking horrified, Donovan put up both hands and shook his head vigorously. "Absolutely not! I'm perfectly capable of..."

Grace couldn't stifle the sigh of relief that escaped her lips. "Then what is it?"

"Grace, I'm not that kind of man. I don't sleep with a woman without first honoring her with..."

"With?" she prompted.

"With more than what I can presently give you. With a commitment, a vow."

"Didn't you pledge me your heart?"

"Yes, but you deserve much more than words spoken privately with no real obligation attached to them. But I can't give it or ask it of you because I may not be around to live it out."

Grace had no idea what he was talking about, but she could see the torment in his eyes.

She took a deep breath. "If that wasn't an issue, if we were just two people in love without the worry of the rest, what would you want to do?"

"Marry you." The response was so immediate that it had to have been at the forefront of his mind.

Sucking in a breath, she put a hand to her heart. "You... You want to marry me?"

"Yes, ma'am; marry you, love you, make a home with you, have children with you, grow old with you, all of it. I know there's no time for any of that, but it's dishonorable to do this wrong, simply because we don't have the time to do it right."

Heart pounding, Grace struggled to breathe, but this time it wasn't due to a surge of passion. This man truly loved her. In all her years of dating, she'd never met a man willing to forego a night of offered sex to honor her with a much truer and more binding act of love. And Donovan, unlike the others, had a legitimate reason to grab every pleasure he could before it was too late.

But that wasn't why he was with her. He wasn't after a good time, a satisfying way to spend his last days. He loved her, genuinely and selflessly. Though he'd spoken the words days ago, until that moment, Grace's heart hadn't fully believed them. Growing up, she'd heard many men say those words to her mother, but they meant nothing at all. There were no actions, no proof. But Donovan wouldn't treat her with less than the highest form of respect, even with the extraordinary circumstances he faced. If that wasn't love, then nothing could rightly qualify.

With a new depth of respect for the man before her, she raised her eyes to meet his. "Donovan, if you're asking, my answer is yes."

He leaned forward, searching her eyes. "You would marry me? Even though..."

"In a heartbeat."

"But we have no time to plan to..."

"I can pull a white dress out of my closet, we can go down to the courthouse, and we can be married by the end of the day tomorrow, if you're indeed asking me." She winked at his stunned expression.

"But don't you want a wedding with a gown, guests, a cake, the whole thing?"

Dismissively, she waved her hand in the air. "We can do that later if we feel like it. But I don't need it. A groom is all that's required."

"You're... You're serious!" he said with astonishment, still scrutinizing her as if expecting her to add a "just kidding" to the end of her sentence.

Opening her eyes as wide as she could, she leaned toward him. "I've never been more serious about anything in my life. I love you. I want to be beside you through whatever lies ahead. Besides, those prison guards at the hospital can't kick me out if I'm your wife." She laughed, but there was a comforting truth in her words.

After a long, silent moment, Donovan took her hand, pulling her to her feet. Then he got down on one knee in front of her. "Miss Sophia, you are my saving Grace, the reason my heart is still beating. For whatever time I have left, I want to spend it all loving you. Of all the things I've done in my life, loving you is what matters most to me. I offer you all of me, my heart, my name, the wrecked pieces of my body, every possession I own, everything I am. Would you do me the great honor of binding your life, your heart to mine by becoming my wife?"

Grace smiled. "Yes!"

Donovan rose and took her in his arms. "I don't have a ring, but I can—"

"No rings, not yet. Until this is over, until Ben and Callie get back and we follow through with their plan, please, let's just keep this between you and me. It will hurt them if they know we got married without them, and it will be a big distraction as I know Callie will want to throw us a party or plan a ceremony. There will be time for that when you're... when this is all over. Please, let this be just ours for now. I promise, I'll let you buy me a big diamond when you're better."

Donovan considered her request. "How about a compromise? I'll buy you a ring, so I can put it on your finger tomorrow, but you can wear it around your neck on a chain after that if you'd like. I want us to have something to remember, something to mark the day."

"I can live with that," she agreed with a full smile.

Donovan called the courthouse first thing the following morning and reserved a three o'clock appointment with the Justice of the Peace in the building's small chapel. The clerk informed him they'd need to bring one witness, and after talking it over with Grace, they decided that Lobster would stand with them.

"He doesn't talk much as it is, so we definitely won't have to worry about him spoiling the surprise," Grace stated confidently.

Though Donovan didn't feel the same need to keep their marriage private, he understood her reasoning and would respect her wishes. It was more than enough for him that she'd agreed to be his wife, despite the fact that he couldn't give her the wedding or the future she deserved.

After spending several hours apart to take care of needed preparations, they met outside the chapel doors a few minutes before three. Grace wore a silky white dress with lace sleeves and a band of lace around the waist. Her hair was up in a loose bun with alluring strands dangling beautifully around her flawless face. But as attractive as all that was, it was her smile that took his breath away. Joy colored her cheeks and glowed in her eyes. As he approached, awestruck and unspeakably happy, he had intended to ask if she was sure, offer her a chance to change her mind, but after seeing her expression, he simply smiled, no longer having a single doubt. She wanted this as much as he did. Whether he lived a day or a hundred years, he would never forget the way she looked at him that day.

With Lobster grinning unabashedly beside them, they spoke their vows, choosing to use the traditional wording. As Grace uttered the final phrase "until death do we part" her eyes grew moist, but she never looked away from him, facing the truth with the courage of a warrior.

As he slipped the ring he'd purchased on her finger, she gazed in delight at its beauty, and Donovan was glad he'd requested that concession. When the Justice declared them husband and wife, Donovan bent to kiss her, sure he must be in some marvelous dream world, as it was more than he'd ever dared hope for, even before he began living under the shadow of a death sentence. When their lips at last parted, she put her arms around his neck, rising higher onto her tiptoes to whisper into his ear. "This is the happiest day of my entire life. I love you, Donovan Bradshaw, now and forever."

As they left the chapel, Donovan paused to shake Lobster's hand and thank him for standing as a witness. The height difference between them meant Lobster had to tilt his neck awkwardly to look up into Donovan's eyes.

"You fixed her heart," Lobster said with a smile. "I wasn't sure anyone could do that."

"And she mine."

Donovan took Grace to an upscale restaurant where he'd reserved a private room for the entire evening. They ate until they were stuffed. Then they danced for a long time, holding each other close as they cherished each sacred, fleeting moment.

Afterward, as Grace stroked the back of his neck as he drove, she abruptly turned questioning eyes to him. "Donovan, you missed the turn. My... our house is that way." She pointed to the right.

"We're not going home tonight, Mrs. Bradshaw."

"Where are we going?"

He grinned mischievously at her. "You'll see."

AN HOUR LATER, they pulled off the dirt road and stopped in front of a quaint log cabin surrounded by towering trees.

"We're staying here?" Grace asked, her eyes dancing.

"Affirmative. I may not have had the time to plan much in the way of a honeymoon, but at least I could offer you this. Private, quiet, and"—he inhaled deeply through his nose—"the fresh smell of nature."

Grace laughed gleefully. "As long as there's no bears."

With an amused grin, he squinted, as if in deep thought. "Never tried, but I bet I could take one down. Hm, but those claws; might be like fighting a man with twenty knives, and if you count the teeth..." He visibly cringed.

"Let's just stick to honeymooning, shall we, soldier?" she said with a giggle.

"Whatever you wish, ma'am." He pulled her hand to his lips, kissing it softly.

When they went inside, Grace shook her head as she admired the furniture and décor, which tastefully combined luxurious with a touch of rustic. A large fireplace took up almost an entire wall, with two cozy chairs in front of it. An enormous clawfoot tub stood on the opposite side of the room, and when Donovan saw her staring at it, he chuckled. "I brought you a clean bath towel," he said with a wink.

The bed was in the center of the room, large and a little intimidating as a sudden shyness made her divert her eyes.

"I... I don't have any clothes. I didn't know we were..."

Donovan turned and lifted a small bag, one of two he'd retrieved from the trunk of his car. "I walked into a women's department store this morning—something I've never come close to doing before—told them your size and the occasion, and..." He held out the bag. "I have no idea what's in here, but I hope it works. I also picked up toothbrushes, toothpaste, and a few other essentials. I'm sure it's not all the luxuries of home, but..."

"It's wonderful, perfect, incredibly romantic! Thank you!" She kissed him on the cheek and took the bag. I think I'll go see what my options are. Maybe you could get a fire going."

"Yes, ma'am. I'm on it."

As she walked toward the bathroom, she glanced back at him, struck by the remarkable fortune of having found such an extraordinary man. It was supposed to be a casual, courthouse wedding with no bells and whistles, but he'd turned the day into a dream, more than she could have wanted if they'd had weeks or months to plan. As she closed the bathroom door, she smiled to herself. She would make sure he had a night that equally exceeded expectations.

Rummaging through the bag, Grace was taken aback. He must have spent a fortune! There were three complete outfits, a silky robe, and five different choices in lingerie, all expensive brand names. The robe was off-white, so she slipped into the tasteful but revealing matching night gown. From her purse, she retrieved a small bottle of perfume, applying it strategically. Before securing the robe around her, she looked at herself in the mirror, turning in a full circle. Through the thin lace, she caught sight of the birthmark on her right side. She hadn't told him about that yet, and she doubted he'd had time to notice it during his brief glance when they'd surprised each other after her shower. Sucking air through her teeth, she felt a little nervous about it, as she'd always found it rather ugly. Shrugging, she pulled the robe around her. Good and bad, she'd offer him all she was.

He hadn't asked her about her past or previous experiences, and she hadn't asked him. She'd watched her mother's promiscuousness all her life, and before she'd made the vow to never again give herself to a man who didn't truly love her, she'd made two mistakes, ones she greatly regretted. But that was years ago. If she'd known that there were men out there like Donovan, she certainly would have made different choices. Her stomach twisted as she fretted about his expectations. Before she had time to make herself sick with anxiety, she sighed and turned the knob. He'd married her without asking the question, so it obviously wasn't a dealbreaker.

When she stepped timidly into the room, Donovan turned from the fire and the look of love in his eyes dispelled her fears. Taking his time as his eyes roamed freely, he approached.

He'd also changed, wearing a simple but pleasingly tight black T-shirt and a pair of gray sweats. His chest and arms bulged with thick muscles and as he came up in front of her, the gold in his eyes danced in the flicker of the firelight. The room was so quiet that Grace could hear him breathing unsteadily as he reached to pull the pin from her hair. As it fell around her shoulders, he softly ran his fingers through it, smiling at her like she was the only woman in the world he'd ever desired.

"Donovan, I... You never asked me, but I feel like you should know..."

He put his finger to her lips. "It doesn't matter."

"But..."

"As you've pledged to be mine alone from this day forward, let's leave the past where it belongs."

"But I wish I..."

His lips met hers, so softly that she almost couldn't feel them.

"We all have scars, Miss Grace. If you can abide mine, I can abide yours."

Lovingly, she traced the scars on his face. "Your scars are beautiful to me."

His lips moved to her ear. "And I'm rather fond of that little teardrop-shaped mark on your side. I've been looking forward to getting much better acquainted with it."

Stunned, she leaned back and looked at him. "Donovan Bradshaw, when did you..."

He laughed and pulled her back into his arms. "You should really be more mindful about the state of your clothing when you fall asleep on the couch in a man's arms."

Playfully, she punched his chest. "I guess all the secrets are out now."

Gripping the tie of her robe, he tugged at it until it loosened. Savoring each second, each touch, he slid his hands inside, around her waist, then up her back, making her skin tingle and her heart race. After a slow inhale, ripe with anticipation, he whispered softly, "There are still plenty I'm anxious to discover."

Releasing her fears and insecurities, she gave herself over to loving him without reservation. No man had ever loved her with such raw passion, yet also with a tenderness that fueled her desire, leaving her wanting nothing more than to stay forever enraptured in his arms.

When they at last lay quietly together in blissful contentment, Grace found it impossible to believe that someone so ill could love her so perfectly, just as she'd always dreamed but had never known. If she had any lingering doubts about the genuineness of his devotion, the way he made love to her had silenced them for good.

"Donovan," she whispered dreamily against his warm chest.

His fingers lightly stroked her back as he answered. "Yes, ma'am."

Laughing, she resigned herself to him never giving up addressing her with such formality. In truth, it was his way of being affectionate. "That was absolutely... it was perfect, but also quite... energetic. Are you alright?"

He turned and kissed the top of her head. "In all my life, I've never felt better than I do right now."

Relieved, she relaxed against him. "That makes two of us. I love you, with all my heart and soul."

"During my recovery, and many times since, I wanted to die, just to escape the relentless pain. But, Grace, you've made me want to live. I'd endure the agony and more for the rest of my life, gladly, if I could just stay with you."

Gripping him tighter, she could feel the scars on his skin. "I'm not going to let you go, soldier. Even if the time comes when you're no longer strong enough to keep it burning, I'll never let your bright light go out."

CHAPTER 13

IN TIME'S CLUTCHES

When Grace awoke the next morning, Donovan wasn't beside her. Gripping the sheet, she raised herself up and looked around the cabin, but he was nowhere in sight.

"Donovan?"

There was no answer.

Slipping out of bed, she pulled her robe around her as something in her gut began to churn.

Walking to the front window, she looked outside. The car was still parked where they'd left it. Where was he?

Gasping as fear overtook her, she turned and ran to the bathroom. There, slumped against the back wall, was Donovan, his face as white as a sheet, a trickle of blood streaming from the corner of his mouth.

"No!" The agonizing cry dropped her to her knees.

Putting her hands on the sides of his face, she called his name, frantic as tears began to blur her vision.

"Please, soldier, please. Don't leave me. Open your eyes."

She felt for a pulse, but her hands were trembling so

fiercely she couldn't be sure one way or the other. Leaning down, she put her cheek in front of his mouth, then let out a soft cry of relief when she felt his breath on her skin.

For another minute, she tried shaking him, calling him, but there was no response. She needed to get help, at once. But she wasn't sure exactly where they were, and how would an ambulance get here in time, way out here in the woods? Then with a surge of hope, she remembered Agent Taylor's card.

Kissing his forehead, she rose and ran for her purse and phone, bringing them back to the bathroom with her. With trembling fingers she dialed the number, thankful that she had cell service out here in the middle of, wherever they were.

"Wes Taylor," came the immediate answer.

"Mr. Taylor, it's Grace. I…"

"Grace. It's alright. Take a breath. What's going on?"

"Donovan collapsed in the bathroom. I don't know what to do. We're in the woods, somewhere, I don't even know exactly where."

"Breathe, dear one. It's going to be alright. I'm tracking your location right now, and help will be on the way in moments. Can you tell me if he's breathing?"

"Yes, but his face is deathly white and there's blood."

"Blood from where?"

"His mouth."

"Is he lying down?"

"No, he's sort of, leaning against the wall."

"Place the phone on speaker mode and set it on the floor."

She did as he asked.

"Now try laying him down and elevate his legs on a pillow or rolled-up rug."

Though it took all her strength and then some, she slowly maneuvered Donovan so that he was flat on the floor. Then she rolled up the rug and put it under his legs.

"Now check his breathing again, Grace."

Stroking his face as tears dripped onto his neck and bare chest, she stifled her sobs long enough to listen and tune in to the feel of his breath on her cheek. "I think, maybe, he's breathing a little easier now. I don't know for sure."

"Alright, Grace. You've done all you can. He's alive and breathing, so he's okay for the moment. There's a helicopter en route. Pack your belongings quickly. They'll be at your front door in less than fifteen minutes. Place your phone where you can grab it, and we'll leave this line open. Keep checking on him every minute or so, and if anything changes, just pick up the phone, and I'll talk you through it, alright?"

"Thank you, Agent Taylor," she said through a sob.

Setting the phone down, she ran to get dressed. Then she began frantically throwing their belongings into the two bags Donovan had brought, stopping each minute to check his breathing. His face was still pale, but he had a little more color than when she'd originally found him. When the bags were packed and gathered by the front door, she heard the distant sound of a helicopter. Lying down beside him, she covered his face in tears and kisses. "Soldier, you have to pull through this. Please. One day as your wife is not enough, not nearly enough. Hold on. Please, hold on."

"Ma'am." A voice in the doorway startled her. She hadn't heard them land or enter the cabin. Her entire focus was directed at praying desperately for his brown eyes to open.

"We're here to help, but I need to get in there to see how he's doing."

A second man, standing behind him, held out his hand to her. "I'll take you to the chopper, miss. We'll get you strapped in where you'll be able to see him, alright?"

She stood and took the man's hand, but she stayed where she could see Donovan.

"I know you want to stay with him, but I need to help my friend here get him onto the stretcher so we can take him with us. In order to do that, I need to get you in the chopper, set to go. Do you understand?"

Numb and disoriented, she obeyed, letting the man lead her out the door and help her into her seat. He pulled a belt around her and patted her shoulder. "I'll be right back. You stay put."

Though it seemed like an eternity, they eventually loaded Donovan into the helicopter, and she watched help-lessly as they attached monitors to his arms and chest and inserted an IV. The man who had helped her into her seat typed information into a small computer and spoke on the phone to what seemed to be the hospital they were headed for.

"Are you his girlfriend?" the man asked, but the ques-tion barely penetrated her consciousness.

"His wife," she said, her voice flat and hollow.

"He's alright for now. It looks like his body went into shock, but I'm concerned about the blood. We should have his file momentarily, but can you tell me anything about his injuries?" He pointed to the scars on Donovan's abdomen.

"He broke his back almost two years ago, and he said his kidneys aren't working right. I..." She put her face in her hands, sobs shaking her shoulders.

"It's alright. That helps a lot." Though he was trying

hard to project positivity, she could see the concern in his eyes.

Though Grace had never been in a helicopter before, she didn't remember the ride. All she recalled was his face, pale and lifeless. When they landed on the roof of the hospital, a team met them and rushed him off before she could protest. A soft-spoken African American woman put her arm around Grace's shoulders. "Come with me, darlin'. They're gonna get him all settled, then they'll come get you. It won't be long."

Grace couldn't remember responding, walking, sitting, or waiting. Her mind had shut down, turned off. All that filled her thoughts was the deep, calming timbre of his voice, the golden flecks in his eyes, the strength of his embrace, the softness of his kiss, the warmth of his body against hers. And the aching truth: if he didn't come back, she would never again know a love as profound as the one she felt for him.

"Mrs. Bradshaw?"

Not accustomed to being addressed by that name, it took her a moment to look up. An older man in a white coat stood staring down at her.

"I'm Doctor Karl. I've been taking care of your husband. We've stabilized him as best we can, but he's in a lot of pain. We're working hard to get that under control. He's in and out of consciousness, but he's called your name repeatedly. Do you feel strong enough to sit with him? It will be hard to watch, Mrs. Bradshaw, but I'm betting it will bring him comfort."

"Yes," she said, jumping to her feet.

Though her whole body was trembling, she followed the doctor down a hallway to a closed door. "He's in critical condition. We are doing our best, but as you likely know, his injuries are extensive and incurable. Trying to minimize the pain is the best we can do."

Despite her distress, she straightened and looked the doctor in the eye as a sudden surge of strength washed over her. "Doctor Karl. My husband was told he had six months to live. That was almost two years ago. He's not going to die in this hospital."

Politely, the doctor nodded, but his eyes betrayed his disbelief. "I'll be back to check on him shortly. Hold his hand, let him feel your presence. It shouldn't be long until the pain medication kicks in." With that, he turned and left her standing alone.

Grace took a deep breath before stepping into the dimly lit room. Donovan lay with his eyes closed, but she could see the pain on his face. "Grace," he whispered her name in desperation, like a dying man begging for water.

Heartbroken at the plea, she rushed to him, grasping his hand, and leaning down to place her cheek against his forehead. "I'm here, soldier. I'm right here and I won't leave you." He exhaled, and though there was relief in it, each halting breath resounded with the agony he suffered.

"I'm sorry."

"Shh. I'm not sorry about anything. You're alive. That's all that matters. I thought..."

After struggling through another breath, he opened his eyes. Feeling as if a knife had pierced her heart, she swallowed hard, trying to stifle a sob as she took in the look of unbearable pain. "I can't fight it this time, Grace. It's too strong."

Tears streamed down her cheeks, and she wiped at them angrily. "I know it's hard. I know you're tired. But this time, you are not alone. I'll fight with you. I won't let it take you. Please, my love, please, don't give up."

Conflicting desires raged in him. He wanted to let go, to rest in peace where pain could no longer torment him. But love held him captive. For a few seconds, she wavered, wondering if what she was asking of him was cruel and selfish. If there wasn't any hope, she'd gladly take the sorrow upon herself and release him. But as long as there was a chance, even a distant one, she couldn't let him give up.

"One more day, soldier. For my sake, can you hold on for just one more day?"

His fingers tightened around hers. "Whatever you ask of me, ma'am. I'll do my best to oblige."

Two hours later, Doctor Karl checked back with them. Donovan had at last fallen asleep after an excruciating hour of labored breathing and falling in and out of consciousness. Grace held his hand, stroked his face, and continued to beg him to hold on.

Flipping through his chart and checking his monitors, Doctor Karl wrote down a few notes before turning to her. "His vitals look a little better, though I don't know why. There's nothing more we can do, except keep him out of pain. We'll keep him under heavy sedation for the night, let his body rest. In the morning, we'll bring him out of it, see how he feels. You should go home, Mrs. Bradshaw, get some rest. Your bags from the helicopter are at reception."

"I'm not leaving."

The doctor tucked the clipboard under his arm and studied her. "I understand how much you love him, and I've been informed about his valor and sacrifice for our country. If there was anything I could offer you in the way of hope, I'd gladly do so. But there's nothing, Mrs. Bradshaw, nothing we can do to save his life."

Grace bit her lip, struggling to stay in control. "Thank you, Doctor. I understand. But I'm still not leaving."

"Alright then. Push the button if you need anything."

When the doctor left, she cautiously lay beside Donovan, being sure not to disturb any equipment. She had no idea what time it was, but she knew hours had gone by without her awareness. The repeated adrenaline rushes had drained her, but she wouldn't sleep without being sure Donovan knew she was beside him, that he wasn't alone.

How could it be that they'd had less than a day as husband and wife and only one night together before their world collapsed around them? She thought about calling Callie but then realized she'd left her phone in the cabin. She was certain Taylor would take care of that anyway. Though she regretted interrupting their honeymoon, this was a matter of life or death. If Ben wanted to save his friend, he needed to act fast.

"Rest for now, soldier," she whispered. "I'll keep the flame burning for both of us."

When Donovan awoke, the pain hit him with such fury that for a moment, he couldn't breathe. Even with the narcotics that were scattering his thoughts and dulling his senses, his whole body felt as if it were burning up on the inside. This had to be it, the end of the road for him. He'd made it longer than anyone believed possible, but he couldn't defeat this enemy. As his mind and heart began to accept the ugly reality, he felt her breath on his neck.

Turning his head, Donovan's gaze lingered on her beautiful face. Sleeping soundly, she had somehow wedged herself beside him in the small hospital bed, her body warm and comforting, making the cold, sterile place feel like home. As he stared at his new bride's closed eyelids, framed by her long, seductive eyelashes, her light pink cheeks, and her soft, full lips, he let his mind drift back to their passionate night together. Focusing his thoughts away from the pain, he replayed every exciting kiss and each thrilling touch. Making love to her had been the most pleasurable and among the most powerful experiences of his life, irrevocably changing something deep within him. Two were now one, their souls fused together forever. He had never dreamed he could love someone this much, with his whole being.

But as the joy of what he'd found filled his heart, the sorrow over what he was about to lose broke it. No matter how much he wanted to, he couldn't stay with her much longer. Though their love was powerful, it couldn't overcome death. One magical night with her was all he would ever have, but he'd hold that memory close, cling to it, and take it with him as the light faded away.

As the agony in his heart overshadowed that which was throbbing through his body, he pressed his lips softly to her forehead and she stirred and blinked. When her eyes met his, she smiled. "Hi, soldier."

"My beautiful Grace." His voice was so weak that even he didn't recognize it. "This isn't exactly how I pictured waking up with you the morning after our wedding day."

Very gently, she kissed his lips, then stroked his face with her fingertips, and the pain retreated ever so slightly at her touch. "No matter the circumstance, any morning I wake up and look into those incredible eyes, I'm the happiest woman on earth."

He tried to smile, but it was impossible to mask the

despair that was pressing in on him. "Grace. If you hadn't been there... but, we were so far out of town. How did you manage to..." His voice trailed off as a surge of pain made him grit his teeth.

Grace took his hand in both of hers. "Ben's father, Agent Taylor. He has a great deal of respect and admiration for you. At the wedding, he gave me his private number, told me to keep it just in case. I don't know how he knew we'd need it, but when I called him, he got a helicopter there in minutes."

"That was kind. Like his son, he's a good man. I wish I could have given you more of a honeymoon."

Inching closer to him, she spoke in a whisper near his ear. "It was a dream, absolutely perfect. Being with you was unforgettable. You set the bar very high, soldier, but when you're better..."

"Grace." He shook his head. "I'm not going to get better this time. Everything inside me is coming apart; I can feel it, and I can't stop it no matter how badly I want more time with you."

Her eyes filled with tears, but she held his gaze. "I know the pain is unbearable. I see it in your eyes, and it kills me. I promise you, if I didn't believe with all my heart that there was still a reason to hope, I'd let you"—a soft sob shook her shoulders—"I'd let you go, release you to rest, and spare you the agony, even though it would break my heart. I would not selfishly ask you to keep fighting. But it isn't time for that yet. There *is* still hope. As long as that's the case, I won't let you surrender to despair or fade into the darkness." She lifted his hand and held it to her heart. "Please forgive me for begging you to suffer a little while longer."

No matter how doubtful he was that he could survive another hour, much less a day, he could not refuse her. "I will try, but when the time comes, when hope is gone and I have no more strength, please forgive me for hurting you, for coming into your life only to break your heart."

As she leaned over him to kiss his lips, a tear dropped onto his cheek and rolled into his hair. "There is nothing to forgive. I know what love is now because of you. But I also know I could never love anyone as I love you. We were meant to find each other, and I was destined to be here, in this moment, to keep you from giving up, to help give you the courage to continue fighting. You said you wanted a life with me, children, growing old together, the whole package. Hang on to that dream. It's not time to give up on it, not yet."

Looking up into her eyes, he lifted his hand and stroked her wet cheek. "If you wish it, I'll do all I can to keep breathing until you're ready to grant me relief and let me go."

Smiling through her tears, she kissed him one more time.

A FEW MINUTES LATER, a soft knock at the door startled them both, and Grace slipped off the edge of the bed and stood to her feet. "Come in?"

When the door opened and Ben and Callie stepped into the room, Grace's tears of sorrow turned to joy. Running to them, she threw her arms around them. Though she was expecting them, she hadn't dreamed they'd get there so fast.

"How in the world?"

"Taylor," Donovan said hoarsely, coughing as he tried to speak loud enough to be heard.

With one look at his friend, Ben rushed to Donovan's

side and gripped his arm firmly. For the first time in more than twenty-four hours, Grace took a deep breath as the pain visibly retreated from Donovan's eyes and color returned to his face. She'd never seen Ben's gift in action before, and though she'd believed Callie's description of it, seeing it play out before her eyes was astonishing. Within seconds, Donovan began breathing normally and he let out a sigh that refreshed her soul. Hope sprang anew as witnessing this miracle firsthand bolstered her faith that a cure was indeed possible.

As she watched Donovan's whole body relax, she couldn't help but think about how strange it must be for him to be at death's door one moment then suddenly restored to perfect health the next. When Ben let go, would the reprieve make the return to torment easier or harder?

As she continued to watch, though Donovan's condition dramatically improved, Ben's face paled as if they'd switched roles, Ben trading his wellness for Donovan's sickness.

"Don't blame him," Ben pleaded. "We're glad he called. This is exactly where we want and need to be right now, my friend."

Though his eyes had brightened with the restoration of strength and wholeness, as Donovan looked at Ben, they narrowed in concern. "Thank you for coming, but I'll never forgive myself for cheating the two of you out of a honeymoon. I'm sorry, ma'am," he said in a clear voice, directing the last few words to Callie.

They both continued to reassure them that this was where they wanted to be and that the honeymoon could be easily resumed when the crisis had passed.

Still reeling from the shock of his sudden restoration to full health, Grace returned to stand next to Donovan, and

Callie joined Ben on the opposite side of the bed, putting her hand around his arm.

"Are you... Are you completely out of pain?" Grace stammered, as she watched Donovan continue to take easy breaths.

"No pain whatsoever." He smiled and held out his hand to her, and she took it, noting his strong grip. "But I'm not going to let my friend drain himself dry keeping me that way." He turned serious eyes to Ben. "When your hands start shaking, you're done here. That's an order."

So, it *was* true. What Ben offered Donovan came at a price. There was a poison pill in all this wonderment, for the giver as well as the receiver. Knowing his heart, Grace easily discerned how uncomfortable it was for Donovan to watch his friend suffer at the expense of his relief.

Despite his own distress, Ben smiled warmly at Donovan's noticeable improvement. "I'll take breaks so I can continue periodically helping you, but—"

Donovan shook his head. "Ben, listen! I'm not going to get better this time. You can't hold Humpty-Dumpty together forever. It's very unlikely I'm leaving this hospital alive."

Grace's heart ached at the hopelessness in his voice, but Ben set his jaw and responded with a tone of unyielding conviction. "You most certainly *will* be leaving this hospital alive. As soon as I can arrange it, actually."

Encouraged by his confidence, Grace wiped a tear from her cheek. "Are you... Is this the plan Callie told me about, the long shot?"

Ben directed his smile at her. "It is. It's still in the works, and not guaranteed, but I'm feeling more confident about the possibility, as all involved seem poised to benefit from the results."

"This is the plan where I become… one of you, Succouri, correct?" Donovan asked, keeping his watchful eye on the progression of Ben's deteriorating condition.

Callie, who was also watching him with concern, nodded and took over the explanation. "That's right. Fortunately, we found a Succouri ready to transfer his gift, but we haven't personally met with him yet. The situation with him is delicate. He lost his wife, his Succouri partner, many years ago and as a result, he's not well."

Confused, Grace raised her hand. "Wait. Wait. Back up. Donovan filled me in on some of the details we didn't get to in our little pow-wow in Mr. LeVray's closet, but honestly, he doesn't know that much more than I do. Watching this all in action is phenomenal, but I think we're both suffering from an acute case of insufficient information here."

Taking a deep breath, Callie briefly glanced at the door before proceeding with her explanation. "The Succouri gift can only be passed along by a mature Succouri, someone who's possessed it for about forty years and has entered what's called 'the ripening.' The recipient must be ill, in need of the powerful healing the gift provides. Through a donation of blood, the gift saves his life and transforms him into the next Succouri; that's how it propagates. But the Succouri is incomplete on his own. As we ourselves have only recently learned, the word 'Succouri' is plural. Alone, he's unable to fulfill his calling and maintain wellness in body and mind. Every Succouri needs a partner. When he meets her—his intended match—a unique bond quickly forms that is unbreakable. In time, the partner develops the ability to physically strengthen the Succouri as he helps others, and restore his strength quickly when it's been depleted." Callie turned to smile at Ben, her eyes shining with love and excitement. "And there are many other extraordinary and beautiful benefits to the bond, but they're best experienced rather than explained. The bond is so essential and tight that the lack of it or loss of it is devastating. We've never met a Succouri who lost his partner so we're not sure exactly what to expect, but the doctor we're working with has met him, and he told us he's deeply troubled."

"I don't quite understand," Grace interjected. "How exactly does the partner help the Succouri?" She stared at Callie, noting how she had both hands wrapped around Ben's arm. "Are you helping him right now?"

Ben nodded emphatically, though Callie answered the question. "We're helping each other. He's giving me sight, and I'm... It's a little hard to explain but I'm giving back to him a portion of what he's giving Donovan, allowing Ben to assist him for a while longer and with fewer negative effects."

The tension in Donovan's face notably relaxed at this revelation.

"But you're not... Succouri. Are you?" Grace asked, wrinkling her brow as she tried to process what Callie was telling them.

Callie laughed lightly. "That's something that took us a while to understand, but yes, I am Succouri, but in a different way. My gift only helps him. I can't do what he's doing for anyone else."

"How did you become Succouri?" Donovan inquired of Callie.

"It's part of the bond," Ben answered. "Though I didn't know that until after it happened. Contact with me, through the bond, changed her." He lowered his eyes, looking regretful about the admission.

"In a good way," Callie quickly added.

There was silence for a moment as everyone took in the information.

"If a Succouri needs a bond and does so poorly without one, how did you escape that fate since you only met Callie a few months ago?" Grace asked Ben.

"We don't have a solid answer to that question," Ben admitted. "We'll try to give you all the information we have regarding the Succouri, but you must resist the urge to apply it to me, I'm..."

"Extremely unique and special," Callie chimed in, love shining in her eyes. "Ben's early and unusual acquisition of the gift means we get to break all the rules and blaze our own trail."

"How old were you, and what's the typical age for a recipient?" Donovan asked.

"I was twelve. I received it when my father donated marrow to save me from dying of leukemia. How he acquired it is another long story. Until now, all involved with the Succouri phenomenon believed it impossible for a child to acquire the gift, but I have disproved that theory, though we don't yet know exactly why or how. The typical age of a recipient is early thirties, but you are well within the acceptable parameters. After donating his gift, a Succouri lives for approximately fifteen more years, but in a significantly weakened state. Even so, that's a pretty good, long life, and you'll live forty of it without any disease or pain whatsoever, as will also be the case for your partner."

Before responding, Donovan glanced down, frowning at the tremble in Ben's hand. "I always thought you were a little different, Ben," he said teasingly. "But different or not, I won't be the cause of you overdoing it and leaving your lovely, but petite wife to carry you out of here, so..." He tugged at Ben's hand, and Grace put a hand to her mouth, bracing herself against the torment of watching the pain return.

"Alright, I'll take a break but not for long. We both need to stay strong so we can arrive at Cape Cod ready for the transfer." With a sigh, he removed his hand.

Though he did his best to mask it with a weak smile, Grace saw the shock in Donovan's eyes as the pain returned with a vengeance. Likewise, Ben agonized as he witnessed the abrupt change in Donovan's condition. His genuine love for Donovan was evident as was his torment at having to let go of him.

"Besides the weakening you described, what are the other costs?" Donovan asked, still cautious to embrace the hope Ben offered him.

"If you choose this path, you'll be different, changed, compelled by a power that will shift your priorities and destiny. You'll live with the constant fear of being discovered and the consequences that could result from that, but you won't be able to walk away from those who need your help. The draw is... unpleasant, yet something you will never be able to avoid, as the voice inside you is relentless in its urgings. The identity will change relationships, cause you to think twice before you touch someone, and pierce your heart every time you're forced to do what I just did with you; let go and watch the pain return. I can't describe the internal agony you'll suffer when that occurs. I love helping Callie, but I hate knowing that whenever I let go, her world dims. And, though there are wondrous aspects to our lives together, I've burdened her with many sorrows, both now and in the future, most of which I couldn't forewarn her about because I didn't know about them myself. I want you to have the choice that, regrettably, I was never offered. This life was forced on me, altering my body and my future without my consent or understanding, but it doesn't have to be that way for you. You have the chance to choose or reject it of your own free will, and I want you to have as much information as we can offer you before you make that decision."

Though Grace appreciated Ben's well-intentioned warnings, she swallowed hard as, in truth, this was Donovan's only shot at survival, which, in her estimation, meant there really wasn't a choice at all.

Looking into Grace's eyes, Donovan took several raspy breaths before turning back to Ben. "What sorrows did you place on her?"

Ben hesitated, looking across the bed at Grace with such apprehension that it made Grace's heart pound.

"Tell me, Ben. Please," Donovan pleaded.

"When I rescued that family in the fire, I used up every ounce of my strength. I was helpless, unconscious for hours. Callie was left alone to save us both from discovery and danger. Then she had to... to take care of me until I recovered some of my strength. The effects of the draw can last for days, especially when the bond is young and incomplete. After he's passed along his gift, the weakening that occurs leaves the Succouri's partner to care for him for years. And..." Ben lowered his eyes, and Grace could see that the worst was yet to tell.

Though the idea of watching Donovan weaken each time he helped someone disturbed her, she felt encouraged by the idea of being able to actually do something to assist him. Since she'd met Donovan, she'd helplessly watched him suffer continuously but she had nothing except words of encouragement to offer. What a relief it would be to bring more than that to the table. But, by the look on his face, whatever Ben had saved for last on the list of drawbacks was clearly the most devastating, and that made her stomach churn.

"Go on," Grace encouraged, despite her fear. "We need to hear it all."

As he continued to gaze into her eyes, Ben's expression suddenly relaxed, as if he'd glimpsed something in her soul that put him at ease.

"Callie and I recently learned that Succouri can't have children."

Grace put a hand to her stomach, feeling as if she'd been punched. A house full of children was something she'd always dreamed of.

"Never?" Grace asked in a whisper, looking at Callie.

Callie shook her head. "But I want to present my side of the story too. Yes, there are costs, I can't deny that, but I love my life with Ben, and I wouldn't trade it for anything, even with the costs. There's purpose, meaning, extraordinary intimacy, and a love that doesn't compare to anything you've ever known. Partnering with him, whether through my Succouri gift or just my human hands, fills me up inside as nothing else ever has or ever could. It's like... like being with him has always been my destiny, and I finally get to live it out. And there are so many other wonderful benefits, which I'll hold close to my heart, and simply say that they're more miraculous than you could imagine. I wouldn't trade any of this or wish it any different. I love this life and this man with all my heart."

Though comforted by Callie's words, when Grace caught the look of shock and sadness in Donovan's eyes, she knew that this news had hit him hard, perhaps hard enough for him to reconsider accepting a gift that would save his life. Though Ben and Callie didn't know it, Donovan and she had already taken vows, pledged their futures to one another. Though she couldn't deny that the costs were significant, nothing Ben had told them caused her to second guess her choice to marry him, but she could see regret on Donovan's face and that pierced her heart so painfully that sorrow nearly overtook the hope that had barely begun to take root and spring to life.

CHAPTER 14

PLANS AND PERILS

Thirty minutes later, Grace sat in the hospital cafeteria with Callie, staring blankly at her untouched sandwich. A nurse had interrupted their conversation in Donovan's room, and when the three of them stepped out into the hallway to give her space to run some tests, Doctor Karl approached them. As he'd been Callie's father's doctor during his hospital stay, he already knew Ben and Callie, and from the look of bewilderment he sent Ben, it was clear he had suspicions about Ben's gift. Since Ben needed to speak with the doctor about transporting Donovan back east, the two of them had retreated to talk privately while Grace and Callie went to get something to eat.

Though she'd barely eaten anything in the last twenty-four hours, Grace had no appetite, but Ben and Callie had insisted, and as she was too tired to argue and she presently needed to stay out of the way of the hospital staff anyway, she'd complied.

"Gracie, please try to eat something," Callie encouraged. "You won't do Donovan any good if you're so weak you end up getting sick."

Picking up her sandwich, she obediently took a few bites before speaking. "Cal, why Cape Cod? It's so far and Donovan might not be well enough for the trip."

"Ben and I will make sure Donovan gets there safely, and we'll help keep him stable until the transfer takes place. There's a doctor there who works with the Succouri. He knows how to do the transfers and has a medical lab in his home. Plus, the man—his name is Ethan Devereaux—who is ready to pass his gift lives within driving distance. Ben has a house nearby where we can all stay during the process."

Grace leaned her elbows on the table and massaged her temples, overwhelmed by what they'd learned in the last hour. "So, if there are doctors who work specifically with Succouri, is this like a widespread thing, like are there a lot of them out there?"

Callie smiled. "I asked the same question not long ago, probably with the same dumbfounded look on my face. Of course, it's exceedingly rare, but there are enough to include a network of people who support those with the gift. It's like a big family, everyone taking care of everyone else."

"And if... if it works, he'll be completely healed, permanently?"

"As if he'd never been injured," Callie answered, the joy in the statement causing her green eyes to sparkle.

When Grace let out a relieved sigh, Callie's expression shifted to delighted curiosity. "You are deeply in love with him, aren't you." The comment was an observation more than a question.

In that moment, Grace wanted to tell her friend everything, but with the mountain of obstacles in front of them, it still didn't feel like the right time. "Cal, I love Donovan with all my heart and soul," she confessed in a whisper.

Beaming, Callie put a hand over her heart. "You found a good man of your own just as I knew you would! My best friend in love with Ben's best friend, and vice versa! It's like it was meant to be. I'm so happy for you both. This has to work; we'll make it work. He'll be okay, Gracie."

"Cal, if he becomes Succouri, will he be different, like a whole other person?"

"Oh, not like that. Not in a way that you won't recognize him. He'll still be your Donovan." She hesitated for a moment, as if deciding whether or not to share the next part with Grace. "I had an encounter with Ben's Succouri during our honeymoon. It... spoke to me, in a way. It's hard to explain."

Dropping her hands onto the table, Grace sat back in her seat. "What do you mean? I thought it was just a... a thing in the blood. I didn't know it was, like alive?"

"No one really knows exactly how to label it. Even Ben has a hard time defining it as a separate consciousness. But I think that's because, when you possess it, it's so much a part of you that differentiating it is difficult, particularly in Ben's case since he's had it for such a long time and he was so young when it came to him. But almost from the day I found out about his gift, I've, sort of, known it, been aware of its presence. It's much like him, their personalities nearly identical. It rarely asserts itself, except of course in providing healing, but it's there, giving him courage, prompting him to act when someone's in need, and drawing us together in wondrous ways." She waved her hand in the air. "You'll see. But the point is, yes, its presence will change Donovan's path in life, though his history of service to others will make the change less dramatic. Your essential role in it will change you too, Gracie. But the change will be for good, and you will still be you and he will still be him. It won't break you apart but will instead bring you closer together, put you on parallel paths as you'll want the same thing from life. You'll still love each other. Actually, you'll have a deeper connection than you could ever imagine; and that's heart, mind, and body."

"It's all so... so..."

"Miraculous? Strange? Overwhelming?" Callie laughed when Grace confirmed her guesses with an exaggerated exhale. "It won't feel that way when it happens. Trust me, he will still be the man you fell in love with, and the process will be exciting and beautiful."

Before Grace had a chance to ask any more questions, Ben joined them, smiling as he took a seat next to Callie and grasped her hand. "We're all set," he said triumphantly. "The day after tomorrow, first thing in the morning, we fly out on a medical transport plane. The doc already had it scheduled for a young girl who needs a specialized heart surgery performed by a doctor who practices in Baltimore. We'll go there with them, be sure the girl makes it safely as well, then meet up with our Succouri doc and head to Cape Cod."

"So, it's... it's really going to happen? How did you..." Grace stammered, shocked that Ben was able to talk the doctor into allowing someone as sick as Donovan to be transported.

"The doc, Callie, and I have some history that worked to our advantage."

"Does he know about your..." Grace asked, and Callie turned curious eyes to Ben as well.

"He does now. Well, at least the basics," Ben answered with a low chuckle.

Grace lowered her eyes, humbled by the risk they were taking to save Donovan's life. "Thank you, Ben. I want to go with you. I have to—"

"Already arranged," he said with a smile.

When the three of them returned to Donovan's room, they found him asleep under heavy sedation. Though it took a lot of coaxing, Callie finally convinced Grace to go home for an hour to shower and change. They promised not to leave his side until she returned.

On her way out, she picked up the bags from their overnight trip, and, after she'd showered and dressed, she sat on the bed sorting through them. Lifting the black T-shirt he'd worn on their wedding night, she breathed in the scent of him and tears sprang to her eyes. She'd give anything to have him there with her. Memories of their extraordinary night together comforted and pained her simultaneously. Even if their crazy plan worked, would she ever have that Donovan back again, the one who had fallen for her, married her, and loved her with a kind of passion she'd never forget? Despite Callie's assurances, Grace had doubts.

Callie hadn't known Ben before he was Succouri, so how could she be sure that the change wouldn't radically alter Donovan's personality, and maybe his love for her as well? But carrying through with this plan was the only way to save his life, so in the end, no matter the consequences, they had to proceed.

At the bottom of her bag, she found the small black box that held her wedding ring. Retrieving a chain from her jewelry collection, she slipped the ring onto it and secured it around her neck. Until she was sure that the new Donovan, the one altered by the presence of a being no one seemed to fully understand, still wanted her as his wife, she'd keep their marriage a secret. But the ring would remain close to her heart always, as she'd never forget the remarkable man who'd stolen her heart.

It was dark in the room when Donovan awoke. Though sharp stabs of pain quickly reminded him of the state of his reality, he could feel the effects of heavy sedation tugging him back toward unconsciousness.

"Donovan, can you hear me?" Somewhere in the distance, her voice echoed, like it was bouncing off the walls of a steep canyon.

"I'm here with you. It will wear off in a minute. Take some deep breaths."

He did his best to comply and gradually, the tugging relented, and her face came into focus. "Grace."

She smiled at him and put a straw to his lips. "Room temperature, I promise."

He took a long sip, grateful as his mouth was dry and his throat sore. When he finished the entire cupful he relaxed back into his pillow, and she withdrew the glass as she stroked the side of his face. "There's more where that came from if you want it."

"How long have I—"

"A day and a half. The doctor wants to keep you rested so you're strong for tomorrow, but I asked him to bring you out of it for a few minutes so we could talk. Do you feel well enough for a short chat with me?"

"As always, I'll do my best to fulfill your every desire, ma'am. What's happening tomorrow?"

She pulled a chair up to his bed and took his hand.

"That's what I want to talk to you about. Ben spoke with your doctor, and they've arranged transport for you for first thing in the morning. We're going to Cape Cod to meet with the Succouri doctor. As soon as we get there, Ben's already scheduled a time to talk with Ethan Devereaux, the man who is going to pass along his Succouri gift to you." She paused to smile again. "It's all working out beautifully, Donovan. We're going to get you better. You'll be strong again, even healthier than before you were injured. But Ben wanted me to speak with you before tomorrow, confirm that this is the course of action you want to take. It's important to him that you are given the choice."

Though her words gave him hope, as the fog began to clear from his mind, he recalled Ben's description of the costs involved in accepting the gift, and he turned to look Grace in the eyes. "I won't hold you to it, Grace."

"Hold me to what?" she asked, leaning closer to him.

"The marriage."

"Donovan! No. I—"

Reaching up, he lovingly stroked her silky cheek, the words he knew he must say bitter on his tongue. "We didn't know all that was involved, what we'd have to give up. It isn't fair to you, and I won't ask it."

Once again, he watched as his wife's eyes filled with tears. Despairingly, he wondered if the day would ever come when he wouldn't cause her pain.

Abruptly, she stood and walked a few feet away from his bed, staring out the window at the dark sky. "Will you answer a question for me? Full honesty?" she asked, though she didn't turn toward him.

"Yes, ma'am."

"If the shoe were on the other foot, if we were just a normal couple who fell in love and got married and a year later discovered I couldn't conceive, couldn't have children, would you leave me because of that?"

"Never! But this isn't the same thing. I pushed you into this because I wasn't sure we had much time left together."

Grace turned toward him. "Are you saying you wouldn't have asked me to marry you if you weren't dying?" A tear streaked down her cheek, and it tore at his heart as he was desperate to hold her.

"Negative. Grace, I've loved you, wanted you since the moment I laid eyes on you, and I will love you until my last breath."

She walked back to his bedside and leaned over him, looking directly into his eyes. "It is exactly the same for me, soldier. I didn't marry you because you were dying. I married you because you are the first and only man I've ever trusted completely and loved with my whole being. There will never be anyone for me but you. I meant the vows I spoke, and I am a person who keeps my promises. But let me tell you this, Donovan Bradshaw. If we hadn't gotten married, if I hadn't yet spoken those vows, I'd still want to be your wife more than anything I've ever wanted in my life. This difficult news, the truth about the cost we must pay to keep our love alive, would not have scared me away or caused me to change my mind, even if I hadn't yet committed my heart. It certainly won't change my mind now that I have." The conviction in her voice and the look of determination in her eyes, left him no doubt, and though he'd cried only once or twice in his entire life, he had to blink hard to hold back tears of gratitude for the priceless, selfless love she freely offered him.

"But what about the rest of it, Grace? The changes for both of us, the redirecting of our lives, the obligation to care for me when I grow weak, the constant threat of discovery, all of it? Doesn't that scare you?"

"A little," she admitted with a half grimace, half smile. "But then I watch Callie and Ben and see how incredibly happy they are and"—she shrugged—"I guess I figure if it works for them, it will work for us too." Though her tone was casual, there was something she was hiding, something about the whole thing that did worry her.

"But?"

"But nothing." She leaned over to kiss him. "I think I'm still just processing the whole idea. It's one thing to know someone who has superpowers. It's quite another to join their ranks, become one of them."

"If I make it that far. There's still no guarantee I can survive long enough to see this through."

"Oh, you will," she said with a definitive nod. "Between Ben, Callie, and me, we won't let you check out. So, just so I'm clear, as Ben wanted a firm answer, you're saying yes, you want to proceed?" The pitch of her voice rose with excitement despite the fact that he was still certain there was something else troubling her.

"This decision impacts both of us equally. The lovely lady votes first."

"That's easy," she giggled. "Yes! Unequivocally, yes!"

Donovan coughed, and his monitor began beeping loudly. A nurse rushed into the room, and Grace stepped back, her smile quickly fading.

"Spike in his blood pressure," the nurse informed her. "We need to put him back under."

"One moment, ma'am," Donovan said to the nurse. He beckoned for Grace to come close, and she quickly complied. "I love you, Grace. I also vote yes. And one more thing. Would you be kind enough to retrieve the letter from my parents so the next time I'm awake, we can read it together?" he whispered in her ear.

"I promise."

Grace returned to her house for a few hours that night, leaving strict orders with the hospital to call if there was the slightest change in Donovan's condition. She washed the clothes from his bag as well as some of hers. Then she repacked for both of them, left a message with her neighbor asking her to retrieve her mail while she was away, watered her plants, took a shower, and returned to the hospital before dawn broke over the horizon.

At five a.m., Doctor Karl checked in. "I've taken him off the sedatives. He'll be coming around soon. If possible, I want him awake and communicative on the trip so he can keep me informed on how he's doing. His vitals are... amazingly stable for a man in his condition." He looked at her and smiled. "Whatever you're doing, Mrs. Bradshaw, keep doing it. You were right about his ability to beat the odds. When he was brought in, I didn't think he would last twelve hours, much less three days. I have no idea how this young man is still with us, but my best guess is sheer willpower. But the pain he's enduring is so excruciating that it easily sends his body into a state of shock. We need to avoid that. I'll be back in an hour, and we'll start getting him prepped to go."

"Thank you, Doctor," Grace said, but as he started to leave, she called after him. "Ben and Callie don't know that Donovan and I are married yet. With everything going on, it's not the right time to tell them. So..."

"It's just Grace then." He smiled, then gestured with

pinched fingers across his closed lips as if zipping them together. With a smile and nod, he headed out the door.

Fifteen minutes later, Donovan stirred, eventually opening his eyes.

"Time to hit the road," she announced with a smile. "Bags all packed and ready."

He took several deep breaths, and she could see the pain ignite, but it didn't appear to be as potent as she'd observed the last time he awoke.

As his gaze focused on her, a look of concern wrinkled his brow. "Grace, as always, you look beautiful, but exhausted. Have you slept at all?"

"A little. I'll sleep when you're better." She winked at him. "Preferably with you beside me. Let that be motivation to hold on," she flirted with a laugh.

"It certainly is." He returned her wink and set his hand on hers.

"For now, I brought you something." She reached behind her and retrieved the letter he'd requested from the small side table. She held it out for him to see. "Still up for reading it? We've got time before the doctor comes to take you to the ambulance."

He blew a breath through his lips. "If you'll do the honors."

She tore the envelope and pulled the small single sheet of paper from it. Clearing her throat, she retook his hand before reading it aloud.

Donovan, Word has come to us concerning your return to the States and retirement from active service. Your name, as well as your acts of valor, are spoken of with the highest regard.

The manner of our parting was most regrettable. It is our wish to set matters right before more time is lost. Kindly consider returning this correspondence or paying us a visit at your earliest convenience.

    Your parents,
    Ivan and Clarice Bradshaw

Grimacing, Grace lowered the letter. "Why not just come out and say 'sorry, son' and 'we're so proud of you'? Why all the cryptic, fancy talk?"

"Believe it or not, that was rather direct and informal for my parents. Now you see what I mean when I say that there's not much warmth there. Talking to them has always felt like a business transaction."

Raising the letter and scanning it, Grace shrugged. "Still, the sentiment is there. I think they are sorry and want to reconnect. Interested?"

Donovan deliberated for a moment. "It doesn't sound like they know about my injuries, and I'd like to keep it that way. I'm not convinced much has changed, but perhaps it warrants at least one phone call, just in case things don't work out as we hope. But I have a condition. Something that requires your approval."

Grace tilted her head in curiosity.

"I want to tell them about us, that I'm married to the most lovely, compassionate woman in the world."

Grace smiled. "How can I possibly refuse?"

Ten minutes later, Donovan hung up the phone and sighed, relaxing into his pillow. He'd done his best to speak with a steady voice, though if his parents knew him at all,

Grace was sure they had to know something wasn't right. As she'd listened to his side of the conversation, she'd smiled at his glowing description of her and the happiness he felt at their marriage.

Near the end of the conversation, her eyes had moistened as she heard his final statements. "Mother, Father, I want you to know I don't hold anything against you. I know you were afraid for me, worried about what could happen, and that fear motivated your decisions. I'm grateful for all you taught me, gave me. I'm happy and loved, and I wish the same for you, always."

When he'd hung up, very cautiously, Grace wrapped her arms around him and put her head on his shoulder. "I'm proud of you. That had to be hard. What did they say?"

"Not much. I think they were stunned I called, and I'm sure it came across as a final goodbye. I didn't want to leave anything unsaid. They want to meet you."

Grace raised her head to look at him. "Really?"

Donovan chuckled, then winced, exhausted by the energy he'd expended. "Very much. That was the most enthusiastic request I think I've ever heard from my parents."

"Are you glad you read the letter, called?"

He ran his fingers through her hair, smiling at the pleasure of having her so close. "It was awkward, and I'm not sure what might come of it if I do survive and become Succouri, but I won't have regrets either way, and that's what's important."

She softly kissed him. "Well, I'm incredibly proud of you, and I'm not afraid to say it straight out, no fancy talk or hidden messages."

Weakly grinning, he raised his eyebrows. "You're next,

Mrs. Bradshaw. When this is over, I want to meet your family, disfunction and all."

"Ugh," she said putting her face back onto his shoulder. "I suppose fair is fair, but don't say I didn't warn you."

DONOVAN DID his best not to visibly react to the sharp pains that shot through his body at every bump and shake as they loaded him in and out of the ambulance, wheeled him onto the plane, and transferred him to the onboard bed. Though he was immensely grateful for the heroic efforts everyone was making to save his life, as he felt his body weakening by the hour, he privately harbored serious doubts that he'd survive long enough to benefit from them, even with Ben's help.

When the medics had secured him, attaching his monitors to the onboard computer, connecting his IV, and buckling three tight straps around his torso and legs, one of them patted his shoulder softly. "I've been doing this job long enough to recognize that look of agony, Mr. Bradshaw. Hang in there. Wherever you're going, I'm praying relief is waiting for you."

"Thank you," he replied, offering the kind man a weak smile.

As Ben and Callie had informed him, a young girl was also being transported on the flight, and when the medics moved out of the way, she offered Donovan a friendly smile from her bed across the aisle. The space was tight inside the cabin, so there was only a few feet of distance between them.

"Hi," she greeted, her dark eyes shining with excitement. "I'm Allie Hughes. And you are..."

"Donovan, ma'am. Nice to meet you."

The girl looked to be about fifteen, but her eyes held a wisdom beyond her years.

"How'd you get hurt, if you don't mind me asking?"

"I was a soldier."

Her eyes grew large with admiration, and she leaned toward him. "So, you're a genuine hero. Are you Ben's friend?"

"Affirmative." Donovan was surprised by the question, as he was sure the girl couldn't have spoken to Ben and Callie for more than a few minutes, yet she spoke of them as if they were her good friends.

With a sigh of relief, she leaned back and relaxed, her long dark hair framing her face. "Then you'll be okay." She turned to look him in the eyes. "Thank you for what you did for our country, Mr. Donovan. I'm glad you'll be better soon."

Puzzled, yet encouraged by the girl's confidence, Donovan smiled at her kindness. "It was my pleasure to serve, Miss Hughes."

Allie looked toward the group of people gathered near the back of the plane. She pointed at Grace. "Is she your sweetheart?"

"She is, indeed," he said with pride.

"She's beautiful. She looks just like a princess. I thought she was your girlfriend because she keeps watching you with that look." Allie giggled. "Like you're the only person in the whole world she can see." She leaned toward him and put a hand to the side of her mouth. "She's totally in love with you, Mr. Donovan," she whispered. "Same as Callie with Ben."

Despite his pain, Donovan chuckled, thoroughly enchanted with this spunky, sweet girl. "That's very reas-suring since I'm head over heels in love with her."

Allie put both hands to her heart. "Oh my goodness! How romantic! Then you must get better soon so you can marry her."

"I'll do my best," Donovan replied, surprised at how easy his smile came now.

The doctor approached and began taking notes and asking questions, but before anyone else joined them, Allie leaned over the side of her bed and whispered once more to him. "A wedding where a handsome hero marries a gorgeous princess. Now that's something I'd really like to see. I hope you'll invite me."

"You'll be at the top of the list," Donovan promised.

Throughout the flight, much more in the way of entertainment came from the opposite side of the aisle, and the distraction kept Donovan from focusing on his growing discomfort. As the girl had a defective heart, Ben had to step in and use his gift to keep her stable during takeoff, which led to the revelation that both the girl and her mother, Jessica Hughes, already knew about the Succouri. Though Donovan didn't catch the details regarding how or why, Allie's mother was noticeably antagonistic toward Ben despite the life-saving assistance he gave her daughter. Allie, on the other hand, was delighted, not only with Ben but with Callie's younger brother Lee, who had also joined them for the trip.

By the time Ben finally turned his attention to Donovan, he already looked tired, both from the aid he'd offered Allie, but also because of the hostile encounter with Jessica.

"No one told me this trip would be so entertaining," Donovan chuckled. "I'm alright, Ben. Take a break and recharge. You've earned it."

Grace stayed close by, but she was quiet, and Donovan's concern grew. Something about the whole plan was eating at her, something she didn't want to burden him with.

When the doctor stepped away from his bedside for a moment, Donovan took her hand. "Grace, please, tell me what's troubling you," he implored in a whisper, trying not to disturb the card game between Lee and Allie taking place just feet from them.

She shook her head. "Just a little tired and…"

"And?"

"And I can see the pain in your eyes, and I hate it! I feel selfish, asking you to continue to endure it just because I can't lose you. I'm sorry."

Though she spoke the truth, Donovan still felt as if there were more to it than she was admitting.

"Do you remember what I told you after we…?" he winked at her.

She nodded.

"I meant it. To have a chance at a future with you, I'll gladly bear all of this and more. And besides, I wouldn't have made it this long without the strength you've given me through your unwavering faith. I'm still here because of you, Grace. Keep believing so I have cause to go on."

Lifting his hand to her cheek, she smiled. "You will make it, soldier. But I'm still sorry for the struggle, the misery this is causing you."

Donovan turned his hand to softly stroke her cheek. "Let's hope that someday soon, this is all a distant memory. I…" At that moment, his head began pounding so intensely that a groan escaped his lips before he had a chance to stifle it.

"Donovan!" Grace nearly shouted in panic.

The next thing Donovan remembered was the soothing relief of Ben's healing as it spread to every corner of his body. He exhaled in a sudden puff of air as if he'd been holding his breath for a long time.

"Good. Breathe, Donovan," Ben encouraged.

"His blood pressure dropped dangerously low," Doctor Karl informed them. "Let me try something. Keep ahold of him for a minute until this has a chance to circulate. Then we'll see if it does the trick."

Donovan kept his eyes closed, unashamedly grasping the moment of paradise Ben offered him. If he did make it, get his cure, for the rest of his life he would never take one moment of wellness for granted.

As Ben watched Donovan's face, he smiled. "You're going to be an extraordinary Succouri, my friend. I don't think there's anyone who's endured pain like you have. Even after years have gone by without feeling any, I'm betting you'll still easily relate to those who are suffering. And unlike me, you also know exactly what the receiving side of this gift feels like, so you'll be able to offer those you help a special kind of empathy. I'm looking forward to working beside you, partnering together to help people."

"It would be an honor."

"Alright, Ben, let go. Let's see if this works," the doctor instructed nervously.

Within seconds, the throbbing resumed, and the doctor exclaimed frantically, "Not working!"

Ben grabbed ahold of his arm again, and the doctor went back to work, trying to find the right combination of medication.

When the second try was again unsuccessful, Grace came up beside Ben. "Donovan, please hold on."

But he could make her no promises. Being pulled back and forth, from agony to ecstasy was horrifying. The sensation of his insides coming apart was spreading, invading his mind, and without Ben's healing, he was sure he couldn't tolerate it.

When the doctor at last warily instructed Ben to let go, the throbbing resumed, but with slightly less fervor.

"That's it!" the doctor exclaimed with a sigh. "Still a little low, but acceptable."

Donovan strongly disagreed. He wanted to unashamedly beg his friend for just a few more moments of sweet relief, but he held his tongue.

Ben placed his hand gently on his shoulder. "I'll be nearby. Try to rest. We're almost there." His voice was strained, and Donovan knew that the intensity of the draw had informed Ben of how serious his condition was.

Leaning down, Grace put her cheek on his. "It's worse now, isn't it?" she whispered.

He struggled to take a breath. "I'm not going to make it, Grace. I'm sorry."

"Here's what I need you to do, soldier. Focus on breathing. That's it, nothing else. Don't talk or think. Just breathe with me, one more time and then another and then another."

She inhaled slowly next to his ear, and he breathed with her, in and out. Someone spoke to her, but Donovan didn't try to listen. He just obeyed her and kept breathing until his world faded to black.

CHAPTER 15

NIGHT OF SORROWS

Grace hugged her arms around herself, chilled by the cool temperature in Doctor Navarro's clandestine lab. Though it had been touch-and-go the whole way, thanks to the expertise of the Succouri doctor who had met them in Baltimore, they'd made it to Cape Cod in one piece.

Upon meeting Doctor Navarro, Grace relaxed as he had a contagiously calm demeanor that inspired confidence as well as a compassionate touch. After landing at the private airport, she and Donovan were loaded into an ambulance by two paramedics who were part of the Succouri network. The young men treated them as if they were family, expressing excitement for Donovan's upcoming transformation and healing. After a short drive, they'd arrived at the doctor's home.

When they'd passed through the front entry, walked down a long hallway, and entered a room with a locked door, Grace found herself standing in a space that looked like it belonged in a state-of-the-art medical facility. The floors and walls were bright white. Medical equipment of every shape and size lined a large portion of the back wall and left side, and there were several workstations around the room, equipped with microscopes and computers.

They'd settled Donovan in a private corner on the far right near the back of the room. Everything in the room was on wheels, which made it easy for the doctor to retrieve what he needed to connect Donovan to various monitoring equipment.

"He's doing well," the doctor announced after rechecking Donovan's vitals. "We'll keep him sleeping and still until right before the transfer. That gives him the best shot and keeps him from suffering needlessly." He turned and looked directly at Grace. "Doctor Karl left a note in his chart about the positive impact of your presence on his condition." He patted her shoulder. "Love is more powerful than medicine sometimes. Keep giving him a reason to stay with us."

Callie put an arm around Grace's shoulders. "We did it, Gracie. We're here. He's still with us. We—"

Grace stiffened as she watched Callie's face drain of color. From the other side of the lab, Lee shouted her name, but Callie had already turned and was running toward him and Ben, Grace following a few steps behind.

In the chaos, she didn't see exactly what happened, but the next thing Grace knew, Ben lay on the ground, pale and unmoving, as Lee leaned over him. Callie stood with her hand over her heart, frozen and silent.

Doctor Navarro responded quickly, kneeling to check Ben's pulse. "He's alive, but his pulse is thready."

Pained for her friend and utterly confused, Grace didn't know what to do or say. She thought Succouri couldn't get sick, much less faint.

As Callie continued to stand, dazed and horrified, the

doctor and Lee lifted Ben off the floor and carried him to a nearby hospital bed. As the doctor examined Ben, Lee returned and put an arm around Callie's shoulders. She kept her distance from Ben's bed, believing his collapse was somehow her fault and that she'd cause him more harm if she got too close.

After attaching monitors to Ben's arms and chest, the doctor stepped back, shaking his head in confusion. "I don't understand. Succouri don't pass out."

"This one does," Lee announced. "This is the third time this has happened in the last two weeks."

Taken aback by this revelation, Grace glanced at Callie. Why hadn't they mentioned this to her and Donovan? With horror, Grace began to wonder if helping Donovan and the young girl during the flight had precipitated the collapse. Maybe Ben had pushed himself too far, as he'd admitted to doing before. But less than an hour ago, he'd been fine; perhaps tired but not unwell. And, if this was a normal consequence of overusing his gift, why was Callie so upset as was the doctor who knew all about the phenomenon?

At the doctor's prompting, Callie did her best to explain, describing two separate instances in the last couple of weeks when Callie had struggled to wake Ben up, the second episode requiring Taylor's assistance to bring him around.

"Also, two days ago, he had a headache while using his gift; a severe one." A tear traced down Callie's cheek, and she held her hands to her stomach as if she were feeling ill.

Without having to ask, Grace knew the headache had occurred when he'd been helping Donovan at the hospital. She'd thought Ben looked distressed, but as that had been the first time she'd ever seen him use his gift, she assumed his reaction was normal.

"And each episode of unconsciousness was predicated by the use of his gift sometime that day?" the doctor inquired.

Lee and Callie nodded.

Now, Grace began to feel sick. Though desperate to keep Donovan alive, she didn't want harm to come to Ben or Callie. For too many days she'd been living the nightmare of watching the man she loved lying helpless and suffering in a hospital bed. She didn't wish that torture on anyone, much less her best friend. And she'd begun to love Ben like a brother, his faithful devotion to Callie and Donovan easily earning him a special place in her heart.

Despairingly, Grace went to stand beside her friend and put a hand on her shoulder. "Cal, I'm sorry. I hope this isn't because he helped Donovan or Allie. I didn't know he wasn't well."

Doctor Navarro stepped away from Ben's bed, and when he returned, he carried a small syringe. He poked the needle into Ben's arm, and when blood gushed into the tube, everyone in the room gasped.

"I don't understand," Grace whispered to Lee.

"Succouri don't bleed like that," Lee explained. "They heal so quickly that there's never more than a trace."

Putting a hand to her head, Grace felt dizzy. There was so much she didn't know about the life she and Donovan were about to embrace. Or, at least, the one they had been about to embrace. Without Ben, the plan for saving Donovan fell apart.

Abruptly, Lee grabbed ahold of Callie, and Grace looked up to see her friend swaying unsteadily. She rushed to retrieve a nearby chair and pull it over to her, and Callie sat with her arms hugged around herself, looking as sick as Grace felt.

Just then, Agent Taylor entered the lab with a woman who looked like she could be his older sister. They both halted and stared in surprise when they took in the scene. Doctor Navarro called the woman over and she began assisting him, but Taylor came up beside Grace, Lee, and Callie.

"What happened?" he whispered to Grace.

"Ben collapsed. The doctor's trying to figure out what's happening."

Though distressed, Taylor didn't look surprised.

"And Donovan?"

"He's stable for now. Thank you for your help the other night, Agent Taylor. I don't know what I would have done if you hadn't given me your number."

"I was glad to be of help, and I'm encouraged he's hanging on. That part is your doing. I knew you were precisely what he needed to get through this." He sent her a look that made her wonder just how much Agent Taylor knew about her and Donovan's relationship.

Before he left the room to study Ben's bloodwork, Doctor Navarro stopped to offer Callie words of encouragement. "We're going to get some answers. Hang in there. Ben needs you to stay strong. He loves you and he'll fight to get back to you. But you need to be strong for him too."

Despite her tears, Callie nodded, but soon after the doctor left, she reached up and grabbed Grace by the arm. "I'm going to be sick," she said frantically.

Understanding her need, Grace took her arm and ran with her to the nearby bathroom. As her heart ached, Grace rubbed Callie's back helplessly as she knelt doubled over the toilet, emptying everything in her. Though the severity of the reaction puzzled Grace, over the last few days as she had watched Donovan's agony, she'd frequently felt sick to her stomach, so it wasn't difficult to empathize.

When the vomiting at last ceased, the two women sat weeping, confused and desperate for answers. Weariness from many days without much sleep weighed her down and made it hard for Grace to offer her friend much except a comforting shoulder.

Grace put a hand on Callie's forehead. "Cal, you're burning up. Are you sick, or is this because of Ben?"

"I can't get sick, Gracie. Not like that anyway."

"We need to get you back to Doctor Navarro."

Callie shook her head. "No, please. I want him to stay focused on Ben and Donovan. If Ben gets better, I will too. If he doesn't, there's nothing the doctor can do for me."

Grace's eyes grew large, and she was sure she must have misunderstood what her friend was implying. "What are you saying?"

"I've suspected for a while, but now I'm certain. My fate is linked with Ben's, and I wouldn't want it any other way."

Grace sat back on her heels, staring at Callie in disbelief. "How... how can that be, and how do you know that for sure?"

"I can't explain it, but every cell in my body knows it's true. It's like... like knowing you'll die if you don't breathe. You don't need proof to accept that fact."

"Is that... Is that always how it is with Succouri and their partners?" Grace couldn't believe Ben would have missed telling them this important detail when he outlined the costs of accepting the gift.

Callie shook her head. "Maggie lost Owen over a year ago, and Louis lost his Succouri gift over fifteen years ago. Maggie and Ms. Essie may be heartbroken, but their bodies are fine." Grace was lost as she didn't know all of the people

Callie referenced, but she wondered if Maggie was the woman who'd walked in with Taylor.

"So, this is because of Ben's... unique situation? I don't understand."

"Because Ben became Succouri when he was very young, it altered his personality and biology. It's not just an addition to his identity, like it usually is. It runs all the way through his being. Because he's different, he needed a different kind of partner, someone who could also be altered to become his perfect companion. I haven't put all the pieces together yet, but I think the constant inflow of strength I've received from him because of my blindness since the first day he touched me may have provided the opportunity for an accelerated bonding and a more permanent one too."

Overwhelmed, Grace fell silent as she tried to process Callie's explanation. When she spoke again, she couldn't raise her voice above a whisper. "Does Ben know?"

Momentarily closing her eyes, Callie shook her head. "I haven't been one hundred percent sure about it until now, and I knew he wouldn't like it. He'll be devastated by this and take the blame upon himself, even though I'm not upset about it in the least, and there was no way he could have known. Since we found out about his altered physiology, his greatest fear has been harming me in some way."

"And you're absolutely sure about this?"

"I am," Callie said, not a hint of regret in her tone.

"Cal, you need to tell the doctor. He may need this information to help Ben, and certainly, he needs it to help you."

Reluctantly, Callie nodded. "You're right. But I'll wait for the right moment when Ben and Donovan don't require his full attention."

Grace took a deep breath and let it out. "I'm here, girly. We're all here with you. You're not alone, and I believe Ben will get better and come back to you."

They embraced, comforting each other in a moment of shared fear and pain. None of this made sense to Grace, but she knew probing Callie for answers right now wasn't what she needed as she was also confused and afraid.

Despite the risk to Ben and to herself, for the last three days, Callie had encouraged him to use his gift to help Donovan. There was no greater proof of true love and friendship than that.

When they left the bathroom, Lee took Callie's arm and Grace went to check on Donovan, needing a moment to refocus and settle her own thoughts as well as her stomach. What had started out as a straightforward plan had suddenly become a confounded mess of confusion and heartbreak. Now, she not only faced losing Donovan, but maybe Ben and Callie as well. The very phenomenon that was supposed to miraculously save the life of her husband was killing her friends.

Though Callie unquestioningly believed in the goodness of the gift, Ben certainly had lingering resentments about his involuntary transformation, which was why it was important to him that Donovan had as much knowledge as possible before making a choice. But there was still so much they didn't know, and her tired brain couldn't sort it all out.

Pulling a chair close to his bed, she took his hand and pressed it to her cheek, comforted by his nearness. She wished he was awake so she could talk with him, but at the same time, she was thankful he wasn't. If Ben didn't recover soon, any hope for saving Donovan would disappear, and she didn't want him to give in to despair and stop fighting. A tear traced down her face as she wondered how she would ever survive losing him.

Shortly after Grace returned to Callie's side, the doctor returned and delivered his analysis. "Perhaps not all of you know this, but Ben isn't like any other Succouri I've ever known. The Succouri and human biology in Ben are inseparable; merged in a way that can't be undone. As I told Ben and Callie several weeks ago, I don't understand how the blood he possesses keeps him alive as it is so drastically altered by the Succouri modifications that it no longer resembles human blood much at all. His body, his brain, and likely his personality and character are shaped by this integration wherein neither identity dominates nor subjugates the other. But it is also the case that neither can function independently. Ben is biologically Succouri in the truest sense of the word. Though science can't explain it, practical observation informs us that whatever the delicate balance is within his body, it's effective as we all gratefully witness him function and thrive. Though I need more time to perform a detailed analysis, what I was able to observe is a retreat or perhaps a dormancy of the Succouri markers in his blood. I can't be sure which is accurate; whether the decrease is a result of a withdrawal, an inexplicable departure of the Succouri presence in his body, or"—he paused to release a distressed sigh—"it is possible that the Succouri in him is becoming inert, whether temporarily or permanently, I can't say."

"Is this..." Taylor started, rubbing his forehead. "Could this be the ripening, like he's at the end of his time as Succouri?"

"Unlikely. Since Ben's system is integrated with the Succouri additive, I don't believe Ben will ever enter the ripening stage or pass along his Succouri."

"Does he need a new infusion of Succouri additive?" the older woman who came in with Taylor asked.

"No one can become Succouri twice, and that's doubly true for Ben. His body wouldn't accept it. Each Succouri is unique, distinctive. Ben has been adapted to accommodate this particular Succouri. Introducing a different one into his system would be like trying to inoculate someone against a specific virus by administering a vaccine designed for an entirely different virus. The effort would be fruitless. There's something systemically wrong here. The Succouri in him is not doing its job."

"What do we do, Doctor?" Taylor asked, shifting the focus away from the painful revelations. "How do we figure out why the Succouri is retreating or falling silent, and how do we fix it?"

"From what Callie told me, this state of unconsciousness is likely temporary, but it seems to be lasting longer each time and it's becoming increasingly difficult to revive him. Each episode occurred subsequent to Ben using his gift. Therefore, until we know a lot more, without exception, Ben must abstain from offering his strength to anyone."

"He's already made us that promise," Callie said. "He promised Taylor and me he wouldn't use his gift again unless one of us were in trouble."

"Under *no* circumstances, Callie," the doctor emphasized. "Using his gift accelerates the decline. He won't like this prohibition and may fight us on it. Even though the Succouri in him is waning, the need and drive to reach out are ingrained in his character. Despite that, we need to protect him from himself to buy him the time needed to figure this out."

Everyone nodded, agreeing to do their part in saving

Ben from his own destruction, but Grace's heart pounded. If Donovan took another sudden turn for the worse, Ben would no longer be able to save him.

"And if we can't wake up the Succouri in Ben, what are the other options?" Taylor asked.

For a long moment, the doctor just shook his head, his tortured eyes avoiding everyone's inquiring gaze.

"Agent Taylor, there are no other options. Ben is fundamentally Succouri. Just as it would be if his human body failed, if the Succouri in Ben ceases to function, Ben won't survive."

And that means neither will Donovan, Grace thought as tears ran unashamedly down her face.

Four hours later, the lab was quiet save for the low buzzing of computers and the rhythmic beeps of Donovan's heart monitor. Though everyone had tried numerous times to convince both women to rest and eat, neither had obliged. Despite their efforts to comfort one another, the weight of each woman's sorrows and anxieties was so heavy that, ultimately, neither had much strength left to share. Grace didn't want to say anything to add to Callie's heartache, and she guessed the same was true for her friend.

"Grace." The woman who'd come in with Taylor approached as she sat by Donovan's bedside, setting a hand gently on her arm. "I'm Maggie. I'm a nurse, and Wes's... well, mother, in a way. Not biological, but by means of the heart." She smiled and her greenish-brown eyes shone with pride. "I wanted to check on both of you. Are you alright?"

Warm and genuine, the woman's kind demeanor put Grace at ease. Still, it surprised Grace that she considered herself a mother to Agent Taylor as they looked to be about the same age.

Doing her best to smile, Grace nodded, knowing if she spoke, her voice would betray her fears and exhaustion.

After checking on Donovan's condition, Maggie pulled a nearby folding chair over and sat beside Grace. "His blood pressure is on the low side, but he's breathing easy, and the sedative is keeping him comfortable. Wes told me all about him," she said as she looked at Donovan with admiration. "I can't wait to meet him and thank him for his service and sacrifice. What a worthy candidate for this extraordinary life!" She returned her gaze to Grace. "You love him very much," she stated with confidence.

"He's... he's a rare, genuinely good man. I didn't think I'd ever be lucky enough to find someone like him." Grace lowered her head.

Leaning forward, Maggie set her hand on Grace's. "Don't despair. As long as he's still with us, there is hope." She paused to study Grace's face. "If anything changes, even just a little, these monitors will alert us. There's no way for you to miss anything. If he does wake up in distress, he's going to need your strength and cool head. If you get a little rest now, you'll have that to give him."

Grace shook her head. "I can't leave him."

Maggie pointed to an oversized cushioned chair a few yards away. "You could rest right there. I promise to check on him every thirty minutes without fail. Even an hour or two of sleep will make a difference in what you can offer him."

Though she intended to protest again, when she looked into Maggie's pleading eyes, Grace knew she was right. Her mind and body were so tired that she could barely hold her head up or process simple thoughts.

"Come with me, brave girl," Maggie said, seeing the surrender in Grace's eyes. She put an arm around Grace's shoulders and helped her to her feet. They walked together to the chair, and when Grace had settled, Maggie covered her with a blanket. The woman's voice carried such tenderness and compassion that Grace now understood how Taylor had easily adopted her as a mother figure.

When she took one last worried look toward Donovan's bed, Maggie retreated, sitting in the seat Grace had vacated. "I'll sit here for a while, and I or the doctor will be nearby. I promise."

Grace pulled her legs up into the large chair and leaned her head back. Though she was sure she wouldn't be able to sleep, within seconds, the world faded away and she dreamed of him, his eyes bright and his smile full. He lifted her into his arms, laughing at her surprise. "You're the one, the only one, Grace Sophia. Never forget me, and how much I loved you."

He set her back on her feet, kissed her lips, and began to walk away as a fog closed in around him.

"Donovan! Where are you going?"

"Where there's no more pain."

"But I—"

As the fog surrounded him, she caught one last glimpse of his peaceful smile. "Please. It's time to let me go. If you love me, don't ask me to keep suffering."

Taking a step toward him, she put out her hand but then lowered it. His expression was serene, and, for once, there wasn't a hint of torment in his eyes. More than anything, she wanted him to be happy. If the price of acquiring that was letting him go, she resolved to pay it.

"Grace, no!," came a familiar voice from behind her. She

spun around and looked into Ben's striking blue eyes. "Don't let him go."

"But you can't help him anymore. The plan has fallen apart, and I can't keep asking him to suffer."

Ben took a step toward her and put out a hand, bidding her to hear him out. "It might appear that way, but things aren't always as they seem. Donovan is exceptional, brave, and good, and because of that, he's been chosen. He has a role to play that is indispensable, as do you. You must keep him alive as only you can, Grace."

Turning back to Donovan, her heart pounded as the fog had nearly overtaken him.

"Hurry!" Ben urged, but when she turned her head to look at him, he was gone.

Rushing forward, Grace caught Donovan's arm. "Sorry, soldier. I can't let you go. The battle isn't over yet. You must keep fighting."

A piercing sound jolted her from sleep. For several seconds, she was disoriented, unsure of where she was. As she looked around, trying to get her bearings, she was surprised to see Ben awake, standing next to his bed. Doctor Navarro and Maggie rushed into the room and headed straight for Donovan, their actions at last enlightening Grace to the source of the noise. Not wishing to interfere with their efforts, she stayed behind them, trying to catch glimpses of Donovan's monitor as well as his face. The doctor calmly directed Maggie, and she responded, moving adeptly around the lab to grab medication and equipment. Although they didn't appear to have met until just hours ago, they worked together fluently.

As soon as an understanding of what was happening registered in Ben's expression, he rushed toward them, but Taylor and Lee stepped in front of him, blocking his way.

Though her focus remained on Donovan, she was vaguely aware of a tense standoff that ensued as Ben insisted on being permitted to help Donovan but both men held their ground as Callie pleaded with him to understand why he couldn't risk using his gift.

Overtaken by anxiety, Grace covered her face with her hands, understanding why they blocked his path, but wishing desperately that Ben could intervene. In that dreadful moment, the tragedy playing out before everyone's eyes broke each heart in the room.

After handing the doctor a vial of medication he'd requested, Maggie stepped back, put an arm around Grace, and pulled her forward. "Talk to him."

At first, she didn't know what more to say as she'd offered dozens of appeals for him to hang on in recent days. But then, she remembered her dream. As if it occurred in the realm of reality, she remembered every detail in vivid color and sound. The prophecy Ben had spoken about Donovan repeated on a loop in her mind.

Leaning down, she pressed her cheek to his, speaking in a whisper. "Because you're exceptional, you've been chosen. You have a job to do, more people who need your protection. You must survive. I know you want to rest, but you can't give up. Keep fighting."

She stepped back, and Maggie smiled at her before resuming her efforts with the doctor. An arm encircled her shoulders, but she didn't look away from Donovan to see who it was.

A few minutes later, the doctor shut off the alarm but continued observing Donovan carefully for a time before at last releasing a breath. "He's alright for now, but we're running out of time." He shifted his gaze to Grace. "Whatever you said made a difference. It was as if he'd decided to give up but suddenly changed his mind."

"No matter how dim, you don't let the light die," Grace mumbled to herself.

"Oh, Gracie." Callie sighed next to her, and Grace looked over in surprise, realizing it was her friend who'd come to comfort her.

"Where's Ben? Is he—"

"He'll be alright," Callie assured, but her wobbly smile betrayed her worry. "I'm sorry he couldn't help."

Turning, she put her head on Callie's shoulder, and Callie leaned on her as well. Releasing hours of pent-up emotions, they gave in to a steady stream of healing tears. The dark night they'd endured was one of the worst Grace had ever faced and she was sure Callie felt the same way. But if Ben was awake and recovered, perhaps a spark of hope still flickered amidst the long shadows of deep despair. She couldn't shake the words he'd spoken to her in the dream, and though it made no sense, the prophetic pronouncement gave her something to cling to as the storm continued to rage around them all.

CHAPTER 16

WAITING AND WONDERING

A short time later, Maggie brought Grace a plate of breakfast.

"Is it morning?" Grace asked with surprise. There were no windows in the lab, and she hadn't looked at her watch in hours.

"Early, but yes."

Though her stomach still felt queasy, Grace ate a few bites.

"Do you know what's going on?" Grace hadn't left Donovan's side, which limited her knowledge of what was happening with the rest of the group, particularly Ben and Callie.

"Lee went to talk with Ben." Maggie paused to shake her head. "None of this makes sense to me, but apparently Ben and Callie are both gravely ill and their conditions are connected somehow. Between finding out about Callie's illness and being prevented from helping Donovan, Ben was distraught, to say the least. It goes against a Succouri's nature to withhold assistance. It's something they can't abide." She sighed. "Still, because of Ben's unique situation, much of this is different from my experience, so I'm almost as confused as you are."

Lowering her fork, Grace considered the kind woman's troubled expression. "So, you were bonded, the partner of a Succouri?"

"I was. Actually, the Succouri Ben presently possesses once indwelled my husband, if that's the right way of describing it."

"But, I thought Taylor—"

"My husband, Owen, passed his gift on to Wes, but after just a few days, Wes inadvertently passed it to Ben." She laughed. "I still haven't figured out how that happened as we were always told children could not become Succouri."

As she recalled Callie and Ben's description of the forty-year term of service, Grace straightened. "But you look so... Maggie, I don't mean to be rude, but may I ask, how old are you?"

Maggie smiled. "I just turned eighty."

Aghast, Grace shook her head in disbelief. "But... you look... You don't look like you could be more than sixty, if that."

"Extended youthfulness is a benefit of the gift, particularly for the partner. During the forty years Owen and I served together, neither of us aged much at all. After Owen passed his Succouri to Wes, the years caught up to him quickly, but that wasn't the case for me, which is a blessing and a curse." She lowered her head. "Living without him doesn't feel much like living most days."

Astounded, Grace shook her head as she wondered what other marvels Ben and Callie had left out in their abridged description of the phenomenon.

"Were you ever sick?"

"Not a single day during our forty years of service."

So, Callie had been right in her assessment that her sudden, acute illness was atypical. As Ben's situation was an anomaly, Maggie was assuredly a more representative source for learning about what life as Succouri would be like for her and Donovan.

Leaning back in her chair, Grace contemplated before asking her next question. "Did you know your husband before he became Succouri?"

"Knew him, yes, but we hadn't dated. He worked undercover for the FBI just as Wes did. It was dangerous work that landed him in the hospital far too often; that is, before he acquired that superhuman healing. I was employed there and treated his injuries on several occasions. The moment our eyes met, something powerful ignited between us. But it wasn't until after he became Succouri that we began dating, though one could hardly call it that since we knew at once we were destined to be together, and we married within just a couple of weeks. It's a long story but, like Ben, Owen didn't know what he was at first, and it took a good amount of research before we at last understood what the bond was and why our feelings for one another were so... overwhelming." She smiled. "Not that we minded the mysteries. The experience, our love story, was a thrilling, wondrous, and beautiful adventure, and I wouldn't change a single moment."

Maggie's eyes shone as she spoke of her life with Owen, and Grace found herself captivated by her story. With ease, she could relate to the instant connection Maggie described, as she had felt the same for Donovan and he for her.

"But if he wasn't Succouri when you met him, why do you think you were so strongly drawn to one another?"

Maggie considered Grace's question carefully. "The influence of the Succouri on the man who possesses it is complex, difficult to judge or measure. At times, there can be no doubt that his actions are directed by its promptings, as when it compels him to touch a hurting soul. But in regard to the bond, I believe it is the other way around; the man taking the lead and the Succouri accommodating. After all, it is the human man who is able to love in heart and in flesh. When his heart is touched by a woman, in that special way, I am convinced the Succouri simply cooperates, opening a conduit for the bond. But the foundation is the genuine love of a human man for a human woman. As there are no secrets between the Succouri and its host, it knows with certainty when he's given his heart, chosen the woman he'll love for a lifetime. Until that moment, it won't initiate the bond. And, of course, the woman must love with equal devotion, or the bond won't take. In some cases, like mine and Owen's, and yours and Donovan's, the choice has already been made; the man has already given his heart before the gift comes to him. As soon as the Succouri integrates and detects the pre-existing bond, it proceeds with adding what is necessary for the Succouri partnership. Whatever the timing, genuine, mutual love is the catalyst. Though our life together was assuredly enriched by the Succouri gift, I would have loved Owen just as faithfully without it, and our story would have still been a beautiful one."

Uplifted by Maggie's words, Grace smiled. "So then, I assume you feel the life, the adventure was worth the costs."

As she answered, Maggie shifted her gaze to Donovan. "I wouldn't have had a life with him if the gift hadn't rescued him, saved his life, so it most definitely was worth any and every cost."

The squeak of the lab door redirected their attention. Ben and Callie entered, smiling, their arms around one another. But despite their contentment, their conditions appeared to have worsened, revealed by their pale complexions and the difficulty with which they weakly stumbled to the nearest hospital bed. Maggie patted Grace's hand before hurrying off to assist Doctor Navarro. Taylor and Lee circled around them, and though Grace was curious about what had transpired over the course of the last hour, she gave them privacy as the doctor spoke with them and ran tests. Before leaving the lab, however, Callie approached, and her weary, yet hopeful smile caused Grace to rise from her chair.

"Ben and Lee are going to meet with Ethan. There's still hope."

"I... but... The two of you don't look well. Shouldn't you focus on yourselves right now, trying to figure out why you and Ben are sick?"

"Taylor and I are on that. We're heading to Philly to meet with someone Owen knew. His name is Carozza. We think he might have some answers for us. Apparently, he has knowledge about the Succouri no one else has. We're going to rest up for a short bit, then the four of us will head out."

Unable to hide her relief, Grace sighed and her shoulders relaxed. "Is there anything I can do?" she asked, feeling helpless as her exhausted and ill friends worked to save not only themselves, but Donovan as well.

Callie turned to Donovan and set her hand on his. "Your job is to keep him alive, Gracie. I know your heart would break if anything happened to him, but so would Ben's and so would mine."

Ben joined them and Grace turned her eyes to him, tears of gratitude welling up. "Ben, are you alright?"

Lowering his head, he put an arm around Callie's waist. "I'm sorry I can't help Donovan, Grace. Right now, I can't help anyone, even if my father and Lee would let me. But regardless, I promise to do everything I can to convince Ethan to come back with us, meet the two of you, and save my best friend's life. I don't need Succouri powers for that. I won't let you or him down. This was my idea, and it's my responsibility to see it through."

Moved by the intensity of his expressed regret, Grace shook her head. "What's happened isn't your fault. You've risked, are risking everything. Without the two of you, we would have no hope whatsoever."

Ben looked into her eyes, his deep compassion warming the cold places in her heart. "Donovan wouldn't still be here without your strength and love, Grace. I hadn't realized how severely injured he was and how little time he had left, until we got back from our honeymoon. I don't know exactly what he went through overseas, but if anyone deserves a miracle, it's him. You've bought us time, given him a reason and the will to fight. When we get through this, and we will, the credit will belong to you."

Though she didn't entirely agree, Grace simply smiled, more pleased than ever with Callie's choice of husband. Despite <u>his</u> waning Succouri powers, Grace understood what Callie meant when she spoke of the Succouri's influence on Ben's character. There was something beyond human about the kindness he exhibited. It held no hint of pride, selfishness, or ulterior motives. It was pure and undeniably genuine. If this represented the way the gift impacted those it occupied, no wonder Callie was certain of the Succouri's benevolent nature.

Before they left to get some rest, Grace embraced them, comforted, despite the unknowns, by friendships that were much more than the word adequately conveyed. Ben and Callie were family, closer relations by far than those she'd had growing up. Though she hated the stress their present situation placed on them—especially considering their deteriorating health—there were no two people in the world she trusted more with her and Donovan's fate.

The hours that followed ticked by much too slowly as Grace paced, held Donovan's hand, chatted quietly with Maggie, and periodically rested in the oversized chair. Doctor Navarro worked like a man possessed at one of the workstations on the other side of the lab. Maggie brought her lunch, but she continued to have very little appetite. As she watched him sleep, though grateful he wasn't suffering, her heart ached to talk with him, glimpse his warm brown eyes, and feel his strong arms around her.

Maggie's and Owen's love story had brought her comfort. If Donovan's choice held precedence in the initiation of the bond, their history would seem to ensure that she would become his Succouri partner. But she still worried about how becoming Succouri, adopting a new life and integrating with a mysterious entity, would change the man she'd fallen in love with. Would they still fit together as they had before? Would she be the right kind of person, have the right heart and demeanor, to help him fulfill such a consequential calling?

Though they were dear friends, she and Callie had different personalities. Callie was trusting by nature, and she possessed an innocence that allowed her to immediately see the good in people. In contrast, Grace's upbringing had left her a little rough around the edges and, in some ways, jaded, particularly when it came to her perception of men. Donovan was the first person she'd ever fully trusted with her whole heart. Even if he loved her in the profound way required for the bond to initiate, her significant flaws might disqualify her from a life where service to others was the primary mission.

As she sat stroking his hand, her heart ached at the horrifying possibility that the very cure that would save his life might, in the end, be the cause of their parting. As she touched the spot where her wedding ring lay pressed against her heart, she recognized that, though her heart would break if she lost him, his happiness and well-being were more important to her. Even if it were the only way to keep him with her, she could never wish him a life filled with pain and suffering.

Just before three o'clock, Maggie brought a small basin of warm water and a sponge to Donovan's bedside. "While everyone is away, I thought it might be a good time to..." She nodded toward the items in her hands. "I can take care of this, we can do it together, or I can leave it with you. Whichever you think Donovan would prefer and you feel comfortable with."

"Please, let me do it," Grace replied without hesitation.

Nodding, Maggie set the items on a small table and left the lab. As presently, Doctor Navarro was not in the room either, for the first time since their wedding night, they were alone together. With a kind of love and tenderness she didn't know she possessed, she washed Donovan's body as best she could, bending over to kiss him frequently as the intimacy of the act made her heart ache for his conscious presence. As she washed his scars, she cried anew, replaying the terrifying story of how he'd come by them. Whether Ben's plan succeeded or failed, she was infinitely glad that his suffering was nearly at an end.

After pulling the sheet back over him and retrieving fresh water to wash his face, Grace lovingly traced the scars above his eye and along the side of his cheek. Ben had no scars whatsoever, and she assumed, after the change, Donovan wouldn't either. No more scars meant no more pain. But still, she would never forget them for they were the evidence of his courage and sacrifice, and because of that, as she had told him on their wedding night, each one was indeed beautiful in her sight.

At about five thirty in the afternoon, the door to the lab opened and Taylor, Lee, and Callie entered. As the doctor had resumed his work in the lab shortly after Grace completed her task, he, as well as Maggie and Grace, turned when they entered. When the three of them took in the sight of Callie, they gaped as they couldn't believe their eyes. She looked normal, her face pink with color and her eyes and smile bright.

As the doctor walked toward her, moving slowly as if he wasn't sure what he was seeing was real, he spoke her name in a hoarse voice. Grace also approached, and Taylor smiled reassuringly at her. She was relieved that Callie was back and appeared much improved, but where was Ben?

"Hi, Doctor," Callie said somewhat sheepishly, her smile growing. "It's a very long story, but Ben and I are alright. You can rest easy, though we are infinitely grateful for your efforts."

"What happened?" he asked in a voice drenched with wonderment.

"Let me ask you a question first," Callie said with a light

laugh. "What did you find in my bloodwork from this morning?"

The doctor shook his head as if trying to clear away the confusion. "To my profound surprise, I found traces of Succouri additive. I've never seen that in a Succouri partner before."

Now Callie laughed freely. "It turns out Ben's Succouri wasn't dormant or lost. It was inside of me, at least a small part of it. We still have no idea why that happened, but I've returned it to him, and that seems to have resolved the whole terrible condition, for him and for me."

"But that's impossible," the doctor insisted. "The gift doesn't move around like that, except when it's permanently transferred through blood. And I've never heard of a partner receiving a portion of it." He scratched his head. "I don't understand."

Continuing to smile, Callie turned to Grace. "Remember I told you how, because of Ben's special situation, we get to break all the rules and forge our own path?"

Grace nodded.

"Turns out, I was right about that, more so than I could have imagined." She shifted her attention back to the doctor. "What we learned today revolutionizes everything, Doctor, about the Succouri generally, but also in regard to Ben. I—"

Once more, the door to the lab opened and Ben appeared, looking as healthy and restored as Callie. Behind him, a thin man with tormented light blue eyes, medium brown hair, and a short neatly trimmed beard entered timidly. Grace held her breath, hoping that this might be Ethan Devereaux.

"Is everything alright?" Ben asked with concern as he

swiftly approached the clustered group, while the stranger stayed several steps behind him.

Callie laughed again. "Everything's fine. We're just, once again, bewildering the good doctor here. I've been doing my best to explain what happened today but..."

"While you're at it," Ben chuckled and put up his hands. "Maybe you can explain it to me. I'm still confused by what you told me before I collapsed."

Though Grace tried to keep up, she nevertheless felt lost in the conversation. Ben had collapsed again? Then why did he look completely normal now?

Doctor Navarro slowly approached Ben, staring at him like he didn't recognize him. "You... You're completely recovered? No different from before this all started?" As he asked the question, he put his hand to Ben's forehead, checking for a fever.

With a look of compassion for the doctor's sincere bewilderment, Ben nodded his head. "I am. Better than ever."

Though she was afraid to hope, Grace's heart neverthe-less rejoiced as she assumed this meant he could once again help Donovan if needed.

"Maybe we should start by filling Ben in on what the doctor discovered in my blood work from this morning," Callie said with a sly smile.

Raising his eyebrows, Ben looked at the doctor.

"I... I found Succouri additive. Just a trace, but unmis-takable."

"So, you were right," Ben said, perplexed as he looked at Callie. "You did feel a draw because you had some of my... my gift."

She smiled satisfactorily.

"Though the fact that my wife was, once again, correct

in her assessment doesn't surprise me in the least, I still don't understand how that's possible. No blood was transferred between us."

Taylor and Callie smiled at one another, then Taylor looked at Maggie. "During our visit to your home, Ben brought up a very interesting question."

"I remember," Maggie responded. "He wondered about how the Succouri gift was transferred before modern medicine, before blood transfusions and transplants. None of us knew the answer."

"Right," Taylor said putting up a finger. "But Carozza did. Carozza believes that the Succouri of old, the Antico as he calls them, sought a perfect match, a specific human soul to unite with, whose heart and character were like its own. The terminal triad, made up of the Succouri, the host, and his partner—called a Datouri—had a special destiny, a mission to carry out for the good of humanity. It often took hundreds of years to meet up with him, but the Succouri was determined and strategic, moving from host to host, each transfer bringing it one step closer to the chosen one. Because the Succouri knew the route, but the host did not, Carozza asserts that it was the prerogative of the Antico, not the host, to select the recipients."

Seven confused faces stared at Taylor.

"But if the host didn't know who was next in line"—Lee spoke up—"how did he know who to give blood to?"

"There was no need for a blood transfer," Callie explained. "At the time and place of the Antico's choosing, it moved to the next host in the same way it transfers healing, through touch."

"Are you saying that, in the last couple of weeks, my Succouri was trying to transfer itself to you?" Ben asked, crinkling his brow.

"No. It's still true that a woman can't be Succouri, only Datouri. Why a portion of your Succouri moved into me is still a complete mystery. What we're telling you is the way that small portion transferred to me was by touch. According to Carozza, that's the only way an Antico should ever be transferred."

"But"—Doctor Navarro objected—"in all my years of working with the Succouri, I've never heard of the gift transferring that way. And if it were truly that simple, why does the host enter the ripening stage at all?"

"To alert him, let him know that his time as Succouri is ending, and to begin the process of returning his body to its pre-Succouri state," Taylor explained. "According to Carozza, originally, a host's term was much shorter than what we see nowadays, typically only ten to twenty years. Because of that, the cumulative damaging effects of the draw weren't as severe or permanent. After the Antico departed, the host could go on and live out a normal life-span without significant weakening."

"But that's not what happens," Doctor Navarro argued, looking increasingly distressed as their explanation unfolded. "I've never known anyone who's had the gift for such a short period of time, nor have I known one who hasn't weakened after the transfer." He shook his head. "I'm not sure this source offered you anything of value; just a lot of unsubstantiated myths."

Looking directly into the doctor's eyes, Taylor answered his objection with a tone of empathy. "I would agree with you, save for one thing." He paused and shifted his gaze. "Ben."

All eyes focused on Ben as another silent moment lingered.

"I don't understand," Maggie at last spoke. "At this

point I think we all know that Ben is different than other Succouri, but Owen wasn't, and Ben possesses his… his gift."

Taylor and Callie exchanged a quick glance. "I'd like to speak to Ben privately about his specific situation before saying more on that," Callie said apologetically.

"Alright," the doctor said with a sigh. "If whatever this man told you about Ben convinced you that he was more than a misguided quack, why don't his assertions align with the experiences and observations of anyone I know who presently works with the Succouri?"

For several awkward seconds, neither Taylor nor Callie answered, but at last, Taylor cleared his throat and spoke softly. "Because Carozza passionately believes that our modern imposition, our immoral meddling in the way the gift is transferred, has permanently altered the phenomenon."

Doctor Navarro stepped back and his eyes grew wide. "How?"

"When an Antico undergoes a forced transfer of the host's choosing, it knocks it off course, making it impossible for the Antico to ever meet up with its intended terminal match. As a result, the spirit or will of the Antico essentially dies. It becomes… inanimate, no longer active in plotting its own destiny. Consequently, the gifts it's able to offer its hosts are diminished. In addition, as the Succouri has withdrawn from the transfer process completely and therefore no longer monitors or modifies it, a longer and thus more damaging term plagues the hosts who carry it. And, as if all that weren't bad enough, perhaps the worst consequence of them all is the unfortunate foregoing of the impactful blessing that the destined triad was meant to bestow on mankind."

Though every face in the group expressed alarm, the doctor's look of dismay was particularly acute. "Are you saying that the blood transfers we've been performing for decades have destroyed the Succouri?"

Callie's eyes filled with tears as she answered, trying to take some of the misdirected heat off Taylor. "That's what Carozza believes."

Though Grace was doing her best, her limited pre-existing knowledge of this phenomenon was making it hard for her to follow the conversation. Still, she understood enough to worry about what the discovery meant for their plan with Donovan.

The man who'd entered with Ben came up beside him, speaking at last. "So, if I give my blood to your friend, save his life, I'm killing the Succouri in me?"

Grace's heart lifted and sank simultaneously. So, this man was Ethan Devereaux. Ben had been successful in convincing him to come and it appeared he was willing to offer his gift to Donovan. For the first time in days, a bright light flooded the gloomy recesses of her despairing soul. But as quickly as the light spread, fear over the consequences of what Callie and Taylor had learned that day threatened to extinguish it.

"No!" Callie exclaimed, turning her eyes to Ethan. "This happened long ago, likely many transfers before you received your Succouri. What's done is done. It's no one's fault. If all of this is true, no one knew. No one, at least no one alive today, did this on purpose."

"And the gift is still beautiful," Grace softly reminded them. "It still saves people, helps people."

Reaching out her hand to pat Grace's arm, Callie offered a weak smile. "It certainly does."

Each of them wrestled with doubts, fears, and questions as a long silent moment hung in the air.

Finally, the doctor blew out a breath and lifted his eyes to Taylor. "How many are left?"

"I don't know. I don't think Carozza knew for sure either, but not many. Perhaps only one." Every eye turned to Ben once more, but no one asked the question.

"And there's no way to right the wrong, revive and restore the original... Antico?" There was a desperate plea in the doctor's question.

"Carozza doesn't believe there is, but he was... severe in his judgments, and I'm not sure his mind was open to the possibility."

"If he knew about this, why didn't he tell anyone, warn the network about the consequences?" Maggie asked.

"I'm not exactly sure," Taylor admitted. "It appears Carozza's been mistreated and outright rejected by most who've heard his theories. Even his own family doesn't believe him. Those experiences have made him guarded and distrusting of people generally and of talking about the Succouri specifically. His attitude is decisively harsh, which is a barrier to hearing him out and accepting his theories."

"But you both believe all of it?" Lee asked, glancing between Callie and Taylor.

When Taylor nodded, all eyes shifted to Callie.

Momentarily, Callie closed her eyes, appearing afraid to speak the truth. "Because of what he knew about Ben, yes, I do."

"Where does this leave our situation?" Ethan interjected, looking toward Donovan's bed in the back corner of the room.

"Donovan doesn't have much longer," the doctor said, his voice tight with stress. "Maybe a couple of days, if that."

Grace lowered her head, feeling that the doctor's estimation was overly generous. She wasn't sure Donovan would survive another twenty-four hours.

Ben sighed and looked around at each person in the group. "We're not going to solve this dilemma in that short period of time. We need more information, much more. I'd like to talk with Carozza myself, see what else he might know. But Donovan can't wait for us to get the answers." He turned to Ethan. "If you're still willing, I'd like to introduce the two of you and give you a chance to get acquainted with him and with Grace."

"That's not really necessary."

"Please," Ben gently encouraged, and Ethan reluctantly nodded.

Letting go of Callie's hand, Ben turned to grip the doctor's shoulder. "Doc, you need some rest. If you think he'll be alright to wait until tomorrow for the transfer, then why don't you go get some sleep? Callie and I will stay close by to make sure Donovan remains stable. The rest of you are more than welcome to head to our place in Cape Cod for a full night's sleep as well."

While arrangements were being made, Grace approached Callie. "Are you sure it's safe for Ben to use his gift?"

"One hundred percent sure. We're not going to leave you or Donovan until the transfer, Grace."

With an audible exhale of joy and relief, Grace threw her arms around Callie, and Callie returned the embrace. "What terrible days of worry we've endured, Gracie! But it's almost over. After we speak with Donovan, you need to rest, really rest. Like, in a bed for several hours."

"But—"

"No arguing. You know he's in good hands with us. You deserve and need a break."

"But you haven't slept much either."

"We'll take turns, but you need to be strong and ready as, by this time tomorrow, you'll have the man you love back, healthy and strong." Callie smiled. "And that will only be the start of the greatest adventure you could ever imagine."

CHAPTER 17

HOPE AND HEARTBREAK

The moment his mind breached consciousness, Donovan recognized the welcome sensation of Ben's healing in his veins. Unlike the gradual emerging from medicated slumber, this was abrupt and untainted by the accompanying resumption of pain. Still, his throat was dry, and as he opened his eyes, he was disoriented by the unfamiliar surroundings.

"Hey, Ben," he managed weakly.

Grace rushed to his side with a cup of water, and he accepted it, drinking heartily as he took in the welcome sight of her loving smile. As always, she was beautiful, and he'd never stop marveling at how someone so lovely, both inside and out, would choose to be with someone so totally broken. Nevertheless, she looked utterly exhausted, and there was a heaviness in her posture, evidence of the stress she was under as she carried the weight of the world on her shoulders. His heart ached as he knew he was the cause.

"Welcome to Doctor Navarro's Succouri hospital," Ben said with a chuckle.

Donovan looked around, squinting his eyes. "We made it. Did Allie make it alright?"

Callie put her free hand on Donovan's shoulder. "Everyone is just fine, including you."

While her words might describe their present status, from the weariness in each pair of eyes, Donovan was certain much had happened while he'd been asleep. "How long have I been out? You all look worn out."

"A little more than a day," Ben answered, under strain as he countered the sedative in Donovan's system in addition to healing his countless injuries.

Frustratedly, Donovan huffed and shook his head, as he turned to Grace. "Not exactly how I would have chosen to spend my last days."

"Not your last days," Grace responded, her sky-blue eyes sparkling with delight. Lifting her gaze, she focused on someone standing behind Ben whom Donovan couldn't fully see.

Continuing to smile sweetly, Grace beckoned with her hand, inviting a thin, anxious-looking man to come and stand beside her, and he reluctantly complied.

"My friend," Ben began with a grin. "I want you to meet Ethan Devereaux. Ethan, this is Donovan Bradshaw."

After a moment of confusion, understanding dawned as he remembered where he'd heard that name. This was the man Ben had spoken of, the one he had hoped to convince to donate his Succouri gift to Donovan. And it appeared, somehow, Ben had done just that.

Handing the cup of water back to Grace, Donovan extended his hand, and Ethan took it. Looking into his troubled eyes, Donovan recognized the look of suffering, but not of the physical kind. This man had deep wounds of the soul.

"Ethan has agreed to offer you his gift," Ben explained with a smile. "If that's still something you and Grace wish to accept."

Donovan kept his eyes on Ethan. "How long have you been Succouri, Mr. Devereaux?"

"Forty years," he answered stiffly. "Fifteen years longer than I wanted to be."

"Forgive me, Ben is the only one I've ever known, and I've only known about him for a few weeks. You don't like being Succouri?"

Ethan lowered his eyes. "Not without... Not alone."

Then Donovan remembered. This man had lost his wife, the partner he loved and needed to fulfill his calling. "What was her name?" he asked in a gentle whisper.

Surprised by the question, Ethan lifted his eyes to Ben, and Ben nodded. "Lexi," he answered simply, sorrow mixing with annoyance in his tone.

Sensing his discomfort, Donovan changed the subject but didn't break eye contact with Ethan. "Before... Did you like being Succouri? Did you find the life it offered you meaningful, worth the costs?"

Ethan shifted and cleared his throat. "I... Well, I..." He let out a long, slow sigh. "Yes, Lexi and I were honored by the gift."

Though he had no desire to make Mr. Devereaux uncomfortable, as Ethan's presence here meant the plan was likely a sure thing, Donovan wanted to be certain it was the right choice, more for Grace's sake than for his own.

"And the costs? Giving up the chance to be a father and all the rest: was it worth it for you and Lexi?"

"Well, we... we already had a daughter before... before I was changed so we were fortunate in that way."

Surprised, Donovan shifted in bed, rising to a sitting position so he could look the man more directly in the eyes. "I see. And what does your daughter think about the Succouri and the lifestyle that comes with it?"

Ethan's eyes again dropped to the floor. "As a child, she loved everything about it." Gesturing toward Callie, Ethan chuckled, momentarily forgetting his pain as he got lost in a sweet memory. "When Lexi would help me like that, Jes would put her tiny hand on top of her mother's pretending to offer her own Succouri power. She would kneel by her bed at night and pray that God would send her a Succouri husband someday, so she could love him like Lexi loved…" His voice trailed off as the reality of the present returned.

"That's beautiful," Grace whispered, and Donovan's heart ached as he wished he'd had the chance to give Grace as many children as she wanted before it was too late.

"Did she?"

Confused, Ethan stared blankly at Donovan.

"Did she marry a Succouri?"

"No. But her husband was a good man. I know they were happy, and Lexi and I were glad she didn't give up the ability to have children of her own."

"So, you have grandchildren?"

Again, Ethan looked to Ben, and Ben shook his head, answering his unasked question.

"Mr. Bradshaw, Jessica Hughes is my daughter. I believe you traveled with her and my granddaughter, Allie."

Simultaneously, Donovan, Callie, and Grace turned stunned, questioning eyes to Ben and he smiled in confirmation. As it appeared Ben was the only one who knew about this incredible coincidence, Donovan was comforted that he wasn't the only one with gaps in his knowledge regarding the happenings of the last few days.

Fondly recalling his charming conversation with the young Allie Hughes, Donovan smiled. "That delightful, spunky girl is your granddaughter?"

When Ethan didn't smile or answer, Donovan's enthusiasm faded. "You've never met her, have you?"

Ethan's silence and diverted gaze were answer enough.

"Until a few days ago, I hadn't spoken with my parents in many years. They didn't approve of my choice to serve in the military, and they took my decision to go against their wishes as a rejection of them personally. I didn't want to die and leave anything unsaid, so"—he paused to smile at Grace—"at the kind nudging of... Miss Sophia, I reached out. It was uncomfortable, difficult, but I'm glad I did it. I said what I needed to say, opened the door, and the rest is up to them. It's worth it, Mr. Devereaux, taking the chance. Whoever's right or wrong; it doesn't really matter. If you're going to help me get my life back, I'd like to help you get your family back, if I can."

"I haven't made up my mind yet. Right now, I just want free of this. Perhaps without it, I'll be able to offer them something worthwhile, rather than just hurting them all over again."

With deep compassion for his obvious turmoil, Donovan considered Ethan for a silent moment. Then he looked up into Grace's eyes. The storm of emotions he saw there made his heart constrict. He wished there were time to talk with her, hold her, act like her husband instead of continuing their charade. But as Ben's hands had already begun to tremble, his time was almost up. Discerning his urgent question, she nodded resolutely and gently took his hand.

"Alright then. If, as Ben suggested, this is a situation where we both stand to benefit, I'll accept your gift of life with boundless gratitude, Mr. Devereaux. But please, consider my offer. And I'll gladly accept any guidance you can give me. I have much to learn."

"I'm sure Ben can help you. I wouldn't be a good teacher as I haven't used my gift in years and my perspective is biased. I'll return in the morning and, if you still want this burden, you can have it. But I warn you, Mr. Bradshaw, though it might seem like a blessing, if it all goes wrong, it will trap you in a kind of death much worse than what you're facing right now. No one ever warned me how relentless the suffering could be, so I'm warning you. Consider that my contribution to your Succouri education."

At that, he turned on his heels and rushed from the room, as they all stared after him.

Grace placed her hand over her heart and whispered softly, "That poor man!"

"He reminds me of you," Donovan said, looking over at Ben, "before you met Callie."

Nodding, Ben sighed in sad agreement. "The pain of a missing bond is severe and perhaps permanent for a Succouri, much more so than the ordinary grief suffered by typical human loss. It doesn't lessen with time. The emptiness is all consuming, growing from a deep gaping hole inside." Ben took a deep breath and Donovan looked down at his trembling hand. "I'm hoping I can help him fill the void with the love of his daughter and granddaughter. Truthfully, I don't know if that will be enough, but I have to try. Though ill-timed, his warning was valid, Donovan. There are grave risks to this life in addition to the benefits."

Donovan offered a weak smile. "If I were afraid of risks, I never would have joined the SEALS, my friend. And let me correct you. *We* have to try. I want to be a part of this, helping him find healing."

"Me too," Grace said.

"But"—Donovan put his hand on top of Callie's—"the two of you need to let go now. Thank you for working a miracle, getting me here, convincing Ethan to give me his gift, and saving my life. I'm indebted to you both. Please, go and get some rest. I know I will." He flashed a half grimace, half grin.

"I wish I could give you and Grace a few more minutes, but I promised the doc that we'd be ready in case you need us during the night, so…"

"Conserve your strength. I understand." Donovan lay back down. "I'll see you in a few hours, and when I do"—he grinned at Ben once more—"we really will be like brothers."

Ben patted his shoulder with his free hand. "Indeed, we will."

When Ben released him and he and Callie moved away, the pain returned as did the fog of the encroaching sedation. But before the world vanished again, he stared into Grace's tired eyes. She bent over him, kissing him softly then laughing as she stroked the rough whiskers that had grown as he hadn't shaved in days.

"I may have to give you a shave while you're asleep," she teased. "As I've never shaved a man's face before, you might be in more danger than during some of those knife fights you told me about."

He smiled weakly as he felt his mind growing increasingly foggy by the second. "Grace," he murmured, and she leaned in closer. "I can only imagine what you've been through in the last few days. I'm truly sorry."

She shook her head as a deeper, more tested kind of love shone in her eyes. "As I've told you before, soldier, you're more than worth it."

He pressed his lips to her forehead. "One more thing," he said, his words slurring as he could barely force them past his lips. "I don't ever want to call you Miss Sophia again, Mrs. Bradshaw."

COMFORTED by the promised joy at the dawning of the coming day, Grace slept peacefully during periodic respites that night. She dreamed Donovan was lying beside her, and each time she awoke, she smiled, hoping this lonely night would be the last of its kind.

With an excitement that mirrored her own, Callie stood beside her next to Donovan's bed early the following morning. Despite their jubilance, both women yawned at the same time, triggering a round of girlish giggles.

"Tonight, we can get some real sleep, Gracie. Donovan should be strong enough by then to not need supervision, and I know we'll all be able to relax knowing he's on the mend."

"How long until he's... changed?"

"It seems to be different for each person. Sometimes, it happens in a few days, other times weeks. But he'll be healthy nearly immediately."

Grace fidgeted with her sleeve as her smile wilted, and Callie squeezed her shoulder. "He's going to be alright. It's extremely rare for the transfer not to take and—"

Grace waved a hand in the air. "It's not that."

"Then what is it?"

Turning toward Donovan, Grace sighed, unable to stay silent any longer about her doubts and fears. "He's going to need a bond soon, right? I mean to be fulfilled and healthy as Succouri."

"He will?" Callie's brow wrinkled in confusion at the question.

"How do I know for sure that... that I'll be the one? What if becoming Succouri changes his feelings for me, or what if his Succouri chooses someone else?"

"Oh, Gracie! That's not how it works. I mean, yes, the Succouri initiates the bonding process, but it won't select someone randomly. Donovan already has a bond with you and you with him. As far as I know, in every case where there's been a pre-existing relationship, the change has served to deepen that connection by adding the benefits of the Succouri bond. Ethan and his wife, for example. The change won't alter his feelings for you. Not in the least. It will enhance them and offer the two of you an even deeper connection."

Grace's shoulders relaxed and she smiled at Callie. "What's it really like, Cal?"

"Like nothing you could ever imagine. Quite literally, Ben is part of me, in my heart and soul. I know him as well as I know myself and we share a... a place, a sacred, intangible space where our thoughts and feelings are known and experienced by the other. It may take you and Donovan a bit longer than Ben and me to develop that but you will."

"And we'll be..." Grace shifted, shy about her upcoming inquiry. "We'll be even more attracted to one another? Physically, I mean?"

Callie laughed dispelling some of the unease. "That definitely is part of it. You'll be drawn together in every way, heart, mind, and body. It's a package deal. Physical closeness is an essential part of the bond because that's how you use your Succouri gift, how he benefits from it. But there's more to it than that. It's difficult to explain." She patted Grace's hand. "You'll see."

Nodding, Grace's smile returned. "I watch you and Ben, and despite all the two of you have been through, I see something I've never seen before. I didn't know that kind of love existed, except in fairy tales. My parents weren't in love, at least not by the time I was old enough to understand what that meant and to notice how they treated one another. When they divorced, I stopped believing in happily ever after, even though deep down, I craved that kind of love story. And then, I met Donovan. When I saw him, that day in your living room, he looked at me like... like he knew me, and I looked at him the same way. Talking to him was like talking to a lifelong friend; easy and natural. When he pulled away because of his health issues, the loneliness I felt at his absence surprised me." Laughing, she gently stroked Donovan's sleeping face. "I thought I was ridiculous. I mean, I'd only known him for a week. I scolded myself, remembering that I didn't really believe in love anyway. But..."

Callie reached out for Grace's arm, begging her to finish. "But what?"

"When I picked him up at the airport—when we locked eyes as he walked toward me..."

"Grace!"

"I saw the same look in Donovan's eyes, the one I'd seen in Ben's when he looked at you. It turned my world upside down. He wasn't Succouri, had nothing unusual inside him drawing him to me, but he loved me with that... that forever kind of love."

Embracing her, Callie's profound happiness for Grace and Donovan raised the pitch of her voice. "There's no need to worry about being chosen for the bonding. There's no doubt at all that it will be you."

Though she still couldn't shake a few lingering doubts, as Callie's words had backed-up Maggie's assertions, Grace began to feel excited for the first time since hearing about the bond. She believed Donovan's love for her was abiding, the kind necessary to initiate the bond. The prospect of having a deeper connection with him than they already shared was assuredly thrilling, though perhaps a little intimidating. She'd barely had a chance to get used to trusting someone with her heart. Now, he'd learn all her secrets and the traumas from her past, and she'd learn his. Having already glimpsed the horrors he'd endured during his years in the service, she felt some trepidation at the idea of experiencing those things directly through his eyes, if that was the way it worked. But if it meant loving him more, enjoying a kind of intimacy few were privileged to experience, she would embrace it wholeheartedly.

Before everyone gathered for breakfast, Taylor came to check on her and Donovan. "What a whirlwind these last few days have been!" he exclaimed, swiping the back of his hand across his brow. "It's a blessing Donovan slept through it. The stress would have been too much for him." He paused to look intently at her. "How are you holding up?"

Though Grace missed Ronald LeVray, she'd begun to believe Agent Taylor might eventually fill the hole left by his absence as he seemed to have a father-like affection for her and she for him.

"It's been a very long few days. Not exactly what Donovan and I had hoped for. But it will all be worth it when we get our miracle."

Glancing around the room, Taylor folded his arms and smiled slyly at her. "Indeed. I would say a solitary night of honeymooning isn't what any newlywed couple anticipates."

Abruptly turning wide eyes to him, Grace sharply inhaled. "How... How...?"

Taylor chuckled, amused by her dumbfounded reaction. "I spoke to Doctor Karl the day Donovan was admitted, told him about his heroism and his injuries. He told me he was concerned that Mrs. Bradshaw appeared to be misinformed about the severity of his condition." He shook his head as he continued to chuckle. "He was absolutely certain Donovan wouldn't last the day. After that, confirming the filing of your marriage license with the courthouse was... Let's just say for someone like me, who's basically worked as a spy for decades, that was child's play."

"Have you told—?"

"Of course not," Taylor interjected. "It's not my place to do so. Besides, I can understand wanting to wait, let this situation work itself out. Everyone has had plenty to handle. But"—he smiled—"Ben and Callie will be over-joyed for the two of you. As am I."

"The desire to keep it a secret was mine, not Donovan's. I didn't want to put any extra pressure on Ben, and I knew Callie would be hurt that they weren't there with us. I'm still not sure how I'm going to tell them. But I'm kind of relieved that someone knows." Shifting her gaze to Dono-van, Grace sighed. "I don't know how to thank you for helping us. I have no idea how you got a helicopter out there in the boonies so quickly, but if you hadn't—"

Taylor reached out and patted her hand. "Everything's worked out beautifully. I have a surprise for the two of you when this is all over."

Grace raised her eyebrows as she turned back to him.

"I'll keep it to myself for now as you've got enough going on today. Plus, I want Donovan awake and fully present when I spill the beans." His grin filled his face. "It's something that should have happened a while ago by my way of thinking, but better late than never."

Though intensely curious, Grace let it go, respecting Taylor's wishes.

"Are you coming to breakfast?"

Grace shook her head. "Maggie's bringing me a plate. The doctor should be here momentarily to withdraw the sedative, and I want to be here when he wakes up, try to keep his mind off the pain until the transfer."

Smiling, he patted her hand once more before turning to go. "Your steadfast devotion has been noticed and admired by everyone. Donovan is blessed, and something tells me he knows that and won't ever forget what you've done for him. It's almost over, dear one. Keep your chin up."

"Mr. Bradshaw, can you hear me?"

Though the agony was all too familiar, the voice he heard as he emerged from oblivion was not. Blinking, he struggled to focus his vision. A kind-faced, older man smiled down at him, his white hair starkly contrasting with his brown skin.

"Good morning. I'm Doctor Ed Navarro. I've had the privilege of supervising your care over the last couple of days along with Maggie Briggs, our resident nurse, and, of course, Grace who has done the most important work of all. How are you feeling?"

Donovan swallowed hard. There was not a single place in his entire body that wasn't on fire. Almost immediately, he knew that the pain medication had been discontinued, making the throbbing intolerable. In addition, though he had no appetite and was certain he could keep nothing down, his stomach twisted with hunger as he'd eaten nothing solid in days. Each breath took effort, and he had to bite his tongue to keep from groaning as waves of intense nausea rose continuously. Too weak to offer the doctor an answer, he shook his head in response.

"I know you're in a lot of pain, and I'm truly sorry about that, but I needed to clear your system of the strong narcotics before we begin the transfusion. I also know that you haven't eaten in a very long time. I've done the best I could to keep you hydrated through your IV, but that's no substitute for solid food. Do you think you might be able to tolerate something to eat or sit up for a bit?"

Again, Donovan shook his head.

Compassionately, the doctor nodded, his eyes tormented as he watched Donovan carefully. "Alright. Understood. We're going to begin momentarily. I'll leave you in the capable hands of Grace as I prepare for the procedure." He set his hand on Donovan's shoulder. "Hang in there, young man. It's almost over."

"Thank you, Doctor," he managed in a weak, breathy voice.

When the doctor moved away, Grace appeared and sat on the edge of the bed, her eyes filling with unshed tears as she studied him. Tenderly, she stroked his cleanly shaven cheek, and as before, the pain retreated ever so slightly at her touch.

"Ben will be here soon. He'll be able to help you with the pain until the doctor's ready. I'm sorry," she said in a tortured whisper as she leaned closer.

Hating the distress he was causing her, he did his best

to smile. "I appear to have survived the perils of the razor," he teased, though he could barely make his voice audible.

Though the anxiety in her face eased only slightly, she laughed. "Only because Maggie helped me. Trust me, that job is much better left in your hands. In very short order, you'll be perfectly capable of taking care of yourself, though I hope you will still find cause to keep me around."

Donovan lifted his hand, and she reached for it, intertwining her fingers around his. "Whether my body is broken or whole, I can't breathe without you."

A single tear slid down her cheek. "Nor I without you."

Pulling his hand to her heart, she lay down beside him, breathing steadily in his ear. As he matched her, heartbeat for heartbeat, breath for breath, the pain retreated even further, and inhaling became easier. This woman was his literal salvation, giving him the strength and will to live second by precious second. Discerning that talking was far too strenuous at present, she was content to lie silently, the warmth of her body like a magnet, keeping his soul tethered to the realm of the living.

Time was meaningless as he focused all his attention on accomplishing his next breath, but eventually the doctor approached, cleared his throat, and spoke, his voice sounding as if he were delivering a dreadful diagnosis. "I apologize for the delay. Are you feeling any better, Donovan?"

"A little," he managed.

Grace opened her eyes, then abruptly sat up. "Is everything alright?" she asked, glancing at her watch.

Avoiding their eyes, the doctor shifted uncomfortably. "I'm sure it will all work out. Any chance you might try some food now? It might give you some strength, and it would make me feel a lot better." He tried to smile, but Donovan could read the panic clear as day on his face.

Something was wrong. Most likely, Ethan had changed his mind, maybe even left. His heart broke at the realization, but not for himself. Either way, within an hour, his struggle would be over. But the woman beside him would be left behind with the heartbreak of coming so close to a miracle, only to have it snatched away at the last second. She'd put every bit of her heart, soul, and strength into saving him despite the odds. Such a tragic ending would crush her.

As the doctor continued to avoid his gaze, Donovan did his best to capture it. "Doctor, I appreciate what you've done for me. Please, give us a few moments, then it might be best to put me back under."

"No!" Grace protested, but the doctor nodded his understanding and walked away, his head hung low.

Rallying every ounce of strength, Donovan raised himself up in bed and put his free arm around her. "Grace Bradshaw, I love you with all my heart and soul. You've been my strength my—"

"Donovan, No!" she pushed against him as sobs began to shake her body. "This isn't over. Wait until we're sure, please!"

"Shh," he soothed, stroking her silky hair. "I know you wanted this to end differently, and so did I. But, from the beginning, we knew this was a long shot. One day, one night as your husband wasn't nearly enough, but it was sweeter, more glorious than I dreamed possible. Your love saved me, kept me alive longer than anyone believed possible, including me. Please, always remember that. Despite the pain, you filled my last days with happiness, beyond my wildest hopes. You are beautiful, gracious, perfect. I want you to go on with your life, find and grasp every opportunity for happiness." He pressed his hand to her heart, "Forever and ever, I'll be right here with you."

"No! Donovan. No!" Grace collapsed into his shoulder, sobbing as she clung desperately to him. "You can't. Ben said—"

"Ben has done all he could, given me his strength more times than I can count. It's best that he's not here right now. He'd try to keep me alive, kill himself giving me everything he had. Please don't let him feel responsible for this. He's been the best friend anyone could ever ask for. Please, be sure to tell him that."

Lifting her tear-stained face, she shook her head repeatedly. "I won't let you go. Not yet."

"Grace, please. I beg of you. Don't ask me to keep suffering. You must let me go. There's no more hope." A groan passed through his lips. "I've fought hard, because I love you, but I can't endure it any longer. You don't understand."

Abruptly pulling away and rising to her feet, she put both hands to her stomach and all color drained from her face. "But I do understand," she exclaimed through a sob. "It's destroying me, Donovan. But I can't explain it. I just know this isn't over yet. Please, just give me thirty more minutes. That's all I ask. Then I'll lie beside you and hold you as you go. Please, soldier. Thirty minutes longer. Please!" Streams of desperate tears ran down her face, each one ripping holes in his heart.

"As you wish, ma'am." He surrendered. "Thirty minutes." He closed his eyes, the pain of watching her heart break worse by far than any hurt he'd ever known.

Ten minutes passed, then five more. Each breath became shallower, and his heart pounded in his ears, like the final beats of a distant drum. Grace paced, watching the door, the clock, and the doctor continuously. When twenty minutes had elapsed, Donovan felt tears on his cheeks, wishing there was more he could say to ease her suffering, but lost for words. Though he regretted the pain he'd brought into her life, loving her was something he could never have avoided. His heart, in this life and the next, wholly belonged to Grace Sophia-Bradshaw.

CHAPTER 18

MORE THAN EXPECTED

When the door to the lab opened, Grace spun around, her heart pounding so furiously that she felt light-headed. She had five minutes left, precious little time to prove to Donovan that all hope wasn't yet gone.

An unrestrained sigh of relief flowed from her when Ben, Callie, and Ethan Devereaux stepped into the room. Turning immediately to Donovan, Grace took his hand. "He's here! Hang on, Donovan."

He nodded but didn't open his eyes. His breathing had become painfully labored, and she wasn't sure he could speak, even if he wanted to.

At once, Callie rushed to Grace's side and put an arm around her. Grace couldn't hear the words as Ethan spoke to the doctor and kept glancing toward Donovan.

When Ben caught sight of Donovan, he rushed toward him, but Ethan intercepted him.

"Ben, let me. I think I still have enough to at least keep him out of pain briefly while we talk. But it would probably be wise for you to stay close by, just in case."

As Grace stared at Ethan, she was puzzled by a new look of peace in his eyes. At Ethan's touch, Donovan's entire body relaxed, but when he opened his eyes, Grace could still see pain. The strong draw hit Ethan hard, looking as if someone had struck him, and he held onto the edge of the bed with his free hand. Ben stayed a few steps back but watched Donovan protectively.

"Donovan, I'm ready to help you now. I'm sorry I caused confusion."

Glancing first at Grace, then at Ben, Donovan squinted, perplexed by the change of heart. Ben smiled and nodded reassuringly.

"I don't understand," Donovan said. "I thought you changed your mind."

"It's a long story. I learned something that upset me, but it wasn't related to you or the transfer of my gift. Unjustifiably, I became angry and said something I shouldn't have. But I do want to give you my gift. I need to..." The strain of the draw cut off his explanation, and Ben shifted closer, but didn't intervene.

Donovan took a deep breath, which brought Grace tremendous relief, but Ethan cringed. "Ethan, I'm at peace with dying. If you have any doubts, any questions about passing the gift to me, it's alright. No hard feelings or resentment." He looked at Ben, holding his gaze for a breath before returning his eyes to Ethan. "When I signed up to serve my country, I knew this was a possibility. I don't regret anything, except for the broken heart I'll leave behind." He directed his mournful gaze toward Grace.

Vigorously, Ethan shook his head. "I haven't changed my mind. I need to move on from this, shed my Succouri identity. It's the only potential path to healing for me."

Grace looked down, noticing that Ethan's hand was already trembling.

"I promise you, Donovan. This is what I want. No doubts, no hesitations."

Grace covered her face with her hands, breathing deeply as her heart settled from the last hour of debilitating anxiety. Callie tightened her hold around her shoulders.

As the trembling spread to his arm, Donovan studied him. "If that's your final decision, then I have one more question before we proceed."

Though Ethan could barely lift his head, he did his best to nod, encouraging Donovan to continue.

"When it's over, and the gift is gone, do I have your word that you won't do anything... rash? I know you miss your wife terribly, but I won't be involved in enabling you to... to harm yourself once that becomes possible."

Again, he tried for a nod, but his body was shaking, making it hard to complete the motion.

Ben stepped forward. "Ethan, you need to let go. You won't be strong enough for the transfer. Please."

Sighing, Ethan released Donovan and briefly grasped Ben's arm to steady himself as he tried to straighten his posture. A strange look flashed across the faces of both men, and they stared at one another.

"Are you... Do you feel that?" Ben asked Ethan, just as Callie released Grace and went to stand beside him.

"I... I can feel strength from you," Ethan stuttered, shock written all over his face. "How is that possible?"

Callie smiled. "Ben has a unique gift that permits him to help anyone, even other Succouri. This has happened before."

"She's right," Ben acknowledged. "But there's something else there too. Do you also feel... I don't know exactly how to describe it: a stirring?"

"Maybe... I don't know. I've never been on the receiving end of the gift, so I don't know what's normal and what's not." Ethan withdrew his hand, and though he continued to look puzzled, Ben returned his focus to Donovan, taking over where Ethan left off as Callie assisted him.

After slowly inhaling deeply several times, Ethan's breathing settled enough for him to answer Donovan's question. "Thanks to everyone's patience and kindness, I have decided to return to my daughter and granddaughter and do my best to repair the damage I caused by the years of separation. Without the consuming emptiness of the absent bond, I'm hopeful that I'll finally begin to heal. I give you my word that my intention is to honor my wife by taking care of our family and passing along her legacy of love." He locked eyes with Callie. "That's what she would want me to do."

No hint of pain in his expression now, Donovan searched Ethan's eyes for confirmation that his words were sincere. Despite his weariness, Ethan didn't look away or drop his head.

Gradually, a smile lifted the corners of Donovan's mouth, the expression revealing the restoration of hope taking place in his soul. "Good enough, Ethan. Let's do this."

Unable to contain her joy, before Ethan made his way across the room to the doctor, Grace caught up to him and tackled him in a full embrace. "Thank you," she said through tears. "He almost gave up. I almost lost him. Thank you for coming back."

Though Grace had no clue what had happened to change his mind in the first place, it was obvious Callie and

Ben were the reason he'd returned. They hadn't abandoned her and Donovan. Quite the contrary. They'd, once again, found a way to save the day.

Though uncomfortable with the sudden embrace, Ethan nevertheless looked at her with appreciation for the kind sentiment. "You will be an exceptional Datouri. I recognize the look of devotion and unconditional love. As Ben is with Callie, Donovan is extremely fortunate."

"May I ask you a question?"

Ethan nodded.

"Did your feelings for Lexi change in any way after you became Succouri?"

"They did," he answered without hesitation, and Grace sucked in a breath as that hadn't been what she'd expected or wanted to hear.

But then, a rare smile filled the troubled man's face. "I loved her more, and I loved her better. She was and will always be my everything. And I have no doubt it will be exactly the same for you and Donovan."

Fifteen minutes later, Donovan and Ethan lay ready for the transfusion, their beds side by side in the center of the room with just enough space between them for the doctor to maneuver. The doctor explained the procedure in a rush, keeping a nervous eye on Donovan's monitor. Though Grace didn't know a lot about the readouts, she knew enough to be anxious as well. Ben and Callie had disappeared again, likely trying to stay out of the doctor's way as he and Maggie wheeled equipment around and repositioned the beds. Grace stood nervously beside Donovan, holding tightly to his hand.

Turning to one patient, then the other, the doctor hastily pulled on a pair of gloves. "Any questions?"

Both men shook their heads. The doctor wiped Donovan's outstretched arm with a sterile cloth, then did the same with Ethan's.

Just then, the lab door swung open and Ben rushed inside. "Hold up, Doc," he said, putting up a hand.

Startled, the doctor took a step back.

"There's another way."

"Did... Did you receive an answer?" The doctor's voice was hopeful. Though Grace knew the doctor unquestionably wanted to save Donovan's life, his discomfort with the procedure, springing from what Callie and Taylor had recently learned from Carozza, had been clear. The idea of harming a Succouri was distasteful to all of them, but they'd run out of time to seek other means of saving Donovan's life.

"Not step-by-step instructions," Ben answered. "More like an arrow, pointing us in a general direction, but I'd like to try if Ethan and Donovan are willing."

"Ben, what's going on?" Donovan questioned, his voice quiet and hoarse.

Though there wasn't sufficient time to catch him up on every detail, Ben and Callie did their best to quickly give Donovan the basics of their discoveries about the Antico and the ancient way of transferring the gift.

"And you possess one of the originals, the kind that still has a will of its own?" Donovan asked, struggling to take it all in.

"I do."

"And that's why you're... different?"

Ben sighed. "It's a big part of the reason."

"So..." Donovan took a shaky breath and everyone in the

room felt the urgency to move forward with the transfer as quickly as possible. "You have no idea how much longer your Succouri will stay with you?"

"Well." Ben cleared his throat. "In my case, I'll remain Succouri all my life. I won't ever pass the gift."

Maggie gasped at the revelation.

Donovan locked eyes with Ben. "You're the one it was seeking, the final host!" he exclaimed with wonder, mixed with a tone of confirmation, as if he already knew that to be the case.

Clearly uncomfortable with the newly discovered truth, Ben offered a weak smile and a nod.

"The chosen one!" Donovan mumbled, his tone still filled with awe, but Grace wasn't sure anyone besides her heard him. "Weeks ago," he continued, speaking louder now, I told Callie I always thought you had a uniquely courageous heart. I guess I'm not the only one who noticed that fact."

Humbly, Ben bowed his head.

Breaking the silence in the room, Donovan's monitor suddenly began beeping, and Doctor Navarro responded, circling around to Grace's side of the bed as she stepped back. He silenced the alarm, but as he took in the information on the screen, the panic on his face was just as jarring as the piercing noise. "We need to hurry," he urged, looking at Ben.

Immediately, Ben turned to Taylor and Lee. "Let's push their beds closer together."

They rolled Ethan's bed directly alongside Donovan's as Doctor Navarro pushed medical equipment out of Ben's way. Then, with Callie by his side, Ben took a deep breath and stepped to the open side of Ethan's bed. "If my Succouri can make contact with yours and wake it up, I'm not sure what you'll experience. I do believe that, for it to leave you and transfer to Donovan, you—the human part of you—must consent. If you resist or refuse to relinquish it, I don't think it can go."

"But, Ben..." Donovan spoke in a barely audible whisper as he struggled mightily to breathe. "If Ethan's Succouri becomes sentient, doesn't that mean it gets to decide who the next host is? How do you know it will choose me?"

"It's my firm belief that you are the intended recipient. The timing of my illness, my loss and then subsequent restoration of healing power is too coincidental. If it wasn't fated for you to be saved by the reception of the gift, why did my Antico work everything out so perfectly, even down to the amazing coincidence of being on the same transport flight with Jessica and Allie?"

Briefly, Ben looked over at Callie and she nodded at him. "You are meant to be the first, the initiation of a new beginning for the Succouri." Ben chuckled. "Or actually, more like a rebirth. Though I don't know exactly how it's all going to happen, this feels, this is right. My Antico's telling me this is the way it should be." Ben held out his hands as if ready to receive a gift. "I can't explain why I'm so certain of this but I am... we are. We're humbly asking for your trust."

Donovan smiled and relaxed. Briefly, he lifted his eyes to Grace, and she smiled at him, providing all the assurance Donovan needed. "I couldn't be in better hands," he declared, with no hint of reservation.

Every eye in the room turned to Ethan, who looked puzzled.

"This must be done of your free will, Ethan. It won't work otherwise."

"I don't know if I believe in all of this. We're all putting a lot of faith in this... Carozza and his unorthodox views.

I've been a Succouri for forty years and besides you, Ben, there's nothing in my experience to support these wild ideas. But I can't deny that what I've witnessed in the last twenty-four hours has been extraordinary; inexplicable by our conventional wisdom." His eyes met Ben's, then shifted to Callie's. "I don't trust Carozza, but I trust the two of you. You've risked a lot to help me. You saved my granddaughter's life, and I believe you genuinely care about my family. If we're all being duped here, so be it." He smiled and nodded at Ben. "I'll cast my lot with yours."

What transpired in the following moments confounded Grace. Though her center of focus remained on Donovan's rapidly deteriorating condition, she was aware of the drama playing out on the opposite side of the adjacent beds.

After grabbing ahold of Ethan with both hands, Ben seemed to enter a comatose-like state, unable to speak and barely able to stand, fully dependent on Callie to keep the group informed on his progress in awakening Ethan's Succouri. Holding tightly to the back of Ben's shirt as if anchoring him, Callie shifted between the real world in the lab and the invisible one playing out in, what Grace could only guess to be, the intangible space of their bond, which she'd described to Grace just a few hours earlier. Helplessly, everyone watched in silent concern, mesmerized and perplexed, but scared to interfere in any way lest they disrupt the process.

As the doctor shifted his gaze around the room, he wrung his hands, uncharacteristically anxious. Though he'd initially watched Ben and Callie closely with the rest of the group, after several minutes passed, Donovan closed his eyes, and Grace watched in fear as his face grew paler and his breathing became increasingly irregular. Taking his hand, she lifted it to her cheek, trying to warm it as it was frigid to the touch.

"Donovan?" she inquired softly, leaning over him, but there was no response.

Doctor Navarro set a hand on her shoulder. "He's failing," he whispered. "If the transfer doesn't happen soon, we're going to lose him."

In desperation, Grace leaned over and spoke in Donovan's ear. "Five more minutes. That's all I need. Keep breathing." But again, there was no response. Maggie came up beside Grace, putting a supportive hand on her back, her expression solemn.

As they all held their breath, the drama playing out beside Ethan's bed abruptly ceased. Though still bent over and unaware of anything around him, Ben's shoulders relaxed. Callie smiled, though her eyes remained closed. As Grace watched, Ethan's countenance also changed, a profound expression of tranquility settling on his face.

Abruptly, Donovan's entire body convulsed, and the doctor began checking his neck for a pulse. "Callie! What's going on?" he shouted in a panic, no longer able to wait for the process to play out in its own time.

Opening her eyes, Callie looked around the room, temporarily dazed. "Everything's alright. The worst is over now," she comforted, at last focusing her gaze on the doctor.

Through clenched teeth, the doctor spoke with urgency. "Callie, we're losing Donovan."

Putting her hand to her mouth, Grace spoke, her voice a cry of desperation. "What do we do?"

Donovan had fought way too hard and suffered way too much to lose now when relief was at hand. But as he'd slipped into a coma, she had no way to reach him, no more power to keep his heart beating.

"It'll be alright," Callie encouraged.

For an unbearable moment, no one moved, unsure what to do or say as Donovan's monitor ominously signaled his faltering heartbeat. Callie whispered into Ben's ear, and he opened his eyes and straightened.

It's up to Ethan now," Ben panted, beads of sweat on his forehead. "He has to choose to let go."

"Did you… Did you wake it up?" Doctor Navarro asked.

Ben smiled at Callie before nodding his response. "My Succouri did. My only job was to hold on for dear life while it did what it needed to do inside Ethan. And that would have been impossible if it weren't for Callie. She held on to me, tethered me to reality. Without question, she saved my life."

Every face in the room held the same perplexed expression.

Ben lightly chuckled at their bewilderment. "Let's just say we now understand why this life, this calling requires the full engagement of all three partners."

The beeps that accompanied Donovan's heartbeat momentarily sped up and then slowed, nearly to a stop. Grace sharply inhaled and lowered her head into her hands.

Alarmed, Ben started toward Donovan's bed, but suddenly halted, as if someone had grabbed ahold of him from behind, restraining his advance. "I can't help him," Ben agonized. "His only chance now is the transfer."

He stepped back and leaned over Ethan. "Ethan, come on. You have to let go."

Donovan's heart monitor beeped, then ceased for five seconds. As everyone froze, suspended in terror, one last heartbeat echoed through the tiled room, and then, silence.

. . .

Donovan tried to move, but his muscles wouldn't respond to his command. Lying face down in the sand, he couldn't see anything, but he felt the hot blood, his own and that of his brothers, trickling down his face in steady streams. Angry shouts and gunfire echoed around him, and he was certain he must be in hell.

The intense burning from two bullets, shot at close range directly into his lower back, made him want to cry out in torment, but he bit his tongue hard, knowing that if he permitted one sound to flow from his lips, the enemy would finish him off. For a moment, he wavered, considering that death might be the more favorable option, but something inside of him wouldn't let him quit. A sharp new pain in his side accompanied the sound of mocking laughter, and Donovan bit his tongue so hard that a fresh fountain of blood spilled from his mouth, soaking the ground. Just let me die! his soul pleaded with God as the agony was more than he could bear.

"You were meant for more than dying with your face in the dirt." He'd heard those words before, but this time, the voice that spoke them wasn't his own, yet it was almost as familiar.

All at once, the pain eased, and the ground underneath him morphed. Lush green grass padded his broken body, and a cool breeze drifted across his sweat-drenched back. Silence descended, like a thick curtain, blocking out the wretched sounds of war.

"Rise, soldier," the same voice gently commanded. "It's time to leave that battlefield far behind."

Though still covered in blood, Donovan rolled over and sat up, looking around him in confusion. The sky was brilliant blue, and the air so fresh and sweet that for a long moment, he unashamedly sucked in glutinous lungfuls of it. Wiping the blood and sweat from his eyes with the back of his hand, he startled at the presence of another soldier, dressed in fatigues, sitting casually just a few yards in front of him. His face wasn't familiar, though he looked a little like himself, same height and build, blond hair, and brown eyes.

"Hello?" Donovan inquired. "How did we get here? What happened to the battle?"

The soldier smiled and pointed to his right. Shifting his gaze in that direction, at first, Donovan saw nothing. But as he continued to stare, Ben's familiar image appeared in the distance, approaching at a swift pace. When he was a few yards away, Ben sat between him and the other soldier, shifting his gaze as he smiled satisfactorily. "Good. Very good."

"Ben! What in the world's going on?"

Ben laughed. "Just saving your life, my friend. And his as well." He pointed to the unknown soldier.

Shaking his head, Donovan squinted at Ben. "Who?"

"He's my brother, as Ben is yours."

"But aren't you..." Donovan started to ask, but as he gazed at Ben, he realized this wasn't his friend, not exactly anyway. He looked exactly like him, but the image lacked depth, almost two-dimensional, like looking at a reflection of Ben in a mirror.

"Are you... Is he... Succouri?"

The image of Ben put out his hands and smiled, as if impressed by Donovan's insight.

"So, you're Ben's..."

The blue eyes of Ben's Succouri twinkled as it nodded. "How?"

The other soldier rose, studied Donovan for a moment, then sat beside Ben's Succouri. "He and I are going to get along just fine," he said, chuckling softly. "Unquestionably smart, exceptionally brave, perhaps a little stubborn, but that will come in handy. Does he understand?"

"Not much more than Ben did when I came to him. But he'll catch on, and you'll learn just as much from him as he will from you." Ben's image redirected its gaze to Donovan. "You are the guardian for the one who is chosen. We saved your life. Before your time as Succouri is over, you and Grace will save ours." As he said the words, the blood on his body and uniform vanished, as if someone had wiped him clean.

"I understand!" Donovan exclaimed in a tone of awe mixed with bewilderment. "I've heard those words since I was young. I heard them again in Boston when Ben... you saved my life. But how is that possible? I only found out about the Succouri a few weeks back?"

"Echoes of the future, resounding in the past. I've known Ben from the beginning. Those he loves, I love also." He pointed to the soldier beside him. "Those you love, he will embrace in like manner. But he's at the beginning of a long journey. Teach and learn. He'll give you a second chance at life, and you'll set him on a straight path. But his destiny will eventually separate you. Even so, you and Grace will always be of us. Arise, Donovan. Embrace life to the fullest. Waste no more time living in the shadow of that dreadful day. The defeated man you perceive there never was, nor will ever be, who you are. A new mission awaits, an entirely new destiny." He smiled, his eyes reflecting pure joy and deep affection.

Strengthened by his proclamations, Donovan stood to his feet and extended his hand, and Ben's Succouri responded in kind. But a second after their hands touched, Ben's image vanished, leaving Donovan alone with his Succouri.

"Are you ready, warrior?" he asked as he also stood and locked eyes with Donovan.

"Affirmative. Will I hear your voice inside my head?"

"Eventually. It will take some time for us to get acquainted." He laughed. "This is almost as new to me as it is to you."

"I don't know why I was chosen for this great honor, but I'll do my best to prove myself worthy of it."

Smiling, the soldier slapped Donovan playfully on the arm. "You and me both. But I already have a pretty good idea of why Ben picked you. We'll figure it out." Keeping his eyes on Donovan, he slowly backed away. "Time to get started. You've been through some brutal battles, brother. I've got my work cut out for me. Slow is smooth. Smooth is fast." He offered Donovan a salute as a blinding white light began to overtake the scene.

Just before he disappeared, his image fading into the colorless brilliance, he spoke once more, his smile whimsical. "I've got your six, Donovan Bradshaw. Just like before."

At his words, Donovan instantly remembered. A second before the blast hurled him through the air, breaking his body and drenching him in blood, he'd heard a voice from behind him. "Watch your six!" it exclaimed, and he turned around in response to its warning. That action had saved his life. It was the same voice, that of his Succouri.

But that was two years ago, he marveled, shaking his head. Long before he knew anything about the Succouri. 'Echoes of the future, resounding in the past.' The incomprehensible explanation repeated in his mind as the world around him fell deathly silent and still.

Gradually, he heard the drums begin anew, this time growing louder and more rhythmic as they approached. His heartbeat, like the synchronized marching of a great army, shook the ground under his feet and resonated through every inch of his body.

Something touched him, then sank deep into his bones. It began to move, starting at his right wrist and spreading, inch by inch, up his arm and into his shoulder. There, it split, creeping up into his neck and down into his chest. He heard himself suck in a breath, and somewhere in the distance, Grace's joyful voice spoke his name.

Within seconds, his whole body was on fire but not from pain. Reminiscent of Ben's healing warmth, the flames consumed every ache and agony as if they were brittle kindling. When the fire reached the crown of his head and his fingertips and toes, it abruptly turned back, crashing over him like a violent ocean wave. For a few seconds, he couldn't breathe from the pressure as it wedged itself against every organ and bone. But then, with a kind of plea-sure he'd never experienced or imagined, it began to settle, soaking deep into each broken place in his being. Like quenching a thirst, he felt the healing begin, moving slowly but deliberately through his entire being.

A long, slow breath flowed from his lips, and for the first time since he'd died, or fallen asleep, he wasn't sure which was accurate, he felt Grace's hand in his.

"His vitals are returning to normal," he heard the doctor declare, and sighs of relief and exclamations of astonish-ment came from every direction.

He felt the tugging as sensors were removed from his chest and a fleeting pinch as the IV was withdrawn from his arm. And then, Donovan opened his eyes.

CHAPTER 19

A New Life

In sharp contrast to the ecstatic shouts just moments earlier when Donovan's heartbeat had resumed, a deep silence now hung in the air as everyone watched him recover. Grace held a hand to her heart, unconsciously gripping her wedding ring through the barrier of her shirt. She felt shy and nervous, like she was about to meet a stranger.

After Ethan had at last roused and reached for Donovan's arm, she'd watched the man she loved transform. His pale face took on healthy color, and the scars, though not completely gone, faded significantly. The lines of pain and exhaustion around his eyes and forehead vanished, making him look ten years younger than he had only moments earlier. Every muscle in his body relaxed, dispelling the look of sternness, which Grace had known to be a byproduct of his unceasing battle with pain. But beyond the discontinuation of that impression, the features of his face changed, becoming visibly softer. Though the change undoubtedly made him appear more approachable and attractive, for Grace, it was bittersweet, as she wasn't sure if the changes on the outside coincided with equally dramatic changes on the inside.

As he took in the ecstatic faces gathered in a tight circle around his bed, he smiled, and her heart found reason to hope as this expression was unaltered. When his eyes found hers, his smile grew as he probed her heart and soul with those familiar golden-brown eyes. As had happened when they first met, Grace was paralyzed, barely able to breathe as his gaze held her prisoner.

Lifting his hand, he held it out, palm facing her, as his eyes begged her to accept his invitation. Timidly, she touched her palm to his, the welcome warmth of it triggering a sudden and unanticipated sigh of relief. Gently, he interlinked their fingers and pulled her hand to his heart, causing her to step closer and sit on the edge of his bed. As she did so, she briefly glanced around, stunned that there was now no one else in the room.

"Hi, soldier."

"My saving Grace." The words conveyed much more than a simple expression of affection: gratitude, joy, relief, hope, wonder, but above all, love.

Grace smiled, and Donovan reached out and swept her into his arms, holding her against him like he was afraid she might disappear if he let go. "You believed," he whispered into her hair. "You always believed this was possible, and because of that, I'm here. I'm alive. How do I ever begin to tell you... to thank you for never giving up on me."

"When your heart stopped..."—her body trembled—"I thought... I couldn't..."

He tightened his embrace. "It's over, Grace. All over."

Tears of joy spilled onto his neck as she melted into him, noting the easy strength with which he held her. "Is the pain gone, Donovan? All of it?"

He laughed. "That's affirmative, ma'am, save for one remaining discomfort."

Alarmed, she pulled back to look at him questioningly.

"I'm literally starving to death. And I desperately need a shower."

Grace giggled. This was indeed her Donovan; the same twinkle in his eye, his habitual use of the word ma'am, and the tenderness in his touch. "I'll get your bag, then I'll fix you something to eat. Do you think you can manage a shower on your own?"

With a wink, Donovan traced a finger down her cheek. "I'll manage on my own this time, but next time, I'll most definitely need some assistance."

"Perhaps something can be arranged," she returned playfully, lowering her eyes as she still felt uncertain about the dramatic change he'd undergone and how all of it would alter their future and relationship.

Donovan released her and put his finger under her chin, lifting her head so she'd meet his gaze. "I know all of this is... disorienting, overwhelming." He laughed sarcastically. "Trust me, I know. We have a lot to talk about. There's so much I want to tell you, and I'm sure, so much you need to tell me. But there's one certainty I can offer you, Grace Bradshaw. I love you, now and always. Whether time goes on or stops. Whether the laws of nature order the universe or everything descends into chaos. Whether you and I are Succouri or human; it makes no difference. My heart is eternally yours."

DONOVAN CLOSED HIS EYES, letting the warm water thoroughly drench him. His words to Grace had been entirely genuine, but besides his anchoring love for her, there was almost nothing else about himself that was unaltered. He felt like a stranger in his own skin. The pain was completely gone, and though that was more than he could've ever dreamed or hoped for, it was a change that would take time to get used to.

For almost two years he'd lived in constant agony, and he'd learned to move, breathe, and survive within those confines. He knew which twists and motions would trigger the worst of it and had adjusted his behavior to avoid or, at least, minimize the suffering. As the water flowed over his head, he forced himself to overcome his fear and lift both his arms, reaching his hands as high as he could toward the ceiling, a motion he'd avoided at all costs, as previously, the pain would have dropped him to his knees. Though he felt some odd pinching in his back, it was nothing compared to what he'd suffered before.

Stepping out of the shower, he stared at himself for a long time in the bathroom mirror. His face looked different, his features even and symmetrical. Though the change was subtle, he began to understand why Grace had looked on him with apprehension when he first awoke. As he turned around in a full circle, he laughed in amazement and delight as every scar on his body had noticeably faded. Even as he watched, he witnessed their second-by-second retreat as smooth, flawless skin took their place.

Though he'd done his best to stay in shape since his traumatic injuries, he hadn't entirely regained the muscle structure he'd lost during his months of recovery and bed rest. But now, his muscles were hard and tight, and he felt stronger than he ever had, even after completing grueling weeks of military training exercises.

But setting aside the drastic physical changes he was undergoing, the swirling confusion inside his mind was what occupied most of his attention. Ordered and linear, his clean and logical thought process had always been a strength, an important asset in his line of work. But right now, he could barely hold onto a single idea for more than a few seconds without another overriding it, and then another. It was dizzying. Were some of these interjecting thoughts coming from his Succouri? Undoubtedly, the reality of having another being inside one's head would take some getting used to, but he had expected his Sucouri's voice to be more distinctive. Currently, it was a jumbled mess. He hoped Ben or Ethan could help him sort it out, as presently it was making him feel unsettled.

As hunger was apparently not a discomfort relieved by this phenomenon, Donovan dressed quickly, additionally motivated by a desire to express his gratitude to everyone who'd selflessly risked and endured so much to save his life.

When he left the lab and stepped into the home's living room, Ben was the first to greet him, his smile unrestrained as he approached and embraced Donovan eagerly. When they released one another, Donovan kept his hand on Ben's shoulder, struggling to come up with words that could convey what was in his heart. Then, seeing Ethan just behind Ben, Donovan beckoned for him to join them.

"There's nothing I can say or do to express my gratitude to the two of you. You saved my life at great personal cost, and I'm forever in your debt."

Ben patted his arm and sent him a teasing smile. "Alright then. Your penance is to be my lifelong friend."

Donovan laughed, but the words spoken by Ben's Succouri in his vision replayed in his mind. "That was already a given, but"—he stepped back and offered his hand—"I accept your terms."

After the handshake, Donovan turned to Ethan.

"I want nothing from you," Ethan declared adamantly. "As I was just explaining to Ben, I've already been compensated far beyond my wildest hopes." He looked down for a moment, contemplating before refocusing on them. "I'd like to help you, Donovan. I don't know how much I can offer since this is an entirely new thing with your awakened Succouri, but I'd like to at least share what I know and be there to answer questions you might have. If that's alright with both of you?"

Ben patted Ethan's back. "That's more than alright. That's the way it should be."

Relieved by his offer, Donovan nodded enthusiastically. "Grace and I will rely on you both. We have much to learn. You look like a different man," Donovan noted as he studied Ethan's clear eyes and confident posture. Knowing that Ben's Succouri had been the main actor in the whole incredible drama, he wondered if he'd had an encounter similar to the one Donovan had experienced, and if so, whether that was the catalyst for the dramatic change.

"So do you," Ethan responded with a low chuckle.

"How do you feel?" Ben inquired of Donovan.

"Let's see…" Donovan grinned but raised his eyebrows and folded his arms. "Here are the things I *can* describe. I feel strong, free from pain, and ten years younger than I've felt in… well, in the last ten years I suppose. But there are also an assortment of new sensations I'm struggling to define. It's disorienting."

Donovan's anxiety retreated even further when Ben and Ethan nodded emphatically, conveying that what he was going through was, in fact, normal.

"Be patient with yourself," Ethan encouraged, "and give it time. It will be interesting to find out what's different about your experience as a result of your Succouri being revived." They both turned their eyes to Ben.

Ben sighed. "I was very young, and my memories are tainted by the confusion and fear I experienced. As I am the last recipient of this Succouri, that sets me apart in some ways. I'm hoping you and Grace will agree to travel with us when we go to see Carozza as he may have more answers to offer us, but according to Callie, the biggest difference will be the indeterminant length of the term you will serve as Succouri. It could be five years or thirty. There's no way to know. The good news is, assuming the term of service is significantly shorter than the previous norm, your body won't suffer the same debilitating effects, so even after your Succouri departs, you'll live a long full life. As I'm also doing, you'll need to learn to listen for your Succouri's voice, as it now has a much louder one to hear. When you enter the ripening, your only duty will be to keep an eye out for those who might be candidates for the transfer but, ultimately, you'll need to submit to your Succouri's will for the selected inheritor. Assuming you've learned to tune in to its voice by then, I'm guessing it will communicate with you regarding its choice. When the recipient is identified, you won't need a blood transfer. Simple touch contact will be all that's necessary for the exchange, just as Ethan did with you. Besides that, there's not much else we know for certain yet. You're a pioneer, my friend."

"Then I'm in very good company," Donovan noted with amusement. "I guess we'll just wait it out and see what happens. How will I know when... when it all kicks in and I can heal like you can?"

As he asked the question, Grace and Callie joined them, and Donovan slid his arm around Grace's waist, his heart aching at the exhaustion in her face and posture.

"It should be at least a week or two, but…" Ben smiled down at Callie. "There's an easy way to test it right now if you wish."

Callie grinned and extended her hand. "Donovan?"

After a second of confusion, Donovan nodded his understanding and took Callie's hand hesitantly, not sure what to expect.

Everyone watched Callie as she blinked and stared straight ahead, but Donovan felt nothing at all.

"Sorry," she said at last, shaking her head. "Not quite yet. But I'm sure it won't be long."

When Donovan released her hand, Ben patted his shoulder. "In my case, it took almost a month before I started manifesting signs of being Succouri. We'll be nearby whenever you want to test it out."

Content to wait for the changes to happen in due time, Donovan sighed. "In the meantime, from the looks of it, everyone in this room could use some sleep. I think I'm the only one here who's had ample rest over the last few days."

"We're planning to head to our place in Cape Cod within the hour. Whoever wants to join us is more than welcome. I want to check on the doc, though, make sure he's alright. Is he still in the lab?"

Donovan nodded. "Before I took a shower, he was already busy running his tests. He seemed shaken up by everything that happened today, so I think checking on him's a good plan."

When Ben and Callie stepped away, Taylor approached and offered Donovan his hand. "Congratulations. No one could be more deserving." He paused to smile at Donovan and then Grace. "It's a strange experience, watching scars on your body suddenly vanish and making room in your head for a strange new voice. I didn't have the chance to see the process through, but I remember how fantastic, yet disorienting the initial experience was."

"Yes, sir. It is that," Donovan agreed with a nod. "Grace told me how you helped her, got a helicopter out to us before it was too late. Thank you."

"And," Grace said, her voice low. "He knows about... about our little secret." She smiled affectionately at Taylor.

Momentarily confused, Donovan looked between them. Grace tapped the spot on her chest where her wedding ring made a small indent in her blouse.

"I see," Donovan exclaimed, grinning. "Hard to keep a secret from an FBI agent, I suppose. In that case, besides Lobster, you're the first person I am fortunate enough to tell how truly lucky I am."

With sober sincerity, Taylor nodded. "That's indisputable. Grace didn't leave your side, not to eat and barely to sleep. I've never seen such devotion, except between Ben and Callie. But I'm equally confident it was well earned. The Succouri may have healed your body, but I'm gratified to see you let Grace mend your heart as, in the end, that's what makes life worth living." He paused to take a deep breath. "I want to meet with both of you as there's something important we need to discuss, but first, take a few days to get your feet under you, adjust to all the changes. I'll be heading back to Boston with Maggie, maybe as early as tomorrow, but we'll work something out." Once more, he extended his hand. "Take full advantage of the new life you've been given, Donovan. Don't waste a moment."

"You can rest assured, I won't," Donovan promised, grasping Taylor's hand firmly.

After everyone in the house had had a chance to congratulate him, and Grace introduced Donovan to Maggie, they moved to the kitchen where Doctor Navarro's wife, Silvia, generously fed them until Donovan couldn't eat another bite. Grace laughed as she watched him, eating a little herself, but nowhere near the portions he consumed.

"I'd caution you not to make yourself sick," she giggled, "but I doubt that's possible, so..." She gestured toward a third sandwich Silvia had just set in front of him.

"In twenty-nine years, I've never been this hungry."

She tilted her head as she smiled. "It sounds odd to say, but in a way, you're sort of eating for two, though I don't know exactly how that works."

Donovan shrugged. "Your guess is as good as mine."

Doctor Navarro entered the kitchen and took a seat at the table with them. Though weary and subdued, he didn't look as defeated as when they'd spoken to him just before Donovan headed for the lab's bathroom.

"How are you feeling?" he asked, studying Donovan carefully.

"Fantastic!"

"Any pain at all?"

Setting down his sandwich, he leaned back in his chair. "It feels wrong to complain in any way but, since you asked, there's a slight pinching sensation in my back, not really painful, just odd."

Grace looked at the doctor with concern.

"I figured it wouldn't be long. You've got a lot of hardware, plates, and pins you no longer need as your spine, if not already, will soon be completely healed, as if nothing ever happened. We'll need to get all that out before the rapid healing fully sets in, making the procedure near impossible and excruciating." He grimaced.

"But I thought Succouri couldn't feel pain," Grace asked in confusion.

"Not so. Succouri feel pain just like anyone else, but as

their bodies heal nearly instantaneously from any injury, it's rare, and when it does happen, it typically lasts only a few seconds. However, if surgery becomes necessary, that's a different matter entirely. Anesthetics don't work on Succouri, and to keep ahead of the rapid healing, continual cutting is necessary. It's miserable for doctor and patient. We have a few days to work with here as your body adjusts and changes. The effectiveness of anesthesia will diminish more each hour and staying ahead of the healing will become increasingly challenging. Therefore, my recommendation is to put you back under as soon as possible so I can remove the unnecessary hardware and—"

Donovan put up his hands. "Hold on, Doctor. I've been awake for less than an hour. I need to get outside, get some fresh air in my lungs and, without delay, I must ensure that my... Grace gets some sleep. Can we possibly put this off until tomorrow?"

The doctor sucked air through his teeth. "The surgery will become more complicated the longer we wait, and if things shift in the meantime, it could become more than just an annoyance. It might really get painful. I wouldn't recommend waiting any longer than first thing in the morning."

"Alright," Donovan acquiesced. "We'll come back first thing and—"

The vigorous shake of the doctor's head halted Donovan's sentence. "You'll need to stay here for at least a few days, preferably a week. We'll make up bedrooms for you and Grace, but I need to monitor your progress and run tests. Besides Ben, you are the very first human I, or anyone else in the network, have known who carry a sentient Succouri. As Ben's a member of a terminal match while you're an interim host, your experiences may diverge, and compared to what we've previously observed, there will undoubtedly be dramatic differences in how the Succouri integrates and affects your body, as well as that of your partner. Ben's going to remain nearby to help us, as he's the closest thing we've got to an expert on this, but though I have no power to keep you here, I humbly ask for your patience and indulgence, both for your and Grace's well-being, but also so we can learn and thus better prepare those who will come after you. Ben believes it is his calling, his destiny to awaken every Succouri in existence. Learning more about the process and the consequences is essential, and right now, you're our solitary subject."

Caught off guard by the doctor's urgent plea, Donovan rubbed his palms together, then turned his eyes to Grace. He understood the doctor's reasoning, and he felt obligated to help as the doctor, Ben, Ethan, and the gift had saved his life. But he'd lost far too much time with Grace already and the idea of continuing to hide their relationship, sleep in separate rooms, and call her by a name she no longer possessed was intolerable. If he had to be trapped here, he wanted to be trapped with his wife.

Reading the message in his eyes, Grace reached across the table and took his hand before turning to the doctor. "Doctor, we haven't told anyone else—well, besides Taylor who came to the knowledge on his own—but given what you're suggesting we need you to know." She nodded at Donovan, bidding him to continue.

"About twelve hours before I collapsed and was life-flighted to the hospital, Grace and I were married."

Surprise flashed across Doctor Navarro's face for less than a second before an approving smile lit up his eyes. "Congratulations are in order then. I'm gratified I won't need to give you the same speech I gave Ben. Starting your

Succouri life with a Datouri already in place simplifies matters tremendously and will make your journey much smoother and easier. I had a feeling there was more to your relationship. I've only ever seen that kind of bond with Succouri partners." He clapped his hands together. "One bedroom it is then. But I still recommend sticking around, just for a few days, and I definitely advise surgery in the morning. As with Ben, after that, we can set up telephone appointments and periodic visits to keep tabs on your progress."

After a contented nod from Grace, Donovan sighed and picked up his sandwich. "Sounds like a reasonable plan, Doctor. We're in."

When the doctor returned to the lab, Donovan had had his fill of food, and Donovan and Grace had explained their plans to remain at the doctor's residence for a few days, with a round of joyful embraces, they bid their friends goodnight. Turning to her with a contented smile, Donovan held out his hand to Grace. "I know you're tired, but would you consider going for a short walk with me? I need to breathe some fresh air."

"I know the feeling," she empathized, accepting his invitation.

It was late afternoon, and as they strolled down the country lane, blinding rays of horizontal sunlight streaked between the thick trees of the surrounding forest. Upon their arrival in Cape Cod a few days before, they'd been rushed from the plane into an ambulance, then directly into the doctor's house, so neither he nor Grace had been aware of how far from the city they were. There wasn't another house or a paved road in sight.

"I suppose, when you're a doctor who works with

magical beings, living off the grid is a must," Donovan mused.

"I suppose so," she agreed distractedly, without looking over at him.

"Grace?" he probed, halting to turn and face her. "I know the last few days have been a nightmare. I can't express how sorry I am for marrying you only to leave you basically abandoned and afraid. But it won't happen again. From this day forward, I'm at your service, ma'am, day and night, your permanent personal bodyguard." He smiled and offered her a shallow bow. "If you'll have me."

Though she returned his smile, her eyes remained shadowed. "Donovan how... how does it feel? Do you still feel like... like you?"

"Mostly," he reflected. "Though the constant pain had become so much a part of my reality that its absence is, of course, welcome, but foreign." He redirected his gaze down the dirt road. "Did you know I used to run daily, usually at least eight miles? I haven't done that in a very long time."

Hearing the yearning in his tone, Grace released his hand and stepped back. "Go!" she ordered, pointing down the road. "Take your new body out for a test drive." She giggled and playfully shoved him forward.

Not certain if she was serious or kidding, he hesitated, but she put a hand on her hip and pointed emphatically again, so he turned, fixed his eyes on a spot far ahead, and took off at a full run. The available power coursing through his muscles astonished him as it propelled him forward with ease and at a speed he'd never achieved before. Even when he was in his late teens, he'd never been this strong. This felt more like flying than running, the wind blowing into his face and whistling in his ears. Apart from the pinching sensation in his back, there was no discomfort whatsoever.

Quicker than he'd believed possible, he reached the spot he'd visually marked and turned back, pleased to see Grace laughing as she watched him. When he returned to her, he swept her into his arms, spinning her in wild, jubilant circles as their laughter rang out, the dream that had felt painfully out of reach now a vivid reality before their eyes.

"That was really fun to watch," Grace said, through the giggles. "I could barely see you, you were moving so fast, and you looked so completely happy and free! It's everything I ever wanted for you, Donovan Bradshaw."

Setting her on her feet, he stared, his expression sobering. "This is *our* new life, Grace. Yours and mine. You understand that, right?"

Dropping her gaze, she didn't answer.

"Grace. What is it? Do you no longer want to be my partner?" he asked, his voice distressed.

"Of course, I do, but..." She looked up, and in her eyes, he could read the question she didn't want to ask.

Sighing, he took her hands and stepped close enough that she couldn't evade his gaze. "I know I look a little different. My scars are almost gone and there's something alien whispering in my head that I can't comprehend yet. From what I understand, the bonding thing will take time to develop, so for the moment, you're probably feeling overwhelmed, and a little left behind. But, Grace, despite the changes you see on the outside, it is still me, your Donovan, the one who fell for you the first time I looked into those sky-blue eyes, the man who bought you that ridiculously tiny salad at the neighborhood deli, who survived your intimidating interrogation, and who cursed having to leave a town I'd only been in for a few hours because you were in it. I'm the one whose heart beat out of his chest when I caught sight of you at the airport, who, in terror, showed you his scars despite being certain you'd think me a monster afterward. I'm the broken man who sat in the car with you, staring up at the stars, telling you a horror story I had never spoken about in detail with anyone else." He chuckled softly before continuing. "I also must confess that I'm the same man who let you believe you knocked me off balance, causing us to tumble to the floor during our improvised training session, when in truth, I intentionally orchestrated the whole thing so I could get close to you, as from the moment I saw you in that bath towel, I could think of nothing else."

Grace's eyes began to shine, even as a tear slipped down her cheek.

"I'm the man who stood with you in that courthouse chapel, fervently praying that God would grant me time to savor even the smallest, sweetest taste of life as your husband." He took her face in his hands. "And I'm the man who made love to you in that remote cabin in the woods, so overcome with passion that, while I was in your arms, I felt no pain. I haven't forgotten one second, one heartbeat we've shared, Grace, and that won't change. This wondrous thing that's happened, this new life, it hasn't replaced who and what we were and are. It won't steal our memories or change our feelings. Please, hear me, Grace. I don't want this life, or any life for that matter, without you. I—"

Before he could finish, Grace released his hands and wrapped her arms around his neck. Slowly, yet hungrily, she kissed him, and inside his chest, something shifted, forever altering the rhythm of his heart. Heat ignited, moving from his toes up the full length of his body. When it reached his lips, Grace gasped and stepped back.

"What... What was that?"

"You felt that?" he asked in surprise.

"I most definitely did." Her eyes grew wide.

"I'm not sure what's happening, should we—"

Cutting off his question, she leaned forward and eagerly resumed the kiss. Once again, the heat rushed through him, rising more quickly this time, as if targeting the point of contact. Though he felt her react to it, she didn't pull away. As the experience was confounding yet thrilling, the sound of their unsteady breathing soon filled the air around them.

Donovan slid his fingers up the side of her cheek and into her hair, and the warmth spread to every point of contact. As it pulsed, it intensified, and he shifted closer, unable to resist the pull, drawing him toward her. Mirroring his action, she wrapped her arms around him and pulled him so tightly against her that he could feel every curve of her body. The light breeze, swaying trees, chirping birds, and even the solid ground beneath his feet faded from his awareness, leaving only the moment to consume him. His entire world narrowed, consisting only of her: the warmth of her flushed face, the enchanting aroma of her perfume, and the harmonious cadence of her heartbeat synchronizing with his. Lost in a thick fog of passion neither could escape, Donovan lifted her into his arms.

"Grace, I—"

"Hurry, soldier!"

Unfathomably, in a new or previously dormant corner of his heart, Donovan could feel her presence, sense her desire for him, and, like pouring gasoline on an already raging fire, it fed the flames, making focusing on where they were and where they needed to go near impossible.

In a daze, he carried her back to the house, up the stairs, and into the bedroom Silvia had prepared for them, driven solely by an instinct, an irresistible need to be alone with her.

When he lay her gently on the bed, she gripped his shoulders, kissing him with unrelenting fervor, as if this were the last time she'd ever have the chance to love him. Sweeping aside her silky hair, he caressed the soft skin of her neck, and she trembled at his touch. When she slipped her hands inside his shirt, the fire engulfed his entire being, and they willingly surrendered to it.

The moments that followed were the most electrifying, yet also the most meaningful ones of Donovan's life. Never before had he felt that connected to someone, sharing emotions and heartbeats as if existing in the same skin. Yet the closeness went far beyond the physical. The fire that moved between them united their souls and their destinies.

Later, as they lay face to face, staring with wonder into each other's eyes, they struggled to process what was happening between them.

"Grace," Donovan whispered, softly stroking her hair. "Do you believe me now? Do you see I'm the same man you fell in love with?"

"Yes," she smiled. "And no." She traced the places on his face where his scars were now almost undetectable.

"Fair enough. Besides the scars."

"Please understand what I mean when I say this," she started hesitantly. "I won't ever forget them. I'll always remember what you suffered, what you sacrificed. It made you the man you are, and erasing the evidence on the outside doesn't mean the effects of it, good and bad, disappear. Though I'm immeasurably grateful for the miracle of a new, full life with you, I won't forget how our journey started."

Leaning in, he whispered into her ear. "And I won't forget that you loved me despite the scars, that you were willing to marry me without a single guarantee that we'd have a future together. I'll remember how you stuck by my side when I was unconscious or in too much pain to offer you anything but hardship."

Gripping him tightly, she smiled, but her expression soon shifted to a look of confusion. "What we're feeling, this connection, the fire, is this the bond?"

"I'm not one hundred percent sure, but what else could it be? It certainly qualifies as extraordinary. Since it began, I can feel you, inside my chest, your emotions, and echoes of your thoughts. There's no reasonable explanation for that, so it must be the Succouri at work."

"Same for me. I feel you too, right here," she said, her voice breathy with wonder as she pressed her hand to her heart. After a deep breath, she giggled, making Donovan smile as her joy and laughter echoed through the corridors of his heart. "I guess all that silly worrying was for nothing."

"Worrying?"

Closing her eyes, she sighed. "Maggie and Callie said it... you would choose me, but I thought maybe... maybe I wouldn't be the right person, not someone suitable for this life. I assuredly understand the Succouri picking you. You've already given so much of yourself, saved countless people. You're a natural fit, but I'm..."

Donovan shifted, leaning away to look at her incredulously. "That's what you've been worried about all this time? After you sat faithfully by my bedside, night and day, not eating or sleeping, you didn't think you were qualified or that I'd choose you for the bond?"

Grace closed her eyes. "I... I wasn't sure, and if you didn't, I couldn't stand the thought of losing you and—"

"Grace!" he exclaimed, the word resounding with deep compassion mixed with disbelief. "Even now, after all we've shared, you don't understand how I love you. Becoming Succouri, as life-changing as it is, could never alter my devotion."

"Maggie told me the Succouri inside a man knows when he's found a love that's true and will last for a lifetime. And it also knows when the partner, the future Datouri, feels likewise. I already knew I loved you in that way, and I was pretty sure you did too, but..."

Donovan's heart physically ached at her insecurity.

Sensing his distress, her eyes moistened. "I'm sorry, but please understand. Insincere expressions of devotion and broken promises are all I've heard from the lips of men all my life. As I was growing up, I heard one man after another pledge their love to my mother, then turn around and break her heart. As soon as the high of the infatuation wore off, they either left or treated her like trash. Before I made a vow to myself to pretty much stay far away from men altogether, the ones I... I trusted with my heart, turned out to be of the same crummy variety. Until I saw the way Ben looked at Callie, and then the way you looked at me, I didn't believe in any of this, Donovan, the true love, happily ever after thing. But you've made me believe in it, though I guess..." She sniffled, and a tear traced down her cheek. "I guess my scars are taking longer to disappear."

Moved by her confession of pain, Donovan set his hand over her heart, and she placed hers on top of his. "I wish the Succouri in me could heal those kinds of wounds. But regardless, in time, you will come to trust in me, Grace Bradshaw, because I'll still be here, and still love you, likely better and deeper. For the rest of my life, I'll need you and want you. That is the solemn vow I willingly and reverently took. We are one, more so now than ever. Whatever's begun inside of us is irreversible. I'm certain of that. Ethan's unending pain over losing his wife is easily comprehensible to me now. There indeed exists such a thing as a faithful, honest man, Grace, and I hope, in time, you will come to believe I am one."

With a new light shining in her eyes, she smiled up at him. "That much I do believe, soldier."

CHAPTER 20

RENEWED PURPOSE

Late into the night, they conversed in whispers. Grace told Donovan about what had happened while he'd been unconscious, and a weight of sorrow burdened his heart when he heard of the troubles Ben and Callie had faced. The fact that they'd still managed to get Ethan to Cape Cod and save his life was astounding, and their selfless efforts were yet more proof of the rare, priceless friendship the four of them shared.

Donovan described his vision, what Ben's Succouri had proclaimed, and how he'd come face to face with the Succouri who now resided in him. Then she shared hers, explaining her belief that it was Ben's Succouri who encouraged her not to give up fighting for his life. In the end, they wholeheartedly agreed that the revelations were not coincidences or random dreams.

"I'm not sure how it will play out," Donovan admitted. "But somehow, my skills, my training, it will be put to good use. Ben and Callie, perhaps the entire Succouri network, will need help and protection. For this time, for this purpose, we were chosen."

"Though I agree, I admit it scares me a little. I hate the idea of you being in harm's way, but I can't deny the truth." She yawned, and Donovan chuckled under his breath, knowing it wouldn't be long until he lost her to exhaustion.

"No need for worry. This will sound arrogant, but that doesn't mean it isn't true. Even before, with my body in shambles, I was a formidable enemy to all things evil. Now, I'm stronger and faster than I've ever been, not to mention I evidently have the power to heal myself nearly instantaneously. Without question, I wouldn't want to fight an enemy with my level of training and experience, who also had that advantage."

"But aren't Succouri supposed to be pacifist, placed on earth to heal and comfort? Ben is strong, and he's certainly protected Callie without a second thought, but mostly by using himself as a human shield. He doesn't strike me as the warrior type."

As he considered her question, Donovan tried to listen for his Succouri's voice amidst the jumbled mess of thoughts in his head. "I think, though you are right about healing being the primary mission, each Succouri is distinctive, just as humans are. They have different persuasions and personalities. Compassion, goodness, and empathy are common, basic attributes, but—I can't be sure yet as its voice still isn't very loud—I think the one I possess has a personality much like mine, just as Ben's resembles his. Even though I'm not its final host, we have a great deal in common. I sensed that when I spoke to him, or it, in my vision. It even looked like me and wore military fatigues. It said something about admiring my courage, even my stubbornness," Donovan relayed with a chuckle.

"It makes sense that, in order for the two of you to live with one another in such an intimate way, like-mindedness would be imperative," she said, her words slurring. She yawned once more. "I think…"

"Grace?"

There was no answer, and Donovan smiled as he pulled her closer, amused by how she could fall into unconsciousness mid-sentence. Though medically induced, he'd had his fill of rest, but he was content to hold her in his arms, enjoying the feel of her warm body pressing against his.

For the next few hours, he listened intently, the task considerably easier in the stillness of the dark night. As dawn's first light spread across the horizon, he grew more confident in his ability to discern which thoughts were his own and which echoed with the voice of the soldier he had met in his vision. Presently, it still spoke too faintly to decode its messages with certainty, but he felt more assured that, in time, its voice would be as familiar as his own.

When he'd first heard about the Succouri, he thought of it as an inanimate power, some kind of magic that infiltrated the body. Then when Ben and Callie described their new discoveries just before the transfer, his perception morphed. At that point, the whole thing sounded like a tame version of *Invasion of the Body Snatchers*, which wasn't particularly appealing, but since he was dying, it was much too late to quibble about the means of his salvation.

But after his vision and a few hours living the life, it wasn't at all what he'd expected. Grace had asked him if he still felt like himself, and besides the radical changes to his physical body, he assuredly did. Though presently jumbled, nothing in his mind screamed for special attention or authoritarian control. Donovan was still the autonomous king of his castle, so to speak. His Succouri demonstrated no desire whatsoever to rule over him or usurp his will. On the contrary, the voice he'd only just begun to recognize spoke in quiet suggestions, all of which condoned his well-being and aligned with his character. Perhaps the intensity of the assertions it offered would increase with time, but regardless, Donovan no longer felt any trepidation or intimidation at its presence.

At six a.m., he quietly slipped out of bed, showered, and dressed, knowing the doctor was anxious to complete the surgery to remove the unneeded hardware from his back. Before he left the room, he stood by the bed, staring down at his new bride.

She slept on her stomach, her flowing hair covering her left shoulder. The fair skin of her back glowed in the soft morning light.

'Beautiful' was far too small a word to capture who she was. Loving her was as easy as breathing. Her faith and her wonderful, stubborn, ceaseless strength were the reasons he was alive. It was true that Ben, Callie, and Ethan had brought him the gift, but without Grace's constant presence, imploring him not to give up, breathing in his ear and begging him for just a bit more time, he never would have lived long enough to receive it. For days on end, he fought for every breath, willing himself to keep the light flickering. He did so for one reason alone: he couldn't leave her, break her heart, or let her down. If she'd ever released him, given him permission to let go, he would have died minutes later. Succouri prophecies aside, Donovan knew God had brought him this angel, for there was no one else who could have had that potent influence over him.

Gritting his teeth at the thought of the worthless men who had hurt her fragile soul, he reminded himself that the best revenge he could extract was to love her faithfully for the rest of his life and hope it would be enough to eventually heal the wounds their wicked actions had inflicted. To do so would be the honor of his life, an even greater one than serving a country and a people he loved.

Though he had begun to embrace the soldier in him as she loved that part of him too, her acceptance of his past and scars had redeemed his humanity, brought back into balance what had become unstable through the decade of combat and killing. As a result, the debt he owed her wasn't just for saving his life, but also his soul.

When he finally pulled himself away from her side and made his way to the lab, he found the doctor already hard at work.

"Don't you ever sleep, Doctor?" Donovan asked, startling him as he leaned over a desk, staring at a computer screen.

"Not when I have the opportunity to study something I never dreamed I'd encounter," he answered, waving Donovan toward the nearest hospital bed. "Where's Grace?"

"Fast asleep, as she should be. She's way beyond exhausted. I didn't figure she needed to be here for this anyhow. Without question, she's been through enough turmoil in the last couple of weeks, and she's certainly put in more than her fair share of time standing by my bedside. My turn to take care of her now, and since there's no real danger in this procedure, that starts with letting her get some well-deserved rest."

"Good man," the doctor praised with genuine admiration. "I used to think I understood the Succouri, Mr. Bradshaw. Then I met Ben. Since then, I take nothing for granted." He sighed and put up a finger. "But I'm reasonably certain there's no serious risk, though I can't guarantee a painless morning."

"Pain and I are very well-acquainted, Doctor. I think you'll find my tolerance level exceeds what you previously believed possible."

Patting his shoulder, the doctor nodded. "After what you've endured, undoubtedly I will."

Just before the doctor administered the anesthetic he hoped would put Donovan under for at least a few minutes, Donovan turned a curious eye to him. "I hope you don't mind, but, given your experience with the Succouri, I wanted to ask you something... of a personal nature."

"Of course."

"I think Grace and I... What I mean to ask is can you tell me what happens when the bond first initiates?"

"Ben didn't inform you about what to expect?"

"Unfortunately, I've been asleep for all but a few minutes since he and Callie returned from their honeymoon. They told us how important the bond is, and how the partner helps the Succouri, and I've watched them in action enough to see how they connect and relate with one another but I don't know exactly what to look for in this regard, how to know if it's begun."

Contemplating, the doctor rubbed his palms together. "There are numerous manifestations, but the most common, and usually one of the first, is heightened physical attraction. Keep in mind, I've never been Succouri myself, so this is second-hand information, and—as the experience is quite... intimate and personal—most prefer to keep it private, so even what I do know is limited. Nevertheless, there seems to be a chemical reaction that takes place, manifesting as a sensation of heat at the point of contact followed by an irresistible drawing of one to the other. My daughter, who married a Succouri, described it to me as magnetism, but at a scale unlike anything typically experienced by human beings. When it reaches full strength, it becomes overpowering, and most can't defy its demands, not for long anyway. That is precisely why I told you having a spouse before becoming Succouri is preferable. Let the bond have its way and develop in its time. It means an easier, happier transition as well as quicker available aid when the Succouri faces the demands and consequences of the draw."

Unable to suppress his smile, Donovan nodded, comforted by the doctor's words. "Thank you. That helps tremendously."

Intrigued, the doctor raised his eyebrows. "Donovan, have you and Grace experienced something like what I just described?"

Donovan held his grin.

"Are you certain?"

"Affirmative."

Disbelief was written all over the doctor's face. "Consider that you were recently married, and you've just been given a second chance at life, brought back from the edge of death. Perhaps excitement over that fact as well as the cessation of pain—"

Donovan shook his head, still smiling at the bewildered man before him. "You forget that we did have one night of honeymooning, Doctor. This was... very different."

Pacing a few feet away, the doctor repeatedly rubbed his head before at last turning back to Donovan. "Well then, it seems we've discovered our first point of deviation from the way dormant Succouri function within their hosts. Even when there is a pre-existing spouse, I've never known the bonding process to initiate before the manifestation of healing power. As that typically takes two to four weeks, you can understand why I'm stunned to learn that, in less than twenty-four hours since your acquisition, you and Grace have already begun the process. As with Ben and Callie, we will need to discard our previous assumptions and take each day as it comes, learning anew about this remarkable gift. Let's just hope the rapid healing hasn't set in on the same accelerated timeline. Otherwise, we could be in for a challenging morning."

With a sigh of blissful contentment, Grace slowly rolled over and opened her eyes. Donovan sat on the edge of the bed, fully clothed, and smiling down at her.

"Good morning."

Alarmed, she sat up. "What time is it?"

"Nearly eleven thirty, ma'am," he informed her with a twinkle in his eye.

Reaching out, she gripped his arm. "Your surgery! I—"

"All done. No more bionic man. I'm pure flesh and blood now." He chuckled. "Well, if you don't count the alien being living inside my head."

Though he was trying hard to allay her distress with humor, their new connection betrayed him, informing her he wasn't being entirely candid. The procedure had been brutal; she was sure of it, and the thought of him facing it alone made her heart ache.

"Why didn't you wake me? I wanted to be there with you; I didn't want you going through that by yourself."

Tenderly, Donovan swept the hair away from her face and leaned forward to kiss her forehead. "Grace, you've done more to care for me than I can ever repay. It was my turn this morning to take care of you, to put you first. You needed rest, and I was at peace knowing you were getting what was required to keep you healthy. And anyway"—he gestured toward himself—"I'm just fine, functioning at one hundred percent, no more pinching. Besides the new ones the kind doctor just inflicted, the scars have completely vanished. The new ones will disappear within a day or so. I'll be back to running eight miles a day or more in no time." He winked at her. "I'm going to need a partner who's fully rested to keep up with me," he teased.

Cringing at the idea of fresh wounds after the countless ones he'd already endured, she nevertheless appreciated his thoughtful choice to save her the torment of watching him suffer further. "I'm sorry it wasn't as easy as the doctor hoped. I appreciate your thoughtfulness, but please, don't go it alone ever again. By your side, no matter the difficulty, is where I want to be."

"Understood, ma'am," he replied, his gratitude expressing itself in his sincere look of adoration.

Leaning back, she at last smiled. "Speaking of being by your side, what are we going to do when the doctor finally releases us from this comfortable, nevertheless confining jail?" She laughed. "We've been so focused on making our little miracle happen that we never once talked about where we'd live."

Acknowledging her point, Donovan nodded. "After we visit Carozza with Ben and Callie, I'd like to take you to Boston, introduce you to my parents, and vacate my apartment. As we've agreed that our destiny intersects with the Sawyers, it follows that we'll need to live nearby. If I promise to unpack my boxes quickly, protect you from all pesky neighbors, give you a lifetime of self-defense lessons at no charge, and only walk in on you in a bath towel with your express permission, might you consider taking me in, and letting me share your heart and home for the next seventy years, give or take a decade?"

With a refreshing giggle, Grace kissed him repeatedly before answering. "Everything I have is yours, Donovan Bradshaw: my home, my life, my heart."

Reaching to retrieve Grace's wedding ring from the nightstand, he slipped it off the chain and took her left hand in his. "May I?"

Grinning, she nodded her approval, so Donovan slipped it onto her finger. "Whether I had lived for a day or a lifetime, I meant every word of the promises I made you when I first put this on your finger."

"As did I. And by the way, we need to get you one of these as well. Don't want single women out there getting any fanciful ideas."

"We'll put that on the top of the list of priorities as soon as we're liberated."

As they held each other's gaze, the sacred moment felt like a new beginning. They'd left behind the shadows of pain and dread and embraced the reality of a future filled with wondrous possibilities. Though there was still much they needed to learn about their shared gift, they no longer doubted that their lives would be filled with enduring love and exceptional purpose.

A WEEK LATER, Donovan and Grace traveled with Ben, Callie, Ethan, and Taylor to Philadelphia to meet Carozza. His health was declining and Taylor suspected he wouldn't live much longer, so this was likely their last chance to learn more about the old ways of the Succouri from him.

It's too bad he won't live to see it all change," Donovan said regretfully as the group reclined in the comfortable cabin of the private aircraft.

"But he'll get to see the beginning and meet the first benefactors of that change," Grace reminded them.

"Yes, he will," Ben agreed. "And that brings me to a matter I've wanted to discuss with you all but haven't found the right time to do so. As soon as the doctor can shift his focus away from your care, Donovan; he, Silvia, Callie, and I will begin the difficult task of tracking down and contacting every Succouri we can find and educating them on what we've learned. Initially, we'll focus our efforts on persuading those closest to the ripening phase, as that's the only time their Succouri can be awakened. Therefore, the urgency to convince them is greater. Though my childhood reception and transformation provide compelling evidence, the strongest proof lies with the two of you. If we have any chance at convincing people of this radically new and foreign perspective, we will need your testimonies."

Donovan leaned forward and started to speak, but Ben put up a hand. "Before you give an answer, please understand the risks involved here. Anonymity and privacy are essential safety nets in this life. Callie and I learned that lesson when we foolishly revealed our names to those we helped in the housefire. Not only did it result in unwanted publicity, but it also enabled her stalker to find us. Despite the need for it, I'm doubtful that remaining anonymous will be possible, at least not within the Succouri network. We'll have to be known to effectively bring about the kind of dramatic change we're seeking."

Apologetically, Ben looked at his father. "As you've now associated yourself closely with us, your job, reputation, and perhaps more may be at risk if we're discovered and investigated. Before he headed home to finish his last few months of high school, we spoke to Lee, and our family has unanimously decided to stay the course as we believe this is our destined path; what we're meant to do regardless of the risks. I wish I didn't have to ask the same of each of you, but without your statements as evidence, I doubt we'll succeed. The blood transfers and the perceived right of each human host to select the inheritor of the gift are ingrained practices and ideas that some won't easily renounce. Please, before you give an answer, consider carefully what you're jeopardizing by partnering with us." He took Callie's hand. "Consider the loved ones whose lives will be impacted and make the choice that's best for you. You won't forfeit my friendship or respect if you decline."

Though Donovan appreciated Ben's warnings, he and Grace had already discussed this at length, counted the costs, and decided with equal conviction that partnering with Ben and Callie to assist and protect them in their endeavor was the central focus of their calling. Without a single doubt, they believed the mandate came directly from Ben's Succouri who had orchestrated not only Donovan's rescue from certain death but also Ethan's redemption from inner turmoil. Though these were pure gifts of mercy and kindness, they did come with a duty, an obligation to offer what Donovan already possessed in service to the cause.

Even without the confirming visions, his integrity as a man and a soldier would have brought him to the same place. He'd chosen to serve his country because he wanted to give back, repay a personal debt he felt he owed for the freedoms he enjoyed. In the same way, he was indebted to the Succouri as the gift had saved his life and given him a future with Grace.

After a confirming nod from Grace, Donovan spoke up quickly. "I may not be able to hear everything my Succouri whispers to me with complete clarity yet, but if there's one thing I'm absolutely sure of, it is this: just as the human part of me is forever indebted to the human part of you, Ben, for saving my life, so too the Succouri in me is eternally loyal and will remain faithful to your Succouri for bringing it back and giving it a new destiny." He chuckled at the truth in his next statement. "I literally couldn't live with myself if I... *we* didn't offer our unconditional, full support."

Ben lowered his head, humbled by their generosity of spirit. "Thank you both."

"But," Donovan added quickly, holding up a finger. "One of the ways I can help is by putting my skills and training to good use. There's a lot we can do to protect ourselves. Between Taylor and me, I'm confident we can put together a plan to effectively accomplish our mission while exercising caution. And even if something does go wrong, we can plan for that eventuality as well; sort of a hope for the best, but plan for the worst strategy."

"I agree, and I'm in," Taylor responded enthusiastically.

Ben sighed in relief. "I was hoping the two of you would offer your expertise in that area. That takes a significant weight off our shoulders."

After Callie and Taylor's visit to his home, Carozza had been moved to a local nursing home so he could receive around-the-clock care. When they entered his room, Donovan, Grace, and Ethan hung back, allowing Taylor, Ben, and Callie several moments of private conversation.

The man's face was wrinkled and his skin pale. Even when Ben touched him, his frail bones and weakened muscles made it a challenge for him to rise to a sitting position. He spoke with a deep raspy voice, the remnants of an Italian accent adding to the sense of mystique projected by his presence. Upon meeting Ben, the man's eyes filled with tears and the homage in his tone conveyed how long he had awaited such an encounter.

"On their last visit, you informed my father and Callie about the devastation caused by the blood transfers and how they had robbed the Antico of their will and their destinies," Ben said, shifting the conversation away from more personal matters.

Raising a tight fist in the air, Carozza's face began to redden with anger. "Traitors! All who receive this miraculous gift, then trample it under their feet deserve to suffer the worst hell can do to them." The man's sudden, fierce anger caused Grace to tighten her hold on his hand.

Shaking his head, Ben kept his voice soft and controlled as he countered Carozza's unjust verdict. "Without exception, every Succouri we've met, as well as those who support them, have been unaware of the truth. I don't deny that those who initiated this practice deserve blame, but neither I, nor my Antico equate innocent ignorance with intentional malice, Mr. Carozza."

Looking like a child who'd been corrected by a parent, Carozza lowered his gaze and softened his tone. "Nevertheless, the sorrow and devastation of losing an invaluable treasure forever is unfathomable."

Ben smiled. "Not forever, my friend. Because of your help, the Antico has not been irrevocably silenced."

Raising his eyes to Ben's again, he squinted in confusion.

Ben turned and beckoned for the three of them to approach, and Grace, Donovan, and Ethan lined up at the foot of Carozza's bed. One by one, Ben introduced them, giving Carozza the pertinent information about their background.

"Before Callie and I became aware of your theories, we

devised a plan to save Donavan's life through the transfer of Ethan's gift. We worked with a doctor in the network to bring everyone together, but before we could go through with the procedure, things went awry with Callie and me. That's when she and my father came to see you. When they returned from their visit, they informed us of what they'd learned, and the doctor, Callie, and I began to ask ourselves some hard questions about the ethics of following through with the blood transfusion, even though not doing so meant certain death for Donovan. Just in time, our Antico gave us the answer, solved our dilemma."

Holding his breath, Carozza put a hand to his chest.

Ben nodded to Ethan, and he cleared his throat.

"Through direct contact, Ben's Succouri temporarily moved into me, awakened mine, and healed the emptiness left by the death of my wife fifteen years ago."

Gaping, Carozza leaned forward so quickly that Ben almost lost contact with his arm. "Awakened? How do you know your Succouri was awakened?"

"I experienced the change, in a big way. It was like a part of your body you've never paid much mind to—like maybe your elbow or knee—suddenly coming alive with sensations unlike anything you've ever experienced. And I heard Ben's Succouri speaking, almost as clearly as his human voice. As it accomplished its task, mine also began to speak, express itself in kind, only less... wise, less confident." Ethan shook his head in frustration. "It's hard to explain as there's no experience similar enough to provide a reasonable comparison. After Ben's Succouri returned to him, there was a time of disorientation as I sorted through the jumbled messages coming from this new, independent voice in my head. When Ben reminded me that Donovan was in trouble, it all fell into place. I understood it couldn't stay with me, and in truth, I didn't want it to. It wanted to leave, and I was ready to be human again. This mutual realization initiated an impulse to reach out to Donovan, the force of which was many times stronger than the normal urge Succouri feel to touch the suffering."

As no one in the room had heard about his experience in this much detail, Ethan had everyone's undivided attention, particularly Donovan's, as he continued.

"When I made contact with Donovan, I felt it go. For a moment, I panicked, hoping its absence wouldn't open another hole in me similar to the one Ben's Succouri had just healed. But as it departed, it felt much more like an unburdening, a lifting of a heaviness I'd become accustomed to throughout the years." Ethan locked eyes with Carozza. "Perhaps it's because of my wife's death that I feel this way, but I've had a week to think about it, and I'm increasingly convinced that it's more than that. I don't believe I was ever meant to be Succouri. It saved my life, gave me many happy years with Lexi and my daughter, and I'm grateful for that, but if it had been the Succouri's imperative rather than my human donor, I don't believe I would have been selected. The Succouri that was awakened didn't resemble me. We didn't fit together, match one another; not like Ben's does with him. When his Succouri spoke in my head, I could have sworn it was Ben, the human being standing beside my bed. If he struggles at times to differentiate its voice from his own, I believe that's simply because there's hardly a discernable difference between them."

Caught off guard by these revelations, Donovan and Ben leaned closer. Though its presence was almost undetectable at first, Donovan had never felt as Ethan had; that the Succouri's nature didn't fit with his own. Their thoughts and characters ran virtually parallel. He'd assumed that was always the case, but Ethan's story countered that presumption, providing further proof that Ben's Succouri deliberately engineered the match.

"But, Ethan, just because your personality didn't align as closely with your Succouri's nature as mine, doesn't necessarily mean you weren't meant to be Succouri."

All eyes turned to Carozza, but Donovan already knew what he would say.

"Though the match will not be perfect until the Antico reaches the end of its journey, each chosen host will have some common qualities, both in personality as well as physical features." He gestured to Ben before continuing. "I've been uniquely privileged to know three hosts of Ben's Antico. Marvelously, each one has had those same unusual blue eyes, and Owen Briggs possessed a nearly identical disposition. As the Antico craves the one-of-a-kind union it will someday enjoy with its perfect counterpart, it will select hosts who resemble him, allowing for effortless compatibility and companionship. The closer the resemblance the faster the integration and the tighter the bond. Of course, all of this was only true before the Succouri were diminished by the blood transfers."

Though Carozza's explanation made sense, Donovan struggled to embrace the idea that he closely resembled a man far off in the future, one who quite possibly wasn't even born yet.

"Then that confirms it for me," Ethan said, crossing his arms. "Once it was revived, we both felt the awkwardness of the incompatibility. We weren't well suited, but I believe Donovan is."

Donovan couldn't help nodding in response to Ethan's statement.

"Then your Succouri voluntarily departed?" Carozza questioned. "You didn't coerce it in any way?"

"None whatsoever. As soon as I touched Donovan, it left."

"But I don't understand," Carozza exclaimed, looking uncomfortable with the admission as he rubbed his nearly bald head. "How could the Succouri be revived when it had long ago lost its path? If there had still been a way to reach its intended, it would not have fallen silent in the first place."

Everyone, including Carozza, shifted their gaze to Ben who closed his eyes before responding. Smiling, Donovan recognized the look on his face. Ben was listening for the voice of his Succouri, seeking an answer to Carozza's question. "My present understanding is that the awakening resets the Antico's journey: assigns it a new ultimate match and a new final mission. Ethan compared the distinction between his newly awakened Succouri and my ancient one to that of a child versus an adult. This makes sense if the awakening was, in essence, a rebirth, not just a revival."

"Then how was it that Donovan, who was chosen by your human impulses, just so happened to be the correct heir for Ethan's particular Succouri?" Carozza asked.

Ben took a shaky breath, and Donovan and Grace noticed Ben's trembling hand. A new and intense urging began to stir inside him.

"In this case, Callie and I are convinced it was my Antico who orchestrated the match. It is the only Succouri in existence who can restore what's been lost: reignite the Succouri's spirit and give it a new purpose. Because of this unique ability, we've come to accept that awakening the Succouri is our lifelong assignment, but convincing others to adopt this new paradigm won't be easy. To convince me and others in the network that your theories were and are correct and that the blood transfers should end, proof was required, a tangible example of a successful rebirth and touch transfer. I don't presently have the strength or time to go into all the details but trust me when I say the coincidences are too numerous and incredible to ignore or dismiss. Ethan and Donovan were intentionally selected to be the first, the authentication of what you've spent a lifetime proclaiming. I'm close to the end of my strength, so I want to say this while you're still well and able to hear it. You've been right all along, and because you spoke the truth, everything is about to change. We won't rest until every Succouri is reborn and the blood transfers are relics of the distant past."

As Ben spoke, two powerful sensations flooded through Donovan's being. First, a renewed urgency to assist Ben and Callie in their mission. More than ever, he was certain their journeys were interconnected. Second, the voice he'd just begun to recognize called out to him, not audibly, but with a message so clear it might as well have been a shout. *Help him*, it exhorted. *Reach out your hand and give.*

With a look of confusion, Grace caught his eye, and he subtly nodded, not sure exactly what she was sensing, but wishing to confirm that there was something important happening.

Carozza's eyes filled with tears, and Ben held on, even as his body began to tremble.

Unable to resist the call for another second, Donovan slowly walked to the opposite side of Carozza's bed. "Ben, I... I think I can help. I feel like... like I should help."

Callie stepped away from Ben and reached her hand across the bed to Donovan. When he touched her, Donovan gasped involuntarily. From every part of his body, strength was forcibly evacuated, as if a suction device had been attached to his muscles. Not only did it drain his strength, but it also took his breath, unsteadied his footing, and scattered his thoughts. Though he couldn't fairly describe the experience as painful, the discomfort it elicited was, in many ways, as distressing as physical agony.

Prior to becoming Succouri, through sheer willpower, Donovan had taught himself to mask the pain of his injuries, developing a mental discipline that allowed him to flip a switch and perform whatever task the moment demanded. But, as the draw hit him hard, he wasn't confident he'd be able to apply the same strategy to this situation. The pull on his strength was immediate, stripping him of his warrior's might and leaving him as weak as an invalid, his head too heavy to lift.

With newfound respect, Donovan marveled at how Ben had endured this for fifteen years, displaying a quiet courage that made his sacrifice appear almost effortless. The thought of how often Ben's gift had relieved his pain in recent weeks churned Donovan's stomach, as he now tasted the actual misery involved in the draw. Yet despite the forceful evacuation of strength, Ben maintained a façade of normalcy, at least until his body betrayed the devastating cost. In describing him, Grace had relayed her impression that Ben wasn't the warrior type. Knowing what he now did, Donovan vehemently disagreed.

Callie laughed in delight and looked at Grace. "He's ready. It's time for the adventure of a lifetime!"

Though everyone else smiled, Donovan wiped his hand across his brow. "You weren't kidding about the draw, Ben, though 'unpleasant' isn't the word I would use to describe it. It reminds me of the torture exercises they put us through during SEAL training to test our physical endurance."

Ben grimaced empathetically. "I wish I could tell you it gets easier or that you'll get used to it with time." He shook his head. "Sorry. I can't. In fact, the draw from Callie is relatively weak. You don't have to—"

"I think you know better than anyone that I have to do this. The voice in my head isn't open to negotiation or compromise. I can take it. I passed every one of those tests with flying colors, though I can't say I enjoyed them." He did his best to offer a reassuring smile before continuing. "I'm certainly feeling substantially more gratitude for what you did for me over the last few weeks. The SEALS would have loved to have you, Ben, as you make this look easy. I had no idea. But this is what I signed up for, so I'd rather just jump into the deep end with both feet."

"Can I help him?" Grace asked, her anxiety for him causing her voice to shake.

"Not yet," Callie answered. "It takes more time to develop your gift."

Though he and Grace had intended to tell Ben and Callie about their marriage that day, the solemn conversation during the flight derailed that plan as it didn't feel like the proper moment for such a revelation. As they'd remained sequestered at the doctor's residence, there hadn't been an opportunity to catch their friends up on the progress of their bond either. Still, according to the doctor, it would likely be a while longer before Grace could help him with the draw as there were changes that needed to take place in her body chemistry before that would become possible.

Donovan sent Grace a reassuring nod before placing a hand on Carozza's arm. He sucked in an unsteady breath and braced himself with his free hand, adjusting to the increased pressure.

The sensation of suction swelled. The force was so powerful that standing became challenging as his legs weakened. His head swam, and before long, he began to feel a slight tremble in his hand.

Ben stayed in place for a few seconds, watching him with grave concern. Setting his jaw, Donovan flashed the 'okay' sign with his free hand, and Ben exhaled and let go of Carozza. "Thank you, my friend."

Ethan moved to Donovan's side. "Without help from a Datouri, you won't be able to hang on for long. Please, don't overdo it on your first day. You will eventually pass out if you aren't careful and recovering alone from that takes days. After using your gift for a while, you'll learn where that line is so you can avoid crossing it, but for now, you should stop when your arms begin shaking. Can you feel the kickback?"

Unable to speak as the effort required to do so felt overwhelming, he wobbled his head at Ethan.

"It's like a drop of cool water on your parched tongue, a slight, inadequate relief, but if you focus your mind on it, it sort of, grows, or at least seems to."

Covering his eyes to concentrate, Donovan slowly nodded his understanding. There was something hidden in the draw, a fleeting sensation of pleasure. Heeding Ethan's instructions, he centered his focus, trying to mentally grab hold of it. Though his efforts were only partially successful, in the few seconds he managed to fix on it, the power of the draw waned ever so slightly. Nevertheless, he was encouraged by the small victory. More practice at employing this countermeasure, in addition to the assistance Grace would eventually be able to offer him, gave him hope that, in time, he might have some potent weapons at his disposal to counter this new and powerful foe.

Everyone, but particularly Carozza, watched with a mix of anxiety and wonder. For the first time, the old man studied Donovan carefully. "Every word Ben has said can be trusted as the integrity of those in a terminal triad is of the highest quality. He says you were the intended recipient, the next in line, and indeed, I see in your eyes a wisdom and courage that will benefit your newly reborn Succouri. It will learn quickly, however, and soon have much to teach you as well. Learn to hear its voice and guard it carefully. Don't allow anyone to silence it again. When the time comes for it to move on, you must submit to its choice no matter how tempting it may be to grasp that power. Most assuredly, there will never again be a Succouri like Ben, who can resurrect the lost, so you must be unmovable in this pledge, and you must charge your inheritor with the same."

He paused, leaning in close to Donovan and staring into his brown eyes. Though the scrutiny verged on aggressive, Donovan didn't look away. The Succouri within him listened with equal interest, and Donovan sensed his reverence for the prophetic words Carozza spoke.

"Because the chosen one and his Antico selected you and granted life to you and your Succouri, it is your obligation, yours and your Datouri's, to stay by their side. You must walk the difficult road with them, clear their path, keep them from harm, and remain loyal for a lifetime, even after your Succouri has departed. This is the unique privilege and sacred duty you're charged with as you were the first to benefit from their calling."

Here was the full prophesy, the one he'd heard in an abridged form since he was a child. The words flooded him with strength, despite the continued draw. He'd been born for this. Without his conscious awareness, this calling had been a big reason why he'd joined the military, acquired tactical skills and battle-tested experience. Though what he'd done during those years of service had been consequential, what he and Grace were being called to do now would change the course of the world. It was an honor he felt unworthy of, yet he knew for sure it was his destiny.

"Gladly," Donovan replied without hesitation.

Ben looked at him with such genuine gratitude that Donovan could scarcely hold his gaze. Ben chuckled softly. "A few days ago, I teasingly informed him that he could repay me by being my lifelong friend. It appears that request was more than wishful thinking on my part."

Looking down, Ben saw the tremble in Donovan's hand. "Can you hold on for one more minute, my friend? There's something I'm supposed to do, but I'll need you to keep him whole while I carry it out."

Though he wasn't sure he could, Donovan nodded.

With his right hand, Ben reached for Callie. He placed his left hand on Carozza's forehead. Carozza sharply inhaled, but then blew a slow breath through his lips as his expression became dreamy. He stared at the ceiling, lost in a private vision that no one else could see.

Mesmerized, everyone watched, silent and still. A nurse opened the door to Carozza's room and Taylor reacted quickly, intercepting her, and cleverly maneuvering her back out into the hallway with an improvised question about Carozza's care.

A few minutes later, the draw abruptly ceased, and Ben removed his hand and lifted his eyes to Donovan. "You can let go now. He's at peace, and his pain is gone."

Donovan complied, and Grace pulled a chair over to

him. Blowing out a relieved breath, he sat and put his head in his hands as he tried to regain his equilibrium.

"For your first time, that was excellent!" Ethan praised. "As the feeling of the draw is unlike any human experience, it's quite a shock to the system, so initially, most can't hang on for more than a few seconds. I'm going to go get you both some water," Ethan announced, patting Donovan on the shoulder before moving toward the door.

Grace gently rubbed his back, and her touch helped him regain control of his thoughts and steady his breathing.

Each person in the room watched Carozza's face, but his eyes didn't open. Gradually, they circled around the bed, Donovan leaning on Grace for support, but Carozza remained still and quiet. Callie took the old man's hand, kindly offering him the comfort of human contact.

Ethan returned and handed each of them a bottle of water, and despite its cold temperature, Donovan drank heartily. Unsure whether Carozza had slipped into a coma or was simply asleep, they waited. No one considered leaving as something compelled them to maintain the silent vigil.

Half an hour passed before Carozza's eyelids finally opened, just a sliver. He weakly smiled at Callie and Ben. "It forgave me, and it took away my pain," he whispered, and they all leaned closer to hear him. "It showed me the future, how it will happen, and it provided an answer to my life-long quandary. What an extraordinary journey awaits you all!" Carozza shifted his gaze around the room, resting it on each of them for a few seconds before moving on. When he looked at Donovan, he smiled broadly before proceeding to the next pair of eyes.

"I both envy and pity you," he continued, speaking to the group as a whole. "Because of you, it was worth it: every loss and each rejection. Though, throughout my life, my voice was muzzled, through you, I will sing a triumphant song that will be heard in the farthest corners of the earth."

Callie and Grace cried softly, and Ben set a hand on Carozza's shoulder. "You won't be forgotten. You'll be remembered as a part of our family now."

"Then I am indeed eternally blessed! *Arrivederci, amici miei.*"

With that, a full smile filled his face, and he closed his eyes and took his final breath.

CHAPTER 21
HONOR AND RECONCILIATION

When Doctor Navarro was informed that Donovan had developed his Succouri healing power, he ran a few more tests, then released him with the promise that he and Grace would check in at regular intervals. The following day, they boarded a plane bound for Boston and, after a stop at a local jewelry store to purchase a wedding band, Donovan drove them to his apartment.

With a sly grin, he twisted the key in the lock and opened the door, but before Grace could enter, he scooped her up in his arms. "I know we've been married for a couple of weeks now, but it's not too late to do this," he explained as she gasped in surprise. Though it had taken him a full day to recover from the draw, he presently felt stronger than ever.

"But this isn't our official home."

"Close enough. I never dreamed, when I left this apartment weeks ago, I'd come back here with a wife and a whole new life."

Grace giggled and Donovan reached to flip on the light. When his eyes adjusted, he froze in his tracks. His apartment had been ransacked. Papers were strewn across the floor and every box had been cut open and their contents spilled out. The pair of barstools lay on their sides and each kitchen cabinet had been emptied forcefully, leaving jagged pieces of glass and the broken remnants of plates and bowls strewn across the kitchen tiles.

"Um... What?" Grace stammered. "Donovan!"

"Don't let this change your mind about taking me in. I promise, I'm not this messy," he said, trying to ease her fear with a bit of humor. "Someone obviously broke in here."

Instinctively, he stepped in front of her. "Stay close behind me. I'm sure the intruders are long gone, but I want to have a look around, just in case."

She complied, and slowly, he walked through the apartment, opening each door looking for evidence the intruders may have left behind. When he was sure the place was empty, he turned and took her hands. "All clear. I need to sift through the mess, see what they took. Are you alright?"

Though she looked frightened, she nodded. "Who would do this and why?"

Donovan scratched his head. "There's a number of possibilities. I've protected some high-profile individuals, taken down some first-rate bad guys, not to mention ticked off hundreds of terrorists all over the globe. But something tells me this is unrelated to any of that. Maybe it's my Succouri's suggestion, or perhaps it's just my instincts."

Sucking in a slow breath, she stepped closer to him. "Can I help?"

"Best not to touch anything, lest we leave fingerprints. As soon as I look around, see what they were after, we're leaving. I won't take any chances, not with your safety. Whoever did this may have more sinister intentions than just a robbery; if that's even what this was. As we're having dinner with him tonight anyway, I'll read Taylor in on this, get his help. We'll stay at a hotel for a few days, then head home."

Nervously, she bit her lip and looked down.

"I won't leave your side." He smiled and tapped his finger to his chest. "Personal bodyguard for life, remember? You're not in any danger."

Though she did her best to smile, the tension in her face only slightly eased. After a thorough inspection, Donovan discovered that his laptop was the sole item missing.

"I didn't take it with me because I had only intended on being in town for a few days for the wedding, and truthfully, I hadn't expected to be alive longer than a week or two beyond that, so I had no active cases," he reflected as they drove to a local restaurant to meet up with Taylor. "The computer's encrypted, so I can't imagine they could get much off of it, but until we know who we're dealing with, I won't rest easy knowing it's out there."

"Why do you think that was the only item they chose to take?"

"That's the important question. This could be simple petty theft, juveniles looking for something of value to sell, but as the front door's lock was intact and there were other items of value left behind, I'm doubtful that's the case. This doesn't seem like the work of amateurs, though the mess they left behind isn't characteristic of professionals either. They were searching for something, perhaps the computer specifically. So, if this was targeted and not random, it could be..."

"Could be?"

"The names of my contacts at the FBI and other agencies were on the computer. That's why I used heavy encryption. And also…"

"Donovan?"

"Remember I told you I did substantial research after I found out about Ben's gift. I went looking for proof, specifically combing through everything written or said about him and Callie in regard to the fire rescue. I put together a hefty file of quotes and observations. It's what helped me finally accept the truth."

"You think this has something to do with the Succouri, or Ben specifically?"

Donovan shook his head. "I highly doubt it, but we need to be sure."

Over dinner, Donovan told Taylor about the break-in and what they knew thus far.

"I concur that it doesn't sound random," Taylor said. "Petty thieves don't go to that much trouble. They grab what they see out in the open and get out. This sounds like a detailed search, targeted and thorough. I'll get someone out there immediately to dust for prints, in an unofficial capacity. There's a file six inches thick on the Succouri at headquarters, though they still don't know the phenomenon's official name. I don't want to provoke further suspicions."

"But if they were after information about the Succouri, why me? I just became one days ago, and until a few weeks back, I knew nothing about it. Right now, there are only eight or nine people who know I'm one. Why didn't they break into the residence of someone who's been a part of this life for much longer?"

Taylor stroked his chin. "These valid questions and facts do appear to eliminate the possibility of the Succouri being the target, unless whoever did this is interested specifically in Ben. You've been his closest friend since childhood, and for the last month, the two of you have remained in close contact. Consider also that Grace has been a close friend of Callie's for years. It wouldn't take long for someone to connect the dots. Ben to you or Ben to Callie to Grace to you. Ben's Boston home has been emptied, everything sold, shipped, or stored as it will soon be on the market. In light of this, as well as the fact that Ben has moved around continually for six years, there's nowhere to break in and steal something of his directly. And anyway, as the saying goes, if you want to know the man, get to know his friends. And there's one more consideration. If they were able to find out about your condition, you might have been the perfect choice as"—he cleared his throat—"a dead man tells no tales. They may have believed they could break into your house and take your things with impunity because you wouldn't be around to report or investigate it."

Tapping a finger on the table, Donovan silently considered Taylor's analysis for a long moment before following it up with a statement. "I'm all too happy to disappoint them. Nevertheless, this living, breathing man suddenly wishes he had his laptop," he said with a chuckle. "Any ideas on a profile, who we might be dealing with if this is, in fact, about Ben? Who would be interested enough to go to all this trouble?"

"Only one name comes to mind, and if he is involved, it's because of my actions."

He and Grace both stared questioningly.

"Carozza's son, Roberto, aka Bobby Carozza," he explained. "When we visited his home, the guy threatened Callie and me, tried to solicit funds in return for access to his father. He's a real piece of work; in debt up to his eyeballs, gambler, drinker, philanderer, the whole sad package. He owes enormous debts to some craven individuals. When I... emphatically denied his request, he wasn't happy. He knows we were there to discuss the Succouri with his father, and he harbors deep resentment for the phenomenon as well as for Carozza, who he believed to be out of his mind. But despite hating it, I think he knows that the gift is real. Our... confrontation in addition to the follow-up calls I made to have Carozza removed from that cesspool, may have ticked him off, perhaps enough to motivate him to seek revenge. I gave him our first names only, and just Callie's and mine, so unless Carozza spilled the beans, which I highly doubt given his reverence for Ben, I have no idea how he would have made the connection. He's not nearly intelligent or crafty enough to do the research necessary, but perhaps he clued someone in who is, in exchange for payment, of course. After all, he had literally nothing to lose. In his mind, the Succouri ruined his family and his life. His father's gone, and he may blame us for that too. It's an unlikely theory, but it's all we've got until we gather more intel. I assume you two aren't going to stay at your apartment."

"Definitely not. And we probably won't stay in town for long either. If there is a threat to Ben and/or Callie, I want to make them aware and stick close."

"Good plan, but I do hope you will pick up your mail and check your messages before you leave." A coy smile lifted the corners of his mouth.

"I will?" Donovan answered, the statement sounding like a question as he was confused by the expression of excitement on Taylor's face.

"Lieutenant Commander Bartlett has been trying very hard to find you for over a week. I think he fears you dead."

Grace looked at Donovan. "Who's that?"

"He was the officer in charge of my SEAL team while I was overseas. How," he started to ask Taylor, but then shrugged and modified his question. "Why is he looking for me?"

Taylor folded his arms and leaned back in his seat, his smile broad and his eyes locked on Donovan. "It has come to my knowledge that you, Donovan Bradshaw, have been selected to receive one of our nation's highest military honors, and rightfully so."

"I... What?" Donovan stammered, and Grace sucked in an excited breath.

"You have been recognized for extraordinary acts of valor during the execution of Operation Lightning Strike and will receive the Navy Cross, presented to you in a formal ceremony at the Pentagon next month."

Gaping, Donovan stared in disbelief. Grace squealed in delight and threw her arms around his neck. "Oh, Donovan! I'm so proud of you!"

"But I... All I did was survive."

Scoldingly, Taylor frowned and shook his head. "I read up on your decade of service, and on that operation in particular. Horrible, tragic day. I know what you miraculously survived, and I've witnessed the results of the wounds you incurred for myself over the last weeks. This honor could not be more well deserved, young man. How you found the strength to endure, remain quiet is... unimaginable. Even before you became Succouri, you had beat the odds, lived well beyond the most generous expectations of doctors, and continued to serve as a civilian despite a level of constant pain that would have caused even the bravest among us to surrender to our deathbeds. Extraordinary valor, indeed: there are no other words to describe it."

"I appreciate the generous words, sir, sincerely, but I…" Donovan lowered his head, unable to finish his sentence as he was overcome by Taylor's praise and the unexpected, extravagant honor.

Reaching across the table, Taylor patted Donovan's arm. "Those who believe themselves unworthy are typically the worthiest among us. Humility is a requirement for greatness." He chuckled. "Just be sure to act surprised when the brass comes calling."

As Grace continued to smile proudly, Donovan managed a nod.

"And that's not all," Taylor continued. "I'd like to offer you a job working with me at the FBI. Someone with your integrity and skills would be an indispensable asset to my team."

Rubbing the side of his head as he tried to process the cascade of unexpected honors, it took him a few seconds to respond. "But I'm… I'm Succouri."

Taylor laughed. "Yes, I am aware. So was Owen and so was I for a short time. That's an asset, not a liability, Mr. Bradshaw."

"But aren't there medical tests and—"

Taylor waved his hand in the air. "Let me worry about that."

Donovan turned to Grace. Though still smiling, her tentative expression reflected his exact thoughts on the matter.

"I sincerely appreciate the honor of being considered, Agent Taylor, and it might be something I'd be willing to consider at a future date, but right now, I have a calling to fulfill, and it must be my singular focus."

Taylor raised one eyebrow. "Does this have something to do with my son?"

"Yes, sir. It has everything to do with him and Callie. Grace and I were chosen by Ben's Succouri primarily because I have the skills and training to provide protection for them as they follow through with their crucial work. You heard Carozza's exhortation?"

Taylor nodded.

"That was nothing new. I'd been given that mandate, repeatedly, from my youth, so his words were simply additional confirmation. Since the moment Grace met Callie, she's felt the same way, like their destinies were linked. Not to say that we won't have other goals and or take other jobs, but I can't commit to anything that might pull me away from what I'm meant to do, the very reason my life was spared. It is our duty to help them, and we've accepted that call willingly, gladly."

Taylor leaned his elbows on the table and folded his hands, looking with pride on him and Grace. "I certainly can't fault you for prioritizing something so worthwhile, not to mention so near and dear to my heart. Ever since I met my son, I've felt compassion for the heavy burden he carries, and this new complex calling magnifies that feeling. Though I'll continue to do all I can for the two of them, it comforts me greatly to know they'll have such loyal lifelong companions to assist and defend them." He paused to sigh. "Very well. The job will always be yours if you should ever change your mind. Regardless, I hope you will consider me a friend, someone you can call upon should you need help of any kind."

With moist eyes, Grace reached her hand across the table, and Taylor took it affectionately. "You're much more to us than that. You're family."

"That sounds exactly right to me," Donovan concurred.

Two days later, Grace and Donovan knocked on the enormous, ornate front door of a sprawling mansion just outside Boston's city limits. Though Grace knew Donovan's parents were wealthy, the size and beauty of the traditional New England-style home, not to mention the immaculately manicured grounds surrounding it, were astonishing and more than a little intimidating.

"Don't be nervous," Donovan whispered into her ear as he put his arm around her shoulders. "They're going to love you."

Though the connection of their Succouri bond was growing stronger by the day, the special ability to tune in to one another's emotions wasn't necessary in this case, as her fidgeting betrayed her frayed nerves.

"You look stunning, the most beautiful woman I've ever laid eyes on," Donovan added with a twinkle in his eye.

She returned a wobbly smile as she smoothed the skirt of the dark green dress they'd bought for the occasion.

When the door opened, a woman, who looked to be about fifty, smiled broadly as her eyes danced in delight. Her black hair was gathered into a low, loose bun and she wore a navy dress overlaid with a white apron.

"Donovan!" the woman exclaimed, reaching to embrace him. "Your handsome face makes my heart jump for joy.

You look so strong and well." There was a note of surprise in her tone.

"Esperanza," Donovan responded with a smile. "It's fantastic to see you again. Please, meet my wife, Grace." He turned his eyes to her. "Grace this is Esperanza. She took <u>good</u> care of me for many years while I was growing up."

Grace offered her hand, and the woman cradled it in hers as she gazed at Grace approvingly. "What a rare beauty! You are a blessed man, Donovan Bradshaw."

As Grace's cheeks reddened at the compliment, Donovan chuckled. "You don't know the half of it," he declared with genuine pride.

"Come, come," she beckoned. "Your parents are waiting in the library. They're anxious to see you."

They stepped inside, but before they proceeded any farther, Donovan put a hand on Esperanza's arm, halting her advance. "Esperanza, are they... Are they well?"

Despairingly, she dropped her gaze to the floor, confirming that Donovan's concerns were well founded. "It isn't my place to say, but I am glad you chose to come home when you did. There is still time to set things right."

For several ticks of a nearby grandfather clock, Donovan was silent, and Grace slipped her hand in his. But at last, with resignation, he sighed and gestured for Esperanza to proceed. They trailed behind her through richly furnished rooms adorned with high ceilings and beautiful artwork, arriving at a set of French doors that opened into a smaller room painted soft tan, its back wall lined with fully stocked bookshelves.

Esperanza announced their presence, turned to smile at her and Donovan one last time, then quietly left the room. Donovan's parents rose from a couch that occupied the center of the room and stepped forward.

As his hand tightened around hers, Grace could feel the pain throbbing through his heart, triggered by their appearance. Though she had no frame of reference from which to draw a fair comparison, the man and woman before her were gray and their shoulders bent. What caught her attention immediately were their tired eyes. Considering the lives of luxury they'd lived, Grace marveled at the palpable heaviness that clung to them as if they carried a physical burden.

Donovan's father wore a black suit and his mother a gray skirt and matching jacket. Though they couldn't be more than sixty five, they appeared older, and she wondered if the years of regret over their choice to disown their only son, and then the subsequent worry for his safety, had caused the premature aging.

"Mother. Father," Donovan greeted, his voice low and pained, as he looked on them with compassion. "It's good to see you again. May I present my wife, Grace Bradshaw."

The woman reached out her hand, first to her son, tears shining in her eyes. "Donovan," she managed, clinging to his hand for a long moment, making Grace certain Donovan was feeling a draw from the fragile woman, though he hid it well. "You appear to be… in good health. We were told—"

"There is no cause for worry. I'm well," he reassured her. Briefly, he glanced at Grace. "I've been loved and cared for by some remarkable people and an outstanding doctor."

After holding her son's gaze for another confused breath, she turned to Grace. "I'm Clarice Bradshaw. It's lovely to make your acquaintance. What a striking young woman you are!" she complimented, and though she couldn't describe the woman as warm, there was kindness in her words and tone.

"Thank you, Mrs. Bradshaw. It's a pleasure to meet you."

Donovan's father offered a similar greeting, but as they all moved to sit, Grace noticed how gingerly he walked, and she guessed that it was his father's health that had been the source of Esperanza's cryptic comment regarding Donovan's timely visit.

"How long have you been back in the States?" his mother asked when they had settled.

"Nearly two years, but I was in the hospital for almost half that time."

Nodding, as if she were aware of this fact, she folded her hands in her lap and continued. "And when were you two married?" Clarice looked at Grace.

"Just recently, a couple of weeks ago," Grace answered.

"Your face is familiar. What family do you come from?"

"Grace is not from around here, Mother," Donovan interjected, rescuing her from the woman's interrogation. "We met through my old friend, Ben Sawyer. You remember the Sawyer family, of course."

"Indeed," she replied, a touch of disdain in her voice.

"Ben was also recently married to a lovely woman who is Grace's best friend."

"I had heard he disappeared. No one knew where he went after…"

"Just as I am, Ben is quite contented now."

"Will the two of you settle in Boston?" Donovan's father inquired, his voice hoarse.

"No, sir. We'll live back west, in the town where we met. We're leaving tomorrow."

Disappointedly, Donovan's mother dropped her gaze.

"Will you have children?" she asked boldly, lifting her eyes to Grace again.

Grace swallowed hard. "Someday, perhaps." The answer was a truthful one as, if Donovan's term was as short as Ben and Callie predicted, they hoped there would still be time for them to become parents after the gift passed on.

After an awkward moment of silence, Donovan's father cleared his throat once more and leaned forward, his hands resting on his knees. "Son, we... We were wrong." He held up a hand. "Not for worrying about you, but for turning you out, pushing you away. It was the biggest mistake of our lives, and we deeply regret it."

Grace held her breath as she turned to look at Donovan, who was blinking hard. "I very much appreciate that," he whispered, and Grace felt healing begin in a place in Donovan's heart that had long been wounded.

"Is there... Do you think you could..." His mother stiffened her back, uncomfortable with the emotions that threatened to overtake her polished manners but determined to say what she must.

Reaching across the space between them, Donovan set his hand on his mother's. "Of course. With great joy."

Grace beamed. Though his courage and strength had impressed her continuously since the day she met him, she had never been as proud of her husband as she was in that moment. The two people who should have offered him the purest and most faithful love possible in this world rejected him for no good reason and had remained stubbornly stuck in their arrogance for a decade. A lesser man would have withheld forgiveness, deciding they deserved a lonely end to their self-centered lives. But she saw nothing but compassion and love in Donovan's tear-filled eyes.

At his gracious forgiveness, the withered, defeated people before them visibly transformed. New life and hope ignited in their eyes and the etched lines on their faces smoothed. Though the expression was unpracticed and therefore lopsided, Clarice Bradshaw smiled, and a single tear dripped onto her designer jacket.

"It didn't change you!" Clarice exclaimed, and Donovan looked at her with a puzzled expression.

"You were such a beautiful boy. Kind and good. I thought war would ruin you, that when you came home, you'd be... broken, a different person. But I was wrong."

Donovan spoke softly as he took Grace's hand in his. "It did change me, Mother, but love has returned what I lost, brought balance, and helped me find new purpose."

With affection and profound appreciation, Clarice Bradshaw smiled, nodding humbly at Grace.

"Then it isn't too late," his father exclaimed with a long sigh of relief.

"Too late?" Donovan inquired, dread in his tone.

"I'm dying, son. Cancer. Doctors say I've got a few weeks, maybe a month."

"I'm... I'm sorry." Donovan agonized as he lowered his gaze.

"When we sent you the letter," his mother continued, "we thought it was you who... We had heard you were badly injured and... Well, either way, we didn't want to leave things as they were. You're our only son, and Grace our only daughter." Grace warmly smiled at the woman, appreciating the offer of full acceptance into the family. "If there's anything we can do for the two of you, throw you a belated wedding reception, or if there's something you need we—"

"We don't need money or parties," Donovan quickly assured them, "though I appreciate the generous offer. I do, however, need my parents as part of our family. I've learned not to necessarily accept the predictions of doctors blindly. They do their best, but they don't take into account the impact love can have on keeping a body strong, a heart beating. But regardless, whatever time we have together, let's make the most of it." He turned to Grace, and she nodded enthusiastically. "In a month, we're going to the Pentagon where I'll receive an extravagant honor I don't feel I deserve."

Grace subtly shook her head in disagreement as his parents' eyes registered surprise at his unexpected news.

"Nevertheless, it would mean the world to me if my parents were in attendance."

"Son!" Ivan Bradshaw exclaimed, the word carrying both pride in Donovan and shame at his own shortsightedness. "Without fail, we will be there."

Late that night, as Grace lay in Donovan's arms, she couldn't keep from smiling as she rejoiced in the peace radiating from his whole being. "You're giving your father what our love offered you when you were in a similar circumstance."

"Hm?" he inquired sleepily.

"A reason to stay with us for a while longer, to fight against the dying light."

He turned and grinned at her. "Do you realize that if I hadn't met you, if you hadn't fallen for a dying, despairing man, the meeting we just had with my parents never would have happened? I would have died, and they would have died without the chance for resolution or reconciliation."

She shook her head. "I don't think there was ever a chance of that. Meeting each other, falling in love; it was written in the stars." She giggled. "Imagine me, a recovering unbeliever saying something so completely sappy."

Rolling toward her, he pulled her to him and kissed her until the fire burned so fiercely that neither could resist it. "Sappy or not, you're absolutely right," he whispered, his lips near her ear. "Whatever comes next, promise me you'll never stop believing that what you just said is the steadfast truth."

"I promise, soldier, with all my heart."

DOWNLOAD **FREE** BONUS EPILOGUE:

NOTE TO READER

Thank you for reading *Against the Dying Light* by Meridith Gibbens.

Please kindly consider leaving a review of this novel at your place of purchase or other book review websites like Goodreads or Bookbub.

This story is part of the beloved Succouri Saga Series. Consider reading the complete *All I Have* Series, which tells Ben and Callie's story in four enchanting novels.

Use this QR code to access purchase links for all books:

To stay informed about new releases and special sales and offers, consider signing up for my monthly newsletter:
Visit my website:
http://succourisaga.com

MERIDITH GIBBENS BOOKS

All novels are available in eBook, paperback, and audiobook format.

List of books in the *All I Have* Series:
    Book 1: *All I Have to Give*
    Book 2: *All I Have to Lose*
    Book 3: *All I Have to Love*
    Book 4: *All I Have to Keep*

Stand-alone or as book 4.5 of the Succouri Saga: Against the Dying Light

ABOUT THE AUTHOR

As an Adjunct Professor of Communication for more than two decades, writing has always been a part of Meridith's life and career. Her novels combine her love for romance and imaginative storytelling with her communication and writing background. Legally blind since birth, Meridith's unique point of view and experiences bring intriguing and fresh perspectives to her storylines and characters. Beyond simple romance novels, Meridith writes unforgettable, epic love stories that sweep readers off their feet.

Meridith resides in Kansas with her husband, Jason, and her two sons.

www.ingramcontent.com/pod-product-compliance
Lightning Source LLC
Chambersburg PA
CBHW030103310726
48970CB00004B/1123